Lifeblood: The Last Vampires Of Hollywood

ISBN: 1-4196-6742-4
ISBN-13: 978-1419667428

Visit www.booksurge.com to order additional copies.

Lifeblood: The Last Vampires Of Hollywood

Shamus Sherwood

2007

Lifeblood: The Last Vampires Of Hollywood

PROLOGUE ix
CHAPTER ONE *MURDER AND A DISAPPEARANCE* 3
CHAPTER TWO *ZIMMER* 25
CHAPTER THREE *AUTOPSY* 43
CHAPTER FOUR *NED & PUDGE....YAK & TOM MIX AND BETTY BOUDIN* 57
CHAPTER FIVE *GOOD BYE JACK* 73
CHAPTER SIX *LONE PINE* 89
CHAPTER SEVEN *BETTY BOUDIN* 111
CHAPTER EIGHT *FUNERAL* 133
CHAPTER NINE *JEAN MARC* 151
CHAPTER TEN *JEFF SMITH* 171
CHAPTER ELEVEN *GREG & LUCILLE* 185
CHAPTER TWELVE *ZIMMER, NED PUDGE & PARIS* 199
CHAPTER THIRTEEN *BIKER HELL* 215
CHAPTER FOURTEEN *POST BIKER HELL* 243
CHAPTER FIFTEEN *LONE PINE 1998* 271
CHAPTER SIXTEEN *RADELESCU* 293
EPILOGUE 325

PROLOGUE

Leaning against the weathered hitching rail, Ned Delacroix squinted through the dust at the gathering pack of horses and men, for the daily turnout at Gower Gulch. It was not quite six in the morning, and the sun had not yet broken above the buildings along Sunset Boulevard, but the heat hung heavy in the air, with a promise of more to come. He couldn't remember the last time he'd felt rain. The summer had been brutal on the men and the animals and he knew that September was usually the hottest month of the year. Besides, he spat; work had been slow all summer long. From the worn back pocket of his Levis, he produced a leather tobacco pouch and carefully rolled himself a smoke. To a passing stranger his great gnarled hands would have given lie to the delicacy he achieved in performing the task. He was a big man, well over six feet, with a bloodline mixed in French and Indian, founded in solitude and toughened by hardship. And Ned was no stranger to those who gathered this morning on the corner of Sunset and Gower, hard men like himself, who had come west, down from the mountains and off the cattle trails, the last of their breed, to seek employment in this new business, this moving picture business, in this last western town called, Hollywood.

"Hey Frenchy! How's about a cup of coffee?" Ned glanced down the boardwalk to where a group of wranglers were huddled around a small campfire, their horses tethered to the same rail against which he had propped himself. Knute Hopkins offered up a charred pot. Around the gulch other fires burned where cowboys had gathered. It was not quite six in the morning, and the fires seemed to be burning off night's fine blanket of darkness. The gulch had once been a pasture, a patch of real estate on the corner of Sunset Boulevard and Gower, just up the street from Paramount Studios, but the daily traffic of cowboys, wranglers and horses had reduced it to a dusty hollow.

"Thanks boys. I could use a cup," he called back as he made his way to the band. "And a job," he mumbled, shaking hands around the group of three.

"Damn, that's a fact," Pudge McCoy chimed in with a tenor's pitch that was but one of the things that set him apart from the others. Pudge stood no taller than five foot four and couldn't have weighed more than a hundred and fifteen pounds fully decked in boots and riding garb. He was as Irish as The Lord made them, with curly blond hair that tumbled over a boyish face. He could sing like one of God's own angels, drink whisky with any man twice his size, and was the best damn trick rider around. No one could recall just exactly how he'd acquired the appellation Pudge, and nobody knew or asked what name his mother had given him back in Ireland, some twenty odd years earlier. He signed all his vouchers, "Pudge" and he was known by all the cowboys and wranglers who convened regularly at Gower Gulch, in fact, by all the men that worked in this new vocation that we know as the movies.

"Thanks Knute. I need a jolt this morning." Ned grasped the hot, chipped mug from the older man. Ned wasn't much older than Pudge. He figured his age at either twenty-six or seven. He'd been pretty much on his own since age eleven or twelve when both his parents had succumbed to a flue epidemic during the winter of 'thirteen. That was back in Guthrie, Oklahoma. He'd come a long way since then and the lines on his face told something of his story.

"What we all need is some steady work," Pudge chimed in. "My horse hasn't had a decent feed in weeks, and I could use a real drink."

"Well there's somethin in the wind. A big one. Lot's of horses, and lots of men. Jack Perkins was tellin me 'bout it yesterday," Ned informed them, and then spat again as if doubting his own information. The men fell into silence, sipping their coffees, waiting. If they were to work that day, they would learn soon enough. Every morning the cowboys gathered. By six, the assistant directors would show, and start picking the men, and they would ride off to work on some picture, either at a local studio, or some nearby site. If the shooting were to take place further away, the horses and riders would load into trucks to be driven to the location. It was sometimes feast, sometimes near famine. Sometimes for weeks, all the boys would go. They couldn't get enough of them. But during the lean times, only the best of them would work, the ones who had earned their reputations through hard riding, persistence, and getting to know and be known by the powers that really pulled the reins. Such was the business of the movies.

Just minutes later a muffled roar arose as a car pulled up to the far corner of the lot, the corner of Sunset and Gower. The traffic on the boulevard was light, and this one stood out. Its deep blue body was polished to a bright pitch. Ned recognized it as a new nineteen twenty-seven Ford. As the wranglers pushed toward it, a young man in a dark suit and wearing spectacles stepped out from the driver's side. In one hand he held a clipboard. As he reached the passenger side of the car, he flicked a white handkerchief from his lapel pocket and as the men surrounded him, he meticulously went about wiping off the quickly accumulating dust.

"Come on Ned," Pudge yelled, as he and the others headed to the spot. "It looks like a good day!" For some reason Ned hung back. If there was work, he figured on being hired. He was usually one of the first to be picked, as his reputation in town was solid. He sipped the last of the coffee and observed the crowd, but his eyes were drawn toward this young man. He had never before seen this one. He seemed short, dwarfed now by the men who surrounded him. His hair was jet black and shaggy and his face pinched and pale; an old face for what was obviously a young person. The man folded his handkerchief carefully, put it back into his pocket, and then Ned saw him tug nervously at his left ear lobe. Ned finished his cup and sauntered in that direction. He was perhaps halfway across the lot when a vehicle passed behind the car to a stop at the corner. Rarely did one see a horse drawn conveyance in Hollywood. Those days had come and gone. Cars and trucks transported both goods and people. And this one was odd. It appeared to be an open hearse on wagon wheels, drawn by two huge grays wearing blinders. The driver was stout and hunched. Spilling down from a tall stovepipe type headpiece, Ned saw the long blond locks of hair. But even stranger than the driver, was the cargo he hauled, for the wagon carried an ornate and apparently weighty casket.

"Maybe," Ned said to himself, "it's some kind of property or set piece for a film." By the time the driver turned the corner onto Gower, Ned figured that it had to be. "Probably going down the street to Columbia Pictures." He wondered who would be doing that picture, figuring that they'd be hiring more horses and riders. Just as it turned the corner and Ned had reached the group, he noticed the driver turn and catch the eyes of the young man who had given up on the polishing and turned toward the crowd. A look seemed to pass between them, and each nodded ever so slightly. To Ned it appeared to be more than a casual greeting, even an acknowledgment of recognition. There was something ominous and sinister about it, as if it were some kind of signal. And then the strangest thing occurred. Although the sun itself had not yet risen above the horizon, daylight had broken. But as this apparition turned the corner and started to make its way down Gower Street, a huge cloud suddenly covered the sky, sucking up the light of dawn, and at the same moment a harsh wind blew down on the horses and men. Despite himself, Ned shivered as the first drops of a cold rain hit his face....................

BOOK ONE

CHAPTER I

Murder and a Disappearance

Detective sergeant Gregory Delacroix takes another sip of his now tepid coffee and turns the weathered pages of one of the family albums. There is a stack of them on his desk. The albums are but one of the treasures he discovered several months back, while rummaging through the attic of his mother's house in the Los Feliz area of Los Angeles. The house had been in the family since the late 'Twenties, when his great uncle had purchased it. It was typical of the style of the mid to late Twenties, Spanish Colonial, with the tiled roof and balcony and the obligatory patio. It was the house of his youth and would one day be his. Through the years, despite some lean times the family had managed to hang on to this house, for to them it was more than a piece of property. It represented a part of history, and a sense of history had always been an important aspect of the education of the Delacroix family. The albums shared not only the family chronicles, but also something of the history of their city, Los Angeles. In the albums Greg had come across photos and letters, as well as magazine articles and news clippings. It is one of the news clippings he recalls glancing at for which he is now searching. Although the albums had been well preserved, on the older ones some of the plastic coverings had cracked, and most of the earlier clippings had yellowed with the passing years. As he turns a page, he glimpses the gold "Citizen" watch on his wrist, one of his few concessions to vanity. It is after two in the morning. As a Los Angeles police detective he is not unused to working odd hours. Outside the shuttered windows of the study the wind picks up. "It's mid October; too early in the season for rain," he thinks, "but you never known." The summer had been unusually hot." The little bungalow he owns on Spaulding is not far from the police station at 1358 Wilcox. The original location for both the firehouse and police station was at 1625-29 Cahuenga. He wasn't scheduled to report for work until the next afternoon and this search was important. The news clipping for which he is looking had to do with a bizarre murder disappearance that had taken place in Hollywood during the late 'twenties. There was a strange similarity between it and an investigation with which he was presently involved. As he turns one more page, he hears the loud snap of a branch breaking on the pepper tree on the front lawn. It sounds like the crack of a whip but he takes slight notice. He has found the article:

THE HOLLYWOOD NEWS
December 14, 1927
MOVIE DIRECTOR FOUND DEAD

Roland Jordan, the dashing Hollywood director who's last picture, "Westward Wagons," was such a smash success, was found dead in his Beverly Hills mansion yesterday. The cause of death is not known, but an investigation is currently underway as foul play is suspected. Police found no evidence of a struggle; in fact, Mr. Jordan was discovered sprawled on the oversized bed in his spacious bedroom wearing only a blue silk bathrobe and crimson silk pajamas. The French windows were open wide despite the inclement weather. "It looks like someone or something woke him," detective Jack McCrae was quoted. Apparently strange bite marks were found on the neck.

"They don't look like human teeth to me," McCrae added, "and there's no dog or wild animal in the house or yard." An autopsy is scheduled and results should be forthcoming within a few weeks.

In a strange twist to the incident, Jordan's girlfriend, the sometimes actress, full time party girl known as Betty Boudin has disappeared. Miss Boudin who was a complete unknown until her great success in "Westward Wagons," will be missed greatly, according to Hollywood sources. She was last seen in the company of the director Thursday evening, the 12th at the fabulous birthday bash for actor Hoagie Coates at his Santa Monica ranch. The authorities have launched a search for Miss. Boudin.

Despite the late hour and the serious nature of his search, the actress's name makes him smile. A part of the history that was instilled in the Delacroix family was their native language, French. As a child Gregory listened to and spoke only French in his parent's house. His mother, Beatrice was born in France, in the North, the Pas de Calais region, and his father Henri, spoke the old French, the patois of the Canadians, the Arcadian French of the voyageurs, the trappers and adventurers who had made their way across the vast wilderness, that was Canada. Perhaps because of its similarity, Greg also spoke enough Spanish to make himself understood. In Los Angeles that ability was a huge asset. Betty Boudin. It was a catchy name for a Hollywood hopeful. Boudin was a kind of sausage, very popular in his mother's part of the country.

The sound of the bedroom door opening pulls him from his reflections on all things past. As he turns, he sees Lucille on the landing at the top of the stairs. Her nightgown is white and her face seems to shine even whiter than the robe in the pale light. Outside, the wind picks up. "God," he thinks, "she' looks like an angel standing there."

"Honey, are you all right?" she asks. "Do you have any idea what time it is? I heard a noise outside, like a gunshot. God, it's awfully windy out there. Come back to bed Honey. I'm cold. I'm cold." She repeats, pleading. He chuckles. Unlike him, she always speaks like this, with the words and the thoughts tumbling out. Like many cops he's sparing on the words. His approach is blunt, direct, just the facts.

"Just a branch Darling. It's OK."

"Please come back to bed Greg," she asks again.

"I think I'm on to something. It woke me up and I have to check this." She catches his hesitation. After three years with him she has come to recognize his nuances, his peculiarities.

"All right," she concedes, "I'll make us a pot of Sleepy Time. I'll sit with you. You won't be long, will you?"

"No," he mumbles. "No. That would be nice. There's another one, an article in one of these albums." As he starts leafing through the next one she is already in the kitchen. He hears the water as she fills the pot.

"What is it? What are you looking for?" she calls. "It's almost three in the morning honey." This isn't the first time since she moved in with him some four months back, that he's risen in the middle of the night to do some work. Most of the times a phone call would wake them. He would hurriedly dress and often still be gone when it was time for her to get up to go to work. Like Greg, she too kept strange hours. Everyone who worked in the film business did. When you were working the hours were long, and in between jobs, the days grew even longer as you waited and sweated over when and if the next job was coming. Lucille did wardrobe, mostly for commercials, although she had worked on some features. At the age of thirty, she had arrived in the business later than some, having had a variety of jobs after graduating from college back East. She had come to Hollywood four years ago. Sometimes she worked as a dresser on the set, sometimes in the trailer or wardrobe house organizing or building the costumes, but her real ambition was to design. She especially liked working on period pieces that required research into the type of wardrobe that was worn during the era when the story took place in the past. That, she knew took time and connections and a great deal of patience. Fortunately patience was one of her attributes as she was now demonstrating as she prepared the tea and would sit with Greg until he had satisfied his curiosity. Then he would take her back to bed. She knew that, as she knew him, and knew that surely she did love this man.

"Here honey." She hands him a steaming stoneware mug. "This will help you sleep. What are you looking for in those old things at three in the morning?"

"Thanks Darling," he says, taking the mug and blowing at the rising steam. "Read this," he tells her, passing her the album. As he thumbs through the other albums he explains: "This case we're working on now is strange. We've got a disappearance along with a murder. George Zimmer is gone. You know who he is don't you?"

"I think so," she hesitates. "Wasn't it in the paper? He's a director. He did The Synergy. I think he did one called, Over The Edge, also. Too bad he never did period pieces. I would have loved to work for him. Heard he was a little strange but his pictures were good and made money and he treated his people OK."

"Yeah," Greg mutters, "in a way he did do period pieces. Do you know that he made a movie back in the early 'Fifties called "Biker Hell?"

"Oh, yeah, Biker Hell, that was his too, but that's impossible! The guy can't be more than fifty. What was he, a baby genius?"

"Yeah, exactly. That's just one of the problems with this case. Blame it all on the face lift. But it's more than that. We can't find any records of his past. No dental records. No birth certificate or passport. . He had a license, and disappeared with a house full of furniture, an open front door, and a dead body. We did trace a Social Security number that we found in a wallet, but it's a fake. The government has no record of it. And if he had a bank account, we can't find it either."

"Who was the body in the guest house?"

"Some guy. A transient. We're working on the connection between them. It looked like they'd had dinner. The table was set for two. Just some guy. We're trying to find out whom he is, and are getting nowhere. We figured a run away, maybe a street hustler. Young guy, maybe thirty years old. No record. No past. We're drawing a blank on him too."

"This Sleepy Time will help you relax honey," she tells him, as if the cup of tea would resolve all the problems of the world, solve all its mysteries. He has to smile.

"Oh Lucille. Honey is that you?" They both laugh. They're the lyrics from the old Little Richard song and a private thing between the two of them. From time to time he sings it to her when she says or does something that he feels, somehow personifies her.

"Well, what does all that have to do with these old family albums?" She smiles over her cup of tea, pale as porcelain.

"I guess I dreamed it. While I was sleeping, I suddenly remembered seeing these old newspaper clippings in the albums. I didn't really pay any attention to them when I first found the books, but something clicked; this similarity between these things that happened so many years ago and this case we're working on now. It's weird. I don't even know why someone clipped them out all those years ago. The whole thing is very strange. Do you think this Sleepy Time stuff really works?"

"Oh, it works Honey. You're just preoccupied with this thing," she assures him. But he's found what he was looking for.

"Damn! I got it. Listen to this Lucille. He moves the album under the light on the desk and reads. "From the Daily Variety, October twentieth, nineteen forty-six."

Bizarre Death and Disappearance

"The partially clothed body of a young woman was found by neighbors in the house of veteran cowboy actor Jeff Smith. The woman, identified by friends as actress Patricia Schreppel was barely attired in a sheer black nightgown and was discovered in the master bedroom. There were no visible signs of a struggle. Although the curtains that covered the large French style windows, were ripped, torn, as if she clung to them before falling to the floor. The detective on the case, a lieutenant Jack McCrae had this to say: "There have been two other murders in the last two weeks, very similar to this one. Both involved transients. And these cases are very much like one that happened some twenty years ago. These marks on her neck look like bite marks, and Mr. Smith has disappeared. That's exactly the same scenario we had in the Boudin, Jordan case back in' twenty-seven. And when the coroner did the autopsy, that Jordan fellow didn't have a drop of blood in his body. We never did solve that one, but we're hoping to crack this. If I could say for certain, I'd say that this is almost supernatural. No blood in the body and teeth marks? You know what I mean?"

Jeff Smith, the well-known cowboy actor of the last two decades has not been seen or heard from for at least ten days. He was booked to play a small role in an upcoming Western at Paramount, his first in about five years. The picture was to be directed by, Jean Marc Descamps, the French director, who authorities have not been able to get in touch with. The name of the picture is, *"The Bad Lands."*

Mr. Smith's well known, Cadillac convertibles were in the garage and there were no indications that he had made any plans to go anywhere as all his clothing and personal belongings seem to be untouched. "There's something very strange about these murders," McCrae added. "Frankly they give me the creeps. I've seen a lot of murder-disappearances over the years, but this one, like those other ones sure gives me the creeps."

Patricia Schreppel, age twenty-six was an up and coming actress who was also scheduled to work on the same picture as Mr. Smith. It was to be her first ingénue lead. A service is planned for Miss. Schreppel next Saturday at Forest Lawn.

Greg slowly closes the book and turns to Lucille who sits reflectively, holding her cup with both hands. "Well, what do you think of that?" he asks, more to himself than to her. She says nothing, waiting for him to continue with his thoughts. "This is so much like this thing I'm working on now. Why do you think these clippings are in the album Lucille? Who do you think put them in there and what's the connection?"

"Maybe it's that cowboy actor thing," she suggests. "Didn't you have a relative in the movies? "A cowboy actor?"

"You're right, Lucille. That might be it. Yeah, my great uncle Ned, My father's uncle. We used to live with him. It was his house my parents bought. I didn't see much of him. I was just a kid then. He was a stuntman, actor in the old westerns. Maybe that's it. He probably knew this Jeff Smith character."

"Oh I know who Jeff Smith was," she tells him. "He did a lot of those B Westerns. You know, what they used to call, "three revelers?" I think he even started in the silent pictures and went on to the talkies. Honey, hasn't that Sleepy Time kicked in yet? This is all very interesting, but it's late. It can wait 'til morning. Can't it?" Take me to bed. We'll talk about it tomorrow." This seems to disrupt his musings, and as he looks at her, he has to smile. He knows just how much he does love this woman.

"You're right. Let's go to bed." They rise and head to the stairs. He holds her small hand in his large one. As they climb toward the bedroom, she wraps her other arm around them and they ascend together. She pulls him toward her.

"Listen to that wind Greg. Will you hold me in bed? Will you?"

The bedroom is cool. He goes to the window to shut it in case it does rain. Outside the pepper tree rocks with the wind. A large branch hangs over the fence where it has fallen. The streetlight forces the other branches to cast wildly dancing shadows along the sidewalk, and across the tops of the cars parked along the street. In the bed she curls into his arms and sighs deeply. The Sleepy Time has done its job. "I love you Honey," she tells him.

"And I you," he says. Her breathing deepens, as he holds her body against his. "I wonder," he mumbles. "I wonder if this Jack McCrae is still around? He'd have to be close to a hundred if he is." Before he falls asleep, he has made up his mind. The first thing he'll do in the morning is to run a search on this McCrae. A branch from the Pepper tree gently caresses the window. "Lousy odds," he mumbles once more before drifting to sleep.

In the morning when they wake, they make love, slowly, tenderly. He loves to love her in the morning, so fresh, so pale. The wind has died down but no sun shines through the windows. The light in the bedroom is as soft and pale as is she. The hour is late. When they do rise from bed. It's close to eleven. They still have time before he has to be at the precinct. She's "between jobs." That's the term everyone in the movie business uses for unemployment. For perhaps a week, between jobs can be almost like being on vacation. You collect an unemployment check, send out resumes, make phone calls for work and try to find the time to catch up on all the things that you never find the time for when you're working sixteen-hour days. After the first week, the panic slowly creeps in, as all the fears and doubts rise. You wonder if that last job was in fact the last one, and when and if the next one will come. And when it does, you start all over again on a new project, often with new people, and so it goes.

Together, they shower and dress. "Let's go out for breakfast," she suggests. "How about that place on Melrose?"

"That's a good idea. We'll take my car," he says. She knows how much he likes that car. It's a black 'sixty-seven Mustang convertible that he's completely restored. Even on Melrose it stands out. "Not the ideal car for a cop," he often says, "but at least the bad guys know it's me and some of them remember." There are lots of places on Melrose but they have one spot to which they always go. Over the past twenty years, the street and the neighborhood have changed completely. It used to be a commercial district of West Hollywood; a lot of stores selling office supplies and housing fixtures. But Greg remembered the old barber shop, "Evan's," where he used to get his hair cut. Evan and his two girlfriends all cut hair together, but Evan also collected antiques, and the shop was replete with wonderful old objects, furniture and collectibles. Nothing was for sale. It was all atmospheric. Evan, who was in his forties and sported long gray hair, lived with the two girls, both barely into their twenties, both of whom amicably shared his affection. Slowly at first and then very quickly, the whole neighborhood evolved. West Hollywood became many things. The Gay Community moved in and elected a gay mayor. The rents and property values started to soar. Antique shops, art galleries and restaurants sprang up everywhere, and unlike most of Los Angeles, where the traffic on the streets is vehicular, the traffic on Melrose and the surrounding streets, was foot traffic. The atmosphere is carnival, with all types of dress and hair in fashion, motorcycles, outdoor cafes, tourists and the constant flux of the high school crowd from Fairfax High on the corner of Fairfax and Melrose.

The two of them find themselves at the little Italian bistro, "Gino's" on the corner of Spaulding and Melrose, and take their breakfast outside even 'though the sun had not broken through. Sunny, hot days are no rarity in LA and both Greg and Lucille enjoy the change in season and climate on the rare occasions they can. They choose smoked salmon on toasted bagels, with capers, tomatoes and thinly sliced onions, along with a light house salad which they share, and plenty of hot coffee. They are both hungry and hold their conversation until the meal is completed and they are sipping the rich coffee. Greg lights a cigarette. "You know," he says, "it shouldn't be too difficult to track down this McCrae character. He worked right here in Hollywood, same precinct as me. Same address too, but the old building. They should have some record of him."

"If he's still alive, he's got to be as old as God. He might not remember any of it."

"You know, Lucille, it's funny. This Zimmer thing just happened a few days ago but nobody mentioned any connection to those two cases in the past."

"Maybe they haven't figured it out yet. That was years ago."

"Yeah," he reflects quietly, taking a long drag on the smoke, "but there is a connection. That's for sure. And somehow someone in my family, probably Uncle Ned, was on to it a long time ago."

"I'm sure you'll get to the bottom of it Honey," she tells him with conviction. She's seen him like this before when he gets his teeth into a case. She misses him already, knowing that there will be other long nights when he is gone and she alone. He glances at his watch. They still have close to an hour before he has to be at work but she knows that he will drop her off at home and leave immediately.

"I'll take care of that branch latter," he tells her when they arrive at the house. "Got to go. See you tonight." She walks around to the driver's side of the car, leans in and kisses him hard.

"You take your time," she reassures him with a smile. "You know I'll be here when you get back. Dinner will be ready whenever you get here. Just call me a half hour before you leave, whenever that is."

"You know I love you Lucille," he says quietly.

"I know that well," she tells him. Halfway down the block he honks the horn. She waves back to her man. For her, it will be another typical day of phone calls and resumes in the never-ending search for the next job.

At the station, he parks on the street and goes through the public entrance. "What it be Gregor?" The big Sergeant, Jim Diehm, one of the two officers at the desk, greets him. Forty-year-old Jim's just a few years older than Greg but they'd both attended The Academy at the same time and since graduation, worked the Hollywood Division. Jim had suffered a back injury after a fall, and mostly ran the desk, although he often worked with the other detectives on their cases while at the station. He has a wife as large as himself and three dogs, all Doberman's, and despite the constant pain, hasn't lost his sense of humor.

"Hey, Jimmy. It is what it is!"

"That's a fact my friend," the big man chuckles. Greg laughs too and starts for the back, but catches himself and stops at the desk.

"Hey Jim. Have you taken a look at this Zimmer case that just came in."?

"Just heard about it. Big director gone and a dead transient. Maybe the guy was in the gay life, and just panicked."

"Naw," Greg shakes his head, "it's way bigger than that. I think I've latched onto something, but it's so weird that I'd like to run it by you before I speak to anyone else. You got some time this afternoon?"

"Sure Buddy," he nods, "I got a break in fifteen minutes."

"Thanks. I'll be at my desk," Greg tells him.

Greg's desk is at the back of the precinct house in the squad room, with other desks and other detectives. When he gets there, he is glad to see that he's alone. It will give him some moments for privacy. A few of the desks are equipped with personal computers. He has one of them. He's had it for two years now, and although he had some difficulty getting used to its functions at first, he's become quite facile with it. He places a call to the secretaries' desk. "Hello Louise, Detective Delacroix here, Greg. Listen. I want to access the records on personnel who have worked at this station. Can I get that? Great." She gives him the access code, which he writes on a yellow notepad that he keeps on his desk. "Listen, it's got to go back a ways. How far back does it go? Shit. Oh well thanks Louise." The records only go back as far as the early seventies. For a moment he sits there stymied, before getting the thought. If he goes back to the earliest records of employees, he's bound to find some officers who knew McCrae.

Just as he's turning on the computer, he sees the Captain walking down the hall on his way to his office. Greg leaves the machine and catches him just in front of his office. "Captain Magness!" The Captain stops and turns. Kerry Magness is a big, tall man in his mid sixties, six foot six, "Another Irishman," Greg says to himself. He knows that the Captain is due to retire at the end of the year. He likes the man. He's always been fair, showing little if any favoritism toward any of the men, but runs a tight ship and sure as hell knows his business. He's only been at the Hollywood division for the past three years, having worked various precincts all over the city, but has been on the force for at least forty years. Maybe he's run into this McCrae character in the past.

"What can I do for you Sergeant?" The big man leans against one of the windows that surround his office.

"This is just a long shot Captain, but I'm trying to locate someone. He was a detective, worked this precinct years ago. Maybe you knew him or know someone who did. He's probably long gone by now, a Jack McCrae." Greg watches a wide smile spread softly, like a rising mist across the face of his superior.

"Crazy old Jack McCrae," he smiles. "Sure I knew him. Years ago. He retired the year I started. Jesus that was forty years ago." He says this as if realizing for the first time just how long he's been at the job. Greg has to smile at the Captain's reaction. "I was working Central Division, downtown, but sometimes we mixed with the Hollywood boys. I heard of McCrae before I met him. Everyone had heard of old Jack. He was a character. Old school. I wasn't at the retirement party, but the next day the story was all over town. The boys handed him a live bat along with the plaque, and whatever else they gave to you back then."

"A bat! What the hell..." The Captain interrupts him. He's a busy man and Greg's surprised by his reaction but anxious for him to elaborate on it.

"Yup, a bat. You see, for years old Jack would bend everyone's ear with this theory he'd come up with. Two cases he'd worked on that never did get solved. Show biz cases, murder-disappearances. Since nobody came up with any explanations, Jack tried to convince the boys that they were the work of vampires!"

"No kidding Captain. That's rich." Captain Magness straightens up and turns toward the office door.

"Yup," he mumbles. "Crazy Jack McCrae. He was quite a character. An Irishman. Irish as God makes them. Boys used to ask him if he thought maybe the Leprechauns did it."

"Look Captain." Greg stops him at the door. "You think this McCrae is still alive? I'd like to talk with him." The Captain turns and grins at Greg.

"You can't be Irish with a name like Delacroix."

"Only on Saint Patty's Day." Greg grins back. "No seriously, I'd like to talk with him if he's still around." He's tempted to elaborate on why he wants to speak with the man, but the Captain's reaction makes him hesitate giving any explanation.

"Well, he had a nephew. Used to live with him. Same last name. Can't recall the first name. Over on Wilton and Franklin. Think the house was on Wilton. Might give him a shot."

"Thanks Captain," Greg says quickly, "I'll do that." As he turns and starts to go back to his desk, the Captain stops him.

"Wouldn't have anything to do with this Zimmer case, would it?" He asks this softly.

"Yeah. Yeah, it would. Thanks again Captain." He heads back, leaving the big man standing by the door, lips pursed thoughtfully.

Minutes later, Jim Diehm pops into the room and pulls a chair up to Greg's desk. He walks with a slight limp, and lets out a sigh as he sits. He's obviously in constant pain. "Hey Jim, Thanks."

"No problem Buddy. What's up?" Greg shakes his head.

"That Captain Magness is a cagey old bastard. Boy, he doesn't miss a beat. Got to hand it to him."

"Why? What's up?" Jim asks him again.

"It's this Zimmer case," Greg starts to explain. "I'm trying to locate an old timer, used to work this division, name of Jack McCrae." He goes on to tell Jim of his conversation with Captain Magness. Jim laughs.

"Vampires huh?"

"Yeah, or leprechauns." They both laugh. Greg fills Jim in on what he's come up with, the albums, McCrae, and the similarities in all three mysteries. "Look Jim," he says, "if you could research those two old unsolved ones, I'll track down this McCrae or someone who knew him. He had to be on to something".

"Who else is assigned to the Zimmer thing?"

"I'm working with Cove. We're still collecting evidence and waiting for the Medical Examiner's report. "

"No problem Buddy. Things have been slow at the desk. The animals must be sleeping. The zoo is closed. Mostly traffic accidents these last few days. I could use something to keep me busy. You know, make the time go." Jim assures his friend. Greg watches him limp out of the room.

"Poor guy," he says to himself. "Living like that day and night."

Greg pours himself a cup of coffee at the coffee station and by chance runs into his partner, Eddy Cove. "Jesus, Greg, it's turning into winter out there. Must be fifty degrees outside."

"Don't tell them that in Michigan, Partner. Take off your coat and pull up a chair."

The two men return to Greg's desk. Eddy Cove is younger than Greg by a few years. Like Greg he's got dark hair, almost black, but it's cut shorter. They're both about six feet. Greg's just a touch taller and Eddy, a bit stockier. This is not their first case together. They work well as a team, each having that special sense of what the other is doing, or going to do, thinking, or about to think. Most cops have it with their partners, sometimes more so with them than with their wives or girlfriends. It's a survival thing above all, but also an efficiency thing. Like any form of teamwork, it develops into a type of communication, often non-verbal and sometimes, very much so. Cops spend long, strange hours together, especially detectives when working on a case. They have to deal with crime scenes, evidence, perpetrators, and district attorneys. There's plenty of time to talk, and the talk is often about things not related to work. There are wives of male cops who become jealous of their husbands' male partners, and husbands who feel the same about their wives' partners, most of whom are males. Like Greg, Eddy has a girlfriend, a new one. There have been a succession of them and Greg hasn't met the one he's currently dating.

"How's things with Liz?" he asks, pleased that he came up with the name.

"I don't know, Partner. Don't get enough time to see her. She's never dated a cop. Doesn't know the routine."

"Well, maybe that's a good thing. She's got no bad souvenirs. Good place to start."

"You always know how to put a good spin on it Greg," Eddy chuckles, and somewhat sadly adds, "Maybe that's why things click with you and Lucille. How is that beautiful girl?"

"You know Eddy; I think I got really lucky. God must have smiled on me when I met her. When I'm just starting a case, she does something that none of the others ever could do. She gives me the space and the time to do what I have to do, and I never feel any pressure, just," he searches for the word or words, "just, love. It's pure love. It's like she releases me to do what I have to do." Greg tells Eddy about her promise to make dinner whenever he gets home.

"You're a lucky man, Partner. You give her my best, will you?"

"You bet."

Sometimes Greg feels a bit like the older brother. The two men go over what they have so far and decide who will follow through on what. There are a lot of holes and not much evidence. The business about Zimmer seeming to have no records of his past, except what he left on film, is very strange. They decide that either there's been a foul up somewhere in the records departments of the various agencies, or they just haven't tracked down everything.

"Maybe he never had to go to a dentist," Eddy smirks. "Lucky bastard if that's true."

Greg shakes his head in disbelief. "It's the age thing that gets me. The guy made a movie forty years ago." Check out the movie magazines, Hollywood Reporter, Variety. See if they have any recent photos. Greg's already filled him in on the Jack McCrae angle and tells him that he'll follow through with the nephew."

"Oh, and Eddy, look into local vampire cults. I doubt if that's going to lead anywhere, but look into it."

"I'll do that Greg, and check back with you later. When are we going home for that dinner?" Eddy asks, as he gets up to put on his overcoat.

"Now you sound like a wife." Greg grins at his partner.

"Bingo!"

"Depends on if I can hook up with this nephew," Greg answers. "Just leave a message. I'll pick them up later."

"See ya."

"Later. Bundle up. Don't let that 'Nor Easter' get you."

Greg's coffee has turned cold. He doesn't need any more. He's had enough.

Outside the windows of the station house, the gray sky envelopes the city of Hollywood. He shivers, despite himself. He'll track down the nephew if he's to be found. He calls information and asks for a McCrae, telling the operator that he's looking for someone with that name, on Wilton Avenue. To his delight and surprise, she finds a name immediately, a Patrick McCrae. He jots down the number, and then decides he'll have one more cup of coffee. The coffee at the station house tastes nothing like the rich Colombian coffee they serve at Gino's. Back at his desk, he dials the number. It rings three times, and an answering machine or voice mail picks up and starts its message. "Shit," he mutters, "no one home." With that he hears a click and a voice breaks in.

"Hello. McCrae here." The voice is medium pitched but firm. Over the years Greg has tuned himself to voices over the phone. The phone is often the first encounter one has with the other person. The quality of the voice, the manner of speaking, the accent, language and grammar, are all clues to the person holding the receiver. Later, when he encounters that same voice in the flesh, he's already got a profile of the person and a plan on how to approach, and deal with him or her.

"Mr. McCrae. My name is Greg Delacroix. I'm a detective in the Hollywood Division.... Right. I know. In fact that's my reason for calling you.....No. I never knew him. My Captain here did.....Kerry Magness....Well, he's only been here three years, but he knew your uncle years ago." Greg is tempted to accelerate the conversation and get to the point, but senses that this man probably lives alone, and has little contact socially. He'll chat with him, before asking if his uncle is still alive, even though he can taste the question on his lips....."Yeah, so he says....a character....yes.....Yeah, he told me the story of the bat at the retirement party." Something tells Greg not to laugh. "No. No, he never said anything like that. He just told me that the boys were having a little fun with your uncle....No, he didn't know him that well but he spoke about him affectionately.....He's not crazy. Then he's still alive?....My God! Ninety-seven years old. The luck of the Irish.... No, French. And French Canadian.... Does he live with you?....Retirement home on Melrose....Oh yes, I know it....Well; I'd like to talk with him about all that. I think he was on to something....I agree....Well, I agree, I think he could be a huge help on a case I'm working on.....A little incoherent sometimes....Well of course you would be there. We could visit him together....That would be great Patrick. You don't mind if I call you Patrick?....OK, Pat. Well I'm Greg..... Listen. Let me give you my home phone number. I've got voice mail there. You can always leave a message. It's 842-3115.... Yeah, Anytime....A good day....Right....Well you just call and I'll drop everything and come over.....Yes, tomorrow would be great....OK, you let me know....Thanks Pat....Right. Thanks.

It was beyond belief. The man was still alive, ninety-seven years of age. If he could just talk with him. And his nephew, this Pat, he must know almost as much about the two cases as his uncle. The whole thing was crazy, but so far it was the one lead that he could go on. The Medical Examiner's report would be out the next day. Greg decides that he'll get home early. He'll spend the rest of the afternoon researching the old files. He finds the Jeff Smith file, and gets through some of it, but doesn't get to the Roland Jordan one. He'll ask Jim to look up the other one. .

At six he calls Lucille. "I'm breaking this up early, Darling. There isn't much more to do today. Tomorrow things are going to really pick up. Let's spend some time together before then." He takes notes; names, times, associates, and writes them down on his notepad. Before leaving, he runs off copies of all that, and adds a note to Eddy Cove. "Double check the files on the two cases. I ran through the Jeff Smith file, but didn't get to the Jordan one. I want to know names of people connected to this. See if you can put faces to any names. Thanks, Partner."

There's a parking spot on the street just in front of the house, a rare occurrence if he gets home after five in the afternoon. The branch still hangs over the fence, shifting with the rising wind, challenging him, taunting, daring him to move it, like a thing with a life of its own. He makes himself a promise that he'll take care of it over the weekend. He'll cut it up and burn it in the fireplace. If the weather continues as it has been, a fire would be perfect.

Lucille opens the door before he can reach the doorknob. The breeze ruffles her long wavy hair. It's amber red glows like a setting sun, or the last embers in a campfire before nightfall. He has never noticed it quite like he sees it at this moment. Her arms wrap him to her bosom. The white wool fisherman's sweater caresses the nape of his neck, rough, but at the same time, tender. There is no need for words. She guides him through the passageway. Inside, he is overcome with the potpourri of smells, her own exotic blend, warm spices from the kitchen, and the soft scent of dry pine as it smolders in the fire.

On the dark carpet, it is she who makes love to him, her lips on his, her breath on his neck, tresses across his nipples and stomach, and thighs, and again, her lips on him. Now he tastes her and loves her taste; moist smoke, pine and cedar and fir, and then, imperceptibly, they are one; one soul, one heart, one body, one bond. . .together, forever, to the stars and beyond.

They savor a cool white 'ninety-four Chignon accompanied by an endive salad with a Poupon marinade, followed by a delicate Capellini Al Pomodoro, sweet basil and angel hair pasta, and garlic, lots of it, perfumed and rich. She asks no questions. He volunteers none. All has been said with the touch. Later, when they're done, and the burned down candles flicker over the remnants on the table, he blows them out and taking her small hand in his, guides her upstairs, to bed.

CHAPTER 2

Zimmer

George Zimmer was dead. At least he certainly appeared to be. Lenny Field regarded the body abjectly. It lay in the elaborately ornate casket that was his master's, as it had always been. The casket was detailed in silver, with strange beasts and brilliant fires, depicting a history as old as mankind itself. For three days, Zimmer's body had lain in its coffin, in the middle of the living room floor of the old chateau that nestled above Sunset Plaza, off the boulevard; the chateau with the turrets and towers that peaked out behind thick magnolia trees. The chateau was in a way the family home. It had been built for them in the late 'twenties before they arrived, and there they had resided since, first only Lenny and Marcus, then Dragan, this Zimmer. Well, at that time he had not yet become Zimmer, and as Lenny regarded the body, waiting for The Change, he wondered who, what, his master would be this time. He had marveled at The Change three times since they had come to Hollywood, and many more times in the past. Both he and Marcus had been through it, in fact they had both just attained their current identities by going through The Change, only weeks earlier. It had always been so. Together they had passed through many countries and countless generations. In the old days, before computers and modern ways of record keeping, they had managed to keep their identities for many years. Ordinary life spans were much shorter then and the world, a much larger place, its mysteries guarded, and held in place through fear and superstition. The modern world brought change. Superstition had mostly been replaced by science, and knowledge destroyed the last remnants of fear. They were among the last of their kind. There still remained a few of the Old Ones scattered across the continents, but the three had first come to America with the initial settlers, over the years, had migrated with the pioneers, before finally arriving in California with the first influx of miners, during the gold rush of 1849. They had traveled through the mining camps in towns with names like, Cripple Creek, Coeur d'Alene, Hangtown, and Carson City. They had never mined for ore or panned for gold. As aristocrats, that kind of labor had never coursed through their blood. Instead they had set themselves up as financiers or shopkeepers when times were tough. The only mining they did, if it could qualify as such, was the mining of the life blood of their chosen victims, for sustenance, and when it became necessary, and for The Change, when their current identities had to disappear, to be replaced with new ones. They could never bring about this transformation at the same time because it required the help of at least one of the two others to achieve it. One of them had to remain with the body during the six-day period that was the amount of time needed for The Change.

The third of their group currently went by the name, Marcus Banning. Over the years, the three of them had acquired many names, many identities. Lenny Field and Marcus Banning no longer remembered what they had been called before the initial transformation, before they had been selected for eternal life by The Master. His name they would never forget. It was a name as ancient and icy as the craggy mountains of their homeland, Transylvania, Hungary, a name that had once sent cold fear running through the veins of the peasants who lived outside his castle walls and knew him then, but spoke his name in a whisper, only rarely, and only after making the holy sign of the Cross; Dragan Radelescu, Vampire, The Living Dead!

Lenny, regarded the seemingly lifeless body before him, and then glanced toward the great brass clock that hung on the wall over the stone fireplace. The time had come. Now the body would start the metamorphosis which would endure over the next seventy two hours, as the body of George Zimmer would evolve into its new form, taking on the physical and mental properties of its last victim, of the generations that had preceded that victim, as well as all those countless lives that had come and gone before, George Zimmer; Patricia Schreppel, Jeff Smith, Roland Jordan, Sylvia, and so on. The Change always started in the face before traveling the length of the body. George Zimmer had been a person of diminutive stature, his victim, the transient, a much larger person. Lenny understood the risk involved in this transmutation. Sometimes, as the body evolved into its new form, the clothes would rip or start to strangle the one who was changing. A vampire could never lie naked in his coffin, and when The Change took place it had to wear the clothes of its last identity. Every aspect of that victim, his dress, the knowledge he possessed as well as his physical appearance and those same things from his gene pool, from the generations that preceded him, go into, and mix with, the vampire's own. Lenny too had transmogrified a number of times since arriving in Hollywood. The long blond locks of hair had given way to shorter darker ones, and the body too had thinned, but there still remained something of the hunch that he had had to endure during those early years.

As the sweat started to break on the brow of the thing in the casket and what had been a seemingly pale and lifeless face, began to twitch, he placed the call. The spacious room was unfurnished. Two chairs, one at the head, the other at the foot of the casket were the sole items of furniture in the place. Tall windows, framed with heavy purple velvet curtains, gave vista to the outside world. On the exterior, these windows were shuttered. At night in any season, they were shuttered closed. Now open, the last remnants of day's end barely broke through the thick glass, giving faint light to the room. Old embers glowed in the fireplace where tiny flames danced before the ritual. Lenny produced a cellular phone from inside the leather vest that was a constant accessory to his wardrobe, and dialed the number at the production company.

"Marcus please," he said to the secretary. Again he glanced at the body. The hair was changing color and texture, and the hard lines that had once etched the face of George Zimmer, were giving way to a smoother, younger flesh. "Erdelyben Kezdott." It was the phrase they had uttered with awe for centuries, each time The Change began. "It started in Transylvania!"

"It's good," Marcus responded, respectful of the power of the thing. "If you need me, let me know. I will sit with him this evening."

"I thank you my brother. The waiting is always so tiring. I must sleep."

"Then you shall. This project is just beginning. I have the time." He laughed. "I shall tell you of it in a few hours. I think you'll find it interesting."

"I need a diversion," Lenny replied. "I shall cook us up something to eat."

Or is it still too early to tell?"

"He will be pleased. He shall be younger this time, more attractive. He was never happy with this last one. He picked well. This one was young and tall. Very fit."

"That is good. There will be less explaining to do." Marcus suggested, then asked, "You say this one was a wanderer, an unknown?"

"Yes, we made sure. He was a Homeless. We found him on Santa Monica Boulevard, but he was clean. No disease, strong body. No dementia."

"You know my brother," Marcus said slowly, "it is a thing of great beauty to see the Master each time in his new form. He will be even wiser, even more powerful."

"Yes," Lenny agreed, his voice filled with reverence, "it is indeed. Only in his eyes do we see the Old One, the one who gave us life."

"I must go. Someone is coming into the office," Marcus cut short the conversation. "I will see you in a few hours. Good bye."

For the next couple of hours Lenny alternated between standing vigil over the changing body and preparing the dinner that he would share with Marcus. It is only myth that suggests that his breed subsist exclusively on human blood, and it is only rarely that their need peaks to the point that it forces them to drink of it. Were they to do so on a daily basis, they would surely be ensnared and revealed as the creatures they are. When they do partake in the practice, they do so much as do the South American bats that bear their namesake, the Vampire Bat. These bats, when they feed, drink only a small portion from an unsuspecting horse or sheep, leaving tiny bite marks on an ear or throat, not much more than a nuisance to the beast and in no way depleting it of its strength. So it is with these bestial things, who when they must feed on human blood, do so with great discretion, finding a sleeping drunk in a park, or a person alone, in a deep sleep, who may have left the bedroom window open, and who will wake the following morning, somewhat weakened and confused. They are also capable of changing a human into one of them, an Eternal, for that is the word they use to describe their lot. And they have never hesitated in taking a mortal life if that human somehow discovered what creatures they really were. Over the years, many who stumbled upon their secret were eliminated before they could reveal to mankind the nature of these monsters. But despite their caution, tales and folklore were passed down through the generations, of these, the undead. Humans call them vampires," but that is a word never uttered from the cold lips of one of them. This initiation is extremely rare, more so now than in the old days, and it must be requested and consented to by the one initiated.

These three came to America shortly after the Revolution, the French one, for they had been two centuries in France living as aristocrats, and as such, were forced to flee as were many others, those who managed to escape with their lives. In all that time only one, a woman had been made one of them, and she had come to a fiery end, tied to a stake in an eastern town called, Salem.

Women had always been a liability. Perhaps it was because when women came into the picture, they brought men with them, men who were humans, and that brought with it, the risk of discovery. Perhaps it was simply, that when they were with women, a kind of love was involved, the only form of love of which these creatures were capable. Then like the humans they had once been, the Eternals were subject to all love's frailties. Whatever the reasons, these three had chosen to live without female company. From time to time, a woman had come into their lives, and in each case, the results had been catastrophic.

Lenny checked the body once before heading toward the kitchen at the far end of the mansion, passing through the great hallway, dining room, and pantry, before finally arriving in the there. The house had been constructed in 1925 and was built in the "Tudor Castle" style very popular at the time, complete with the mandatory gargoyles. But unlike many other similar houses that employed stucco exteriors, Dragan had imported huge granite rocks from Colorado, and for the interior, marble from Italy. The gargoyles were replicas of the ones on the Notre Dame Cathedral in Paris, a city he had come to know rather well during his two hundred year stay there.

When Lenny arrived in the kitchen, he looked around and smiled with satisfaction. It was a kitchen that would delight any chef or gourmet. It was replete with vast counter and cabinet space, all kinds of cooking utensils and accessories, two refrigerators and a large freezer, all of which were laden with wide varieties of meats, fresh vegetables and exotic delicacies. Adjacent to the kitchen was a wine cellar that was no doubt the best-unknown cellar in Los Angeles, probably in all America. Everything was constantly stocked and maintained by the three of them with much of it, not consumed and latter discarded.

There was another room next to the wine cellar, but sealed with a simple padlock. It was in this room, that Dragan, perhaps due to egotism, perhaps, some form of sentiment, kept his souvenirs. This chamber, this sanctuary, housed those rare things from their past that, over the years, with each move, from country to country, he had taken with them. In this room, he could touch the original coat of arms of the Radelescu family, re-read a letter addressed to him, by Marie Antoinette, and a note from Leonardo DaVinci, or linger over a photo, dated, 1898, of his residence in San Francisco. And he could pause over stills from films, he had directed, including, *"Westward Wagons,"* and *"Biker Hell."*

He had carried, and collected these pieces of his past, throughout the centuries, and in each place he had lived, created a sanctum in which to enjoy these memories. He understood the risk involved in so doing; that if a stranger were to stumble into one of these "museums," a connection might be drawn, and his secret revealed. Dragan had cleverly kept his past lives, secret. He was a prudent creature, but, like the man he had once been, he had also retained a certain degree of vanity, which he might prefer to call, sentimentality. Since their arrival in Hollywood, this house had always been the main house, their headquarters. The Master had in the past, with each new identity, taken another residence. That had been a precaution.

An aquarium stocked with live shellfish caught Lenny's attention. He decided on a Chinese meal. For the next two hours, he passed the time alternating between the kitchen and the living room. The body kept mutating, growing longer and fuller. On one visit he loosened all the clothing. As it transposed it would twitch and shudder, appearing to a first time observer that it was a live thing. But Lenny knew better. In fact, The Old One was in a coma-like state, feeling and knowing nothing. Only when the process was complete, would the eyes slowly open, and with it the mind, and when that happened, all the power and knowledge from countless generations would once again come to life.

By the time Marcus arrived and the outside daylight had given passage to that of the moon and the stars, the meal was complete and the table elegantly set. Before doing anything Marcus paid his respects to the changing body of his master. When he had satisfied himself that everything was as it should be, the two of them moved to the dining room to eat by candlelight.

"This was a good choice Lenny," he complimented his associate after tasting the appetizer of stuffed squid. It was accompanied with green tea and steaming sake. They all cooked, but it was probably Lenny, who enjoyed it most. Of the three of them, Marcus had probably physically altered the least since first arriving in Hollywood, despite having gone through The Change a number of times. He was still small in build although he had filled out some and grown a few inches. The hair had become sandy brown, the face fuller and less pinched, but it was still an old face and he still wore glasses. In fact the last mutation, which he had just gone through with, had added perhaps ten years to the man Ned Delacroix had encountered for the first time that morning at Gower Gulch, one Peter Weir. He did not, facially resemble Peter Weir in any way. He had however, retained one mannerism that had been Weir's. He still tugged at his ear, the left one, when agitated. Of course like the others, once he had transformed he stayed at whatever was that age. They were both famished and didn't say much until the second course of fresh crab with ginger and black bean sauce.

"What was it you were going to tell me?" Lenny asked Marcus.

"Oh that!" He chuckled softly. "I never told you what this new project was. Well it's very new. Only had it three days now but the money's all there and we've decided to go with a fresh cast, mostly TV actors from some of the hot shows."

"What's the story?" Lenny questioned him. Marcus took a moment before answering.

"This crab is excellent, as always," he said. Lenny just nodded, pleased by the complement.

"I'm going to be producing this one, and The Master, in his new form, as Richard Stewart, will direct. Of course I shall hire him, even though he will be unknown in the business. This has always worked in the past. In any case, we're going ahead with it. We've read the script. The story moves and the characters are interesting but a little naive. I'll have to work on that a bit. What's the next course?" He asked, licking his fingers all the way to the ends of the sharp white nails. Lenny knew Marcus almost as Marcus knew himself. He had always been that way, carrying on multiple conversations and thoughts, segueing but always returning to each concept in its own time.

"We will have some more squid with fried egg noodles and then for dessert, leeches' in syrup. Does that please you my brother?"

"Yes, that is a most satisfying combination when one must settle for what humans eat." Satisfied that his fingers were clean, he leaned in and mouthed, "It is a vampire story that takes place in another town called Hollywood. It's called, "Life-Blood, The Last Vampires of Hollywood."

Lenny stopped eating and stole a look toward the living room. His usually ruddy complexion turned sour, pale. Then looking across the table at Marcus said, "I don't know if I like this idea. It is something we've never talked about because I believe we all knew that that was a subject that we wouldn't become involved in. Over the years we've done all kinds of pictures; Westerns, Comedies, Dramas, but we've always avoided anything that comes close to us, to The Old One." Again he glanced toward the room that housed the coffin.

"I know," Marcus responded. "What you say is true, but this one has such possibilities. At last we can present it as it really is and kill these foolish myths and notions that we have had to endure for so long!" Lenny gazed intently across the table but seemed to see only his own reflection in the glasses that Marcus wore. That made him turn away. "The Master and I have already spoken of it when he was George Zimmer. He simply warned me to be careful. He too thinks that if we can put to rest some of the crazy notions that humans have, and then we shall perhaps lead more comfortable lives here, with less chance of being found out. After all, as the producer, I can make them very sympathetic."

"If he has sanctioned it, then it shall be so. Perhaps we should check him once more before the leeches' are served." So the two of them rose from the table and went through the vast house to the living room at its far end.

He lay there much as he was when Lenny last left him. The breathing was slow and shallow and the face no longer twitched. The transformation appeared to have subsided some. The sweat on the brow had dried, and color had seeped back into the face. Over the next two days the process would complete itself. He had the look of a younger, more physical man than he had been as George Zimmer. Both Marcus and Lenny were pleased. "Everything is as it should be. I don't anticipate any problems. What do you think Marcus?"

"I think The Old One will be most pleased with his new form, and I think you are right. It's always at the beginning of The Change that if there are to be problems, they will come then."

"You will sit with him tonight?"

"Yes." Marcus assured him. "It's my duty to do so. You sleep my brother."

"First we will taste the leeches'," Lenny said with some pride. "I think you will find them refreshing."

When they had finished the meal they took care of clearing the table and cleaning the dishes. "Go to bed and sleep," Marcus ordered Lenny. That too was part of their relationship. They both obeyed Dragan's every wish and command, but between the two of them, it was Marcus who usually directed Lenny, Lenny often taking the more servile role, the cleaning and fetching, the labor, and always, the driving. In fact it was a rare occasion that brought them together in the kitchen after a meal doing the dishes. But then, this was indeed a rare occurrence, and Marcus was not unsympathetic to Lenny's needs. "Sleep well. Dream beautiful dreams," he said, as Lenny started to ascend the spiral stairway.

The bedroom in which Lenny slept was dark and spacious in oak. A bathroom furnished in marble, with silver faucets and a deep free standing tub with clawed feet, accessed the room. Here too, the windows were shuttered on the exterior, and framed with the same heavy velvet drapes that were found downstairs. But the bed stood out, and other than its size which was appropriate for the room, seemed misplaced. Lacy white curtains draped from a frame above the bed posts, completely enclosed it, like a coffin or death bed, and the wood frame which could be seen through these curtains, was of maple, soft and light in color and tone. He was so exhausted that he fell asleep fully clothed on top of the silk comforter with the flowered prints, daffodils, all yellow. He dreamt of times gone by, forever lost; of wild dogs running with the wolves through the winter forests in an ancient land that he had not seen for a long time, of dark forests blanketed in snow, and tall pines reaching toward a yellow moon. And he dreamed of the loves he had known, so rare, so long ago, and he dreamed of death, eternal peace and wondered what it could be like.

He awoke sometime around nine in the morning and found Marcus slumped in the chair at the foot of the casket. The body had filled out and the face looked to be settled into the visage that would be its own, unchanged until the next transformation. He brewed a pot of hot Turkish coffee, still a favorite from their days in that part of the world, and gently woke Marcus. "Get up my brother. I am here now. Here is some coffee before you leave for work." Marcus took the cup gratefully and inspected the body before him.

"He is doing well. Soon it will be done," he said to Lenny who had taken his place at the head of the casket. They drank the coffee but shared no thoughts or conversation. Marcus noted that Lenny seemed to be worried or preoccupied with something. He asked him about it on his way out.

"My head is full with many things Marcus. Last night I had strange dreams. I dreamed of death, and that scared me. I've never thought of that before. And this movie worries me. We've always had our own way of doing things. Once, I made a terrible mistake, but I have paid for it, and I understand now. There are rules that we abide by, and the rules have reason, and it is that reason that has protected us, all these years, all this time. It surprises me that The Master agreed to this abomination of a movie. And there is another thing that worries me. The Master has chosen to lodge here in his new form. We've always had another residence, for security, so that they could never trace us to this place." Marcus regarded him gently.

"The times change my brother. We have seen them change in countless countries for centuries. The times change and the people change, and our kind have always survived by changing with them. The master knows this. Watch him well. Be tranquil. It will be as it has always been." With that he was gone. Lenny stood in the open doorway. The sun was out. He didn't like the sun. He had learned to tolerate it to some degree. When he had first become an Eternal, he could not survive the sun for more than a few minutes a day. He lived at night and slept by day. But as with human food, he had slowly acclimated himself to it. Still he did not much care for the sun. This was true for Marcus as well. A flash of sunlight shot off the back fender of the silver Mercedes convertible as Marcus pulled out the drive. Lenny winced and retreated to the darkness of the castle.

The production office for the film was in one of the bungalows on the lot at Raleigh Studios, over on Melrose almost across from Paramount. The whole lot had been upgraded several years before with new, high tech sound stages. It had always been a pretty busy place in the past, catering to mostly commercials, with some films shot there as well, but now more and more film production was going on, and getting on and off the lot was usually a messy business for the traffic. It was really an ideal location for film production, right in the center of Hollywood with all the support industries close at hand. Nearby, are film and sound labs, special effect houses, camera and lighting equipment rental houses, as well as property houses and greens companies for the rental of all kinds of plants and grass mats, artificial snow and such, in fact all that is necessary for bringing the outdoors inside, and re-creating it on a sound stage. Marcus loved the movies. He loved the films, the fantasy, the suspension of disbelief, and he loved the business of making them, the producing and directing, the long hours, the stress and the thrill of the gamble. It was a wild ride for an adventurer and he was surely one of the world's last. And he knew the movies and the business of the movies perhaps better than any living man, which of course he was not. He had after all been involved with the moving pictures since the late 'twenties, just as the "talking pictures" were beginning to take off. Over the years, he had been witness to all the innovations that came to film making, new methods in style and color, equipment special effects and genre. The movies had come a long way. Now, computers could digitally replace scenery and even actors. He could smile with satisfaction, knowing that they would never replace producers or directors.

This new film would be unlike any with which he had been previously involved. It had not been his idea to go ahead with it. When the proposal was sent to his office along with a script and loose budget, he had at first dismissed the idea, knowing that there existed a non-verbal understanding among them that this was a subject that they would never breach. But there was something in the script that drew him into it.

The story takes place in a small western mining town in the early nineteen hundreds. Strangely enough, the name of this place is, Hollywood. After years of wondering to avoid detection, three Eternals find themselves in this Hollywood, just prior to a violent storm that completely floods and ravages the community. The town has vital mining interests and in addition to the physical damage done to the community by the storm, it also kills most of the population. Following the tempest, looters and opportunists descend on the town, resulting in a running feud, a blood bath among the various factions for control of the village and the mining fortune at hand. Eventually, the group led by the Eternal Ones regains authority, and over the years these three become the town leaders. Slowly but methodically, they convert the population into their own kind. It becomes a community of vampires with complete power and autonomy. Eventually, only a handful of humans are left. By then they have discovered the town's horrible secret. Led by a Doctor Van Helsing, the village doctor and his son, Jonathan, they face off against the vampires and destroy all but the leader who is forced to flee. There is a love story that runs through the main story line that follows the traditional Bram Stroker, Dracula story, as the head vampire, whose name is Borisa has designs on Jonathan's girl, Lucy.

Perhaps it was similarity of names and events; three of The Old Ones, the name of the village, it being a western mining town, perhaps simply the timing of the thing coming across his desk, he wasn't sure what induced him after reading the script, to take it home and show it to Dragan. He did so on a night when he knew Lenny would not be present, sensing that Lenny's response would be negative, and guessing, correctly that Dragan would see what he had seen in the story.

"I think the time has come when we can address this kind of thing," Zimmer said, thoughtfully handing the manuscript back to Marcus. It had taken him less than two minutes to thoroughly read the thing. "Information rules this new world; information and misinformation that is properly conveyed. I want you to go ahead with it my son. Besides, it's been years since we've done a film project, and I miss it. I will direct it, in my new body, as one, Richard Stewart."

"I felt that you would see it that way," Marcus said with some relief. "Besides," he added, flashing a twinkle from behind the thick spectacles, "it will make a hell of a good movie!"

"You and Thalberg." The Master said almost affectionately. "You two always were like boys when it came to the movies." He regarded his protégé. "You've far surpassed the boy genius now Marcus."

"That was his choice," Marcus seemed to snap back. "I gave him the chance to become one of us, but he refused. In fact I still think it was that, that killed him."

"It is just as well," Zimmer said. "I was never convinced of his loyalties." Marcus shook his head but said nothing. "You will wait to tell Lenny," Zimmer instructed him. "Wait until I am three days into The Change. He will be troubled but he will not protest. If you must, tell him that I said that you would go ahead with this film."

That had happened several weeks earlier. "We shall see. We shall see," Marcus said to himself as he pulled up to the studio gate and nodded to the uniformed guard who immediately recognized the car and the man, and waved him into the bustling movie factory.

Over the remaining time needed to complete The Change, the activities and routine around the castle remained pretty much as they had been. At night when Marcus returned from work, he was welcomed with a carefully prepared and very edible meal, although the conversation at the dinner table was minimal. Marcus knew that Lenny remained disturbed because of Marcus' activities at the studio, but he also knew, knowing Lenny as he did, that all this would pass when The Old One had again risen in his new form. Lenny continued to carefully watch over the figure that was metamorphosing in the coffin, while at the same time tending to the everyday activities required around the house. Exactly six days, one hundred and twenty four hours from the moment that George Zimmer had sucked dry the corpse of the transient that he had housed and so carefully prepared for this moment, at twelve, midnight, on the morning of Friday, the sixteenth of October, Richard Stewart blinked once, then slowly opened his dark eyes.

Both Lenny and Marcus were witness to the event, one at the head, the other at the foot of that casket that had once been horse drawn down the streets of this city, Hollywood, the city they now claimed as their own. Both were dressed entirely in black, black turtlenecks and slacks, "Perry Ellis", and black ""Gucci" shoes and socks. Each held components of identical wardrobe for The Master who when the eyes did open, was naked but for the powdered ashy remnants of the apparel that had once covered the body of George Zimmer. This, they carefully dusted off as they meticulously dressed him. Although fully awake, he did not move to assist them in any way, allowing them to complete the task before rising to a seated position. Having done so, he held out both his arms so that they could aid him as he descended from the box. For a moment he seemed to stand on unsteady legs much as would a baby colt who having just been birthed, discovers for the first time that he posses that capability. When he spoke, the voice was strong, commanding, a much different voice from that of George Zimmer. "You have done well my children as I knew you would. I think this Richard Stewart will serve our needs most admirably." The two appeared to glow with the acknowledgment. Perhaps it was simply the light from the flickering candles that surrounded the casket and sent shadows skipping across the walls and over the heavy velvet curtains, now drawn.

Outside, the wind rustled the branches of the trees in the yard, and down below, the city, Hollywood, and The Strip burned in all its incandescence.

"You must be hungry Master," Marcus stammered, still in awe after all those years at the wonder of the thing.

"Yes," he replied. "Yes I am. We must feed. It has started!" They walked together to the door that was the front entrance. Lenny reached it first and held it open for the other two, first The Old One, and then Marcus. A gust of the night wind blew into the hallway and as one; the three stepped into the darkness.

Down the hill on the Boulevard, three musicians had just stepped out of the restaurant, "Sushi on Sunset." They were doing a gig at The Roxy and staying across the street at the Hotel Marmont. All three had partaken in great quantities of sake as well as other intoxicating substances. All of a sudden the tall one reeled and shouted, "Jesus Christ! Did you guys see that?"

"See what?" the bearded one asked.

"Bats! Great big sons of bitches! Three of them. I swear they were as big as dogs!" The two others stumbled with laughter.

"You're wacked Tony," the shortest screamed over the horns. "You're pissed!"

"Yeah, you're stoned man," the other joined in. "Wake up. Christ, it's nineteen ninety eight!"

CHAPTER 3

Autopsy

On Friday morning, the sixteenth of October, the fax from the Medical Examiner's office finally rumbles through the machine at the Hollywood precinct. It's a day late. Sergeant Jim Diehm brings it back to the squad room, where Greg is on the phone with Patrick McCrae. Jim stands, resting his weight on his right leg, holding the pages in the right hand, and a steaming mug of coffee in the other, waiting for Greg to finish the call.

"That's great Pat. I'll be there at one. Sure, we can grab some lunch. Well maybe we should see him first. Oh he does. Well OK, we'll get a bite at Gino's. Oh, no problem. Yeah Pat, they've got real food too. Yeah, Italian. Yeah, they've got steaks but I'd recommend the salads. Very nice. OK, see you then. Right Bye."

"Jesus. He's got you by the nuts Buddy," Jim laughs, then asks, "Who's that?"

"That's a long story, is what that is," Greg tells him. "That the autopsy report?" Jim hands it to him and pulls over a chair from one of the other desks.

"You're not going to believe this Buddy," he mutters, settling into the worn and patched Naugahide seat. As Greg scrutinizes the two-page report, Jim sips his coffee. Through the windows, the endless sounds of traffic and the din that is life in Hollywood filter into the room. A bluebird, a rare sight in this town, lights on a branch of the Magnolia tree that graces his view. Greg tosses the report on his desk and runs a hand through his hair.

"Jesus Christ," he whistles. "The guy was bone dry. He didn't have a drop of blood in his body!"

"Yup," Jim nods. "I read it. Thirty-one years old. Perfect health. No broken bones. No holes. No cuts. No nothing, but those bite marks on the neck."

"Jack McCrae's vampires," Greg mutters, as if to himself.

"What's that Buddy?"

"Jack McCrae's vampires."

"Oh yeah. The leprechauns. Part of that long story?"

"That was the nephew on the phone. He's going to take me to his uncle this afternoon. Lives in that retirement home over on Melrose. By Gino's."

"Yeah, I know the place. Don't know how healthy it is for those old timers sitting outside, watching all those cute gals strut their stuff."

"Probably what keeps them alive," Greg laughs. "What's the status on the corpse?"

"They're keeping it on ice for a few more days. Still haven't ID'ed it. Did you read that stuff on the bite marks?"

"Yeah. Similar to canine teeth. Unknown source. That's a big help."

"What about this Zimmer. Anything on his whereabouts?"

"He's still a suspect, but I'm beginning to think that's going to run into a dead end," Greg tells him.

"I almost forgot," Jim says. "Cove dropped off some magazine stuff this morning." He gets up from the chair. "It's out at the desk. Mostly pictures from the trade papers. And he found a file in Records, on the Jordan murder."

"Good work! Thanks."

"This Jack McCrae should be able to help, if he's not some drooling vegetable. Can't believe the guy's still around. Tell you one thing. He kept good notes. I've been looking through these. Must have been a good cop. Good detective."

The remainder of the morning Greg spends looking through the magazine clips and attending to the usual police business. He holds off on the files. The traffic through the station is endless, with officers booking the usual array of junkies, prostitutes, petty thieves and crooks. His desk is like an island in a sea of confusion. All around, phones ring, arguments erupt, and doors slam, and outside above the sound of the city, he can hear the wail of sirens and the squealing of tires, as patrol cars are called out.

The photo clips are from what the film industry calls, "The Trades." They consist almost exclusively of The Hollywood Reporter, and Daily Variety, the two papers that give the industry news; what pictures are in production, costs, stock quotes, casting, hiring and firing, as well as the gossip columns, which often include photos of celebrities. Both these papers came into circulation during The 'Thirties, first The Hollywood Reporter, on September 3, 1930, then three years later, Daily Variety, the offspring of Variety, came out on September 6, 1933. Cove had dug up back issues of both papers dating to the 'Fifties, and left them in three huge cardboard boxes that included the files, and a note:

"Greg. Haven't gone through these. They only go up to the early 'Sixties. Figured that would be enough for now. We've got current photos of Zimmer. Compare them to anything you find here. Good luck buddy. That's a lot of wading to do. Eddy There's also a P.S., and a manila envelope. Found these in with the Roland Jordan files in with Records." Inside the envelope are three spiral notebooks, each with McCrae's signature scrawled on the green, cardboard covers, now weathered by time.

Greg first looks over McCrae's notes on the Jeff Smith mystery. They were, as Jim had described the official file that McCrae must have written, detailed and precise, scratched out in the notepads. There are references to "these horrible creatures," and, "the living dead." On the last page of the third notepad written in red ink in a hand that seemed less steady than the original one, Greg reads these words:

"These murders were not committed by anything human or animal. I am convinced that it is the work of some supernatural force. If anything can account for it, it has to be the work of vampires. This file is still open. This horror will continue. We have not seen the last of it. If YOU are reading these notes, then you too have suspected what I am saying here! Look for a Dragan Radelescu. Look to a George Zimmer."

It is signed, "Jack McCrae, July 5th, 1984.

"Jesus," Greg murmurs, "He names Zimmer. What does he know? That old bastard is a pit bull. He must have come back in here long after he retired and added this." He looks at his watch. Still early. He is looking forward to meeting this old timer. He just hopes, that as Jim somewhat expressed, the man still retains some of his mental faculties. He pours a cup of coffee and settles down to the task of rummaging through the piles of magazines. It doesn't take him long to find the first picture of George Zimmer. It's from The Hollywood Reporter and is dated, June 16th 1955. There's a headshot of Zimmer and a brief blurb underneath referring to "Director George Zimmer and his new movie, bound to be a cult classic, Biker Hell." It gives the movie an excellent review, mentions the cast, all unknowns at the time, but Greg recognizes the names, Brick Lacey, and Niki Starling, an actress, now in her sixties. Brick Lacey has died, but Greg figures he can look up Niki. But what really grabs him, like a hand at his throat, is the picture of the man. The picture is that of a man perhaps in his late forties, with dark hair, and is not noticeably different from a current picture of Zimmer, used to ID him a few days ago, when he first disappeared. Zimmer's current age is listed as fifty-five. In the present photo, he has gray hair, but the face is not much changed from this earlier photo. "Jesus," Greg mutters, forty years have gone by, and the guy's hardly changed at all!"

With an urgency approaching desperation, Greg shuffles through the magazines, passing from week to week, year to year, searching for a second photo. He finds it an hour later. He's just about to give up his search for his meeting with Pat McCrae, when he discovers it in an issue of Variety dated, December 23, 1965. It's a picture from the gossip page, of some swank Beverly Hills party, where individual couples are shown and named, and the reason for the party given. In Hollywood they are mostly fund raisers, or awards events. This one was some charity function. "They're always giving it away," Greg shakes his head. The photo is of Zimmer and a woman. Greg hovers over the page, like a bird of prey waiting on a meal. Again, facially there is very little change, despite the ten years between pictures. He wonders about the hair. If McCrae is anywhere near to the truth, and somehow this man is not a man, and is not capable of aging, then that secret would be a liability. He decides to run it past Diehm on his way out for the meeting. At noon he grabs his nylon windbreaker, and heads to the front desk. He too, notices the bluebird in the Magnolia tree. He smiles. There is something calming about seeing the bird.

"Suppose you couldn't age?" He asks his friend, then repeats himself. Suppose you couldn't get older, but you didn't want anyone to know? I mean if you had nothing to hide, and everyone knew, you'd be phenomena, a celebrity. Geez, you'd be huger than any movie star or politician. You'd be world famous!" Jim laughs as he thinks on that.

"Yeah, just think of all the child support you'd be paying. You'd have to be famous, and filthy rich!"

"Right. But what if you didn't want anyone to know, and you couldn't change it. Oh, you could dye your hair. I suppose you could get some face work done, or put on makeup. I mean this would be a huge problem. Like Dorian Gray, your friends all around you are getting older, and you aren't. What would you have to do? Think about it Jim."

"I see where you're going," Jim nods. "I guess you'd get to a point where people would start asking questions." He pauses, and then adds quietly, "I guess you'd have to just disappear."

"Yeah, but where do you go? Brazil? Kenya? Bora, Bora? You can't disappear anymore. The world's too damn small!"

"Well, with the plastic surgery, burn off your prints..." The two men just look at each other, reflecting on the impossibility of it all, perhaps neither one daring to say what he might be imagining, perhaps neither having arrived at that conclusion.

"Listen Jim, thanks for the help. Think about it. I'm off to meet old Jack McCrae." Jim pats Greg's shoulder and regards his windbreaker.

"Well Laddie," he says, with a bad Irish inflection, "you'll do well with the old leprechaun. You're wearing green."

Pat McCrae's house is a little wood framed bungalow style place right on the corner of Wilton and Franklin. Greg finds a spot close by on Wilton, and parks the Mustang in the shade of one of the trees that line the street. As he crosses the street, he smiles. McCrae's house is Emerald Green, with even greener trim. Pat McCrae answers the doorbell immediately. He too, has a windbreaker in hand, and like Greg's, it too is green.

"Ah Greg," he thrusts out a short arm and seizes Greg's hand. "I see you're wearing the colors." Greg knows immediately that Pat has no intention of inviting him in, and is in fact, all set for lunch at Gino's. Greg doubts that he'll be able to sell him on the salad.

"Nice to meet you Pat," Greg releases his hand after its being pumped by this short, very intense looking fellow. "We'll take my car, the Mustang." He indicates the car with a toss of his head. Crossing the street he takes a real look at the younger McCrae, and figures his age to be somewhere in the early sixties. Pat bounds across the street with the energy of a teenager. "Must run in the family," he mumbles to himself as he opens his door. McCrae has already taken a seat, and is busy attaching the seat belt.

"Always wear my belt Captain," he assures Greg.

"Listen Pat. It's Greg and I'm only a sergeant, but I'm glad to hear that."

"Oh the kids hot rod down the block all the time. Very dangerous neighborhood," Pat confides with a touch of pride. Greg has to laugh. If old Jack is half the character that this one is, he's in for a long afternoon. "Can't wait to try one of those steaks you recommended at Dino's," he says, and winks at the driver. Greg let's it pass. No sense in correcting him, or even hoping to talk him into a cheaper menu item. On his way down Hollywood Boulevard to Highland, Greg turns occasionally toward his passenger, who is full of energy; a man on a mission.

At Gino's, they find a table outside. The place is busy with the noontime customers, but Gino comes out to greet Greg, who introduces him to Pat. "Hear you've got great steaks here," Pat tells him, rubbing his hands in anticipation, much as would a child in an ice cream parlor.

"Oh yes. We got the best on Melrose," Gino assures him. This time it's Greg's turn to wink, or wince. The day is a sunny one, with a light breeze, a perfect day for two green windbreakers.

Over his almost raw steak, Pat McCrae launches into a monologue on what is indeed his mission, that being the validation of his uncle's theory. Basically he tells Greg, that vampires have been living and killing in Hollywood, since at least the time of the Betty Boudin, Roland Jordan incident back in 1927, that his uncle Jack was the only sane man on the police force, and that anyone who disagrees with his theory is an idiot and a blasphemer. Greg listens quietly, as he slowly eats his Caesar salad and sips an iced tea. He finishes his litany, by leaning in toward Greg and wagging his fork very close to the detective's face, and then in almost a whisper adds, "You know Captain, there's still some fools out there that believe that The Little People don't really exist!" With that, he makes a final stab at his steak, swallows the red meat, takes a deep breath, and leans back into his chair with folded arms. Greg decides that lunch is over.

They wheel old Jack McCrae down, out through the elevator into the lobby to where Pat and Greg stand waiting by the front desk. Two big African American orderly types dressed in crisp whites are his escorts. As soon as the elevator doors open, Greg hears the raspy voice barking orders, and catches the amused looks of his two bearers.

"Thank God you've come," he cackles, thrusting out a blue veined and liver spotted hand to Greg. "You know how long I've waited for one of you boys in blue to wake up and see the truth around here?"

"Well, I'm here now Jack. All right if I call you Jack?" Greg asks. He nods and continues his onslaught.

"Only reason I ain't dead is I've been hangin around to fill someone in, someone with some brains. They all thought I was talkin about leprechauns all this time," he croaks, as if the bile has backed up over all the years, and needs a way out. Greg chuckles. Jack McCrae is no disappointment as a character. He is reminded of the movie, "Little Big Man" staring Dustin Hoffman. The old Indian fighter that he portrayed, the one hundred plus year old scout, who had lived through the entire history of the wild west, was not unlike this fellow, both in looks and in manner. Even the name Jack, was shared by the two. This Jack McCrae is bald as a hawk, with a sharp beak, and tight pinched cheekbones, over which the pink, spotted skin is stretched tighter than an old tom, tom. Although he is seated in a wheelchair from which he looks like he is ready to fly at any moment, Greg is sure that when upright, he is no taller in stature than his nephew Pat, whom he now addresses.

"This the one you told me about son? You didn't bring along the partner now did you?"

"Oh this is the one," Pat assures him. "This is that Delacroix fellow, the Irishman." Again, Greg winces.

"He ain't any Irishman!" Jack bellows. "This here is a Frenchman. Matter of fact, he's got the same last name as an old friend of mine, cowboy fellow that old Pudge McCoy and I used to hang around with. I do miss the two of them."

"That was probably my great uncle Ned," Greg tells him in a soft voice.

"That's right!" Jack hollers. "Ned Delacroix. Tall fellow. Taller than you," he adds, darting his old beady eyes over Greg's person as though challenging him to grow a few inches on the spot. Greg tenses as if punched in the stomach.

"Jesus," he utters to himself. "He knew my great uncle!" And with that thought, a hundred more pour into his psyche.

"Good rider too, both of them. They made them tougher then. Real men, not like these youngsters today!" Again he darts those piercing ancient eyes, this time landing on the two orderlies, both of whom stand well over six feet and are built like wrestlers.

"Oh chill Jack," one of the two says affectionately to the old geezer.

"Why if I was ten years younger..." Jack lets the promise trail off, and seems to settle down a bit. Both orderlies grin at Greg, who smiles back. "Well get me the hell outside. Somewhere where we can talk. Alone," he adds, again challenging his two assistants who are more than ready to comply.

Outside the three of them sit around a table on the southern, sunny side of the street. "Oh what a lovely day," Jack intones, as he peels off a bright green, heavy knit sweater. Greg hears the Irish accent for the first time and asks Jack where he's from. "Why the old country lad. God's greenest acre. Course that was a few years back. Old Pudge was from there too. We're both Dubliners," he says, now speaking of Pudge in the present tense, as if he's still alive. Pat returns to the lobby for a couple of cold drinks from the vending machine, leaving the two of them alone. Jack starts to ramble on about his old country, and Greg steers him back on course.

"Tell me about my Uncle Ned and this friend of yours, this Pudge McCoy," he coaxes the old timer, when Pat returns with the drinks.

"Oh, old Pudge was quite a character. Lord he had a beautiful voice. Tenor it was, like one of God's own angels." Again he let's out a howling cackle. "But he had quite a temper. Backed down men twice his size. He was an Irishman, truly. Used to fight real professional boxers over at The Hollywood Legion Stadium, on Hollywood and El Centro over there," he gestures north. Again he diverges into his past. "Put up a great fight against old Henry Armstrong, welterweight world champion! Oh those were the times I tell you. Used to see the likes of Mae West, the Marx Brothers, Fairbanks, Valentino, every Friday night." Greg starts to interrupt but Jack waves him off and somehow gets back on track. "Hell of a rider too. Trick rider. Did that Roman stuff. You know, two horses with one fellow standing, straddling them both. Full gallop."

"So you knew my uncle, Ned," Greg urges him on.

"Oh them two were pals. We all were," he says, remembering. " He was no slouch either that Frenchman."

"And those murders? That message you wrote in your notes?" Jack McCrae seems to just stare past him, his drink in hand and his eyes focused on some place that he alone has been and will never see again, but in moments like these.

"What's that?" he asks.

"The murders. Jordan, and Jeff Smith. That memo you left in your notes about vampires."

"I knew that you'd found them notes. That why you come, isn't it? Had to sneak those things into the old file back in 'Eighty four, when that horse's ass, Keenan, was the Cap."

"And the vampires?" Greg reminds him again.

"Oh them," McCrae intones. Now his eyes are back, piercing blue into Greg's own. "Yeah," he leans close and almost in a whisper adds, "they're here all right. Old Pudge, and your uncle were on to them too. They run the movies. Producers!" He spits on the sidewalk. "Producers, directors. They run the business. And they kill."

Greg can see that the old man is exhausted. He now looks as old as ninety-seven years can look. Greg has one more question he wants to get out before the orderlies who have arrived take him off. He glances toward them, holding them off for a second, and this time it is Greg who leans in. "Jack," he says, touching the man's knotty wrist. "Mr. McCrae! What do they do? How do they do it?" The ancient cataractous eyes gaze into Greg's own, and in them, Greg sees the fear and the loathing, as well as the years of frustration.

"Why they kill their victims, and suck the body dry. . .dry as old dust. And then, why then, they just vanish like the creatures they are."

"Then Betty Boudin, and Jean Marc Descamps, and. . ."

"Were all vampires! And so was George Zimmer, but I could never pin it on the son of a bitch! And now the bastard's disappeared. I know. I read about it! I've had my eye on him for forty years!"

With that, the old man takes a deep sigh and leans back into the arms of his wheel chair. One of the attendants nods at Greg and reaches for the chair, but Greg still has another question.

"Who's this Dragan Radelescu?" he shouts at the old detective. But Jack McCrae has drifted off to some other time, some time when he, as a younger man, still had the stamina to fight ancient vampires. He doesn't answer Greg's question, and the attendant takes hold of his wheel chair.

"Come on Jack," he tells the old man. "Time for that afternoon nap." There is no time for good-byes. The two orderlies wheel the old fellow through the doors, leaving Greg and Pat standing on the now darkening sidewalk in front of the home.

Dusk settles, as Greg pulls the Mustang in front of the little house on Spaulding, and guns the rich engine once before shutting it down. The branch lies sprawled across the yard with the tips of the limbs reaching through the fence, "like grotesque fingers," he thinks. It's been there for close to a week and his intention was to remove it over the weekend, but something about it offends him and he decides that he can't wait. In the pantry next to the kitchen he finds a saw amongst the tools that he keeps, and once outside, goes about the business of carefully breaking and sawing the thing into burnable lengths. He stacks them neatly in a pile next to the door for firewood. As he places the last bundle on the pile, the headlights of Lucille's Volkswagen van cut through the darkness. She pulls into a free spot several car lengths away from where Greg has parked.

"Hi Honey," she calls to him as she gathers herself, portfolio, sweater and purse. "Help me with these, will you?" she asks, pulling out a couple of brown shopping bags and placing them on the hood of the car. "I've got food!"

"Well what do you know," he laughs.

"And great news!" He wraps both arms around her full ones, then hoists the shopping bags from the hood of the van. "Oh," she sighs as with relief, "you got rid of that horrible branch!"

"We'll burn the bastard over dinner tonight," he promises and closes the door behind them. Outside, the wind picks up and Greg shivers despite himself. "What's the good news?" he asks Lucille as she arranges her things.

"Oh, I'm saving that for dinner," she says. "Look Honey. I'll make us some steak tartar. You like that don't you? Don't you?" He nods. "It's perfect for this weather. Isn't this weather unusual Greg? I mean it's still October. It's always been hot in October. Not like this. Not with the rain and the wind. I kind of like it. It's cozy," she says and hugs him.

"Maybe it's still that El Nino thing," he passes it off, his mind fixed on old Jack McCrae and his ramblings. Again he shivers. "Do you want a drink?"

"No Honey. You have one. I'll fix the dinner. Make us a great big fire with that horrible branch." Greg pours himself a couple of fingers of Dewar's and takes a sip, before venturing out to fetch the wood. As he builds the fire, she prepares the meal; raw round steak, finely diced and mixed lightly with virgin olive oil, capers, grated hard boiled eggs, and minced onions, then molded like a small volcano with a raw egg yolk dropped neatly into its crater. She decides to accompany it with a chicory and romaine salad, and a French dressing of Dijon mustard, vinegar, salt and olive oil. Greg, having finished with the fire, watches her soft ballet in the kitchen. He tells her of his meeting with the two McCraes. She laughs at his descriptions. "What a pair. One's as crazy as the other. Really, Honey. Vampires! Isn't that something? Vampires and Leprechauns. Really!"

"Yeah," he mutters, looking deep into the racing fire, "vampires." Before sitting at the table, Greg opens a bottle of a '96 California Beaujolais, a light red wine to go with the heavy meal. He pours two glasses and she lights two candles for the setting.

"What do you think Honey?" She leans toward him, as he tastes the dish.

"It's delicious," he tells her sincerely, for it is one of his favorites and she makes it as he taught her to, soon after they first met. "It really is." He smiles, remembering how difficult it was to get her to try the raw meat, and how she truly enjoyed it, having finally dared to taste it. "Now, I'm dying to hear the good news. It's your turn. Tell me."

She beams a broad smile and her eyes seem to light. "I got a job! A movie! And guess what Honey? It's exactly what I was looking for. A period piece! And Dan Richardson is the costume designer!" Greg nods blankly but encouragingly at that. "It's not a huge, huge feature but it will give me a lot of opportunity and I'll learn a lot and I'll get to work with Mr. Richardson."

"That's wonderful Darling! That's great news," he says, so happy for her happiness. What's the name of the movie?"

"I think it's got a catchy title. It's called, Lifeblood, The Last Vampires Of Hollywood."

CHAPTER 4

Ned and Pudge, Yak and Tom Mix. . ...And Betty Boudin

Betty Boudin would be more than a simple party girl, much more. She was to be in fact a creation; one might go so far as to say that the plan was for her to become Dragan Radelescu's first Hollywood production. The horse drawn hearse that Ned Delacroix saw that September morning in 1927 was not headed toward any Hollywood studio. The driver of that bizarre vehicle was Lenny Field and the man on the corner of Hollywood and Gower; the young man in the dark suit, wearing spectacles was Marcus Banning. At that time they had other identities, having not yet evolved into their current forms or taken their present names. The hearse was en route to the mansion off what is now called Sunset Plaza, and as was always the case, the driver was Lenny, who's name then was George Craft. It was The Master's custom to travel in the ancient style, and Lenny had picked up the freight at Union Station, in the downtown area of Los Angeles.

Its prior address had been San Francisco, an old Victorian house in The Haight area. Marcus and Lenny had been in Los Angeles for a little more than a year while The Master organized his disappearing act from The Bay Area. The rapidly expanding mercantile store with the cavernous warehouses, that sprawled along the waterfront, had to be divested and the moneys hidden, before Dragan felt secure in his impending departure. It was all part of the plan that he had devised before his two subordinates were sent south to pave the way for his arrival in Hollywood. It was a variation on a process that he had followed throughout countless decades in numerous countries. As usual, much work had to be done. The manor had to be built precisely to Dragan's blueprints. Marcus and Lenny were to infiltrate the booming motion picture business, with Marcus more of the above the line type and Lenny with his diminished capabilities, the below the line infiltrator, if necessary. That way, once Dragan set up shop he would have access to everything that took place both on and off the set. There had been talk and rumors about a soon to be made movie called, "The Jazz Singer" that was about to change the whole moving picture business. It was to be the first "talkie," a film with sound, with actors really speaking their lines on screen. As was his custom, Dragan had his ears and eyes tuned to the ever-changing history of the world. This had invariably been necessary for his very survival. The years had finely tuned all his instincts and senses. Like a wolf or a wild dog, he sniffed opportunity and then, having found it, pounced, with both ears back and fangs thrust forward. He knew that this picture would change the course of the cinema and that the moment had come to climb aboard.

By the time Dragan arrived, that rainy morning, while Ned and Pudge and all the other wranglers and cowboys stood on the corner of the area of town known as "Poverty Row," much of that plan had been accomplished. Once settled in the mansion on Sunset, the next step would be to find a body with which to initiate The Change.

"We're shooting this picture in Lone Pine. You fellows ever been up there?" Pudge asked Ned and the others. They had all been hired on by the second assistant director, the spectacled young man who called himself Peter Weir and would one day become Marcus Banning. Ned and Pudge, and Knewt were sitting in a booth at Musso & Franks Grill on Hollywood Boulevard. They'd settled down to a steak and potato dinner, washed down with lots of beer and frequent shots of whisky, in celebration of their newfound employment and the end of the summer draught.

"Yeah, I been up that way," Ned told the two of them and took a long pull on the hand rolled cigarette that he seemed never to be without. "That'd be up by Mount Whitney. Bout a hundred an forty miles north of here. Beautiful country. Shoot a lot of them blood and thunder quickies up there. Rough terrain." Having said that he finished his mug of iced beer and surveyed the restaurant. Musso & Franks was packed with the regular noontime crowd. A few booths away, Douglas Fairbanks held court with a group of newspapermen. The whisky was flowing at that table too, and just behind him, Ned spotted Tom Mix sitting with Yakima Canutt. He nodded greetings to the booth, and Yak waved back. They knew each other having worked on a couple of pictures together. Yak had been three times world champion rodeo rider and the first cowboy to ride the famous bronc, Tipperary, who had thrown over eighty riders before Yak set him straight. He'd been in the business longer than Ned and had innovated the first gags, stunts involving horses and rigging. Years later in 1966, he went on to receive The Academy Award, the only stuntman to have ever done so.

By the time the three men had finished eating and drinking, the clock on the wall showed it to be almost three in the afternoon. As they got up to leave, Yak and Tom Mix stopped at the booth on their way out. "Howdy boys," Yak greeted the trio. "Looks like you got in some celebrating."

"Picked up some work in Lone Pine through the Burwillow studio. That Roland Jordan fellow's the director."

"Oh, I've worked with him," Yak told them. "He's pretty good with the action stuff. Little flashy, but all right." With that Ned couldn't help but glance at Tom Mix who had a reputation for flashy dressing. Even there at Musso's, he was decked up like a birthday present in black and silver. Yak caught his glance and helped out. "You boys know Tom Mix?" he asked. None of them did, and their awkwardness was immediately replaced with respect as introductions were made all around. Tom Mix was still a big western star that had earned his rank. Besides his reputation for fancy dressing, was his renown as a teller of tall stories. A lot of folks said that it was his tall stories that first got the attention of the Miller Brothers, who brought him into the picture business.

"Well you fellers behave yourselves up there in Lone Pine," Tom warned them as they all headed outside into the afternoon sunshine on a busy Hollywood Boulevard. "Watch out for them rattlers up there. They're mighty nasty." After Tom and Yak had left, the men said "so long" to one another.

"See you boys next week on the first if not before," Pudge said, then wheeled and took a careful step before heading west on the boulevard. Ned and Newt watched him head down the street, straight as an arrow without the slightest stagger, all five feet four of him.

"Son of a bitch can sure hold his liquor," Newt noted with some degree of admiration. Ned just nodded silently in acknowledgment.

"I'll see you partner," he said, tipping his hat to Knewt, then turned east and headed on foot toward the house he had just bought in Los Feliz, the Spanish one with the balcony and patio. "Keep the jobs coming so I can pay for it and hang on to it," he said to no one in particular as he made his way through the warm late September afternoon.

By the time the cowboys were ready to head north to Lone Pine, Dragan Radelescu was well ensconced in his new fortress on the hill. All had gone precisely as he had planned, so far. When he left The City on the Bay, he had parted in the body and identity of one Victor Comte, a French aristocrat, a descendant of one of the royals who had been forced to flee during The Revolution. This was not far from the truth, as he had once been one of them, but that had been almost two hundred years and many Changes earlier. Of course he spoke French fluently, as well as about fifty other languages and dialects including a variety of Asian ones. Being known as a French aristocrat in the San Francisco of the early part of the twentieth century, had been most advantageous to his position, giving him access to the more evolved social milieus, the connections and opportunities derived there in. Hollywood on the other hand, was in every way, the new world and the new way. The royalty of Hollywood were the stars and the power brokers. This was a land of opportunity where a poor man's son with little or no education but with enough grit and determination mixed in with a little bit of luck, could become a movie star or run a studio. Dragan understood this concept, this phenomena and his scheme was to work it to the utmost.

While he was still tying up the loose ends in San Francisco and the mansion was just being completed, he directed Marcus, whose name at that time was Peter Weir, get a position with the Burwillow Studio over on Santa Monica Boulevard. He had no trouble selling himself as a useful assistant to the director of their next picture, a Mr. Roland Jordan who was about to shoot a western whose working title was "*Westward Wagons.*" Lenny, or George Craft as he was then called had other duties. He had to oversee the finalization of the estate, and it was his assignment to pick up the master when he arrived at Union Station and stay with him when he went through The Change.

One evening during the last week of October that autumn of 1927, just about the same time that Ned and the boys were celebrating their job status at Musso's, Dragan, Marcus and Lenny sat down to a dinner of pepper seasoned grilled duck, applesauce, and butternut squash, served by Lenny, and accompanied by several chilled bottles of a 1921 vin d'Alscace. Lenny had laid out the candles all about the dining room and their lights mingled together in a macabre dance across the heavily plastered walls. Outside, the moon hid behind dark clouds.

"We must find a woman to complete The Change. And it must be soon," Dragan informed the two, as Lenny served neat portions on gray stoneware plates.

"Hollywood is full of these young starlets, runaways Master; farm girls with no family, willing to do anything for a part in a movie. It should not be a problem," Marcus assured him.

"Yes," Dragan nodded, almost sadly, "such is the nature of the movies, and the frailty of the human flesh."

"It is to our advantage Master, as it has always been. We should have no trouble finding the perfect one for you," Lenny agreed.

"This Change will not be for long," Dragan interrupted him, and then took a sip of wine. "Excellent Alsace. It was a good year there in 1921."

"It was a good year in San Francisco too," Marcus chuckled at some thought.

"I will assume her body only long enough to get to this Roland Jordan. It is really he who I wish to appropriate."

"I know the perfect place to find one such as you want," Marcus said calmly. "The Montmartre Cafe, Eddie Brandstatter's place on Hollywood Boulevard. It is teeming with these young hopefuls. We shall easily find one there."

"Good. Then it is settled. We shall take care of that business tomorrow. Tonight I shall feast on this wonderful duck. Tomorrow on the rarest of all delicacies." Dragan lifted his glass in a toast to the two and with that promise on his pale lips.

That night The Old One slept for the first time in the master bedroom, up on the third floor of the mansion, under the turrets that looked out above the city. The whole third floor had been built with this bedroom being the only room, that and the adjoining bathroom. For a long time he stared out the window trying to catch a glimpse of the moon that ducked and weaved behind the night clouds. All his senses came alive, the senses that he had honed and refined over all those centuries. He tasted the autumn air on his tongue and allowed the breeze to ruffle through the long dark hair that hung to his shoulders. His fingers gripped the sill with an intensity that would have strangled a mortal, so badly did he want to fly into the night. When the moon finally found a moment to break through the covering, he let loose a long, deep sigh. Those who lived in the neighborhood, those still awake at that late hour, never heard Dragan's sigh, and would never have guessed that a monster such as this was so close to their homes and hearths. What they heard, those who could, was the answering wail of the coyote packs that roamed the Hollywood hills, and theirs too was a horrifying timbre.

The following day was Friday. Dragan had not had much sleep. It had been well after three in the morning before he retired to his bedroom and the enormous four-poster oak bed that was his other lair. It didn't matter much. He had little need of sleep. It was only the time needed for The Change that required that deep slumber, and that would come soon enough, for this night was the night that he would find his victim, drain dry her body of its life sustaining blood, and assume something close to her physical proportions, while adding to this new form, all the lives, all the shapes and hearts and minds, of all his victims of the past. He did not need Marcus or Lenny to accompany him to The Montmartre Cafe or to assist him in any way with the work he would perform. He alone was the master of this kind of travail, for it was to be a seduction and he had spent centuries perfecting the art of the seduction.

He dressed carefully for the evening in black tails and cumber bun, a pale silk shirt with a black bow tie and black and white wing tipped shoes. As the night's air carried a slight chill, he completed his wardrobe with an ink black cloak with an ermine lining. Marcus was enjoying a Pernod in the reading room that was just to the left of the main stairway when the Master descended and appeared in all his splendor in the doorway. Even he was overwhelmed by Dragan's presence and could only stammer, "You are exquisite, divine, my Lord." Dragan's lips spread in a thin smile.

"As I should be if I am to have my pick at the cream of Hollywood's hopefuls." He produced an ornate gold watch at the end of a gold chain from the inside pocket of the tuxedo jacket, studied it for a moment and then regarded Marcus. "It is now ten o'clock," he announced, and settled himself in the oversized high backed armchair that was his alone to enjoy. "A Pernod will suit me fine, thank you, while George is preparing the Bentley."

"Of course," Marcus responded already half way to the bar. As he dropped two ice cubes in the crystal, and neatly poured an exact double shot of the yellow liquor, Dragan asked him how things were going at the studio and what progress had been made on "Westward Wagons."

"Everything is going smoothly," Marcus told him, and with a note of pride in his voice, added, "This Jordan fellow is quite pleased with me. Every day he seems to depend more and more on me, just as you predicted he would."

Dragan took the drink that Marcus extended to him. There was no need or reason to thank him for it as it was but one of his duties and over the years, both Marcus and Lenny had become well versed in their individual duties, and the protocol required.

"Of course you will become most indispensable to him," Dragan assured him as one would a child. As they enjoyed their cocktails, Marcus filled him in on the goings on at the studio. Dragan was interested, not just in the progress of the project, but also in every other detail; who was involved, and as much personal information about each one as Marcus had acquired, time schedules, budgets and accounts and so on. Dragan had always paid attention to detail. It was inherent to his survival. At ten twenty two Lenny arrived in chauffeur's attire.

Dragan felt the night chill and wrapped the ermine lined cloak tightly around him as he watched Lenny open the door of the black Bentley. He liked the cooler weather. It reminded him of home. "You will take me to The Montmartre Cafe. I'm sure they will want to keep the car parked out front. It's good for business."

"Oh business is always good there Master. The Montmartre and the Brown Derby, and The Pig'n Whistle. They're all the places to be. There will be lots of stars and of course a good turn out of the genre that you are seeking, the starlets." Once his master had settled into the back seat and he had closed the door, Lenny gunned the rich engine and carefully exited down the drive. He had always been drawn to all things mechanical, and he loved the car and cared for it, as would a mother of her first born. They headed east on a busy Sunset Boulevard then turned north on La Brea.

In 1923, Eddie Brandstatter had opened the Montmartre Cafe on the second floor of the C.E. Toberman Building to immediate success. By 1927 it was running in full swing and was definitely one of Hollywood's hot spots, replete with movie stars, politicians and other celebrities. Lenny pulled in front, and almost before he had stopped, the passenger door was opened by a valet in a red vest and cap. The sidewalk teemed with patrons and passerby's and the street, with cars dropping off their passengers, honking and maneuvering for the limited space available. Dragan smiled at the chaos. He had always reveled in confusion. When Dragan arrived in Hollywood that September of 1927, he had arrived as an unknown. No calling cards had been sent to announce his impending arrival and to pave the way for an easy transition. He had arrived as one Victor Comte, but Victor Comte's worldly stay was at its end and when he disappeared, Dragan wanted to be sure that he left no traces and no secrets that would come back to haunt him. So it was that the last year he spent in San Francisco, much of that time had been spent arranging for Comte's disappearance. His plan was to assume the body of a young and beautiful girl who through her "graces" could get to Roland Jordan. When he took over the body of Roland Jordan, with it he would acquire all the knowledge of the up and coming director. He had researched Jordan. He was smart, aggressive, and he understood the business of making movies, specifically the western movie which at that time was all the rage. Jordan also had a reputation as a playboy and a gambler with some shady connections. This background, Radelescu figured would play in very nicely with his disappearance and because of it, perhaps less questions would be asked, and less of an investigation would ensue. He would find that girl at The

Montmartre Cafe that night, seduce her, suck the lifeblood from her body, and then go through The Change. In the new body of yet another starlet who would go by the name, Betty Boudin, he would invent a background and go about the business of seducing and then consuming this Jordan. First, Jordan would have to hire Betty for his film, *"Westward Wagons."* Betty Boudin was a catchy name and Dragan's perverse sense of humor had come up with the French word for sausage in the name, Boudin.

Despite his anonymity, his entrance upstairs at The Montmartre did not go unnoticed. He was immediately ushered to one of the better tables in the center of the room. The smaller tables were round and the larger ones rectangular. All were covered with fine white linen cloths and surrounded by high back smartly varnished wood chairs. The place was recklessly alive, a bustle of sound and commotion. A five-piece orchestra belted out vivacious numbers, couples danced while waiters scurried in and about the maze of activity. Dragan ordered a very old and expensive Spanish cognac and as he sipped it, surveyed his surroundings. He recognized some of the patrons. A couple of the Marx brothers were seated at a table just to his left. Six or seven young women, all in varying degrees of intoxication, accompanied them. A magnum of Champagne jutted out of a silver ice bucket, while two empty ones rested neck down in two other buckets. At another table Mae West entertained a group of handsome young men and several conspicuously silent girls. He couldn't make out the conversation but could easily see that she held their undivided attention. As he sipped his drink and took note of all the activity, he breathed in the heady ambiance of tinkling glasses and bawdy laughter. It mingled with the notes played by the orchestra, and filled the room like a dance.

It did not take him long to spot her. She was with three other girls at a table like his. They all sipped drinks, giggling amongst themselves while casting glances about the room, but despite the company she kept, she seemed to somehow be alone or at least off to herself. He guessed her age to be somewhere near twenty-five and she also appeared to be slightly older than the other girls. She was certainly the most attractive one in a group of pretty young women. They were all similarly attired in the flapper look; short tight skirts, mostly dark colors, hers being a deep almost royal shade of blue, and blouses that did little to reveal their breasts. It was a gamine look that made the women appear even younger than they probably were. Her clothes, unlike those worn by her girlfriends, were of good quality and not inexpensive and Dragan, always a master of intuition, figured that her education and background were probably a little more evolved and of a higher level than that of the company she kept. As he appraised her, she turned and caught his eye. This was not shear chance for The Master had willed that she turn and see him. This ability to direct, even force the will of others, was but a small example of his incredible power, and once touched by that force, the victim was almost always captured and obliged to continue. As she caught his eye, a shadow seemed to cross her face and her brightly rouged lips, parted ever so slightly. For her part, what she saw, was a strikingly handsome man in his early fifties with thick wavy shoulder length black hair streaked subtly with gray, heavy eyebrows over piercing opal eyes, set between high cheekbones and a clean angular jaw. His lips, she noticed were pale but full. She couldn't help but shiver for what she saw before her pleased her greatly and sent a warm pulse to her loins. She had, she decided in that very moment, never seen a man who elated her in the way that this man did. Dragan saw the look and understood, and those full lips parted in what could be described as a sneer, although not so by her. There was no compassion in his heart. His bait had been set, his prey ensnared. As if in a kind of trance, she rose and approached his table where he now stood and gracefully pulled out the chair for her to sink into.

"Thank you," she said breathless now, and as pale as his lips.

"It is good of you to come my dear. How lovely you are tonight." He glanced about the room and gestured, "A flower among the thorns."

She blushed like a soft rose and asked three questions. He smiled, for they always asked more or less the same three. "Who are you?" What is it? What has happened?"

"I am Victor Comte, lately of San Francisco. A traveler of the world at large and you have waited a long time for me. How did you know that I would be here this evening? That you would at last find me?"

"I don't know," she stammered, now completely confused, yet thoroughly under his spell.

"It is of no matter my dear," he assured her. "It is enough that you have come." For her the rest of the room had simply vanished. She had forgotten where she was and why she had come, or that she had not come alone, that the other girls were just a few tables away and were now looking in her direction. She heard none of the ambient noise, no tinkling glasses, no lively conversation. The only music that she perceived was the intonation of The Master's voice and it was the loveliest music she had ever encountered. It was that fast, that smooth. His skill was frightening and he had passed centuries perfecting it. He knew that it was time to leave. He was also quite aware that many had seen him and that this encounter with the girl would be recalled when the police returned to question her girlfriends and the other patrons. But at the same time he knew that this body that was and had been for some time one Victor Comte, would be no more. It would never be found because it would cease to exist. It would however live on in the body that would transform from this young lady whose name he had no desire to learn but who's pending incarnation, he had already named, Betty Boudin.

He rose without words and once again held the chair for her. She followed his lead.

"Where are we going?" she mumbled obediently as she took his arm. He smiled at her and placed a finger over her lips. On the way out he passed the maitre d' a handful of bills. She had left her coat at the table with her girlfriends and one of them grabbed it and started after them.

"Sylvia!" she called out, but the two of them were already gone. Lenny was ready with the door open, and then Dragan was seated beside her. She said not one word during the brief trip to the castle. It was as if she dreamed. She felt his cold breath on her cheek, the caress of his hair, like a whisper on her ear and neck and she knew that she would go wherever he asked her to go and would always do whatever he dared her to do.

He carried her up the stairs to the bedroom under the turrets. She weighed nothing in his powerful arms, and he laid her gently down on the enormous bed. Thoughtfully and most carefully he removed all her clothes, savoring each moment, each item, much as would a gourmet prepare a great delicacy before settling down to enjoy it. For her part it was as if she were dreaming. She was aware as if from a great distance of what was taking place but not quite a part of it. She felt a great peaceful comfort and a trust that she had never known. And although it all seemed so far removed, she felt a longing and desire, an appetite that was at the same time, unquenchable. When she was quite naked, he went to the shuttered windows and flung them open, letting the amber moon flood into the darkness of the room. He tasted all of her, every pore, every crease, each hair on her body. For hours, he did so, absorbing her, knowing her and filling his void with that most intimate of knowledge. And then he was in her. He did not undress but he was there, inside. So intense was it that all consciousness slipped and fled from her body. She had orgasms followed by even more furious ones, over and over and over, and finally when his teeth pierced her neck, the same teeth that had smiled her way only hours before, before growing long as fangs, the orgasm that was her last, in its violence, snapped her like a whip back to reality. When her eyes flashed open and she drew in her last breath, she saw with horror, the monster that was on top of her, with its foul breath and horrid red eyes, and as she grasped for a scream that would not come, in absolute terror, she died again and again and again.

CHAPTER 5

Good-bye Jack

"Jack McCrae's dead!" Jim Diehm stops Greg in his tracks as he comes into the precinct house Monday morning. As usual, the station is a hub of activity, and Jim's words reach only Greg, who after digesting this, moves to the watch desk and leans in close to his friend.

"Say that again partner."

"Sorry Greg. He's dead. The nephew called this morning. He asked for you. Told him I was your friend. Had to make that clear, and told him we were working together trying to locate these vampires." He chuckles at that, and then, somewhat embarrassed by his own response, adds, "Poor old fellow. Must have died in his sleep, even though the nephew, this Pat, is convinced that there was foul play, that the bats got him." This time Jim can't hold it back and bursts into raucous laughter. "Oh yeah, they were probably trying to seduce the old gummer, make him the bride of Frankenstein!" He stops laughing as he catches Greg's reaction to the news.

"Isn't that something," Greg utters slowly, then looks hard at his friend. "The man lasted ninety-seven years. Refused to go away or die until someone heard his crazy story. Not just heard it, listened to it, but he made damn sure I believed it as well. He hangs on all this time just to get the message out, to pass it along, and then he checks out." For a moment Greg fidgets with a pen he's found on the desk until Jim cuts in.

"So you don't think the bats got to him?" Again Greg regards him closely but with an intensity that sobers Jim somewhat.

"I think there's an element of truth here. Maybe even more than that. Old Jack was a character, that's for sure, but he must have also been a hell of a good cop. Anyway, he kept good notes. And I doubt he was crazier than the next fellow. Maybe, just had a lively imagination"

"Yeah," Jim smiles. "That he did. Poor old bastard. Imagine spending your whole life like that. Chasing after vampires and everybody treating you like some old fool." Jim sneaks a self-conscious look about the room, making sure that no one overheard them. Then he leans in to Greg and asks," What are you going to do now?"

"Did he mention anything about a funeral?" Greg asks his friend.

"Said he was going to bury the old man over at Forest Lawn. Said his uncle picked out a plot there back in 'forty-six."

"Well the price was right back then. Greg turns to go back to the squad room. "You know that cowboy actor, Jeff Smith, they buried him over there in 'forty six, what was left of him that is"

"Same year Jack bought his plot, huh?" Jim winks.

"Think maybe I'll attend the funeral. You never know who will show up."

He spends the remainder of the morning going through Jack's notes, and making phone calls. It's strange reading the notes, and knowing that the man who wrote them is gone, and that Greg, barely had a moment to meet him. The murder of the transient and its apparent connection to the disappearance of George Zimmer, are not the only cases that he is working on. It is usual for him to be busy with several cases at the same time, unless, as is sometimes the case in Hollywood, if a famous person is involved in some horrid crime. Then the public and media pressure to solve the crime, forces the department to make it top priority. In general the cops don't much like that kind of prioritizing, but that's part of living in the world's most famous movie capital.

Just before noon, he stops by Captain Magness' office. The captain is alone on the phone; sitting behind a very neatly arranged desk, blue shirtsleeves rolled to his elbows. He sees Greg standing at the door and beckons him in as he finishes his conversation and hangs up. "What can I do for you detective?" he asks. Greg seems uncomfortable, not really knowing where or how to start. "Have a seat," Magness indicates one of the two other leather-backed chairs in the office, and Greg pulls it to the desk and sits.

"Well Captain, this is going to sound kind of strange, but I've got to consider this vampire angle." He suddenly has an urge for a cigarette and looks out the window. It's a sunny, breezeless day on the outside. He continues: "You know I'm French, Captain, not Irish like yourself or old Jack McCrae. I don't believe in fairies and leprechauns and the like…" He pauses, still looking for the right way to say what he wants to say, but the captain interrupts him.

"So you went and got a hold of old Jack McCrae. Is that where you're going?" Greg looks at him and nods.

"Yes sir. I did." Again Magness cuts in.

"It's all part of this Zimmer investigation, isn't it?"

"Yes sir. It is." Again he looks to the outside. Wishing that he were there, wishing that he had some answers, some explanation, wishing that old Jack was still alive and sitting next to him, and able to explain to the captain in his wonderfully unique way, this theory that in 1998, there are vampires roaming the streets of Hollywood, killing people. He snorts. "Jesus," he says to himself, "vampires who are directors and producers. Is that redundant or what?"

"So McCrae is still alive. Imagine that," Magness whistles softly.

"Not exactly Captain. I mean he was alive and I did see him and speak with him, just a few days ago, but Diehm tells me he's dead. It just happened."

"Jesus," Magness whistles. " He must have been over a hundred."

"Ninety seven, sir, and as spry and sassy as they come."

"And he was still going on about this vampire theory of his?" Greg takes a deep breath.

"Yes sir. That he was. And as crazy as it all sounds, there's something there. It's like he's been waiting all these years to find someone who just might believe in his theory and then when he got it off his chest, it was like his mission was accomplished and he could pass on."

"You want a cup of coffee, detective?" Magness gets up from his desk and goes to a small side table with a coffee machine, and a half pot of steaming brew.

"Thanks, Captain," Greg says, feeling somewhat more relaxed.

"Why don't you tell me all about your visit and your investigation so far," the captain tells him, as he hands Greg a tar colored mug of the steaming coffee.

So for the next forty-five minutes Greg fills him in on everything he's come across. He begins with his uncle Ned, and the articles in the family albums about the strange disappearances and unsolved murders in the past, and how McCrae was involved in both of the ones he's aware of, and he continues through discovering the urgent message in McCrae's notes, the one he added years after he had retired from the force. He tells him that McCrae knew both his uncle Ned, and another cowboy called Pudge. He fills the captain in on the investigation to date; the autopsy, the pictures in the Hollywood trade papers, and now feeling comfortable with the captain's response, he shares with him his theory of switching forms, the Dorian Gray idea. Finally he brings up his next two moves. "I'm going to get in touch with an actress, an old timer from the 'fifties, by the name, Niki Starling, and see if she can add anything to all this, and I want to hit the funeral of old Jack McCrae, just to see," he adds. The two men stand and Greg puts his empty coffee cup, the third cup he's gone through, on the table by the coffee machine.

"You ever watch The X Files?" Captain Magness asks him as Greg opens the office door. He can't help but blush.

"I've seen it, Captain. I don't watch much television, but yeah, I've caught an episode or two."

"Well," Magness grins at him. "I happen to watch it every week. Love that show." Then as Greg walks out into the hall, Kerry Magness calls after him.

"I haven't figured out if the leprechauns really do exist, but there might just be some kind of vampires out there. You keep doing what your doing son, and let me know what you find." Greg smiles comfortably.

"Yes sir. I'll do that."

He finds more than a few Niki Starlings in the Los Angeles' phone books and decides to go through Screen Actor's Guild to get the one he's looking for. Screen Actor's Guild is the actors' union or more specifically their guild, and anyone who is a member will have a listing either through an agent or their own private number. Niki Starling no longer has an agent representing her. Greg figures she's probably been retired for some years from the business, but he does get an address down in the

Miracle Mile area of Hollywood on Cochran Avenue, at Number 535, just north of Wilshire Boulevard.

As luck would have it, she's at home when he calls and tells him that she would be very happy to share some of her memories of the real Hollywood with him. "When people made quality movies, not just a bunch of special effects with explosions and all that killing."

"That would be wonderful," Greg says. "How about two o'clock?"

"Oh Honey, give this lady a little more time than that to get ready. After all I don't get many gentlemen callers these days and you sound like a nice boy."

"Yes Ma'am, I'll do that. Would three be all right?" he asks with due respect.

"That would be just fine," she agrees, then adds, "Now Delacroix, that's a French name, isn't it?"

"Yes Ma'am. Yes it is."

"Funny," she says. "I knew a Delacroix once, a cowboy. Of course he was somewhat older than me," she adds coyly. "I was just a young thing and brand new to the picture business, but he was quite a gentleman." Greg feels his heart skip a beat and quietly asks the question.

"Was his name Ned Delacroix, Madame?" He slips into the French form of address.

"Why yes it was Honey, oui, oui, and he was something to see on horseback, or on a Harley, like in the movie I did with him. 'Course those boys were the real McCoy back then." Then realizing that Greg had asked the question, asks, "Was he some relative of yours?"

"Yes Madame. Yes he was. He was a great uncle of mine." He hears a slight gasp on the other end of the line.

"My, my!" she exclaims. "Isn't that something? The world is indeed a small place. In that case Honey, you come by at three thirty. I'll need a few more minutes to get ready."

At three twenty, Greg is looking for a parking space on the five hundred block of Cochran, not an easy task with busy Wilshire Boulevard and its tall office buildings just at the end of the block. The block has mostly apartments and houses, all stucco although there is one brick building, and the inhabitants are either very young, students and such or older retired people. Being a cop, Greg knows the area. On the last Thursday of each month, all the retired couples stand vigil on their stoops, waiting for the mail person to arrive with the Social Security checks. Niki Starling's place is close to the end of the block, a yellow stucco and stained wood apartment in good shape, and surrounded by a wonderful variety of brightly colored flowers, mostly daffodils. As he crosses the street and looks up toward the shaded balcony with all the hanging plants he sees a little woman with beautiful red hair, sporting sunglasses, and wearing a tightly wrapped flowered, orange and white pareo. He knows right away that it is she, and she smiles and waves down to him, almost in recognition.

"Come on up, Honey, I've made us a couple of tall mint teas."

At the door she greets him. She is tiny. "Why entrez, entrez Monsieur Delacroix. Vous savez, je parle français, mon mari était un réalisateur français, et j'habitais dans le pays." She says, in French.

"Je le sais Madame, Vous étiez bien connue en Europe." Greg answers.

"We shall sit on the balcony," she slips back into English, and starts to lead the way through the most colorful room he's ever seen. She glances back to him. "You're not quite as tall as your uncle, but you're a good looker just like he. Can you ride?"

"Thank you Ma'am. No Ma'am. Just a little." Everything in the place is stuffed; stuffed animals, mostly rabbits, colorful quilts, overstuffed armchairs, even the bright pictures on the walls, the paintings of flowers and gardens, have quilted colored frames. Greg notices that the paintings are all signed N.S. It's like a child's palace, a dream, or fantasyland.

"Oh." She laughs when she notices his look. "I paint now, just for fun. Give most of them away. Once in a while, I sell one or two."

"They are quite lovely. I like them very much," he says sincerely.

On the porch they sit on wicker armchairs. The iced tea and moist crystal glasses wait on a wicker coffee table. Greg also spots several aged photo albums. The afternoon sun is out, but the balcony is shaded with all kinds of hanging plants. He sits as she pours two mint teas. To his surprise she goes directly to the point.

"I know you're not here to talk about your uncle, that it's about George Zimmer that you've come. What is it that you wanted to know?" Greg reaches into his shirt pocket and pulls out a photo.

"Do you know that he has disappeared and the body of a transient was found on his premises?"

"Yes," she says, "I heard that. Maybe I read it in the paper."

"Did you know him Ms. Starling?"

"Oh you go ahead and call me Niki. Yes, I knew him. He directed me in "Biker Hell." Did you see it?"

"No, Niki. Sorry I missed that one. That was in 1955 wasn't it?"

"Yes it was. I was the ingénue and he escorted me to the premiere. You know we all went to The Cannes Film Festival. The Europeans just loved the movie." Greg shows her the picture. It's one that Cove came up with, again some Hollywood party shot. There are a few other people around him and it's a couple of years old.

"Is this he?" He passes it to the little lady who inspects it closely.

"Oh yes indeed. That's him all right. And that man next to him is that creepy driver he had."

"So this is what he looked like when you knew him?"

"Oh yes, that's him. Nothing like your uncle who was tall and rugged. But Mr. Zimmer had strength about him. We all worked very hard for him. He had a kind of power. Sometimes it was a little frightening even." She smiles at Greg. "You know your uncle thought he might be, a vampire," she laughs. "I thought so too, for a while, but I think he was just different."

"My uncle told you that?" he asks.

"Oh, yes, both he and Pudge were pretty convinced of it, and so was that detective, McCrae."

"Did you ever talk with McCrae?" he asks.

"Why, yes, he came by once."

"Did he talk about vampires/"?

"Yes," she smiles, "he thought that Mr. Zimmer might be one. It sounds so silly now, doesn't it?" Greg lets that sink in, and then returns to the picture.

"Do you know this picture is only a few years old?"

"My goodness! Some people have all the luck. I wonder who did his lift. Wonderful job. Hasn't aged a bit."

"Tell me about this driver he had. Did he live with him?"

"I don't really know. He was always around him. I believe Mr. Zimmer had several residences. That driver was horrid! He made advances at me!" Greg sips the refreshing tea and asks her to tell him what happened.

"It was late; most of the crew had gone home. I was alone in my dressing room. I had left the set because I wasn't feeling well, I think that was it. I was asleep on the bed when I suddenly woke and found this horrible man on top of me, almost like a dog, he was, with his teeth on my neck. Of course I screamed, and chased him out of the trailer. I insisted that the man not be allowed on the set after that."

"And was he?" Greg coaxed her.

"No, no. I never saw him again. Of course Mr. Zimmer was furious with him. For a moment, outside, I thought Mr. Zimmer was going to break him in two." She takes a long swallow on the iced tea and seems to recover. "Anyway, that was a long time ago. It all seems so hazy now." She stares off, as if into a distant place, but catches herself, and smiles at the detective. "Would you like to see some pictures from the days when they made real movies? I even have one of your uncle in one of these albums." She's already thumbing through the pages for it. Greg senses that this is about all the information that he's going to get from her but he still has one last question.

"Niki. Do you have any idea where his other residences were located? Did you ever hear anything?"

"Well maybe I just assumed that there was another place. On several occasions I heard that driver talk about the castle. I think it might have been off Sunset somewhere. I don't know. Maybe I'm wrong. It was so long ago." She seems to drift off for a moment and then returns to the album. "Look!" She exclaims, and passes him the album. "Here it is. Here's the picture of your uncle Ned. He was the second unit director on "Biker Hell." Greg shakes his head and places the empty glass on the table, carefully taking the photo album. He sees a young, petite, and quite pretty red headed Niki Starling with an arm around his uncle, who has that rugged cowboy look, complete with a white mustache. She's sitting on a '53 Harley K. R. and Delacroix stands well above her, with his arm draped over her shoulder. Greg remembers his uncle. He had lived with Greg's parents in the house on Los Feliz, when Greg was still very young, before selling it to them, and moving into a smaller place. He has fond memories of the man. Besides the white mustache, Greg sees wisps of white hair from under the wide hat. He figures his uncle was in his mid to late fifties, but fit and most definitely a handsome fellow. When he knew Uncle Ned, he was older.

"Yup, that's my uncle all right."

"Well he was a real gentleman. He taught me a lot about the business. I was brand new to Hollywood, and of course he had been around for a long time. He and that adorable friend of his, Pudge. Pudge was such a sweet fellow and very funny too. He used to have this very strange hairpiece that he was always adjusting," She laughs at the memory, shuffling through the album, before finding what she is looking for. "Look," she exclaims, "here's a photo of his friend Pudge." Greg looks at the photo. It's of a dapper little fellow, in a very large western hat.

"I spent a lot of time with the two of them. They were the ones who warned me not to get too close to George Zimmer, and to stay away from that driver. After that episode, the two of them walked off the movie and suggested that, if I wanted to, I should do the same. They did tell me that they thought I would be all right, that Mr. Zimmer wouldn't harm me. He never did. In fact, he was very nice to me. I owe him a lot. It was really through that movie, that I had a career. I don't really believe in vampires, but at the time, it almost seemed possible. After they left. I missed your uncle and Pudge. I never saw them again, but they left quite an impression."

She walks Greg through the wonderful world of color and form that is her apartment, to the door. As he reaches it, he notices for the first time, the silver crucifix mounted above the door jam. He stops. "Are you Catholic?" He asks the actress.

"No I'm not," she replies. I almost forgot to tell you out there on the balcony. Maybe it was the iced tea," she giggles. It was your uncle, Ned who got me the crucifix. Those last days of the filming, I always wore it. And I wore it to the festival in Cannes, also. Later, years later, when nothing happened, I hung it here in my house." She leans toward Greg and, almost in a whisper, days, "You know the two of them were sure it was vampires, that Mr. Zimmer and the producer, and that horrible driver, they were all vampires! That seems so silly now. Don't you agree?"

"I don't know what to think," Greg tells her honestly.

"They were such nice fellows, those two cowboys. Almost the last thing Ned said to me that day that he and Pudge walked off the film, was that one couldn't be too careful, and that The Lord watched over beautiful girls like me." She smiles at the memory. "Of course, I figured he was Catholic. Most of you French are, aren't you? My husband was French, and he surely was"

"Yes Ma'am. We are and he was as am I." It occurred to Greg that he hadn't been to church in years.

"You don't believe there's any truth in vampires existing, do you Greg?" she asks on his way out. "You don't believe in them?"

"I don't know Ma'am. The whole story is pretty strange, and I don't know the half of it."

Outside the door, he clasps her tiny hand in his large one. "Thank you for all your help. It was a pleasure meeting you and I'll try to catch "Biker Hell" when I can."

"The pleasure was mine young man. You do remind me of your uncle."

"Oh," Greg remembers," what was the last thing he said to you?" She tilts her lovely head back and laughs. To Greg her laugh sounds like a thousand chimes. "Why, he told me that if he were thirty years younger or I thirty years older, he would have swept me off my feet and we would have ridden off together into the sunset."

It's not far too his place and about four-thirty. Lucille went in to work that morning, telling him that she should be back at a reasonable time. He knew that once she really got going, they would see little of one another. "And she's working on a vampire movie," he says aloud in the car. "It's like they are everywhere." He touches his throat. Niki had really given him a lot to work with. "This driver was on top of her with his teeth on her throat. Maybe he would get a crucifix. After all, he was Catholic. And he'd get one for Lucille too, to wear to work. It's all so crazy. The business about having two or more residences made sense as well. Where did they go after the murders?" He decides to stop at the Ralph's grocery on the corner of La Brea and Third and pick up a couple of New York steaks for dinner.

Greg arrives home before she does, and after putting away the groceries, decides to set a fire. There's still a lot of wood from the branch, and the autumn evenings now carry a chill. He carefully sets the fire, starting with the kindling and a few crumpled pages from the L.A. Times, the editorial page, and finishes with the larger branches. As he places the last branch on top of the stack, it catches his wrist. He curses, and immediately drops it. The precisely laid fire tumbles, and as he grabs his wrist he sees blood flowing from a nasty, two inch cut. "Damn branch!" he mutters.

Minutes later Greg is at the kitchen sink rinsing off the wound when the door bursts open and Lucille arrives, arms loaded with paper work, purse and a huge bouquet of assorted fall flowers. "Hi Honey. I'm home!" She announces, as charged with energy as she is with items. Then seeing him leaning over the sink asks, "Are you OK? What happened?"

"I was setting a fire and that damned branch took a bite out of my wrist. It's nothing, but I've got to reset the fire." She's already found some gauze and as he turns to greet her, she holds his wrist and kissing him lightly on the lips, wraps the bandage around the wound. "Thanks, Darling. You look beautiful and so happy."

"Oh I am. I am. Are you OK?"

"Yeah," he assures her. "I'm fine. I got us some steaks and French cut string beans. We'll open a bottle of that 83 Villa Mt. Eden Cabernet and then you'll tell me all about your day."

"I had a wonderful day, Honey. Oh I'm so glad to be working on this film and that Mr. Richardson is so sweet. I'm going to learn so much from him. Are you sure you're all right?" She holds his tightly wrapped hand.

"Yeah, I'm fine. The flowers are beautiful," he adds, knowing that she needs the time to settle down after her first real day on the new job.

So while Lucille arranges the flowers and all her other affairs, Greg pours himself a glass of Dewar's on the rocks and after resetting the fire, lights it. Outside, the wind has picked up again and he hears the whoosh, as it sucks the flames into the chimney, and the heat out into the chilling night air.

The steaks are delicious and the beans cooked perfectly, crisp, with melted butter, a touch of lemon and freshly grated Parmesan cheese that they buy along with other deli items at The Monte Carlo Delicatessen over on Magnolia. Both Greg and Lucille like to cook. He was the one who encouraged her to try new foods and discover new ways of preparing them, along with the traditional methods. The wine is from several cases of aged Cabernet that he found at Baron's for less than five dollars a bottle. It's fifteen years, has given it a unique rich flavor. Lucille has presented the flower arrangement on the table, and surrounded it with scented candles. The fire roars, consuming the monstrous branch.

Over dinner she tells him of her day. "I met with Dan Richardson over at Patty's in Tuluca Lake for coffee this morning and followed him back into Hollywood to the production office at Raleigh. He's a nice guy, maybe forty five, very thin and very bald." She laughs. "He's always rubbing the top of his head. I think he's straight although I'm not sure. You know, Honey, a lot of these designers aren't. Anyway, I don't care. I know I'm going to learn a lot. Some of the work will be on location. I'm not sure where, although there was some talk at the studio of shooting some of it up in a place called, Lone Pine. It's been a location for westerns ever since the early years, and Marcus Banning, that's the producer, he says that he's worked up there before and says it's perfect, but a bit isolated."

"Well I know how things are when you get working. We won't be seeing much of each other," Greg says quietly, looking at her in the soft candlelight.

"Oh don't be silly. It's not that far away. There's the telephone, and roads and guess what, Honey?" She laughs a rippling laugh. "They've even got planes today. You could fly up and see me." He smiles at her exuberance. He's so happy for her.

"I don't know," he tells her. "I'm still bogged down on this Zimmer thing. I might be at it for a while." Seeing her like that, so happy, so alive makes him miss her already and some thing forces a shiver. A live coal pops in the fireplace, slamming up against the screen before falling back into the pit. Greg sips the wine and watches Lucille attack the bone of the New York steak. She sees him watching her and smiles.

"I do love you Greg. You know that, Honey. Don't you?"

"I know that Darling." He searches for the right way to propose the next suggestion, knowing how odd it is going to sound to her. "Look," he says, "this film is about vampires, isn't it?"

"Oh yes," she nods her head, "but for me it's more than that. It's a period piece. I'll get to do some interesting work with Mr. Richardson, and the script is really different. Mr. Banning is doing some of the re-writes and he's really, really talented.

"Well I'm working on a kind of vampire theory myself. I think I'm going to get us a couple of crucifixes to wear." He laughs, trying to make light of it. "You know, kind of for good luck. Kind of like some token that will remind us of each other when we are so far away. What do you think of that?" She throws her head back and laughs.

"Oh you are a dear. I think that's a wonderful idea. I wonder if anyone else on the set will do the same thing. I love it. I'll wear it all the time and be thinking of you." She clicks her glass to his. "That's such a wonderfully thoughtful thing to do. I do love you, Greg."

Later in bed, they make love with a kind of rare, and for Greg, almost desperate passion. He touches every part of her and lingers, memorizing, devouring, savoring all of her; her hair, each aspect of her face, her breasts and taunt stomach, her loins and legs, with his hands and his lips and his tongue, and when she orgasms, her cry is loud, almost a howl, long and full and deep, and when she pulls him to her, into her, he feels the tears, so warm and salty yet so sweet on his cheeks and forehead. He holds her with all his strength, so very tightly and swears to his soul that he will never give her up, never desert or loose this woman he loves with all his body and heart.

CHAPTER 6

Lone Pine

Betty Boudin took the usual six days to come to life. The body of the girl called,

"Sylvia" lay in the casket at the mansion on Sunset, kept vigil day and night by Lenny. He was aided somewhat by Marcus during the first two days of The Change, the most critical time. Marcus spent the first two nights beside the Master although that didn't interfere with his daytime activities on the picture that Jordan was about to direct. The second week of October 1927 on the third day of The Change, Marcus left with Roland Jordan, and in a separate car, the production crew, for Lone Pine. The construction crew had already spent the last week building the set, the additional pieces, as the location picked had been used in other westerns and many of the buildings were used over and over with only the set dressing and story lines changed. The area they had chosen for the film which was to be called, "*Westward Wagons,*" was an area right outside of the little village of Lone Pine that later became known as, "The Background Rocks," because it became the location for numerous westerns including, *"How The West Was Won", "Lives Of A Bengal Lancer"* numerous TV shows as well as the great epic, "*Gunga Din,*" that wouldn't be made until ten years later in 1938.

Marcus drove up to Lone Pine with Roland Jordan and a young girl, a production assistant to both of them, whose name was Dorothy Doty. She was a bright attractive brunette, no more than twenty-two years of age, who unlike the majority of the young women in Hollywood, had no aspirations about becoming an actress, and who had chosen the production end of the business. This was indeed a rarity for the times, as the picture business was completely dominated by men. She came from a well to do eastern family, had graduated with honors from Bren Mawr, and then relocated to Hollywood. When several days after arriving in Hollywood, she showed up at Roland Jordan's production office with her college diploma, a bright smile and unlimited enthusiasm, as well as an extremely attractive body, he immediately offered her the job on the picture.

Roland Jordan was a tall, dashing figure of a man who could have easily found employment as an actor, and perhaps even attained some measure of stardom in the rapidly growing movie industry, but had instead opted, like Dorothy, for the production end, knowing that success there, if attained would probably prove to be more lasting and could if properly played, achieve greater power in the new industry. Power was something Jordan had always sought, power in its many configurations, including the power that could be exercised over women. That too was another of his reasons for choosing the production side of the industry. Women, and beautiful ones at that were a common commodity in Hollywood. But Jordan, when he first encountered Miss. Doty, was intuit enough to recognize that behind the fresh beauty she possessed, resided a facile mind, and that mind could enhance his own reputation. So although tempted to romantically pursue the young girl, he quickly decided that conquest was out of the question. Besides, he figured, just having a pretty young thing by his side could be pleasure enough and would help when dealing with others. It was really his assistant, Peter Weir, who would end up carrying the torch for Dorothy. Jordan too, was an East Coast displacement having been born in Boston's North End. The son of Irish immigrants, he was born on Christmas day, in the year 1888 and at his baptism, the priest called him by his given name, Seamus X Flaherty. He was a bright boy, perhaps too bright or at least too impatient to spend much time learning the rote they then passed as education at the local school, preferring instead, to roam the streets with the local Irish gang who were at constant odds with the Italians who dominated that part of town. Although well built and taller than the other boys in the gang, he preferred to avoid as much as possible the physical confrontations that were part of the everyday life in that working class neighborhood. This aversion to violence would have been badly viewed by the other members of the coterie had it not been for the fact that he possessed a mental facility for ambush when it came to fighting, and extortion, where money was concerned, and was therefore relegated to the role of leader.

After graduating from the boyhood gang, he was recruited by the Irish mobsters who were forever scouting and then recruiting the best and the brightest young hoodlums. He achieved some notoriety as a local thug, again more so for his skills as an organizer than for his hands on participation, but on the one occasion that he did partake in an actual robbery on a shipping warehouse at the harbor, he was nearly apprehended in a shoot-out with the police, who despite his detailed planning of the hold-up, were in on the plan. During this shoot-out he suffered the bad luck of killing one of the local law officers, was identified by the same informer who had tipped off the cops, and became, that same night, a wanted criminal. Within twenty-four hours, he had changed his identity, packed a select few possessions, emptied the gang's coffer and left town. That was in January of 1918. Unlike the majority of young men at the time, he never did go overseas to fight The Great War, but instead, headed west. That first winter he nearly froze to death in a barn just outside the Kansas City limits, but somehow managed to make it to St. Louis where he resided for several years, pursuing more or less his old métier, although constantly honing innovations to the con, the swindle, the grift. By the time he arrived in Hollywood, once again in January of 1924, he had perfected all these skills as well as could be expected of any man. He quickly found out that he was not the first such grifter to come to town, and after several close calls, decided to go legit. The movie industry seemed the perfect venue, and with his looks, his glib tongue, and a certain artistic creativity that he soon discovered he was capable of producing on demand, his transition into the picture business was complete.

By the time he and Marcus and the attractive Dorothy Doty were headed up to Lone Pine, Richard Jordan, his name since arriving in Hollywood, (he liked the sound of it), had directed five pictures; all westerns, each one a step up in terms of budget and star, and his name was now known and bandied about town as an up and comer.

"I've reserved three rooms at The Lone Pine Hotel," Dorothy informed them a few miles south of town. The trip had been uneventful. Marcus was driving. He liked to drive and rarely had the opportunity as that was and had always been Lenny's job. The scenery had been impressive as they climbed out of Los Angeles and headed northeast towards the base of Mt. Whitney, up through the low and high deserts with their short scrubs and rolling hills, and endless rocks. There had been stretches of road where the wind threatened to blow the Ford off the road. "Isn't this beautiful country?" Dorothy had sighed a number of times.

"You'll get used to it my dear," Jordan told her each time, turning to the back seat where he had decided she would ride alone. The thought of passing all that time beside her without being tempted to squeeze or touch or caress, had made him decide to ride up front with Marcus. "After three weeks up here, you'll be ready to return to that little bungalow of yours on Starling."

"Oh I don't know, Mr. Jordan. I've always wanted to see this kind of country. It's so, western!"

"Well don't get too rustic on us." He nudged Marcus who flinched at his touch, and inadvertently, tugged at his ear lobe. "Don't get to thinking about camping out with those men in that tent city over there at the location. You stay there in the hotel in town with us. You'll have time enough to be out there in the high country. Right Peter?"

"Yes Sir." Marcus obliged. He had other thoughts on his mind. He knew Dragan's plan. It hadn't taken Marcus long to come to despise this man, this Roland Jordan. He couldn't wait for the plan to fulfill itself. He knew that within days of the beginning of shooting, an accident would happen to Sally Smyth, the young heroine in the picture. He hadn't figured out exactly how he would do it. He would decide once on location, although it would probably be a fall from the rocks. Of course he would taste her blood before doing her in. It had been a while since he had partaken of human blood and the longing for it was building. There would be the usual panic, the rumors, the fear that the picture was jinxed and the frantic casting call to Hollywood for the replacement. He would oversee all that and when he returned with Miss. Smyth's alternate, it would be one Betty Boudin, known to Marcus by many, many names over the years, but referred to as The Master. He smiled at the genius of it all.

"What's so amusing?" Jordan asked him as they arrived in the little town of Lone Pine, and pulled up to the hotel.

"Oh, nothing really, Roland." He now addressed the director by his first name, knowing that he could get away with it as Jordan had come to expect miracles from him.

"It's just that with all these beef cattle around, I'm hoping they can cook us up a big fat juicy steak at the hotel. I've got a hankering for some rare red meat!"

That evening they all ate steaks before retiring to their hotel rooms. Marcus didn't go right to sleep. He pulled a chair to the shuttered window and opened it wide, letting the moonlight drift across Main Street and on into his room. The wind howled down the tiny western street, and out beyond, straight ahead he knew lay the location, up there in the rocks. And beyond that loomed Lone Pine Peak at almost thirteen thousand feet in altitude, and just behind it, Mt. Whitney, the tallest mountain in America. He sighed deeply and maybe even shivered a little at the wonder of it all. The wind and the mountains rushed back memories of his homeland, but this was all so different. After all these years of wandering, all the professions he had aspired to and achieved, all the lives he had lived, he had finally found his niche; something to which he could really relate. This was true fantasy. This was Hollywood!

"I just love the movies," he said out loud as he tucked himself under the heavy blankets and closed his tired eyes.

When Betty Boudin came to being, to life, three days after Marcus' departure, she was, in Dragan's opinion, everything that he had hoped for, at least on the surface. Interiorly, she was of course, The Master. Each time any one of them went through The Change, he had a pretty good idea of more or less what the physical manifestation would be, but it was still not an exact science. If he consumed the blood and soul of a strapping six foot four inch man, odds were, that the transformation would be similar in body and facial structure. Exactly what it would be, how it would appear, could not be projected until the actual birth of that new creature. Everything inside was a culmination of all the past people that had been consumed. With Betty Boudin he had chosen well. The girl, Sylvia had been young, well educated and therefore more sophisticated than were her contemporaries, and she had been quite beautiful, but when Betty Boudin rose from the coffin, her beauty would have put Sylvia to shame. She was stunning! Even Lenny was in awe of the thing when it rose and addressed him.

"Meet Betty Boudin and tremble at my beauty and power!" For a moment he didn't know how to respond. Over the centuries he had rarely seen The Master take on the form of a woman. On the infrequent occasion that he had, it had always been for a disingenuous plan of seduction. He was not in the custom of seeing his master like that and in his astonishment, fumbled for a response.

"You are beautiful, Master," were the simple words and the plain truth that spilled forth from his dull lips. Dragan gracefully stepped out of the casket and elegantly walked about the spacious living room. Lenny watched in fascination. Betty Boudin was perhaps five feet six inches in height with an exquisite figure, short-cropped jet-black hair styled in the Flapper mode, with crystal blue eyes that flashed out from under long lashes. Her cheekbones were high with an aristocratic delicacy that was both refined and commanding, and her lips were lush and full, and dark as blood. Lenny had never seen a creature of such beauty. Knowing that it was the middle of the night, when she reached the first set of windows which were opened behind latched shutters, she flung them open and let the cool moonlight play across her face. As the night breeze ruffled through her night hair she sighed deeply and this time listened for the answering howls of the wild coyotes in the hills just above the mansion. Lenny, staring in wonder at The Master's transformation muttered the sacred words, "Erdelyben Kezdott." It started in Transylvania.

The next morning as Lenny served Betty Boudin a breakfast of fresh fruit in one of the crystal bowls they had acquired two centuries earlier in Florence, Italy, the phone call came from Marcus. "Master. It is done as you commanded."

"Good. You have done well. Then she is quite dead?" Marcus too had to take a moment to contain himself when he heard for that first time the voice of The Master, Betty Boudin.

"Yes. It all worked exactly as you said it would. Jordan has just given me instructions to return to Hollywood and find the replacement. I shall be there tonight. Are you quite ready?" Over the phone he heard the long delighted laugh and couldn't help but smile at the cleverness of it all.

"Of course I am ready. This isn't my first starring role you know, although it is the first one I will have ever done on film."

"I told him that I had someone in mind; someone who would put Sally Smyth to shame, a complete unknown, and that we would be back by tomorrow night. He is frantic. I have him eating out of the palm of my hand. When he lays eyes on you, I'm quite sure that he will be smitten."

"Oh, that he will be," Betty smiled into the phone as she observed her reflection on the shiny silver surface of the spoon. "He most certainly will be."

"Then I shall see you tonight," Marcus promised and then hung up. He shivered. He couldn't help it. There had been something in The Master's voice that had even frightened him, and he was one who knew no fear.

The next morning after the steak dinner at The Lone Pine Hotel, Jordan called a meeting with the rest of the production crew who had also arrived the same day as had they. The sets had been completed. A rancher had rounded up all the local horses and cattle that were to be used in the film and assembled them in a series of corrals not far from the base camp near the film location. The actors were due to arrive the following day, including the stunt men, some of whom would be convoying up in trucks with horse trailers, as they would often ride their own mounts. Also coming were the technicians, the electricians, camera crew, grips, and so on. The entire hotel had been booked for the film crew and actors with the remaining ones staying with families that rented out rooms. Of course there was also the crew that slept in the tents that were part of "Tent City," as it was called. Filming was due to start the day following the group arrival. The first assistant director had broken down the script into a shooting schedule and as it all stood, the filming was to last about three weeks. They wanted to wrap the film before the snow started descending the mountains and before the conditions became intolerable. The meeting went well. Jordan was extremely pleased and most eager to get going.

That evening over dinner with Dorothy, he thanked Marcus for his help. Marcus sensed that despite the man's inherent hustle, there was a note of sincerity in the thanks and took some pride in that. Of course he knew of an agenda that the director had no idea was about to be played, and he realized that the more he ingratiated himself to this arrogant fool, the greater would be the achievement of The Master's plan.

"Honey, you attack those steaks like a real cowgirl," Jordan commented to Dorothy during dinner. He was eating pork chops and washing them down with some eastern beer. Marcus hated pork and had little taste for beer, preferring instead a fine cabernet. He liked red wines and red meats, and he too had chosen a thick Porterhouse for his second dinner in Lone Pine.

"I guess it's the weather up here, Mr. Jordan. It's that chill in the air, and the sage that blows into my room. I don't know really. I've just got a hunger, an appetite since we got here. Must just be the excitement. You know, I used to collect those dime novels about the west. And now we're here. Right here in the real west." She eyed Marcus' Porterhouse and added, "Right Peter?" He looked at her and couldn't help but smile. He liked this girl. She made him feel almost human.

"Why yes. You're absolutely right, Dorothy." He looked about the dining room which was filled mostly by their own people although there were a few locals. The place was alive, rich with the ambient noises that accompany good dinning. There was smoke and laughter, and the lull of voices. He remembered the years traveling through the real old west, the years before they finally arrived in San Francisco, and felt something of what it had been. She was right. "Yes. This must surely be something like it was." Jordan took a quick glance at the two of them. His instincts sensed a camaraderie that immediately posed a threat.

"Well, here's to the old west," he raised his mug in toast. The three clinked glasses. Marcus said little during the remainder of the evening. He wanted Jordan in his palm, and was not about to alienate the man, but at the same time he decided that he really liked this Dorothy Doty, that in fact, he couldn't remember the last time he had been so attracted to a mortal woman. He decided that night in Lone Pine that if there were a way to take her with him, once Jordan had disappeared, that he would. He too had plans. He was going to launch himself into this movie magic, and he knew that to be successful he would need support. "Perhaps..." he said to himself, "Perhaps a partner for all time?" But this was not the first time that such a thought had passed through his head. He smiled and shook his head at the thought. Again, Jordan asked him what was so funny.

"Can you imagine, Roland, what it would have been like if we had had film cameras sixty years ago when we were conquering the west? Can you imagine the history they could have recorded for all eternity?"

"I don't know," the director responded blankly. "What difference would it have made?"

"Of course you don't," Marcus said, locking Jordan's eyes with his own and grabbing at his very soul. "Of course you don't. And you never will!" This he almost spit at the director, but Jordan didn't follow. Marcus had accomplished what he had come to do. He now owned Jordan. He had set him up, pampered him, seduced him, and then cast the spell, and now Roland Jordan belonged to Marcus and would shortly be blinded and then destroyed by the beautiful Betty Boudin.

When Sally Smythe arrived the next day, complete with an entourage of dressers, gofers and lackeys, Marcus immediately upon witnessing her grand entrance let go of any doubts he might have had regarding her immanent demise, although it is unlikely that he housed any to begin with. They pulled up to the front of the hotel in a cloud of dust and honking horns. It was somewhere around three in the afternoon. Ned and Pudge had left earlier with the other cowboys and teamsters and gone directly to "Tent City" at the location. The male lead, the star of the picture, a certain Hoagie Coates had driven up with them. The difference between the male and female stars was as clear as day is to night. Hoagie Coates was a veteran; a veteran cowboy, having spent the first part of his life on the plains wrangling cattle and doing the rodeo circuit, and a veteran actor, having started as a stuntman and working his way up to leading roles. He was an attractive fellow in his early thirties, with the rugged good looks that come from hard work and honest living; a man who each night before falling off to sleep, thanked God for his good fortune and pinched himself a tad, not quite believing it himself. He preferred the company of other men and women like himself, to the Hollywood life style so embraced by his counterpart, the spoiled, pampered, non talented but beautiful, Sally Smythe. That by the way was not her given name, which back in Oklahoma City had been, Maude Jones.

Hoagie knew Ned and Pudge both from the rodeo days, as well as having worked on several pictures with them. He had never quite adjusted to not doing his most difficult stunts and having to allow the younger men to stand in for him sometimes, but they were all good buddies and had a fun time together on the trip north in a World War One surplus army truck which carried Punch and Judy, respectively, Pudge and Ned's horses. Hoagie was booked into the hotel as befits a star, although after dropping off their things at "Tent City" before heading back into town for an evening meal, Hoagie couldn't stop gazing off at the high peaks and asking himself if he wouldn't be better off after all just camping out here with the other men in the heart of all this beauty. Besides, he'd been hearing stories about his co-star and was already suffering a nervous stomach at the thought of having to deal with her for the next three weeks. The boys offered him a shot of whisky or two, to settle his nerves and by the time they arrived back in town at the local tavern for a few more drinks and some grub, they were all pretty much in the bag. As the shooting was to start the following morning, they didn't tarry long over dinner and by nine the boys were back on location wrapped up in sleeping bags and Hoagie was asleep in his hotel room, dreaming about the night stars over the wide open range.

When she first arrived at the hotel, along with Roland and Dorothy, Marcus went down to greet the very intoxicated Miss. Smythe and company. It became immediately apparent that the actress had accessed herself to at least one of many jugs of pre-mixed gin martinis that were along with her entourage, her constant companions. At age twenty-three, the still gorgeous girl was just beginning to show the tell tale signs of early alcoholism, with the slight puffiness in the cheeks and under the eyes. Marcus knew that although the film might be kind to her, there wouldn't be much of it wasted before she came to her end. Jordan however, immediately knew that he was faced with a potential problem, so while she was ordering her crew on the proper way of extracting her abundant baggage from the three cars, he pulled Marcus aside.

"Peter, we might have a problem here. I heard that she was a little difficult but I wasn't aware of her fondness for gin."

"Don't worry Jordan," Marcus assured him, while waving and smiling at the stumbling, slightly hysterical Sally Smythe, "I'll have Dorothy stick with her day and night and make sure that those drinks are watered down as much as possible. Thank goodness it's gin and not whisky. We can get away with more water." Jordan beamed at him, once again thanking his lucky stars that both Marcus and Dorothy had found their ways to his office door.

"Carry that G..damned bag right side up Buster!" she screamed at the boy who served many functions at the hotel, one of which was that of porter.

"Yes Ma'am. Right." He stammered and cast an eye at Jordan.

"I'll kick your scrawny little ass if anything in there is broken!" This she shouted after him as he scurried through the main entrance.

"Did you say she was originally from Oklahoma City?" Dorothy asked Marcus in a hushed tone.

"Yeah Dorothy," Marcus hissed. "By way of Tombstone."

It took some time to settle the agitated actress into her quarters. That was accomplished sometime around six that evening, whereupon the woman fell soundly into a deep stupor where she remained until six the next morning when Dorothy, who had risen several times during the night to monitor her state, awakened the then sober and somewhat contrite Ms. Smythe.

Marcus, once again didn't go directly to bed. Again he sat by the window, but this time, plotted out his next move, having decided that the accident would happen sometime tomorrow. The Change was almost complete back at the chateau. The Master, as always, would be most prepared, and this Sally Smythe was so completely insufferable that to put up with her for more than one day would be out of the question. Besides, he reasoned as the producer that he was becoming, why waste the film? Her intemperance would only support the theory that it had been an accident, and less questions would be asked during the investigation.

The next morning the entire cast and crew were assembled at the first location near the rocks. A small village had been assembled at the rocks, with a saloon and general store. The story line was pretty simple; the trail west, a love story between the wagon master and the young woman, Indian attacks, outlaws, and finally the settling of the town where Hoagie would be the sheriff who would have the obligatory shoot-out with a bad guy, over the affections of the lovely heroine. The stunt guys would double everyone, good guys and bad, women and in Pudge's case children, and the wranglers-teamsters, would see to the maintenance of the livestock, both cattle and horses. About fifteen covered wagons had also been procured for the scenes west, and to be later dismantled for lumber to build the town.

The first day's shooting involved an Indian attack, an ambush from a group of high rocks now known as Three Passes, also used later in many pictures including *"The Lone Ranger"*. It was a big shooting day with many extras and lots of action, and Marcus counted on the usual confusion associated with the first day of shooting, and all those people. Jordan had wanted to get this one out of the way first while the weather was still good and to give Hoagie and Sally time to get to know one another. Both were involved individually in the scene. Sally was to flee two Indians by running up into the rocks to hide. That scene would be shot toward the late afternoon and that was the moment Marcus had decided to employ his plan.

It was a picturesque morning with high cumulous clouds drifting above and beyond the distant peaks, and a warm easterly breeze blowing in from the desert and Death Valley. The first set ups, were for shots of the wagons and livestock crossing the high desert. Ned and Pudge and the cowboys did a lot of riding and some doubling, and by lunch Jordan was well pleased with the progress they'd made. He was shooting with a wild cam, as no sound was needed. That would be over dubbed back in Hollywood. When they did shoot with sound they used the old blimped camera with the large cover.

Sally Smythe and her entourage arrived at one when they wrapped for lunch. Her morning display of good behavior had apparently been short lived because sometime around eleven she had discovered the martini pitcher. This had not been sheer accident as Marcus had instructed the diligent Dorothy to return it to her room at just about that hour. So when she arrived for lunch she was well on her way. Her language had returned as well when she addressed Cookie, the caterer who had set up a barbecue of ribs, corn and collard greens, and set the long tables for the cast and crew.

"What the hell is this stuff?" she demanded, waving a spoonful of the greens in his face.

"Why, Miss. Smythe," he responded in a rich baritone, as silky as a viola, "that's the finest collard greens you is going to find this side of the Mississippi." He chuckled deeply.

"I don't care where it comes from. I don't eat this kind of crap. Find me something that I can swallow," she ordered the rotund black chef with the wide smile.

"Well yes ma'am, whatever you say," he said and shuffled off, the smile now wiped from his jolly face. Ned and Pudge were sitting with Hoagie and a few of the boys at the other end of the table and having witnessed for the first time, Miss Smythe's style, Pudge turned to his friend and said,

"Why if she was a man, I'd knock her ass right off that bench."

"Cookie's a nice feller and a damn good cook," Hoagie muttered to the boys. "This one looks like trouble." Hoagie's stomach took a turn for the worse.

"Hell, Hoagie," Ned dismissed it; "you'll break her in just like any old saddle horse."

"I reckon you're right," Hoagie mumbled, not sounding too convinced by his own words. The rest of the meal continued pretty much along the same lines. Sally Smythe didn't eat much of anything but the boys noticed her attention to the martini pitcher, as did the rest of the crew and the director, who ordered Dorothy to remove it when the actress stumbled off to relieve herself.

The extras showed up after lunch, as there was no need to feed them before they worked. They arrived in wardrobe, Indians and settlers, and the assistant director gave them their directions and locations for the battle scene in the rocks. Jordan shot the long shot of the battle during which Ned and Pudge each did a fall from one of the galloping horses and Hoagie gallantly led the settlers through the skirmish. It was then time to set up for the individual scenes which would be followed by the medium shots and close ups. Of course the whole battle was to take several days of filming before Jordan would have enough footage to edit the thing together.

At about four in the afternoon, before the sun had quite begun to settle behind the mountains, Jordan set the blocking for Sally Smythe's run for cover up into the rocks. Marcus had really set up the shot and convinced Jordan that he should do it that way, a common situation even today in Hollywood, when the director knows less than some of the real artists with whom he's working. Sometime just prior to shooting that sequence, Marcus found an excuse to absent himself. The sun had just about hit the highest peak and the shadows would soon sweep down from above. They had arc lights and reflector boards for situations like that but Jordan hoped that if everything went as planned, this would be the last shot of the day and none of that equipment would have to be employed. Dorothy had managed to sober up the somewhat dazed Ms. Smythe enough for her to make the run and climb out off camera, out of sight. Jordan smiled. Actually her stumbling bewildered state was perfect for the scene. By the time the action was called, Marcus had positioned himself at the spot where Sally was to stop after she'd cleared the camera. He was alone, about twenty feet above the ground and almost completely surrounded by huge boulders. Only a small ledge gave access to the backside of the rock and the drop to the ground.

The assistant director called, "Action!' Sally scrambled across an open space and clawed and scrambled her way up the steep rock, looked back at her pursuers, and then disappeared behind the boulder. There she stopped cold. Marcus stood in silhouette, arms outstretched, coat sleeves hanging low, like a great bat. He seemed so much taller than she remembered. In fact she wasn't even sure if it was he or some ancient desert creature, just emerged from centuries in hibernation. What she did know in that instant, was that her life was over, and death imminent, and in her realization, even then as the muscles in her jaw started to move for the mouth to open and the scream to emerge, she saw the fangs, and then he was on her. In a split second he snapped her neck like a child snaps a twig and then almost lovingly the sharp fangs pierced Sally's lily-white flesh, and he sucked the lifeblood. He did not suck her dry. He only tasted it, savored it, noting the unmistakable hint of Seagram's Extra Dry Gin, and it was so, so good.

He swept up the lifeless body of the dead heroine as if it weighed nothing at all, and almost casually, tossed it to the ground where it fell, sprawled across the pebbles and sharp smaller rocks below. Like a mountain lion, he leapt from the heights, landing next to her body. Just once for the briefest of moments, he glanced at his work and then sprinted like a cat for the cover of the distant rocks. In the background he heard the assistant call,"Cut!" and the dull applause of the crew, for Sally had just completed her one and only stunt.

As Marcus fled out of sight behind the adjoining rocks, what he did not know, but perhaps sensed, was that he was not quite alone. Ned had dropped a horse, made it fall very close to the point where Sally's body lay. His stunt was on camera although her body was just off the camera angle. As his horse picked itself up and galloped away and Ned slowly rose, now off camera, brushing the dirt and debris from his clothes, he suddenly spotted her body lying in a heap on the rough ground. At the same moment, he saw the fleeing figure of the man he knew as Peter Weir.

"Hey! Here men!" He yelled to the nearest group of riders. "Come quick!" As they started toward his cry, he rushed to the body and reached for the neck, hoping to find some sort of a pulse, yet at the same time knowing that she had to be dead. By the time the other stunt men and extras started arriving at the spot, they found Ned standing by the body, but looking off in the direction that Marcus had fled.

Within minutes, more of the cast and crew had arrived, including Jordan who came in the Ford accompanied by Dorothy Doty. To Ned's astonishment, none other than the same Peter Weir chauffeured the car. He couldn't believe his eyes, being absolutely certain that the man he had seen running away only moments earlier was the same one, even to the way he was dressed. It was this assistant to the director, this Peter Weir. As he stared, transfixed on the driver, the man caught his eyes, tugged nervously at his left ear, and returned the look. Ned Delacroix was a man of some experience, a man who had survived a hard life by his wits and his instincts. What he saw in the regard that this man turned his way, was a look, so stern and menacing that even this tough western cowboy felt a cold chill run down his spine. No words were exchanged. It was for a moment as if the two of them were alone up there at those rocks on the high desert.

That was all. Sally Smythe's incipient acting career was at an end, her body a cut and broken mess. Several teamsters placed it on a wagon and carried it back to camp. The only doctor in Lone Pine, who also served as the coroner, was summoned. He inspected the body and pronounced her quite dead. By then Ned had told Pudge and Hoagie what he thought that he had seen, because by then, he too was beginning to have doubts. It had been physically impossible for Marcus to be in two places at once. There had definitely been someone. "I'm sure it was him," he told Pudge, "but...Damn. That's just not humanly possible."

"We'll keep an eye on him," Pudge whispered, looking around to make sure that the man could not hear him. The boys looked over at Hoagie Coates who stood by the coroner with a strange look on his rugged face, a look that was at the same time one of extreme shock, and great relief.

"These marks on her neck are a bit peculiar," they overheard the coroner say. "Never seen anything like them." The boys walked over to get a closer look. "Well, could be that the sharp ground rocks pierced her skin when she fell. She's got cuts all over her body, and Christ! She stinks of gin. I'd say," This was directed at Roland Jordan who was standing next to him, his face as pale as a freshly washed sheet, "I'd say that the lady was drunk as a skunk and she just took a fall."

"My God," Jordan sighed. "We had no idea that she drank. She seemed like such a sweet kid. Didn't she Dorothy?" Dorothy was learning fast. She then uttered her first Hollywood lie.

"Oh, she was such a sweet thing. Everyone liked her. We shall miss her terribly." When Marcus heard those words drip like honey from her lips, he made a mental note to take her with him on his next picture, and the next one, and who knows. He wondered how her blood might taste, and if she too would want and dare to live forever.

That evening a deadly calm settled over "Tent City" and felt its way to the Lone Pine Hotel. As those who stayed there took their evening meals, that ambiance that had been so alive was blatantly missing. They ate in silence. Any death on a movie location leaves a cold feeling among the cast and crew, and this news had infiltrated the residents of Lone Pine and already reached the ears of the studio bosses back in Hollywood. Out in the hills, Ned mused over his encounter with the fleeing figure and hashed and rehashed it with Hoagie and Pudge.

"Look here Ned," Pudge advised him. "All's we can do is keep an eye on this Weir fellow. He's creepy anyway." Ned nodded and sucked on one of his hand rolled smokes. The stars were out and the sky was bright with their light even 'though the moon was just a pale yellow shade behind the thick clouds.

"You know Pudge; them marks on her neck didn't come from any fall no matter what that old coroner thinks."

"Yup," Pudge agreed, rolling his own smoke and sipping some whiskey out of his tarnished silver flask. "I've seen enough animal bites to know what one of em looks like. Those weren't any scratches all right."

"Well they'll have to bring in someone else," Hoagie added. "Just hope the next one don't have a fondness for Seagram's." He took a pull off Pudge's flask. The three men sat for some time into the night. Hoagie had decided to camp out with the men, not feeling real comfortable back at the hotel digs.

Back at the hotel after dinner, Marcus, Roland and Dorothy pow- wowed in the director's room. "Do you know anyone we can get right away?" he asked Marcus, who was well prepared for just that question, having just called The Master.

"Why yes I do, Roland. I know just the one. She's got real talent, drop dead good looks, and she's got no taste for anything but fine wines which she partakes of with moderation."

"Thank God. I don't know what I'd do without you," the director gushed. For a minute Dorothy thought he was about to kiss the assistant with the dark glasses. "What's her name?" Roland finally asked.

"Betty." He said softly. "Betty Boudin. She's going to be the next great star. You'll just die when you see her."

CHAPTER 7

Betty Boudin

Following the phone call Marcus made to Dragan who then, as Betty Boudin, was enjoying the dish of fresh fruit, he departed from Lone Pine, to return with Betty as the replacement. He packed an overnight bag for the round trip to Hollywood. Shooting had not entirely stopped. The morning after the incident was canceled so that the assistant director could re-schedule the shooting, but the cast and crew were standing by to start in the afternoon. Jordan, who was working with the AD, came out to see Marcus off.

"I'm counting on you, Peter. If what you say is true and this Miss. Boudin is as stunning and talented as you say, then I'd say good riddance to that drunken tramp, Sally Smythe. Her little fall saved us the trouble of firing her."

"Oh she was a poster child for the temperance movement all right," Marcus chuckled, and then slipped on his black leather driving gloves. "You won't be disappointed. I can assure you of that." He winked confidentially at the director, gunned the engine, and left Jordan brushing the dust from his safari suit.

Marcus drove with all haste down from the high desert. Like a Sidewinder rattler on the hunt, he had a mission and time was of the essence. Marcus already possessed a moviemaker's obsession for cutting costs and he knew that the picture couldn't be saved and moral restored, before the replacement ingénue arrived. The Ford flew through the curves and raced the clouds all the way to Los Angeles, and then through the late afternoon traffic to the mansion off Sunset where The Master awaited him.

When Marcus stepped into the great living room and encountered for the first time, The Master in the form of the spectacular Betty Boudin, his jaw dropped and the gasp that followed, made its way to the kitchen where Lenny was packing a picnic basket for The Master's voyage north.

"Master. You are ravishingly divine," were the words he heard Marcus utter, as Lenny arrived in the living room. It pleased Lenny that Marcus' response had not been unlike his own. By then, Lenny had grown accustom to Dragan's new form, which despite its beautiful shape, was still The Master.

"If this pleases you so, then I am convinced that our Roland Jordan will come to me as do bees to honey." He chuckled deeply at his allegory and both Marcus and Lenny laughed with him. Lenny proffered the straw basket, filled with sandwiches, fruits and several bottles of chilled Le Montrachet white Burgundy, a delightful and quite rare wine from that region in France.

"I shall miss the two of you but will keep things in order here," Lenny said rather sadly to the two of them, looking through the windows of the Bentley where Betty sat as pretty as could be in the back seat, with Marcus at the wheel. He had already loaded all her various wardrobe, which he had just acquired from the finest boutiques in Los Angeles. With that they were gone. The plan was to arrive sometime during the night. Jordan had been alerted to that, and then in the morning, Betty was to arrive at the set for breakfast. This Marcus had assured Jordan, would give the cast and crew the confidence, the boost, to give their best efforts, and the film would not only be saved but would be a success. The one hundred and forty mile drive was again, uneventful, other than for the speed to which Marcus pushed the car. He liked speed, and decided that he would drive more often, especially while on location, if Lenny was not around. Dragan said little during the drive, but Marcus did catch his master, on several occasions, primping in the rear view mirror.

They arrived around two: thirty in the morning while everyone slept. Marcus showed Betty to her room, which had been Miss. Smythe's. Betty was delighted to find a bouquet of desert flowers with a note from Jordan:

"Welcome to Lone Pine Miss. Boudin,

I eagerly wait our introduction and the great honor of working with you. I have heard so many favorable things about you from Peter as well as all sorts of people in Hollywood. Please accept my invitation to breakfast with me on the set tomorrow morning. Sincerely,

Roland"

Along with the note, was a bottle of some California Merlot of little distinction. Dragan and Marcus laughed quietly at the note, and sniffed with distaste at the poor choice of wine.

"Both the note and the wine seem to accurately characterize or dear director," Betty said, and smiled a smile so enticingly evil that Marcus shivered, knowing full well of what Dragan was capable. Marcus was ancient and wise with the wisdom that comes with age, and he was one of them. He too was a vampire. He knew full well that whatever the rest of the world would see and take to be this ravishing beauty, Betty Boudin, would never the less always be, The Master, Dragan, in all his power and infinite cruelty; that he would stop at nothing to survive. For all three of them could and would die a horrible death if they were found out. The legends and lore that had always surrounded the vampire story had some thread of truth. Long ago they had learned to adapt somewhat to human ways. They did not thrive solely on blood. They had learned to eat the same foods, as do humans. In fact with their travels throughout the world, they had come to appreciate all the finer foods and recipes, the grand wines and the delicacies. They had no problem with garlic. They never had. That was pure myth. They had adapted to light so that they could function in daylight as well as in the dark, which was their preferred medium, and they held no aversion to seeing their own reflections mirrored, indeed vanity demanded it. They did need human blood on occasion, and they used The Change only when it was necessary to move on in another body form and identity. But there remained two myths that were entirely accurate. They could not enter a church or approach someone wearing a crucifix without extreme pain, which to a human would feel like severe, excruciating burning, and they could be utterly destroyed if pierced by silver. Then death would be horrible as the body disintegrated to hoary dust. Dragan read Marcus' mind and smiled more benignly. "Wake me for breakfast," he said sweetly.

Marcus had decided that Betty Boudin would arrive about ten minutes after the morning call while the men crew were grabbing something to eat, and just going about the business of setting up for the day's shooting. The morning was again, beautiful, much like that of the first day's shooting, and Marcus drove Miss. Boudin to the location where he arrived with much show and honking of the horn. No one could help but take note, and by the time Betty stepped out of the car at the long tables where Cookie held court, a crowd had assembled.

"Damn. She sure is one sweet looking filly," Pudge said to Ned. The two were seated at one of the tables eating cornbread and smoked beef strips.

"I don't know if I'd call her sweet," Ned nodded in her direction. "Looks like she might have a heck of a kick."

Roland Jordan who had been up for hours, nervously drinking cup after cup of coffee, immediately went to the car door where, after opening it, in a gallant attempt to extend his elbow for her to lean on, managed to stumble, and fell headfirst into her ample bosom. It was perhaps at that very moment that the spell was cast, for from that instant on, Betty Boudin became Roland Jordan's obsession.

Breakfast lasted past the given time, with many introductions, and much fussing and fawning by the flushed Mr. Jordan, who couldn't do enough for his exquisite new leading lady. Even Hoagie seemed taken with her. Of course Betty had no designs on anyone other than the director, and sensing her leading man's nervousness, did her best to put him at ease. She wanted him to look as good as possible on film, as it was Dragan's intention that Miss. Betty Boudin, whose life would be short lived, would none the less, achieve one moment of greatness to be stored forever in future film archives.

Jordan decided that they would keep the footage that Miss Sally Smythe had done of the run to the rocks. He didn't want any harm coming to his lovely star. Since she was to wear the same outfit, he'd just use her in the close ups and medium shots and no one would ever know the difference.

The next few days were spent finishing the battle scene. Jordan by then was in no hurry either to see "that big dumb cowboy," Hoagie Coates wrapped up in an embrace with the fabulous Betty Boudin, even 'though he knew it would come, as they did have a love scene.

"You think that love scene is really necessary?" he asked Marcus during a break the next day.

"Absolutely essential for the continuity and believability of the project," Marcus assured him in his best Hollywood pitch language. Inside he chuckled, knowing how obsessed the director had become with Betty who was playing that part, as well as she was doing her on camera role.

"Well that old horse faced cowboy better get it right the first time because he's only getting one shot at her," Jordan mumbled disgustedly." Betty who was sitting in a director's chair not far away, winked at Marcus. All three of them had hearing much more sensitive and highly tuned than humans. Their hearing was more like that of wild coyotes or wolves, both of which roamed those very hills. Everything seemed to turn to magic with her arrival. The crew got along fabulously and worked hard. The stunt guys performed all sorts of amazing feats, falls, and fights without any mishaps. Miss. Smythe's horrible hoard of hangers on had disappeared with her, and Cookie had returned to his usual jolly self, which reflected itself in the fine food he prepared three times a day. On the one hand Jordan was thrilled. It was a director's dream that life on and off the set should run so smoothly and that the footage that he shot could look so good with so few takes and set ups. On the other hand, poor Roland was miserable with the unfulfilled love sickness of a schoolboy. He felt so close to her; so proud, so protective, so, so in love. It was like a hole had formed in his pounding heart and through it every hour, every minute, blew the desert wind with its tiny granules of sand eating away at its very core.

Marcus observed his master with a similar pride for he knew exactly what Dragan was doing, and thrilled the way he played that fool Jordan like a cheap violin, bringing forth amazing notes of pathos and yearning.

"You notice that Weir fellow don't act the same around Miss Boudin the way he did around that foaming nag Sally?" Pudge asked Ned one night while the two boys were having a smoke and a few sips off a bottle of Jack Daniel's. The stars and moon were shining brightly across the desert sky with a slight breeze in the air, and the smell of sage mingled sweetly with the sour mash.

"Yup," Ned squinted at his friend. "That's a fact. He pays close attention to this one. 'Course she's got a bit more breedin than that other one had. She's no sausage either," he laughed. "That's a fact too."

"What's that?" Pudge asked.

"Why boudin is a kind of sausage we French like. Real tasty." Ned told him. "I still don't like his looks. I'm sure it was him up there in the rocks. I know he had something to do with her death."

"Yeah, I bet you're right. But it sure runs a hell of a lot smoother around here with this Betty. Even old Hoagie's picked up a mite. He ain't moping around like he was when that Smythe was hittin the gin."

The picture was moving along very smoothly. Each evening the daily rushes were sent back to Hollywood, hand delivered to the lab by a production assistant. Back there the word was out that Jordan had a fine picture going, and the rumors were started about this complete unknown, this Betty Boudin who was giving a performance unlike anything in recent years. Meanwhile, Betty was sticking to the plan. Jordan couldn't leave her alone for an instant. His love grew into an almost psychotic paranoia and jealousy. He was constantly looking about to make sure that none of the other performers or crew paid her more than what he considered to be the appropriate attention. Word soon spread through the camp that the boys should have as little to do with the star as possible, or run the risk of being fired. Two of the stunt men had already been evicted from the set and sent south. Hoagie picked up on Jordan's insanity and suffered for it, as he got to kiss the stunning girl before the director had done more than brush his dry lips across her hand.

From that moment on Jordan treated Hoagie liked an old dog or a hired hand even 'though he was the male lead. Any other cowboy star of the time would probably have had the upstart director fired, or punched the daylights out of him, but Hoagie was a rare one, who after years in the business had just not given up his old ways and still pinched himself every night, not really believing that he was anything more than he had ever been. Jordan, sensing his naiveté, took full advantage of it, and even got to the point of bullying him in front of the crew, finally telling Hoagie one day that he should have stayed fixing fence posts and milking cows. The fence post part didn't offend the cowboy at all, as that had been good honest work, but when the smart mouthed director accused him of milking cows, a job that Hoagie had never done, he had gone too far, and Hoagie got a bit upset, as did the other boys who thought of Hoagie as one of their own, as indeed he was.

"Listen, you chicken necked, big mouthed son of a bitch," Hoagie cut him short that Friday afternoon. They had just shot the scene where Hoagie confronts the villain, a sweet guy in real life whose name was, Willard White and who had the fortune or misfortune of having been born with one of the meanest, nastiest looking mugs Marcus had ever seen, as well as a fine wall eye that was constantly scanning off to the horizon on his left. "Listen here and listen good. I might not be the best damn actor in town, or even here in Lone Pine, but the next time you accuse me of milking a cow, I'll knock your stupid ass all the way to Bishop. You got that straight?"

The entire crew rejoiced at his outburst as no one liked the man, and even Betty smiled, behind his back of course. Dragan too had come to like the tough old cowboy, and as Betty, had given him high grades for his film kiss. "And from now on you can call me Mr. Coates," Hoagie added, before stomping off the set.

"Yes sir Mr. Coates," the poor director called to the retreating Hoagie. "I'm terribly sorry. I don't know what came over me." Hoagie didn't return to work the rest of the day, choosing instead to go down to Lone Pine and tie one on. The rest of the afternoon didn't amount to much as the crew, entirely in Hoagie's corner took their time getting anything accomplished, leaving the already frustrated Jordan, a complete nervous wreck, so much so in fact, that he had to cancel his usual dinner date with Betty. She went down to the tavern and had a few drinks with her co-star while the director spent his evening throwing up Cookie's lunch of New Mexican chili and corn on the cob.

From then on until they wrapped the film, to the great delight of the crew, Jordan addressed Hoagie as Mr. Coates, and kept himself at arms length from the sturdy cowboy. Of course everyone on the film, right down to the lowliest production assistant, called him by his first name and adored the man. If Jordan noticed, he kept it to himself, choosing instead not to take that trip to Bishop, a hundred miles away, at the end of Hoagie's fist. Hoagie's performance improved as well, thanks in part to Dragan-Betty's skill as an actress. They even spent a little free time together and Betty introduced Hoagie to some fine vintage wines, something he had never tasted. Still there was something about Betty that raised the hair on his neck. It was that sense of danger that he had honed during the years on the plains, the sense that he might be dealing with a rabid coyote, or a mountain lion might be stalking his camp. He couldn't really put his finger on it but he did discuss it with Ned and Pudge one afternoon over Cookie's lunch of barbecued ribs and beans.

"I don't know what it is fellers. She's such a sweet looking little filly, but there's something skittish and maybe even a little dangerous there."

"Like she might throw a hoof when you got your back turned?" Pudge asked.

"Naw," he answered, taking a bite off a juicy rib. "Damn, Cookie sure does a fine job with these ribs." He wiped the grease off his mouth with the border of the tablecloth. "Naw, it's more than that. It's something secret, something she's capable of doing. Like you get yourself a mare that you swear could fly if she wanted to. You know what I mean boys?"

"Yeah, I know that feeling," Ned nodded. Boy don't she have that candy assed director by the reins 'though." They all laughed and looked over to the adjoining table where Jordan was serving Betty a second heaping plate of ribs.

"She does have a hell of an appetite for meat, don't she," Pudge added with a note of awe. Both Hoagie and Ned nodded with appreciation. Marcus no longer sat with Jordan during meal, leaving Dragan the space to do the job he had set out to do, the total seduction of Jordan. He and Dorothy took their meals together at a different table. Marcus had grown quite attached to Dorothy. Ned saw Marcus sneak a glance in his direction and he couldn't help but shiver. He sensed the danger in this little man. He decided that Peter Weir had the coldest blackest eyes he had ever seen, and had no doubt that his heart, if he had one, was no different.

"That Weir fellow knows I'm on to him," he muttered to the others. "This ain't the first time I've caught him staring at me."

"Well, not to sound cold," Pudge said, "but things sure are a hell of a lot better around here without that Sally Smythe. You know, maybe he did. These producers will do anything to cut costs. This picture might have been a disaster if she'd still been on it."

Ned looked at him. "Well, hell, they could have fired her. Course that would have taken some time."

"Just tread lightly," Hoagie told him. "You get this picture under your belt and then we'll see what happens."

When the picture wrapped after three weeks, it wrapped right on schedule. Everything had gone even better than Jordan and the producers had expected. There had been no further incidents, no accidents, some exciting footage, thanks largely to the stunt men and in particular to Ned and Pudge, who created some new falls and gags using special rigging and a lot of heart. And the new ingénue, this Betty Boudin had done an amazing performance on film, full of love and tenderness for the man she loved, played of course by Mr. Coates, but she had also brought to the role a strength and determination of character that few female stars to date had achieved. There was even talk that she might be up for the new award, The Oscar that had just been created in 1927, along with the Academy of Motion Pictures Arts and Sciences. It didn't go to Betty Boudin that year. Instead it went to Janet Gaynor for "Seventh Heaven."

Dorothy organized a wrap party at the Lone Pine Hotel, but there wasn't really enough room, as there were more people than just the cast and crew. A lot of the residents of Lone Pine had participated either as extras, or support groups like the tavern keepers and restaurateurs, shop keepers and ranchers, and they too were invited so that the party kind of spread through town.

During the entire three weeks of filming, Jordan, despite his best efforts to romance Miss. Boudin and get her into his oversized bed at the hotel, got no further than a simple kiss on her most elegant hand. He had never even dared to put his longing arms around her waist or shoulders, knowing instinctually that if she were to reject his move, he would never ever see her divine beauty in its naked form. He was convinced however, as he had convinced himself during many a sleepless night made longer through introspection, that she did love him with something akin to his own passion. He was sure that conquest was possible and would be all the sweeter with the grueling anticipation, and was certain that it would happen back in Hollywood. He had made a solemn oath to himself that upon his return; he would give up his old philandering ways and devote himself entirely to Betty.

"My God Peter," Dorothy noted to Marcus over a bottle of Batard-Montrachet and some fois gras that Lenny had shipped north, "Roland looks just awful!" Marcus was very pleased with Dorothy as his student. She took to the finer things in life with the same zeal with which she took to work. He was also well aware of the director's physical deterioration since Dragan's arrival.

"He's just put a lot of himself into this project," he dismissed the obvious. Jordan, who was hand feeding Betty, oysters on the half shell, (they too had arrived with the fois gras,) did indeed look terrible. His once solid frame had shed at least twenty pounds and his face, once bright and attractive, looked as weathered and craggy as some of the older rocks up in Lone Pine. Marcus made a note to himself that Dragan had better fatten him up before he took over the body during the change

The party was a huge success. Ned, Pudge, and Hoagie, along with some of the other cowboys filled themselves on Cookie's spread of southern fried chicken, sour brisket, roast beef and fried rabbit, and partook with enthusiasm of the unlimited supply of whiskey and draft beer. Around midnight they all mounted up. Pudge and Ned took Punch and Judy, and went for a wild midnight ride.

"Are those gunshots I hear?" Jordan was heard asking Betty, who smiled languidly and said,

"I do believe those are. I think the cowboys have ridden off to stare at the moon." Something in the way she said that at the same time, both chilled and thrilled Jordan, who looking deeply into her sapphire, blue eyes, couldn't help but wonder how many times she had done the same thing.

The following morning the whole cast and crew said good-bye to one another and each one headed back to Los Angeles by some means of transport. Some hitched rides in the grip and lighting trucks that were returning equipment, some in cars, and a few by train from the Lone Pine Depot, a mile north of town. Before leaving, Hoagie made it up to Jordan. He was just too decent a guy to leave without setting straight his accounts.

"You and Miss. Boudin come to my birthday bash in Santa Monica at the ranch on the twelfth of December. 'Course I'll see you at the premiere. But don't forget my party," he instructed them pleasantly. The premiere was tentatively set for the fifth of December. The editing of the film had already started and the studio wanted the picture out before the end of the year in order to qualify for the new Academy Awards. Dragan made a mental note of the party. Before leaving, he discussed it with Marcus.

"I will do it after Hoagie's party," he told him. "By then he'll be dying for it."

"He already is, the miserable fool," Marcus laughed.

"Besides," Dragan added. "I want to enjoy this new found celebrity that Betty is about to have, before I leave her body for good." He threw his head back and laughed like a schoolgirl.

Betty Boudin was to take the train back, despite Jordan's insistence that she go with them by car. Marcus would of course pick her up at Union Station after depositing Jordan and his protégé, Dorothy Doty.

"Please Betty," Jordan pathetically pleaded. "Please, can we see each other for dinner next week? Perhaps The Montmartre Cafe? Or The Roosevelt Hotel?" Betty smirked at Marcus.

"How appropriate," she thought, The Montmartre Cafe, where life began." The glance between the two of them only spurned Jordan on.

"Well if you can't make it next week. Perhaps the following week?"

"Of course I can make it next week," she assured the distraught man, "but only if you promise to take me to Hoagie's birthday party. You have buried the hatchet. Haven't you?"

"Oh Hoagie's a great guy. I wouldn't miss that for the world." The director swabbed at his perspiring forehead with a khaki bandanna that matched his now baggy safari suit.

"Good bye, Peter." Betty offered her cheek for him to kiss. "It's been a real pleasure working with you. We'll have to do it again."

"The pleasure was all mine. Believe me," Marcus winked at his master, "Perhaps we can do lunch together sometime in the next couple of weeks."

"That would be a rare treat," Betty laughed a tinkling laugh that ran right down Jordan's spine. "Bye everyone! And thanks!" She waved to the group before getting into one of the cars to be driven to the Depot.

On the way back to Los Angeles Jordan sat in the back sat and said not one word. Marcus dropped the director off at the studio and took Dorothy to her apartment on Starling.

"We shall see each other at the premiere," he promised her. "It's been fun. You and I shall work together again. You have a special talent for the picture business." In the years to come, she often heard this phrase uttered, and on more than one occasion it was utterly hollow, but when Peter Weir said it to her that late afternoon in early November of 1927, she believed with all her heart that it was sincere, as indeed it was.

Back at the chateau, Lenny was very happy to see the two of them. Over the centuries that they had wondered the world, there had been few times of absence and they had all, even Dragan come to depend upon one another. For their return he had prepared a sumptuous Chinese meal of snow flake crab-meat soup, followed by Yu Shiang beef, Szechwan spicy honey shrimp, and steamed bean curd with broccoli. They enjoyed the meal with cold rice wine, related stories from the set and plotted the future seduction of Roland Jordan which would take place following Hoagie Coate's birthday bash. That night Betty sat by the window watching the clouds fly across the southern sky, wishing that she could once again fly with them, but knowing that, that day would come.

The next few weeks flew too in rapid succession. Betty met Roland Jordan at the Roosevelt Hotel on Hollywood boulevard across from Grauman's Chinese Theater.

"I look forward to the day when they put your footprints in the cement," he toasted the actress. Dragan knew that the seduction was complete.

"Eat Jordan," he implored the man. "You look terrible. Put some sour cream on that baked potato. You're as skinny as a junk yard dog." Jordan, always anxious to please, complied and even ordered a second slice of apple pie. Since the word had spread through town that Betty Boudin was slated to be perhaps the next big star, their appearance at the hotel did not go by un-noticed. Several photographers who followed the movie crowd, snapped their pictures, and a reporter from The Hollywood News, briefly interviewed them. The next day the picture was in the paper and Jordan was quoted as saying,

"You'll see at the premiere on the fifth of December that this lady, this accomplished and most beautiful Betty Boudin gave the performance of a lifetime and will be the next great star." When Dragan read that the succeeding day, he did so with a touch of dismay, knowing how short lived that stardom was to be.

"Oh well," he said to Marcus, "it often is. Perhaps this Betty will become a kind of legendary figure when she disappears forever."

The premiere of *"Westward Wagons,"* took place right across the street from where the two had dined. Many of Hollywood's royalty turned out for it, including Mae West, The Marx Brothers, Douglas Fairbanks, and many others, as well as the press, and of course most of the cast and crew. Ned and Pudge were greeted by name by Mr. Tom Mix who still drew a crowd, and autograph seekers swamped Hoagie. The three of them had met earlier at Musso & Frank's and had a few shots. There was a fourth man with them, a friend to both Pudge and Ned, a young police detective by the name of Jack McCrae. They introduced him to Hoagie.

"It's a real pleasure meeting you, Mr. Coates." Jack shook his hand. "I've been a fan of yours for a long time. You lads aren't no pansy assed sissies. You're the real thing. You're not part Irish by chance, are you?" he asked.

"Don't rightly know just what I am, but thanks Jack," Hoagie said. "I guess we sure were back then. And you just call me Hoagie like the rest of the boys do." It had been Hoagie who had never been real adept at this kind of Hollywood function and had insisted that they have a few drinks before arriving. That was just fine for both Ned and Pudge. Hoagie had recently lost the one and only wife he'd ever wed, and was in no hurry to date, so he accompanied Betty and Jordan amidst much popping and flashing of bulbs and rounds of applause. Neither Pudge nor Ned were involved with any one girl, so the three of them left the party at The Roosevelt early and finished off what they had begun earlier at Musso & Frank's. McCrae was working on a case and had to be somewhere early so he declined. Over drinks Hoagie asked them about Jack.

"Does he always wear them bright green clothes boys?"

"Well," Ned explained. "He's pretty young to have made his detective grade and I think he was in a hurry to get it so he could take off the blue uniform."

"Well, I bet he makes a pretty sight at a crime scene," Hoagie laughed. "Nice feller 'though."

Betty left after the party, in a Bentley driven by a stout, hunched fellow with long blond hair, and Jordan was distressed to see Peter Weir leave with them. He suddenly realized that he had no idea where Betty lived and that the only way he could get a hold of her was through Peter, and now that the picture was all finished, he wouldn't be seeing him every day at the studio.

"Don't worry, Jordan," Betty patted his hand from the back seat of the Bentley. "I shall pick you up for Hoagie's party. Until then," she called after him as the car pulled out into the busy traffic, leaving him standing forlornly on the sidewalk.

He stood there for some time, until the lights along Hollywood Boulevard started blinking out, then walked all the way home to his place in Beverly Hills. Roland Jordan had finally found someone other than himself into whom he could focus all his energy, all his love. He'd never known anything like this feeling, yet at the same time he found himself helplessly miserable.

The twelfth of December blew into town with a gust of wind and some nasty rain. Lenny and Marcus set the coffin in the living room. Dragan had decided that after the birthday party at Hoagie's, he would return with Jordan to his estate. He knew that he had a big house in Beverly Hills and figured that it would be the ideal location for the deed. After Jordan was dead and his body had been sucked dry, just as The Change was beginning, he would have Lenny who would be waiting outside in the Bentley, drive him back to the manor off Sunset. Driving was not the only means of travel for these creatures. There had always been another myth surrounding their kind and it was also based in fact. Vampires could change form. This could only be accomplished under extreme duress or when all the senses had been heightened by some event. It was almost akin to the adrenaline rush that humans experience when frightened or extremely anxious. It was a survival thing. If discovered and then pursued, when all other means failed, it was possible that this power could come to them, allowing them to escape by changing form. There were tales of vampires turning into animals, bats or wolves, or coyotes. This was possible. The problem was that they had no control over that change so they could not count on its occurrence. Sometimes this came over them when they sucked the blood from a body that would be the source for The Change. It was almost a sexual act, and the intense thrill of it could set this off. Dragan however was taking no chances. Lenny would be waiting for him with the car and would return him in whatever form he was, to the castle.

One thing could be said for that old cowpoke, Hoagie Coates, and that was that he knew how to throw a rip-roaring party. Maybe all the birthdays he had passed on the plains, either alone with the livestock or with just a few of the men, had left him wanting, because the party he threw that night for his forty second year on the trail of life, made the front pages of the trades the following morning. Marcus had no idea how many folks showed up for the thing. And it wasn't like any typical

Hollywood type event with a bunch of old stiffs in suits and young, beautiful women who had had too much to drink. Oh that group of Hollywood executives with their girlfriends or wives was well represented. As Ned commented to Pudge,

"That Hoagie ain't no fool. He knows he just did a fine picture and he's got all the Hollywood crowd here too."

"Yup. That's a fact Ned, but old Hoagie didn't forget any of his real friends. Why this thing reminds me of a roundup. Haven't seen some of these boys in years." In fact Hoagie had sent out invitations months earlier and they had made the rounds through most of the still remaining cattle camps from Amarillo to Kansas City and beyond, and a fair group of the guests looked like they'd arrived pretty much right off the cow trails. Of course they had done a little sprucing up for the bash. So when the reporter who covered the party described it in the Hollywood News the next day as, "an eclectic group," the general reading public probably had no idea just how diverse and wild it really was. Fortunately Jack McCrae wasn't the only police officer that Hoagie knew. The LAPD too was well represented and so there was no trouble with either the guests or the locals who had all been invited. His ranch was a big sprawling estate right next to what is now Leo Carrillo State Beach. Leo was another cowboy star.

Lenny with Betty had picked up Jordan at his home in Beverly Hills. Betty was pleased to see that the director had put on a few pounds since their last meeting, days earlier. In fact he had been eating constantly, as his heart sickness had manifested itself with a new symptom, that being a bad case of overeating.

"You look so much better, Darling," she greeted him as he slid himself into the back seat. "Your safari suit fits you again like it used to."

"Oh Betty. Oh Betty," was all he managed to mumble, so overwhelmed was he at once more being with her.

"You know Darling; it was beginning to look like you'd draped some dead jungle beast around you. I've been waiting; it seems like forever, for this evening." He patted his forehead with the bandanna. The morning rain had stopped but the weather was brisk. Despite that, Jordan couldn't seem to stop perspiring and asked Betty if she minded the window being open. "Of course not, Dear. This evening is for you. Whatever you desire."

"I, I, I don't know what to say," he stammered.

"Don't say anything." She touched her fingers to his lips. "I will do everything."

When the two of them left the party at around midnight, just after the cake had been presented by a group of cowboys on horseback, Jordan's recollection of what he had done during the past few hours was a complete daze. He kind of remembered hugging Hoagie. This feeling of love had enveloped his whole body with a magnitude of emotion that he had never known. He recalled drinking some sweet punch that had been well spiked with Tequila. He retained a sweet memory of dancing with Betty; of his arms around her and his head leaning on her bosom, and he was almost certain that after one of the many dances, she had held him in her arms and kissed him deeply, kissed his very core, and touched his eternal soul.

She put him in the Bentley and directed Lenny to return to the director's house. All the way there, he smelled her sweetness and felt the soft flesh of her arm around his neck and his heart and all his senses swelled, almost to the point of bursting. Never had he felt such a closeness, or warmth. "Perhaps," he thought, "when I was a child, a boy in Boston, so long ago."

It was Betty who took his keys and once inside led him upstairs to the master bedroom all done in pastels and velvet. He seemed to come to his senses somewhat, once upstairs, and begged her a moment to change into something more comfortable than the safari suit.

"By all means," she encouraged him. "We have all eternity. Take all the time you want." When he retreated to the bathroom, she went to the French windows and opened them all the way. If Dragan were to change form, if he were to transpose into a bat, or some other creature, which was a possibility, he needed an exit and the windows would serve. Moments later he returned wearing a blue silk bathrobe and crimson silk pajamas. He seemed to have regained some sensibility and the old nervousness was back.

"Lie down, my Darling," she instructed him. "Lie your tired body down and let me do everything."

Like a child, he obeyed and once on the bed she again brushed her fingers over his eyes, which he closed. And then she was on him, with her fingers, her hair and her mouth. He had never felt such pleasure. He was sure that he would burst but dared not to open his eyes lest this delectation stop. For what seemed to him to be a long time she touched every part of him through the silk pajamas. She had no intention of removing them. When he could no longer stand the ecstasy, could no longer keep his eyes closed, for he had to see the women that he wanted and loved, just as they fluttered open, she was on him, her fangs in his neck, her horrible smell all around. He did not see Betty Boudin, the creature of his dreams. What he stared at was a monster with eyes as black as the darkest of nights and claws like those of a vulture. He saw his past float before him, his sins flow like ripples on dark waters, and the horror of it all forced open his mouth. When he screamed, he cried to the god that he had never known or dared to know.

"My God!" he yelled with his last breath, and just before he died, the last thing he heard was a shrilling ghastly laughter, and the words,

"You will not find God here!"

CHAPTER 8

Funeral

It was the day for the funeral. Greg still hadn't bought the crucifixes, and over coffee and fresh croissants that he has just picked up from the little bakery a couple of blocks away on Larchmont, makes a note to himself that he will do so today before the funeral, which is scheduled for one in the afternoon. He's not sure why, but he's had an uneasy feeling since deciding to buy them, and senses that it will fade once he's done so. After breakfast Lucille gathers up her work things and Greg accompanies her to her Volkswagen van. It's a beautiful late autumn day with a fine breeze and few clouds. Greg looks at the gapping cut on the pepper tree, made by the torn branch. It's obtrusive, almost like an insult. He figures he'll cover it with a little pine tar. That will make it go away.

"You have a good day, Darling," he tells her in a quiet voice. "I'll see you later."

"What's the matter Greg?" she asks, discerning something in his voice.

"It's nothing, Babe. Just a lot on my mind," then adds, "Today's old Jack McCrae's funeral. I'm going to be there. Might take Cove. We're just running into dead ends. No pun intended. I liked that crazy old man. I wonder who will show up?" She can see that he's to say the least, preoccupied, and is concerned.

"Honey, everything's going to be just fine. You'll see. He snaps out of it and leans in to kiss her cheek.

"Yeah. You bet. Give em Hell over there!" They both laugh, the tension now gone and as she drives down the block, she honks the horn and waves. Raleigh Studios is not far from where they live. That too is reassuring to the detective.

"Oh well," he says to himself. "We've still got a few weeks before she goes off on location. Maybe we'll get to the bottom of this silly thing by then. Hell, Leprechauns and vampires. For God's sake, this is nineteen ninety-eight!"

Before leaving for the station, he leaves Cove a message on his service, telling him to meet him at the entrance to Forest Lawn at twelve-thirty; that he wants the two of them to make it to check it out together. Once at the station Greg checks in with Captain Magness.

"Cap, I'm hitting old McCrae's funeral at Forest Lawn this afternoon. I think I'll take Cove with me. You know this Zimmer thing is going cold. We never got anything on that transient. We passed the picture around on Santa Monica Boulevard, with the runaways and the hookers. A few of them said that he looked familiar, but nobody could positively ID it. The face was all sunken in by the time we got the photo taken. Couldn't even match it up to a "missing persons," and it doesn't look like Zimmer is about to show up again. They didn't run any further autopsy tests on the transient. All we've got left is what we always had, a bloodless stiff with strange bite marks on the neck. And now they've cremated the body, so we don't even have that."

"What do you think about all this, Greg? Pull up a chair." They've walked back to the captain's office and Greg sighs deeply and sits.

"Captain. I know this sounds damn crazy, but I don't have any human explanation for any of this, and old Jack McCrae seemed to be the only one making any kind of sense." The captain grins a mouthful of white teeth.

"The vampire thing?" Greg feels himself blushing and loosens his tie.

"Yeah, Cap. Vampires. It's got to be some kind of vampire, if the blood is sucked dry. You know there are all kinds of crazy cults; kids walking around committing murders and calling themselves, vampires."

"Have you checked into that?" Magness asks.

"Oh yeah. There's been nothing like that here, not serious anyway. There was some "vampire killing" in Florida, but it was a single incident. This thing has been going on here for years. It's different. And McCrae wasn't the only one who was a believer. I told you that I found these clippings in my family albums, clippings from my uncle, of past murders and disappearances like this, cases McCrae worked on, and they all had the same MOs. They knew each other you know?"

"Who did?"

"McCrae knew my uncle Ned and his buddy Pudge, a couple of cowboy stuntmen."

"Is that so?" Magness leans back in his chair and crosses his arms behind his head.

"Yeah, they did. And then I talked with this Niki Starling who was an ingénue in one of Zimmer's flicks. She told me some strange story about Zimmer's driver attacking her one night when she was asleep, and waking to find him biting, or about to bite her neck. She says that my uncle warned her about Zimmer. You know he worked with that Jordan and Betty Boudin too. They were the first case back in 'twenty-seven." Magnus takes it all in and nods.

"More and more like The X Files," he declares softly. Greg begins to feel more comfortable. He expands on his theory of Dorian Grey and how these vampires if they are indeed such, could only stick around for so long without raising questions.

"Look, Cap. If this is true, these things have been around Hollywood for seventy years at least. Somehow these vampires are tied up in the film business." Magnus chortles a big man's laugh.

"Why son, you've had to work with some of these film people too." Greg ignores the joke. Now he's on a roll and doesn't want to stop before he's said everything on his mind.

"Captain, if this is true than there are a couple of things. Firstly, we've got to assume that this Zimmer was one of them and that he's still around although not as Zimmer but as someone or something else. So he'll pop up again. Also he's got to be the same one, or one of the same ones, who was here before, as Betty Boudin, who also disappeared."

"So assuming that it's possible, and they are here, how many of them do you think there are?" Magnus asks.

"Seriously sir, I don't know. It would make sense that there is more than one. It helps them work together and cover for each other. Besides, Miss Starling told me that story about Zimmer's driver. There must be at least two."

"Go on," Magnus encourages him.

"The problem sir is that we don't know who they are and we have no idea where they live. I know that sounds obvious, but the address thing is interesting. There has to be more than one address. There's the one they or he is living at as whoever he is playing in real life, and there's got to be another place where they live as vampires; like an office, or a kind of headquarters." Magnus leans forward over his desk and nods.

"Go on detective. You've got my attention."

"Well sir, this Niki Starling mentioned something. It's real general but it might be something. Anyway, she was talking about a long time ago." He hesitates.

"I'm listening."

"She mentioned something about a castle somewhere off Sunset."

"She's crazy," Kerry Magness shakes his big Irish head. "There are no castles in L.A. that I know of."

"Well, maybe she's referring to some kind of estate. You know Sunset Boulevard is lined with those huge residences. Like the one those Arabs bought some years back and painted pubic hair on the statues." They both laugh.

"Well, that burned down after that scandal. Insurance thing as I recall," Magness adds. They are both cut short by a phone call to the Captain's office. Greg waits, and Magness hits the hold button. "Look Greg, I've got to take this call. If vampires is all we've got going for now, then you've got the go ahead. Follow that in any way you can. Check out anything that might fit the bill in that area. I doubt that these folks, if they do exist, move every few years. They probably want to keep as low a profile as possible."

"If they do exist, they sure picked a hell of a profession to get involved with for maintaining a low profile. Thank you sir. I'll let you know if anything pops up, at that funeral."

"Give my condolences to the nephew, and be careful." He returns to the phone call and nods as Greg closes the door behind him.

Outside Greg hears sirens and there is a lot of scrambling of personnel. He returns to his desk and gathers his things. At the front desk he asks Jim what's up.

"Hold up at The Bank of America on La Brea." Jim tells him, as all around uniforms as well as plainclothes men and women are rushing out.

"Shit," Greg mutters. "Well that's not me this time. They can get a hold of me if they need me. I'm off to a funeral."

"Let's just hope none of our people are," Jim says solemnly. Greg is just about to leave but Jim's comment reminds him of the note to himself.

"Hey Jim, you're Catholic aren't you?"

"That's not a trick question is it?" Greg smiles.

"Naw. It's just that I want to get a hold of a few crucifixes. You know somewhere around here where I can get a couple of silver ones?" Now Jim does raise an eyebrow.

"You need them for old Jack's vampires, Greg," he asks, suppressing a smile. Greg realizes that Jim Diehm, the nuts and bolts type guy that he is, is not about to buy into this vampire theory and that from now on, Greg's going to pursue it on his own, with Captain Magness' sanction.

"Yeah," he laughs. "That's right. You know a place?"

"There's a novelty store on Melrose. Over by San Jean Vincent. They've got all sorts of stuff, religious, occult. Books, trinkets. You know the style. Tarot cards. I'm sure you can find them there."

"Thanks, Jim. You take care," Greg tells him on his way out. Jim hollers after him.

"Pick yourself up a string of garlic while you're at it." Greg hears Jim chuckling as he walks out and crosses the street to the spot he always tries to park the Mustang.

Before heading to the Valley, Greg takes a ride over to Melrose. He has no trouble finding the shop. A middle-aged woman with long braided dark hair with streaks of gray is setting up a display of incense holders. Incense fills the small room, which is abundant with all sorts of items. She stops her work, and smiling at Greg, asks if she can help him.

"I see you've got some crucifixes. Are these silver?" he asks, pointing to several in a glass case.

"Why yes, they are," she says, and pulls them out to hand to him. They are plain crosses with chains, perhaps four inches in length, exactly what he had in mind.

"I'll get them," he tells her reaching in his pocket.

"Are you sure there isn't anything else you want?" she asks him when he has paid. There is something in the way she asks the question that stops him. It's almost like she knows that she can help him. She's not just trying to make a sale. It puts him at ease, as does she.

"I see you have all sorts of books," he says. "You wouldn't have any on vampires would you?" She nods, looking deep into his eyes.

"I think you will be able to use this," she tells him. Instead of going to the shelves where the books are arranged, she reaches into a drawer and pulls out a small book with a worn green cover. She hands it to him. The title is simple and faded. It reads, "The Real Vampires." He opens the aged cover and looks for the date of publication. It says, Cheshire, England. Regents Publishers, 1903.

"This is very old," he mumbles. "I'm sure it's more than I can afford." Again she smiles at him and he feels like she can read into his soul.

"It's not for sale," she says. "But you can borrow it. I know you will return it when it's over." He doesn't quite know how to respond. She's completely stunned him. All he can do is mutter,

"Thank you. Of course I will. Perhaps this will make things more clear. Thank you." As he starts to leave, something makes him turn back. He thinks he might have a question, but once again she is there before he is.

"They are here too, you know. You have yet to meet them, but they are here, and you will. From now on both of you wear those crucifixes. You'll need them."

"I shall," he promises, and walks out of the incense and into the sunlight.

All the way into the Valley Greg ponders the event that has just happened. There was something about that woman. At stop lights he thumbs through pages of the book. He decides he'll look through it that night.

Eddy Cove is waiting for him at the entrance to the cemetery. He gets out of his Buick and walks over to the Mustang.

"Hey, Buddy. The service is down at the burial plot. I've got the directions. Shall we take my car?"

"Sure," Greg agrees and parks his own on the street out front. "How're things with Liz?" He asks Eddy as they weave their way toward the site.

"It's over. Just didn't have the time. No hard feelings. She's a nice girl. Probably will do better with someone who's not a cop.

"Sorry to hear that."

"Naw. It's okay. How 'bout you and Lucille?" Greg smiles and touches the crucifix around his neck.

"She's fine. She's working on a movie about vampires." Eddy whistles.

"That's some kind of coincidence!"

"I sure hope not," Greg says soberly. He glances at his partner. If Eddy harbors any skepticism, he isn't about to show it to Greg. He'd go with any leads that came their way. "The captain gave us his go ahead. He's an X Files fan." Cove chuckles.

"I wonder if our Jack McCrae caught any of those episodes?"

"Check this out." Greg passes him the book. Eddy glances through it as he drives to the site. He hands it back as they get out of the car.

There are perhaps a dozen cars lined up along the drive and maybe fifteen people already assembled at the grave. The casket is a simple on made of pine and covered with a modest arrangement of flowers and draped with the Irish flag. Standing next to it is Patrick McCrae. Patrick is wearing his green windbreaker open as the sun shines brightly. He spots the two cops exiting the car and ambles over to greet them. Greg can see the sadness, the sheer distress etched in the man's face. He also smells the familiar scent of Jamison's Irish whiskey. As if catching Greg in that observation, Patrick reaches into the coat and produces a silver flask.

"You want a nip, Captain?" He offers the flask. "My uncle would have wanted everyone to have a few nips to his everlasting health and happiness."

"No thanks, Pat. I'll pass." He introduces his partner.

"A good Irish name as well," Patrick assures him. "Surely you'll drink to Uncle Jack?"

"Sorry. We're both on duty," Eddy chuckles.

The three then walk back to the grave site where a priest is about to start the service. Patrick introduces the two cops to those present. All are close friends and family. Just as the priest is about to start, a taxi pulls to the curb where the other cars are parked and a man gets out. He tells the driver to wait. Greg glances over once the engine has stopped. The man appears to be in his thirties, is tall and good looking, well built, even powerful looking with dark wavy hair. Greg notes that he is dressed with good taste. Besides the dark slacks and expensive shoes, he sports a fine blue blazer. The man approaches the group. Few notice his arrival other than Patrick and the two cops. Instead of joining the group, he positions himself away under a magnolia tree.

"Do you know him?" Greg asks McCrae.

"Can't say I do, Cap. Uncle Jack had a lot of friends," As if struck by his own words, Patrick sniffles and looks at the meager group of mourners.

"And you know all these others here?" Greg asks him.

"Oh, yes Captain. I'm sure a lot of Uncle Jacks's friends had to go to far or just couldn't make it. Greg took another look at the man but the priest's words turned him back to the casket.

The service is brief but well done. The priest, besides performing the Catholic service, gave the eulogy. And despite his age and frail appearance, his voice is strong and rich with the distinctive Irish lilt to it, and he touches on something of the spirit of the man Greg knew so briefly as Jack McCrae. The eulogy is not without its fair share of Irish wit. Patrick stands quietly, head bowed, with tears falling softly on the thickly carpeted grass beside the open pit. As the eulogy draws to a close, Greg whispers to Eddy. "Eddy. When this is over, I want to follow that cab and see where he drops that fellow off. Drop me at my car and we'll both follow him.

"Right, Eddy agrees. "We'd better get a jump on him. I've got a feeling he won't stick around for the personal condolences."

Greg tells Patrick how sorry Greg is for his loss; that he liked his uncle and is still working on the case. "I'll be in touch," he promises.

The two cops slip off. The others don't seem to notice their departure. Eddy drops Greg off at his car and they both wait on the street. Within a few minutes, Greg spots the cab as it pulls out onto the street. As they had anticipated, the man had not stuck around after the service. The cab passes Greg's Mustang where he slouches in the seat. Then, after waiting for another car to take up the spot behind the car, both detectives pull and follow. They continue behind as the taxi heads over the hill into Hollywood where it takes a right on Highland onto Sunset Boulevard and continues west. Just before they reach La Cienega, Greg finds himself directly behind the cab. Suddenly the passenger turns as if he knew he was being followed. The man glares out the back window. There is something in his look that sends a cold chill down Greg's spine. The man holds his stare as if challenging or somehow mocking the detective. The man holds the stare for maybe fifteen seconds as the cab slows, and then suddenly pulls ahead, just clearing the yellow light and leaving Greg stopped at the red light. By the time the light changes and Greg again spots the cab, it is parked outside the huge office building at nine hundred Sunset. Greg pulls to the curb behind the cab, but it is empty and just as he stops, the chauffer pulls out into the traffic. Greg slams his hands on the steering wheel just as Eddy slips in behind him. Both men understand that there is no way they can find the stranger inside the enormous building.

"Jesus. He beat us," Cove says through Greg's window. Greg glances at his watch. It's one-thirty.

"I don't know," Greg answers. We can look at this a couple of ways. Either it's nothing or everything and he's on to us. He's no friend of McCrae's. If he's playing us, he'll slip up somewhere. Ego has a way of doing just that.

"Yeah. If he plays. Did you get a good look at his face?"

"Yeah, Eddy," I'll get it sketched out as a composite and run it on the computer. I've got a feeling though that not too many people are familiar with it. It's interesting that he went down Sunset. That fits in with Niki Sterling's notion that they live in this area.

Eddy whistles and looks up to the clouds.

"You know, Partner. You're talking like you buy into this vampire theory. Until today I wasn't But I've got a spooky feeling that you're on to something and you've got me hooked as well. Without knowing, Greg touches the crucifix around his neck.

"Yeah. Me too. I've got that spooky thing too. We'll just see where this thing takes us.

Once inside the building Dragan relaxes, and decides to go directly to the coffee shop. He knows that the two cops won't bother to look for him. The office building is much too extensive, and the two cops too smart. He sits with a cup of poor coffee and reflects on old Jack McCrae. He was a worthy adversary for a human. Dragan will miss him, of that he is sure. It has always been this way. The mortals that he has come up against, and let live, have amused him for a while, but after all, they are only human. Perhaps, he thinks, the detective will prove as stimulating as McCrae had been. He's convinced that the two men are cops. The waitress smiles coyly at the handsome man.

"Would you like anything else?" she asks him.

"No thank you," he tells her, looking at his watch. He has an appointment to keep. He must meet this cop's girlfriend, the one who is working on the picture he's set to direct. "Yes," he says to himself, "perhaps this one will live up to McCrae."

Lucille pours a second cup of coffee for herself and Dan Richardson, and then pulls a chair up to the large drafting table where she has arranged the costume designs. "They're fantastic! Oh. They're just great."

"Well, I kind of like them too," Dan says modestly, rubbing his bald dome and leaning in for closer inspection. "Of course, now we just have to build them."

They spend the morning drinking plenty of coffee and going over the plans for the film. Lucille, as the assistant, will oversee most of the work with Dan's approval. He's hired other members of the wardrobe team; both those who will work in the shop as well as on location with the film, the onset people who make sure that the actors are wearing the correct wardrobe for any given scene or shot. It's called continuity. For example, if a gun shot during a prior scene stained an actor's wardrobe with blood, the continuity people would have to make sure that the actor wore the same clothes at a later date.

Lucille understands all this but remains attentive as Dan hands her a Polaroid camera.

"I want pictures, pictures, pictures, Lucille. There can never be too many pictures. Make sure the whole crew knows this."

"I will, Dan," she assures him. She had just begun calling him by his first name with his encouragement. "I'll keep everything neat." He beamed at her, liking the girl and his decision to give her a try.

"Neat! That's the word. Pictures make a show neat and a neat show is a well run show with pictures to prove it." Lucille smiles knowing that he's repeated that pronouncement on more than one occasion and she's sure she won't forget it. "Now," he continues, "the rest of the crew will be here this afternoon. I'll introduce you to all of them including the director, Richard Stewart."

"That Mr. Banning sure gives the impression that he's not new to the business. You get the feeling that he really loves the picture business."

"Oh yes he has indeed," Dan continues. "He's one of those producers who aren't so obtrusive. They're more interested in the quality of the film than in their own self promotion. Besides, he's a writer as well as a producers so that gives him insight that most producers don't have."

"I sure like what he's done with this script," she says. "The vampires are so different from what you usually see in the movies." She remembers Greg's promise to get the crucifix and is about to mention it to Dan but decides that it would sound too silly. "I'm looking forward to meeting Mr. Stewart. Have you ever worked with him?"

"No," Dan answers, "I don't know much about him except that he's apparently worked with Marcus before and comes highly recommended."

Lucille loves the buzz on the lot, the comings and goings, the trucks and crews and equipment. At lunch time, she and Dan stop to eat at the commissary. As usual, it's packed. Lucille is thrilled to see some well known stars..

"Isn't that Brad Pitt, she asks?" She nods toward the table where the actor is lunching with two unfamiliar faces.

"Yes. That's him all right," Dan tells her. "I worked with him on Babel," he adds proudly. Lucille notes that Dan doesn't say in what capacity he did so. The vampire picture that they were working on was not exactly in the same league as Babel. She picks at her Caesar salad not really hungry. It's a beautiful day and she's about to embark on a journey she's been dreaming of since arriving in Hollywood, assisting a costume designer on a feature film that's sure to offer challenges and opportunities. At three, just before the other members of the wardrobe team are about to show, Marcus Banning and Richard Stewart appear in the wardrobe room. Marcus does the introduction.

"Lucille Salvatore, I'd like you to meet our director, Richard Stewart."

"How do you do Lucille." She touches his large smooth palm. She feels some incredible heat or energy radiating from his hand, and his eyes search deeply into her own. "The pleasure is mine," he assures her. "Marcus is very pleased with your enthusiasm." He is impressive, this tall man in the neat blue blazer. "He told me that your remind him of an assistant we once knew, a young lady much like yourself named Dorothy Doty." Marcus smiles.

"Everything running neatly," he asks? Dan beams.

"Yes, fine," he assures the producer. "We were just talking about keeping everything neat. Weren't we Lucille?"

"A neat show is a well run show with pictures to show," she reiterates. The men chuckle. With the introduction done< Marcus and Dragan start to leave. At the door they both stop at the same moment. For a second it seems odd to Lucille. It's like they were one and the same person so precisely did they stop and turn.

"By the way folks," Marcus announces. "We've decided that the major location for the picture will be up in Lone Pine. It's a beautiful spot. I've worked there many times before." He smiles at Richard who nods and continues.

"We figure on heading up there in about two weeks. I know that's not a lot of time for you to get ready but we've hired a great crew and have our dates set. Thanks you."

"Lone Pine?" Lucille asks Dan when the two men have left.

"Up there near Mount Whitney. Lots of snakes during the summer but with winter setting in we should be safe." He winks at Lucille. "It's way out there; a small town but there is an airport if we need something in a hurry."

The remaining few hours of the day are taken up with the arrival of the rest of the wardrobe crew. There are two young women who are going to work directly with Lucille, Barb and Beth. Jake, fresh out of college makes up the rest of the team. Both Dan and Lucille are pleased when the time comes to wrap the day's work. They have a good crew and everything seems to be running smoothly.

"We'll meet in the commissary tomorrow at seven-thirty," Dan tells them as they head out to the lot where the cars are parked.

Greg is waiting for Lucille when she gets back to the little house on Spaulding. The autumn air has once again brought with it a little chill and Lucille is greeted by fire burning in the fire place. "That's the last of that branch," Greg tells her. "From now on we'll have to buy wood. They dine again by candle light on some Chinese take out that Greg had ordered as she tells him about her day. He's surprised by her appetite. She describes in detail and includes the strange sensation she felt when she shook hands with the director but does not describe him physically. Greg grins. "Well he's the big chief. Hopefully you won't see him go on the warpath."

"Yes," she agrees. "The shows all about all of us and he's got to be the chief." Greg doesn't go into his day. He knows how important this job is for Lucille and gives her the stage. But his thoughts do wonder back to old Jack and Uncle Ned and the yellowed pages in the family album. But mostly he thinks about the stranger at the funeral, the one who got away On the way up the stairs he mumbles. "The X Files," he says.

"What's that," she asks?

Did you used to watch the X Files?"

"No. Can't say that I have. Why?"

I've caught a couple of them, but Captain Magness is a big fan." As he is undressing he suddenly remembers the crucifix and reaches into his pocket to retrieve it. "I almost forgot," he tells her. "I picked up two of these today in a little shop on Melrose. Here," he says, placing the chain around her neck. He bends and kisses her lightly on the neck. "We'll both wear them. See. I've got one too. I know it might seem silly but let's try anyway." She smiles and nods her head, holding the cross in her hand.

"I can do that," she assures him. "Besides, it's very pretty."

Later, in bed he holds her tightly. "Did I mention that we are shooting the film in Lone Pine," she asks? He says nothing. "You will come visit. Won't you, Honey? They've even got an airport there and it's not far from L.A."

"Yes," he says quietly. "That's wonderful. Now sleep, Darling. Sleep." It takes her no time to drift off to sleep, but Greg lies there awake with his pulse beating on his temples. Finally, unable to shake it, he gets up quietly. Going to where he had hung his jacket, he removes the little book from the shop on Melrose. He pads downstairs and sits at his desk where he adjusts the light and again looks at the title. It reads: "The Real Vampires" by Dragan Radelescu

CHAPTER 9

Jean Marc

Dragan, when he was quite done, entirely satiated with the life blood of what had once been Roland Jordan, dashing Hollywood director, crawled to the open French windows, pulled himself to his feet, and still panting from the thrill of the kill, gazed out into the night. The fangs had retreated and the body returned to the form of Betty Boudin. A passing stranger, looking up to the window, would have seen a beautiful woman, and not the monster that was Jordan's last vision. Still, there was blood smudged about her mouth, like a lion's after a kill, and there was too, a savage beastly cast to her beauty.

For a moment she clung there, leaning into the cool night air, breathing deeply of all its scents and sounds, waiting to see if she would take on another form, if she was, once again, to fly like a dark bat from Hell across the night sky. From his place on the street, Lenny spotted The Master at the open window, and for a moment, he too waited to see if he would take a new shape. But nothing changed. Only the curtains moved with the breeze as Dragan waited, poised on the sill. Lenny opened the back door of the car and stood beside it, and then, Dragan dropped. He leapt from the window, like a panther leaps from a rock, and just as easily, as lightly and with a similar grace, he landed beside the car. Neither of them said a word. Lenny could smell the kill on Dragan's breath as he closed the door and climbed into the driver's seat. It made him long for the ritual, long for the rare taste of human blood. Inadvertently, he licked his lips. All the way back to the mansion, Lenny could smell The Master's cold breath, and could feel the churning of wanting, eating at his insides.

At the castle, he gently escorted the almost unconscious Betty into the grand living room where the coffin lay spread open and waiting, lined with fine, black satin and surrounded by yellowed, smudged candles that breathed soft, muted light. Marcus was there too, waiting. Carefully and with a kind of tenderness, they aided the comatose body into the casket and placed her in a prone position. The Change was just beginning to set in. As they stood over the body, they could barely make out the almost indiscernible signs of changing, as the face softened, loosing the distinctness of its features. It was Marcus' turn to stand watch that night.

"You must sleep, Lenny," he instructed the other one. "I will stay watch."

"You know, Marcus," Lenny said, his voice edged with a hint of regret. "I shall miss this one. This Betty Boudin. Even though it was The Old One, it was nice having female company around here."

"I understand. She was wonderful too in the picture. I was very proud of her performance. And she won't be missed by only the two of us. All Hollywood will mourn and wonder where she has gone and what she could have been. Now sleep."

On the thirteenth of December, a delivery boy, finding the door to Jordan's house open and no one there to answer it, ventured into the estate, and after spending some time admiring the fine furniture and movie mementos, wandered upstairs, where he discovered the body of the director. He wasted no time in calling the police who arrived immediately.

Among those on call was young Jack McCrae who had just gotten his detective grade. For some reason, the squad commander hadn't assigned another detective with him, despite that being the usual procedure. Jack had the training and the instincts for the job, and set about the on site investigation according to the book, making sure not to contaminate the crime scene or misplace any of the evidence. Unfortunately, from the onset, he realized that he had very little to go with. It didn't look like a robbery. There were no signs of struggle, and no obvious wounds. He dusted the place for fingerprints, made detailed notes and directed the uniformed cops on hand. It was on his third inspection of the body that he noticed the marks around the neck. He had never seen anything like them.

At about that time, the reporters started arriving and clamoring for details. Jordan's movie, *"Westward Wagons,"* had just opened to great success. The only mistake that McCrae made, and he realized that after the fact, was that while being interviewed by the reporters, he mentioned Betty Boudin as having been in the company of Jordan, the night he attended the premiere. "I've got to get a hold of this Betty Boudin," he said during the course of his own inquisition, "she should be able to shed some light on this thing." A reporter from The Hollywood News took that piece of information and ran with it. To say that she could not be found was slightly premature, but it made good copy. It wasn't until some weeks later that Jack realized that not only had she disappeared, but also she had apparently never been. It was then, he discovered that she had no address, no birth certificate, no history, and if the fingerprints that he found all over the window sill in Jordan's house were hers, he would never know, as they were not on record anywhere and led him to a dead end.

So while Lenny and Marcus took turns standing vigil over the ever-mutating body, the body that was slowly taking on a male form, as Betty Boudin slipped into a thing of the past, Jack McCrae was pursuing the newest and most fascinating of Hollywood crimes. Already, news of the strange murder and disappearance was spreading across the country, and when the coroner's report came back, stating that the body contained no blood, the murder became the talk of the town. From The Brown Derby to the Pig'n Whistle, at any table, one could overhear the whispers,

"And they say her performance could get her The Academy Award!"

"She was a wonderful actress. I did a play with her on Broadway."

"She worked as a domestic in my house when she first came to town. Wonderful girl. Kept everything so clean."

"That's odd. I heard that she came from a good family in Boston. Finishing school. Upper crust."

"Oh, the two of them were lovers for years."

"Really? I thought he was queer."

That was the talk that kept the town buzzing, but Jack McCrae was interested in the facts, and none of these seemed to fit. She had come from nowhere and vanished into thin air. Of course *"Westward Wagons"* became a hit, a must see and the offers for work started flooding the offices of Hoagie's agents over at The William Morris Agency.

"I can't believe it, boys," he remarked to Ned and Pudge one afternoon over a couple of beers at The Formosa Cafe, where the regular clients, most of whom worked in the business had been stopping by the table all afternoon, offering their congratulations, "but Betty's disappearance is changing my life. Feel kind a bad 'bout that. Kind of took a hankering to that old gal."

"Well, it's even too bad about that Jordan, 'course he would have had it coming anyway with that attitude of his. But he sort of straightened up there at the end," Pudge said, sipping an icy one. The three of them were waiting for Jack McCrae who had suggested that they meet at The Formosa. He had a bunch of questions to ask them about Betty and Jordan.

"Figured you lads might throw a little light on this investigation, Pudge. Why don't we meet there at three?" The boys had arrived around two and by the time Jack did get there, they were feeling mighty chipper. "Well lads, I guess I could have just one. It's three and I'm on my own time now," McCrae conceded, when asked what he would be drinking.

"You remember Hoagie, Jack?" Pudge re-introduced them.

"Why yes I do. I'll tell you lads, I've seen that picture three times now, and I must say you all did one lovely job. I recognized you two fellows as well, I'll have you know," he toasted the three of them. The boys returned the toast.

"Thanks, Jack," they all grinned into their mugs.

"Lads," he continued, "I want to know all about this Betty Boudin. I understand that there was an accident up there and she replaced the leading lady?"

"And thank God for that," Hoagie interrupted. "That drunken nag Sally was real trouble. Course I would have been happier to see her depart by some other means."

"Yup, we all kind of liked that Betty, and Hoagie here says she was a real good kisser to," Ned told him. Hoagie's rough, tanned cheeks blushed at that.

"Well tell me all you can," Jack implored them.

Ned did most of the recounting. Basically he told the story in sequence, right through discovering her body. It was not without some humor when he described the raucous Sally Smythe. When he got to the strange business about spotting the fleeing

Peter Weir and then, only moments later seeing him arriving in the car, Jack stopped writing in his note pad and listened attentively, and when he described the marks on her neck, McCrae's ruddy Irish complexion lost a shade or two of color. "Course I'm not real clear anymore on any of that. It's just impossible for a man to be in two places at the same time, and the coroner said the marks on her neck were probably cuts from the fall. She did get banged up pretty bad, not to mention that her neck was broken along with most of the other bones in her body."

"Yup," that's right," Hoagie agreed. "And that old country coroner didn't waste any time getting rid of the body as she didn't have no relatives or anything, and Jordan was in a big rush to find a replacement. It's pretty desolate up there in Lone Pine. Might have been different if we was shooting down here in Hollywood."

Jack decided to have another beer and maybe a shot of Jameson's to go along with it. He leaned in toward the others and whispered.

"You know, I found some marks on Jordan's neck as well. Of course that was in the papers already. I should have kept my big mouth shut, but I never seen anything quite like these. They looked like dog fangs or something. But how in the world could a dog have gotten upstairs into the bedroom and then closed the door after himself when he left?"

"Well, I don't care what that old coroner said," Ned interrupted. "Them marks I saw on old Sally's neck, sound just like the one's on Jordan's." Jack had downed the whiskey and ordered another round.

"Fellows, you say it was this Peter Weir who found the replacement? It was himself who fetched Miss. Boudin from Hollywood?"

"Oh, yup," Pudge nodded. "He was back the next day with her too." Jack noted all this in the pad and continued ordering drinks. They'd all taken to the Jameson's followed now by beer chasers, and all the while, they were greeted by grips and electricians and other stuntmen who told them how much they had liked the picture. By five that afternoon, the three men were well into their cups. The talk of Betty and Jordan had given way to more tales, stories the men told of life in the West, before they had arrived in town. Jack and Hoagie talked like old friends do, and Jack's pad had long ago disappeared into his green blazer.

When it came time to leave, just as they were rising to go, Jack popped a question.

"You lads ever hear the tales they tell back in Ireland of The Little People?" He directed this more to Hoagie and Ned than to Pudge who was as Irish as was he. The two just grinned back at him, figuring this to be another tall tale from the Irish angle. "Well, I tell you, I believe that this might be true. There's many a strange thing out there in this grand world. We cops are taught to see everything in a logical way, based on hard facts, but there's many a time when the facts, no matter how you twist them, just don't make any sense at all." Ned nodded.

"It sure didn't make any sense that, that Weir fellow could be in two places at the same time."

"Exactly my point, Ned," Jack continued. Again he leaned in toward the others, but looked around the room before speaking. I think this strange business could be the work of a horrible creature of the night, a beast as old or older than The Wee People."

"And what would that be?" Ned demanded with a wide grin spread across his face.

"That laddy would be the vampire!" Jack spit the word from his lips like a bad taste. "They are horrible creatures that have been around for centuries. These murders, no matter how you dress them up, have the smell of that beast." By then they were all standing. For a couple of seconds, Jack's outburst seemed to sober the others up. Then Ned broke the silence.

"Maybe we all had a bit too much of that Irish whisky Jack. I'm a practical man too, and vampires are a stretch in my head."

"Well, you think about that when you're sober, and I'll do the same. Meanwhile, I'm going to track down this Weir fellow and I'll see you lads at The Hollywood Legion Stadium for the Friday fights."

The last remnants of the sun left long shadows on the sidewalk, when the four men finally stepped out of The Formosa. After saying their good-byes, each stumbled off in his own direction, each carrying some fresh ideas about not only the Roland Jordan murder, but how and if it was tied into the inexplicable accident that befell one Sally Smythe, the former Maude Jones, of Oklahoma City.

Jean Marc Descamps stepped from the silver lined casket precisely six days after Betty Boudin leapt from Roland Jordan's window sill. Only Lenny was there to welcome The Master's new incarnation into the world. Marcus had other duties to perform. He had been busy looking for an appropriate dwelling for Dragan's new form. Lenny was pleased to see that there was something of Betty Boudin in Radelescu's current identity. Jean Marc was smaller in stature than Jordan had been, and facially carried some of the refined beauty that Betty had possessed, notably the high cheekbones and full lips. The hair too, was dark, as had been Betty's. Of course Dragan had not foreseen exactly what his new person would be, but he knew that it would be a man, and he had taken the appropriate measures as Betty, to slip easily into his next character. With both Lenny and Marcus, he had chosen the name and the background that he would use. Jean Marc Descamps was to be a French import, a prodigy of the new French cinema. Photography was really a French innovation and Dragan planned on exploiting both the ignorance of the Hollywood establishment as to the current state of French cinema, as well as the exotic nature of the Europeans, to establish himself as the next great Hollywood discovery. He had already learned that Hollywood had a penchant for discovering, or more precisely, claiming to have discovered any new and upcoming talent or personality. Of course his knowledge of France, and for that, all of Europe, was complete, and he spoke French fluently.

"Bonjour mon fils," he greeted Lenny, who had guided him out of his satin confinement.

"Bienvenue, mon Maître.» Vous faites très français."

"Comme il faudrait, mon jeune." Lenny and Marcus were fluent as well. "Peter is closing the deal on the house he has chosen for you. It's in Beverly Hills, right off Beverly Boulevard. It is a Tudor design, similar to Pickfair, and was modified to the Regency look by Wallace Neff, the same architect who did Fairbanks's house. I think Jean Marc will find it suits his style."

Over the centuries, the three had amassed enormous financial resources, which were spread throughout the world. They had avoided taxes in their effort to keep their anonymity. Had they wanted to, they could have purchased all of Beverly Hills.

As before, Dragan threw open the shuttered windows and breathed deeply of the still night air. Below, the lights flickered about the town. In one quick motion he turned and addressed Lenny. "And how is Peter?" He asked. "Is it as I said it would be?"

"Yes, Master. It was wise to find another place. We shall keep this place a secret, and keep it always. And you were correct too, about this detective, this Jack McCrae. He is making inquiries. He has already been to the studio and has met with those two cowboys. And he is asking questions about Peter. Perhaps, Peter too, should undergo The Change."

"No!" Dragan hissed. "It will not be necessary. McCrae has nothing on him. Sally Smythe is forever buried, and there never was any connection between the studio and Peter. He handled it all through Jordan, as I instructed him to do. His check has been cashed at the studio's bank. There are no records of calls, no connections at all. There is only a contract with his signature on it and a credit in the film. Hollywood is now aware of our talented Peter Weir. It would be a shame for him to vanish when he could be such a support for Jean Marc Descamps. He will be my introduction."

"You're right Master. He tells me that already the offers for work are pouring into Burwillow Studio. But what about McCrae. Should he be eliminated?" Dragan again turned toward the open windows and stared hard at the sliver of the moon that shimmered down through the branches of the tree. He laughed.

"My dear George," he smiled gently. "We can not kill McCrae. It would draw too much attention. After all he is a policeman. Besides," he scoffed, "I like a challenge. Life as we know it can become boring. This McCrae can keep it interesting. Now. I am fatigued. You will wake me in the morning. Bonne nuit."

That night, it was Lenny who did not go immediately to sleep. He had always relied on The Master and Peter to plan the next move. Perhaps it would all work out, still, he was troubled. He sat all night, gazing at the sliver of the moon until it disappeared in the early light of dawn.

Lenny had the right information on Jack McCrae. The day after spending the afternoon at The Formosa with the three cowboys, Jack went to the studio, pad in hand and started checking into both the whereabouts and the history of a certain Peter Weir. This was met with almost no information or hard facts about the man who was rapidly becoming one of those over night Hollywood success stories. In fact, much as in the case of the vanished Betty Boudin, the rumor mill had started, and the facts that he did get amounted to nothing more than a series of myths and exaggerations.

"The nicest guy you'll ever meet. Worked with him back in New York. Big Broadway producer."

"Been in town for years. Just waiting for that break."

"Used to be a carpenter. Did all the cabinetwork on my house. Etc. Etc."

Friday night as planned, Jack met with Ned and Pudge at Hollywood Legion Stadium, on the corner of Hollywood and El Centro. The stadium, first built outside in 1922, and then enclosed the next year, was one of the town's biggest draws, with its rough mix of the famous and the unknown. On any given Friday, one could see an array of stars, like Mae West, Valentino, Gable and so on. And in true Hollywood fashion, they mingled comfortably with the local residents and regulars. The place was also richly salted with gangsters and racketeers, some as well known as the stars themselves. It was one night here that Pudge took on Henry Johnson, the world welterweight champion. Both Pudge and Ned were regulars and as such were greeted by others like themselves. The Legion was also frequented by a lot of the cowboy stuntmen, and on this particular night, the boys ran into Knute Hopkins. McCrae was waiting in the bleachers when the three of them got there. Ned made the introductions.

"Got any new theories?" He winked at Jack who decided to wink back.

"So you've done some thinking about what I said, once you were in a sober state?"

"Well, it's crazy as all get up Jack, but I know what I saw, and that just don't make any human sense at all."

"What are you boys talking about?" Knute wanted to know. So sitting up there on the wooden bleachers, breathing in the smoke and rich smells, and taking in the wonderful ambiance of it all, the three of them filled him in on the story as they watched the bouts.

"I heard this Roland Jordan was some kind of bank robber back east, before changing his name and coming out here," Knute informed the group. "And that this Peter Weir fellow was tied in there as well."

"Did you now?" Jack asked, having heard something very close to that story himself, about the director. And so the evening went. McCrae was getting used to the rumors. In any case, Jordan was dead, dry as a bone. Boudin was gone, and Jack was beginning to think that she too was dead, and the only thing he had, that could put them all together, was this Weir fellow who had not yet surfaced. He'd run a check on the man and come up with nothing. It was odd, but not unheard of at the time. Hollywood was, and still is, full of people with shady or altered backgrounds.

The fights were all good ones, the men not at all disappointed, and as they left the packed stadium, slowly moving out with the crowd, McCrae said to the others. "Look lads. If you run into this Weir fellow again, let me know. And if there's an opportunity to work for him, take it. Just watch yourselves. He may be on to you."

Marcus closed the deal on the house, and with Lenny, under Dragan's supervision, had it furnished. Dragan still had access to the huge warehouses in San Francisco, where he stored much of his enormous collection of furnishings. Of course he had other holdings scattered throughout the world. Like his fine wines, his antiques, his furniture and accessories would have rivaled any collection at any of the world's most famous museums. Dragan's plan was to establish residency as Jean Marc in Beverly Hills, and keep the Sunset mansion as the real headquarters.

On January 29th, 1928, at a huge party at The Montmartre Cafe, complete with all the news media, celebrities, and hangers on, Jean Marc Descamps was presented to Hollywood by Mr. Peter Weir. He was introduced as a French prodigy of the cinema, and Weir's choice for director on his next picture, *"The Long Trail."* At Peter's side, was a radiant Dorothy Doty, the associate producer on the film. Also in attendance, was detective Jack McCrae. A number of the Hollywood police had been hired as off duty security, and McCrae had placed himself on that list. After leaving the party, McCrae followed Peter Weir and Jean Marc Descamps to a house off Beverly Boulevard. He took note of both the licensee plate and the driver, a short hunched man with long blond hair. Upon checking the plates, he found them to be registered legally to M. Descamps.

The following day, Hollywood was hit with five bank robberies, all executed at precisely nine in the morning, and spread throughout town. The investigation that had been in progress regarding organized crime linked the robberies to the same. Within a week, a series of brutal slayings, all of crime figures, took place. The headlines screamed of gang warfare, and all of Hollywood shuddered. Roland Jordan had been dead and buried for approximately six weeks and no breaks had come in the case. Jack McCrae had been tempted to run his vampire theory past the brass, but being new on the job and not really having any hard evidence to support the theory, decided against it. Although the investigation remained officially open, McCrae was called off the case and assigned to the gang murders.

Jean Marc Descamps gained great recognition as one of Hollywood's most innovative and exciting directors of especially action pictures. His strange disappearance became a Hollywood tale. At his side, throughout his career, guiding the master was the equally celebrated Peter Weir. Along with Irving Thalberg, Louis B. Mayer's "boy genius" over at M.G.M., Weir was considered to be one of the best and the brightest. Despite the competition between the two, both Weir and Thalberg were friends. Thalberg's early death, although attributed to a bad heart, was not entirely due to that. He, along with Dorothy Doty, who gained equal success as a producer, were both given the opportunity to become one of The Immortals. Both declined.

It was with a horrible sense of reluctance and loss that Marcus disposed of his beloved Dorothy. Jack McCrae, who had quietly followed the workings of Peter Weir, took some note of Dorothy's demise, but Marcus, who was well aware of McCrae's interest, chose to end her life through mortal means. This was accomplished one lovely Sunday morning in July of the year 1941, as she drove her new Sportster convertible down Pacific Coast Highway. Somewhere near Zuma Beach, the brake lines, which had been cut by Marcus, were asked to perform an emergency maneuver. They could not. A pedestrian, later interviewed by Detective Jack McCrae, said he could hear her scream for a good fifteen seconds, as the car plummeted off the road and over the adjacent cliff. Her death made all the headlines. At the funeral, again at Forest Lawn, Dragan grimaced when he saw Marcus briskly swabbing his moist eyes. McCrae, also in attendance, noted the same thing and reluctantly put to rest any suspicions he had regarding Marcus' involvement in Dorothy's death. Still, he did not trust either Marcus or Jean Marc, or the strange driver that seemed to make up the trio.

Pudge and Ned never again worked for Peter Weir. They would work for a later incarnation of him. Nevertheless, both did very well. By the time Dorothy passed on, they were both doing far less stunt work. That had been replaced by second unit directing and stunt co-coordinating the younger breed of up and coming stunt men and women. Among those women, Ned found his wife and probably the only love of his life. Her name was Suzanne Farley, and her soul found a path to his heart. In the autumn of '44, when she was killed in a freak accident on the set of a western, over at The Porter Ranch, she left this life with a piece of that heart.

For the next two years, Ned pretty much dropped from sight. McCrae and Pudge were the only company that he shared when they visited him at his place in Los Feliz. He suffered a brief interval with the whisky bottle during that time, but it was short and he came off it well. He did not return to work until 1946.

Hoagie Coates, who had never considered himself an actor, packed his bed roll several years after his one hit film, and retired to his Santa Monica ranch. He never did get married and kept in touch with his old cowboy pals. The public never forgot old Hoagie, and were reminded of him each year on his birthday. His birthday bash became the thing of legends. His ranch was also a hangout for many of "The Beat Generation" during the 'Fifties, and well into the Hippie era, a journey to Hoagie's was a kind of rite of passage.

Jack McCrae continued to work in the Hollywood Division. He was instrumental in getting a strangle hold on some of the major players in the crime breakout back in '28, and was respected as a good cop, but for being slightly eccentric. Over the years, he shared with more than a few colleagues, his theory of vampire slayings. Of course no one took him seriously, and most of them attributed his tales to the well-known bent of the Irish, to exaggerate. Privately, his fellow cops joked about it, as no one would have dared say anything to his face. Jack McCrae was also known as a no nonsense scrapper when the chips were down. Besides keeping a constant eye on Weir and Descamps, he spent considerable time in the L.A. Public Library. Among the books he uncovered, was one titled, "The Real Vampires." It is an old book with a worn green cover.

One day in late September, 1946, Dragan, who was standing in front of the large mirrors in the master bedroom of the Beverly Hills estate, carefully applying gray to his thick dark hair, stopped, and called Marcus who was in the adjoining room going over resumes of actors. "You know Peter," he said, regarding him in the mirror, "the time is at hand for all three of us to move on. I can not play this thing out any longer. Jean Marc Descamps has left his mark on Hollywood, as did Betty Boudin. She, at least, had the good grace to go early. There is nothing shabbier, or potentially more dangerous, than a late exit."

"You are right Master. I too, have been thinking along the same lines for some time now. McCrae is still out there. He looks good for his age, but he's eighteen years older now, and it shows."

"Yes," Dragan sighed with a tinge of regret at perhaps the loss of being capable of aging gracefully as do humans, "it does show. Besides," he added, "you can not forever play the other boy genius of Hollywood." They both laughed.

"Poor Thalberg," Marcus muttered, really thinking of his Dorothy. "You know, George told me that McCrae picked up the copy of your book. He's been keeping an eye on him." This time Dragan laughed loudly.

"Then if he reads well, he should be well versed in our ways. It is decided then. We shall all three go through The Change. We shall take turns during the next three weeks. I shall go last. We shall simply abandon this house and find another. That will convince McCrae if he's still harbors any doubts that he was right and we do exist."

"As always, you are most wise." With awe, Marcus looked at Dragan's reflection in the mirror. "You have become fond of this Jack McCrae, haven't you Master?" Again Dragan laughed.

"Life can become tedious without conflict. McCrae is a worthy opponent. We've had some good ones over the years," he reminisced. The two looking at their reflections in the mirror, stared long and hard, and were in fact, looking deeply into all their pasts. "Come." Dragan finally commanded him. "We shall eat the fine meal that George has prepared and tell him of the plans, and," he touched Marcus' shoulder, "we shall drink a toast, to the future!"

END OF BOOK ONE

BOOK TWO

CHAPTER 10

Jeff Smith

On October nineteenth, 1946, sometime during the early morning hours, Dragan Radelescu, as Jean Marc Descamps, took the life of Jeff Smith. The act was accomplished in the traditional manner. As in each case, the victim's death was a most horrible ending. In the case of the veteran cowboy actor who had made a transition similar to that of Hoagie Coates, (the two of them knew one another, but had never been friends), the act was not achieved without a considerable struggle. Jeff Smith had a moment to realize what kind of monster was upon him, and the quickness of body and mind that had come from those hard years on the trail during his youth, almost saved him.

Both Marcus and Lenny had taken their respective turns and gone through The Change. Both had found transients, unknowns. Jack McCrae was already following the two murders that fell one week apart, both in Hollywood, both corpses having been left in abandoned buildings on two of the smaller streets off the boulevard. McCrae's suspicions were aroused and he had ordered autopsies after discovering the two bodies with the telltale teeth marks on the necks.

Dragan had chosen Jeff Smith as his victim for a number of reasons. Smith was in his early fifties. He was small, short but wiry like many of his colleagues who had once made their living on horseback. Smith also had a good knowledge of the movie business, having been a part of it since the very early years. Of course Jean Marc Descamps had picked up a few tips over the years as well. But Dragan also had a personal reason for choosing Jeff Smith. Jeff Smith had stared in Jean Marc Descamp's first feature, and had also made life miserable for the then unknown French director. Jeff Smith was no Hoagie Coates. Unlike Hoagie, who never quite got used to his role as a movie cowboy, Jeff Smith had embraced that role with the same gusto that he had had as a young cowboy, who after weeks on the trail, rode into the cattle towns with guns blazing and whip cracking. Jeff Smith lived the Hollywood life in grand style. His expensive cars were decked out with cow horns on the hood, and his house in Beverly Hills was a standout for extravagance. Many a tourist stopped in front of its Texas style front gate, to stare in wonder at its outlandish western motif. He had always surrounded himself with beautiful things; beautiful women, expensive, if garish, objects of art, luxury cars, and so on. Dragan, besides despising the man for the way he had treated the aspiring French director, equally loathed Smith's flamboyance and lack of taste. It was for these reasons that Dragan targeted Jeff Smith as his next victim, and the opportunity to do so had come at just the right moment.

Jean Marc Descamps was scheduled to direct what was to be perhaps the grandest, most epic and largest budgeted Western feature to date. The cast would include all the biggest of Hollywood stars. Many of the old cowboy actors had been coerced out of retirement for one last screen role. The movie was to be a plum, and everyone wanted a bite out of it. Jeff Smith's career had skidded to pretty much of a standstill over the past five years and he was hungry. He had never again worked for Jean Marc Descamps, but had watched from a distance, as Descamp's own career and renown as a director had grown.

"Monsieur Smith." He had winced at the French form of address when after almost twenty years, Descamps had called to reconnect.

"What can I do for you Descamps?" he had asked, immediately recognizing the voice.

"There is little you can do for me, my dear friend, but there might be something I can do for you," Jean Marc smiled into the phone.

"And just what would that be?" Smith wanted to know. Of course he had a very good idea. Everyone in town knew of the picture, and Smith had prayed that he might get a shot at it.

"Well Jeffrey, (Smith hated that too.) "Perhaps you've heard that I'm about to direct a feature, a Western?"

"Well I've heard something to that effect," he answered with a pounding heart.

"Why don't we let bygones be bygones," Jean Marc continued, laying on the French accent that he knew so irritated the actor.

"Well, I guess that's all right by me," Smith mumbled.

"Good. That's settled then. I have a wonderful part that I would like you to do. Perhaps I could personally come by your place one evening and we could discuss it over a few drinks. Would that suit you?" Jeff Smith couldn't believe his ears. He was up to his neck in debt with few prospects. This could be the start of a huge comeback. He could hardly restrain his enthusiasm.

"Why, that would suit me just fine Jean Marc. Why don't you swing by around ten tomorrow if that's not too late for you?" Again, Smith winced when he heard Dragan chuckling on the other end of the line.

"Ten's just fine. Despite working in the film business," Dragan rubbed it in, "I've always been a creature of the night. I shall see you then tomorrow."

So it was settled. Jeff Smith was so elated at his sudden twist of fate, that he took his big Cadillac convertible, the one with the steer horns as the hood ornament, and drove it throughout town, making sure that as many people as possible were aware that actor-cowboy, Jeff Smith, was out and about. Of course in that get up he hardly ever went un-noticed.

Dragan, on the other hand, shared the conversation he had just had, with Lenny and Marcus over a dinner of pan fried pork chops wild rice and pilaf, mixed with Parisian mushrooms, and several bottles of the Beaujolais Nouveau that had just arrived from France.

"You know my friends," Dragan said to the other two as they sat sipping expresso coffees, savoring the end of a fine meal and their last evening in the house, "From now on, when we make The Change, we must do so as we did this last time. We must all go together, one after the other, and then re-establish ourselves in a new place, with our new identities. It is too risky otherwise. None of us should be associated with any one of us that McCrae or anyone else might suspect."

"That is a good plan Master," said Peter, whose name was now, Theodore Schreppel. John Joachims, who had been known as George Craft agreed, as was his nature.

"When I have finished with Jeff Smith, we shall return to the chateau on Sunset until Theodore has settled all that is still to be done with the new place on Craig Drive." Dragan had chosen the little street that climbed off of Barham Boulevard into the Hollywood Hills as his next locale. The location was perfect with the modest wood framed house nestled in the hills overlooking Universal Studios and Warner Brothers in The Valley, yet still just a beat away from Hollywood with all its studios and activities. The Valley was just beginning to open up, and Dragan, with his usual vision to the future, guessed that it would be the place to be for the next period of years, before the next time came for The Change.

Once again, Lenny drove Dragan, this time, to Smith's house, that evening of the nineteenth. Dragan made sure to arrive exactly twenty minutes late. This time, he sent Lenny off, telling him to return just after midnight. As he had suspected, (he'd heard the rumors), Jeff Smith was well on his way to inebriation. His liquid choice that evening was Scotch. Despite the fact that he poured Dragan a tumbler of the stuff from a bottle of twenty-year-old Balentine's, Dragan knew after taking the first sip that it was of a much cheaper variety.

"Very tasty, this," Jean Marc raised his glass to his host. "Your taste is impeccable, Jeffrey." Smith flinched, not sure of Descamp's sincerity or motive. He glanced about his western quarters.

"Thanks, Jean Marc. Don't believe you've ever been here. Have you?"

"No Jeffrey, I've never been invited. Perhaps after we talk, you would honor me with a tour of your habitation." Despite his doubts, Smith felt somehow flattered.

"I'd be happy to old Hoss, after you fill me in on the picture and the role you want me to do." Dragan smiled pleasantly. He was going to enjoy this evening, all the way to the very end.

"Well," he began, "it's called, *"The Bad Lands,"* but the title is of little importance. What is, is the role I have for you." He continued. "It's the story of a man of the West, a man of character, a lawman who was tough but had honor as a young man. But he has fallen from grace. He's taken to drinking cheap whiskey and taking up with whores. Worse than that, to supply his habits, he has also taken to robbing and killing. In the film, we find him at his very lowest, a bum, living in a small town in Kansas. A band of outlaws come to the town and terrorize the citizens and he is forced to make a choice. Will he go with them, join them, or will he; can he find something of his old character and save the town and its people?"

"That's real good, Jean Marc. Another refill?" Smith asked, pouring one for himself.

"Of course, my friend." Dragan handed him the glass, which he filled.

"So what does he do?" Smith asked the Frenchman who chuckled deeply.

"Why, he goes with the side of the citizens, the side of law and order and cleans out the bad guys. After all Jeffrey, this is a film for public consumption." Smith couldn't restrain his eagerness.

"That's perfect. What a wonderful role for me. You know," he admitted with some reluctance, "the public hasn't seen old Jeff in a couple of years now. They'll eat it up!"

"Then you'll do it?" Dragan asked, with much the same exuberance as Smith's own.

"Of course, old Hoss! Of course I'll do it!" Smith got to his feet and hastily downed the last of his glass. He then went to the bar and extracted a new bottle of Balentine's twenty-year-old Whiskey. This bottle, Dragan noted with a sneer, still had the seal unbroken. The old fool was all ready to celebrate. Dragan decided that the end was at hand. Smith filled his glass and in afterthought asked Dragan if he wanted another.

"I'd love one more for the road. I shall discuss the money with your agent. I'm sure money isn't the deciding factor is it Jeffrey?" He threw that in just to annoy the man further, knowing full well how badly he needed not only a hit role but the money that would follow.

"No problem, old Hoss. Let's drink to the success of our project. Then I'll give you a tour of the old place," he chuckled, full of his own smugness.

"That was exactly my own thought," Dragan answered Smith's toast with a clink on the old cowboy's glass tumbler.

"Well come on, old Hoss," he instructed Dragan. "I'll lead the way." It was Dragan's turn to cringe, as Smith led him through the garish, sprawling estate. It was, Dragan decided, a monument to bad taste in its most extreme display. The tour took some forty-five minutes, with Smith affectionately and most egotistically pointing out every object and each photo, and further disgusting Dragan's sensibility with a story featuring himself that accompanied each one of these things he so loved.

As Dragan had anticipated, they wound up in the master bedroom upstairs. Jean Marc was not surprised to notice that along with the enormous bed with the carved bisons on the headboard, there was also a matching full bar. Smith, whose drink had long since been emptied, immediately went to the bar to serve up another. Dragan had tolerated this man long enough. After close to twenty years of loathing, he decided in the instant that Smith reached for the fresh whiskey bottle, that the time was at hand and that Mr. Jeffrey Smith had served up his last cocktail.

Like another creature of the West, the mountain lion, Dragan leapt on Smith's back. And in the same motion, clawed the denim shirt in two, making sure not to leave any scratches on the man's back. Smith turned, dropping the twenty-year-old Scotch on the floor and somehow managing in the motion, to fling Dragan from his back. What he saw before him, was a monster, too loathsome to describe. Never, during his years on the plains, never, during his most horrifying moments with man or beast, had he felt the sheer terror that he felt at that moment. But old Jeff Smith had not lost all the fighting determination that he had known as a youth, and worked with to become one of Hollywood's most famous cowboys. In the same instant, he reached behind for the curtains. Somewhere in the back of his head, he remembered disarming a man who came at him one night with a gun, while he was visiting one of Dodge City's more famous bordellos. That night, he had done so by entangling him in the heavy velvet curtains that hung from that second story window. On this particular tepid night in October of 1946, he got no further than ripping the curtains, for while his hand still clutched the paisley material, two vicious fangs pierced his throat.

"Old Hoss!" he choked with his last breath, as his bloody saliva oozed from his mouth and he stared in absolute astonishment into the cold eyes of the Frenchman he had once humiliated so many years before. "Old Hoss," he gasped one last time, as the final curtain came down on the life of cowboy, actor, Hollywood celebrity, Jeff Smith.

As he had done after killing Roland Jordan, when he had sucked the life and blood from the body of the late J. Smith, Dragan, still breathing heavily from the heat of the kill, he flung open the windows, and stared hard into the chilly autumn night, waiting to see if the body would take on another form, if he would once again fly as in the old days. Below, he spotted Lenny, who stared back at his master. He too was waiting. But again, it did not happen, and again, Dragan, after looking down the darkened block to make sure there were no witnesses, leapt from the second floor window to the ground below. This time Lenny drove both of them to the mansion off Sunset, the house on the hill, the house with the turrets and towers and gargoyles.

They had seen the last of the place off Beverly, the place Jean Marc Descamps had called home for the past eighteen years. Hollywood was no longer a small town. It was coming of age. The Second World War had come and gone, and in its wake it had left a rapidly growing population. The San Fernando Valley, which had once been vast farmland, was being quickly filled with tract housing and apartments. Many of the servicemen who had been housed and fed at "Mom's" Hollywood Guild and Canteen, and rubbed shoulders with real movie stars, now returned and took up residence.

And a new war was waging, and the battleground was Hollywood itself. In 1938, Congress created the House Committee on Un-American Activities. By the end of the war, many felt that influential people in Hollywood were in fact, anti American. There had always been a communist party and Hollywood had been, and still is, a liberal bastion of thought and politics. The war had staved off the inevitable inquisition, but by 1946, when Marcus purchased the house on Craig Drive, the "Commie Scare" was in full swing. Over four hundred writers, actors and directors were blacklisted from the film industry. Many simply vanished, others fled overseas to work in foreign countries, and those who remained, those who had named names and betrayed friends, or even done and said nothing, were now looking over their shoulders in fear. The panic did not cease until the mid 1960's.

Dragan had sensed the coming change. He had seen and known change for hundreds of years in countries all over the world. It was this instinct for survival that had kept him and the others, not only alive, but also unidentified as the fiends they were. He knew that McCrae had his suspicions, and he hadn't ignored Ned and Pudge and even Hoagie Coates. He could have killed them. But if Dragan and Marcus and Lenny shared one human trait with those unlike themselves, it was vanity. Perhaps because they had once been human, they retained this potentially fatal flaw. These creatures could live forever, but they too were mortal, and could also be killed. It had been vanity that had induced Dragan to write the little green book that he had

had published years ago in England. It would also be vanity that would lead him as Richard Stewart, to direct the movie, *"Life-Blood, The Last Vampires of Hollywood."* Something in his soulless being urged him to in some way, explain himself, to explain who they were, and from where they came. It was for this reason that he revealed in that little green book, just how he and the others could be stopped.

Jack McCrae had that book. He had found it at the public library, downtown, and despite his naturally honest nature, and despite the fact that he was an officer of the law, somehow he had just never found the time to return it when it was due, and as time passed, he conveniently forgot that it had ever belonged to anyone other than himself. He read it from cover to cover, again and again.

"Vampires are not a myth. They are as old as mankind itself, and they will outlive all of you. I know this to be the truth, for I, Dragan Radelescu am a real vampire. I was born in Transylvania, in the year 1283. I am a descendent of an Ancient One, an Egyptian, and therefore have the oldest lineage, for we were an invention of the ancient Egyptians, and I am a direct descendant. I have lived many lives. I have seen much of history, in many countries, and I speak a multitude of tongues. There are only a few of us scattered throughout the world, but we are here. Make no mistake about it. We live!"

That was the first paragraph. McCrae read it for the twentieth time. He was sitting in a police cruiser outside the house that belonged to Jean Marc Descamps, the Descamps that he had long suspected, the man who had suddenly, along with the strange Peter Weir and grotesque, George Craft, disappeared, vanished as if they had never been.

"What's that little book you keep thumbing through there LT?" the uniformed patrol officer who was the driver, asked.

"You wouldn't want to know, Laddie," Jack answered, not bothering to look up. If he had, he would have caught the smirk on the young man's face. He'd already seen the cover, and couldn't wait to tell his pals at the station house. Jack McCrae's vampires were a constant source of amusement for some of his fellow cops. "Just run in there and tell the two officers that I don't want anyone crossing that line.

"Yes Sir, LT," he said, opening the door. "I'll do that."

"As far as I'm concerned, this is a crime scene. You got that?"

"Yes sir," the man answered smartly. He didn't want to cross old Jack McCrae. He'd heard those stories too.

While the officer went about that business, McCrae reflected on the events. There had been three murders in three weeks, all involving teeth marks. This last one was then four days old, and like the others, there were no suspects. Of course Jack suspected Descamps and company, but Descamps had vanished. The last murder had been that of Jeff Smith, the guy that Hoagie Coates had called, "The biggest back end of a mule, this side of The Rocky Mountains." McCrae knew that Descamps was to have directed a picture, and Smith's agent had called the precinct after the murder, telling Jack that Jeff Smith had mentioned to him that he was to have a meeting at his house with Descamps the night before the murder. It all looked pretty clear.

But where was Descamps? Jack had immediately gone to the house off Beverly, and found it to be apparently abandoned. He'd had it staked out for the past three days and no one had returned. Meanwhile he was going cold on the murders. The two transients had already been cremated at the city morgue, and Smith's funeral was scheduled for that afternoon at Forest Lawn. He planned on attending it. Descamps had vanished, taking nothing with him. His disappearance had made all the papers. Already they were looking for a replacement to direct *"The Bad Lands."*

"They've got your orders LT," the officer told him and got into the car. McCrae looked at his watch.

"Take me to Forest Lawn," he told the man. "We're going to a funeral."

No one from the castle off Sunset was going to the funeral. Dragan's orders. Dragan, of course, was unable to go anywhere. He was stretched out in the coffin with the black silk lining. Already, the other two could see the affects of The Change. The body that was transforming was shorter than Descamps. The clothes hung loosely about the frame, and the man was older. Dragan had already created the identity that he would play out until he no longer could. Lenny and Marcus returned to the great room after lunch, at just about the same time that McCrae was pulling into Forest Lawn.

"So this will be George Zimmer," Lenny said softly, almost worshipfully.

"Yes John, George Zimmer, the director," Marcus agreed. "And I shall be Theodore Schreppel. Perhaps, I shall play my hand at the agent game, just for a while."

Jeff Smith would have enjoyed his own funeral. Perhaps he did. It was pure Hollywood. His agent, Cappy Spindlier, who was also the executor of his estate and perhaps, what passed as his only true friend, had pulled all the stops. He had figured that despite the fact that Smith was practically broke, Cappy was going to sue the studio for what would have been Jeff's salary. He knew that Descamps was a suspect, and Descamps was gone. That was a breach of contract wasn't it? Besides, Smith's house was worth some good cash in the new booming real estate market. Spindler knew he'd make a bundle on the house. Why, it was practically a museum. Anyway, he justified any expense with his own sentimentality. They'd been good friends. Everyone knew that, and after the funeral, all of Hollywood would know just how much Cappy cared. Everyone would want to be on Spindler's list.

McCrae figured that there were at least three hundred people turned out at Forest Lawn. All the famous faces were there, although notably absent were the three cowboys that Jack knew.

Hoagie, Ned and Pudge were all sitting at Musso's eating lamb chops and home fries, and washing down the heavy course with large pitchers of beer.

"Ain't that something about that Jeff Smith? I mean him bein dead, and that Frenchman gone?" Pudge stated to the table.

"Yup, sure is partner. That Descamps was old Peter Weir's little prodigy. Heard he's gone as well," Ned agreed.

"Hoagie, you never worked for him again after that first time with Boudin, did you?" Pudge asked.

"Never did, boys. None of us did. But I'll tell you, that Peter Weir was talking to my agent about doing this Descamps film, *"The Bad Lands."* Said he had a part in it for me "for old times sake," whatever the heck that's supposed to mean."

"Well the whole thing stinks," Ned picked a chunk of gristle from his teeth. "Jack called me the other day. He's convinced that they're just a bunch of vampires and they keep changing form. That's why they disappear. It's taken me twenty years now, but I'm beginning to believe that, crazy as that sounds, he just might have a point there."

"Well if they was vampires, then old Hoagie here, is the only man I know to have kissed one and lived to tell about it," Pudge chuckled. The three of them laughed at that. They'd all had more than a few beers.

"Yup," said Ned, "and he said that old Betty was a real good kisser too!"

"Speakin of vampires," Hoagie cut in, "heard old Jeff's agent was throwin a hell of a funeral for that conceited, drunken, old, jack ass." As the boys were re-filling their glasses, Yakima Canutt came in to the restaurant by himself.

"Well hello there Yak," Hoagie stood to shake the stuntman's hand. "Why ain't you over there throwin flowers on old Smith's grave?"

"Well fellows, probably for the same reason that you boys are here. Never could stand that son of a bitch."

"Well sit and have a drink with us," Hoagie volunteered.

By the time the four of them left Musso's, the funeral was just about wrapping up.

It had been a hell of a send off, done entirely in Smith's inimitable style, complete with the steer horns on the hearse, and pinto colored limos in the procession. It was in fact, such a success, that it even got reviewed in the next day's trades. Jeff Smith would have been proud to know that his last review, although not for the film he had anticipated doing, was nevertheless, an outstanding one.

Two days later, exactly six days from the moment that Dragan had first tasted the blood of Jeff Smith, he rose from the satin lined coffin, decorated with the silver etchings, in his new incarnation, that being one, George Zimmer.

CHAPTER ELEVEN

Greg and Lucille

Years later, Greg often asked himself how things would have been different, had Lucille described to him, the man she met that afternoon, the director of the movie, Richard Stewart. Even then, years after the fact, Greg could still see him, with the wavy hair, dark slacks, and blue blazer. But what stood out forever in Greg's mind, was the look that Dragan had given him from the back seat of the taxi; the sneer, challenging him, taunting Greg to catch him. Of course, looking back was an inherent aspect of Greg's job, but if she had described Stewart to him that night, the night of McCrae's funeral, the evening after Dragan had given them the slip in the 9000 building on Sunset, so much could have been avoided.

The following few days, neither Greg nor Lucille see much of each other. She's busy with the pre-production, the costume gathering and building, and all the things that go along with her job, as well as having to sit in on production meetings with the other department heads. Although she is not the department head, she is pleased, even flattered that Dan has asked that she be there with him at all the meetings.

"I want you to know as much as I do about every aspect of this film," he tells her one bright late autumn day over lunch at the outdoor cafe. "This is the way I was brought into the business. I had someone who placed his trust in me. In the long run, besides learning a lot more, you'll find that it will help all of us, because you will be able to cover for me in emergencies, and you know, in this business, emergencies are an every day occurrence."

"I sure appreciate your trust Dan. This is a big break for me and a great learning experience." She touches the crucifix through the thin blouse she is wearing, and Dan takes notice.

"What is that Lucille?" he asks her. His question momentarily embarrasses her, but she realizes that wearing a crucifix, although she never has, is not anything unusual.

"Oh," she says. "My boyfriend is a cop. He got it for me. Thought it would bring good luck. After all," she laughs, "this is a vampire movie. See." She pulls it out and shows it to him.

"You know, Lucille, I think that's a clever idea. Maybe I should pick up some of these for the wardrobe crew. Ask him where he found that and what it costs. Would you do that?" She's pleased at his response.

"Why, of course I will. I'll let you know tomorrow."

Meanwhile, after the holdup at The Bank of America, Greg gets a new assignment from Magness. The robbers, all three of them, managed to get away with a considerable amount of cash. They'd hit the bank just as the armored truck company was making a transfer. One of the two drivers was shot, and being treated at Kaiser Hospital, on Hollywood Boulevard. Despite the shooting, the bank people and some of the detectives assigned to the case were fairly convinced that it was an inside job, and somehow involved the guard who was shot. The other guard had already been cleared. Magness calls Greg into his office.

"Greg, how's that Zimmer thing going?" He asks the one question Greg was hoping to avoid. The Zimmer case was just about dead in the water. The transient's body had been disposed of; there had been no sightings of Zimmer. He had never returned to the house on Craig Drive. Everything was left as it had been, and no one had come forward as a relative or executor for his estate. He'd simply vanished as though he had never been.

"May I sit, Captain?"

"Sure, pull up a chair," he gestures towards one of the wooden chairs.

"Well, Sir, we've kind of run into a dead end. There was a fellow at the funeral, McCrae's funeral. We followed him. He came in a taxi, but gave us the slip at the 9000 building on Sunset. I've got a strong feeling that he's involved in all this business some way. I put together a composite of his likeness. Got a pretty good one too, and ran it, but nothing came up, no matches."

"Look, Detective," Magness, takes a long sip from a stained coffee cup, "I'm going to have to pull you from this one. There are no relatives or associates of his, screaming to solve this thing. We'll leave it open, but I want you and Cove to work with Kibler and Colton on the B.of A. holdup."

"Jesus, Captain, I just know that I'm close to this. I can smell it." Greg leans in to the Captain. "I just have this feeling..."

"Well, we don't close any of these things. So you and Cove still have this one. But it's got to be on your own time. I'm closing down the surveillance on Craig Drive, pulling my man. If anything more comes up, you keep me informed." The captain stands, indicating that the meeting is over. Greg's feeling of frustration and failure is complete. He starts to leave, and suddenly remembers something. Reaching into his jacket pocket, he withdraws the little green book.

"Captain, I almost forgot. Take a look at this!" He thumbs quickly through the book, and then finding what he is searching for, hands it over to Magness who reads:

"Although we prefer to take on the physical properties of a male, it is possible, when going through The Change, to assume the body of a woman. Although over the years, we have rarely done so, it has been achieved. Usually it is done for a specific reason, to reach a goal, such as the seduction of a man. In that case, we do not inhabit the female body for any great length of time. In the ancient times, we had less need to go through The Change. We simply moved on to a place where no one knew us. In this modern world, we are forced to do so more often. To acquire the female form, the last victim must also be female."

Scratched in faded ink, next to this passage, which falls somewhere near the beginning of the book, are the words, Betty Boudin, and the initials, JM.

"Good God!" Magness exhales, JM. Must be Jack McCrae. Where did you find this?"

"I found it in a little shop over on Melrose. The same shop where I found this," he pulls the crucifix out from under his shirt. And it is Jack McCrae. This book once belonged to the downtown library." Greg laughs then opens the back cover for the captain. "See. Here's the library card pocket, and here's McCrae's signature. It doesn't look like this book was a real popular one, judging from the three names here, but McCrae was definitely the last one to take it out." The captain inspects the scrawl on the faded card.

"That's got to be our McCrae all right. I wonder how it ended up at that shop on Melrose?"

"I don't have any idea Cap, but the lady who lent it to me, she wouldn't sell it, told me to read it, and seems convinced that there are vampires out there, right now in Hollywood, and have been for years." Magness seems to think about this for a minute, then shakes his head.

"Well Greg, if they are out there, they'll just have to wait. Right now I've got the city coming down on my ass over this holdup, and no one's calling for vampires. You know how it is in this town, no matter who you were, once you're gone, you get about twenty-four hours of press time, and then they forget all about you. They've already forgotten Zimmer. This thing is very interesting, but we'll just have to wait and see who or what surfaces. In the meantime, you and Cove check in with Kibler and Coltan."

"Yes, Sir, I'll let Cove know," Greg tells him on his way out the door.

"Look, Detective," Magness calls after him. You keep your eyes and ears open, and keep me informed. I'd rather you don't share anything with anyone else around here. They don't watch "The X Files." Greg smiles, somewhat relieved. At least Magness didn't dismiss him entirely. He'll work on the other thing, but like the captain said, "Keep his eyes and ears open." Later, as he's leaving, he touches the crucifix. He'll make sure to wear it too at all times, and insist that Lucille do the same.

For the next two weeks, Cove and Greg work with Kibler and Coltan. They spend time at the hospital interviewing the guard. He wasn't hurt seriously and is released after a couple of days. It was the nature of his wound that first lead the detectives to suspect that he might be involved; that and the detailed way that the heist was pulled off. It could never have worked that smoothly without some inside line, and both Cove and Greg quickly come to suspect that the guard with the flesh wound to his calf is a perpetrator. The detectives take turns watching his apartment just off La Cienaga Boulevard, waiting to see what kind of visitors show up. The four of them run the operation in shifts. The getaway van, which had been ID'ed, is found abandoned and empty near the Santa Monica Pier. When it is dusted for fingerprints, none are found. When they run the vehicle, it turns out to be stolen, but stolen south of the border in Tijuana. Their break finally comes when a car shows up at the guard's place. They run the plates and find that this too, is a stolen vehicle. Instead of busting the occupants of the vehicle, they wait 'til they've gone inside, then, call in a search warrant for the guard's apartment and serve it while the visitors are still there. Their suspicions are well founded. They find stacks of currency that match the serial numbers supplied by the bank, along with weapons, suspected of having been used in the robbery. One of the guns, a Smith & Wesson three eighty-caliber semi automatic, proves to be the gun that fired the bullet into the guard's leg. At the hospital, because of the investigation, when the bullet was removed, it was saved, in the event that it could be matched to the weapon. The case is not only solved, but makes the papers. The four detectives are even called for a news conference that runs on the major networks.

The next day, Greg gets a call at the station house from Patrick McCrae.

"Hey Captain, I saw you on TV last night. Congratulations. Fine job you fellows did. Course, I never put my money into The Bank of America. Italians run it, you know. But fine job anyway." Greg has to smile.

"How you doing Pat? Have things settled down?"

"Oh yes, I do miss Uncle Jack. He was a good man, and not as crazy as everyone thought."

"I have to agree with you there Pat. I think he really was on to something," Greg starts, but is quickly cut short by the exuberant Patrick McCrae.

"Say, Captain, you know I've been going to Dino's once in a while. Nice fellow too, that Dino. Always asks about you."

"Well that's nice Pat. Listen, did your uncle ever mention a little green book to you, about vampires?" There's a short pause on the other end of the line.

"I know that book!" Pat says excitedly. "That was Uncle Jack's book. He gave it to me years ago. Don't have it anymore. Lent it to a lady. How do you know about it?" For the first time in two weeks, despite their success with the robbery, Greg feels that he's made some progress.

"Well, Pat. I've got that book. Found it in a little shop, over on Melrose." Again, Pat cuts in.

"That would be Andrea's shop, wouldn't it be Captain? Over by San Vicente?"

"That's where I found it. Well, actually, the lady, Andrea, she lent it to me when I went in there one day to get something else."

"Well, that's what I told her to do Greg. You see, I lent it to her and told her that she should hang on to it. Why, I've read it cover to cover, more than a few times. I said to her that if ever, she felt that it was right, the right person, that is, that she should lend it to him too. There are so many non-believers out there Captain, but Andrea, she believes. That's why I go over there from time to time. She's got all sorts of interesting books and things, from all over the world. Even has a few on The Little People."

"I know she believes," Greg says softly. "She told me that they are here, have been for a long time. It was like she knew or something, knew that I was looking for it."

"Of course she knew!" Now it's Patrick who laughs. "She's clairvoyant. She's Irish too. Why she learned to be like that from the fairies!"

"Well," Greg mumbles, "wherever she learned it, she sure had me pegged."

"Have you read it Captain? Have you gone through it?" Pat demands.

"I've been reading it," Greg tells him. "I wonder who this Dragan Radelescu was? I wonder what his real name was?" He hears Pat whistle.

"It's not who he was Captain. It's who he is. Who he might be. Might he be here Captain? Was he Zimmer? Was he Betty Boudin? My uncle thought he might have been. Have you got to the end of the book yet Greg?"

"Yeah, I've read it." Greg says.

"Well read it again Greg. Read it again. And if you have any questions, you go back to Andrea. Perhaps she can help you out."

"I'll do that Pat, and thanks for your help. You know where to get a hold of me. You do that if you hear something. OK? The fairies huh?"

"The fairies Greg. My uncle was a smart man, smarter than most of them that he worked with."

"Although this book is published in England, we are in America now. We have been here for some time. They didn't have much sympathy for the Royalists, in France, during their revolution, and we are, and always have been of royal lineage. America is truly the land of opportunity. We arrived in Boston, and unfortunately settled in Salem during an inopportune period in history, but we got out in time, and slowly made our way West. We are but three, here in this vast country. San Francisco is a beautiful city. It is a city of opportunity, and ideal for our needs. Culturally, it is not lacking, and financially, it offers much; everything that we need for our lifestyle. Being a port city, it is full of transients and travelers. The pickings, when they are necessary for our survival and continuation, are bountiful. For those of you who read this, those few who read it and believe it to be true, we welcome you to San Francisco. If you qualify, and so desire the gift of everlasting life, we chal-

lenge you to find us and perhaps join us. For those who seek to destroy us, we welcome you as well. Eternal life can become so tedious without some form of conflict."

Dragan Radelescu. 1903

Greg again reads the closing passage of the book, the passage referred to by Pat McCrae. He shakes his head. It's so compelling. Part of him wants to reject the whole idea as impossible, after all, he is a reasonable man, for God's sake, he's a cop! But there's another part of him, a growing part that is convincing that skeptic side, that this is true, and can be the only possible explanation for these abnormal events. He's met Jack McCrae. He's read his notes. His Uncle Ned must have been convinced as well. Despite his "Little People" and his reputation for exaggeration, Jack McCrae was a smart man. Perhaps he was the only one with any sense among his colleagues.

Later, Greg returns home, still puzzled "There must be something else," Greg says aloud, "some other clue. A note perhaps?" He decides to once again, go through the family albums, and is half way to his feet, when he hears the front door open, and Lucille rushes in. As usual, she has her arms full. She drops everything in a heap in the hallway and comes to him.

"Oh, Honey, I'm so glad to get home, so glad to see you!" She wraps her arms around him.

"You're freezing," he tells her, holding her even tighter.

"Oh, Greg, it's so, so cold out there!"

"Well, you get warm, maybe I'll cook us a little something to eat, and I'll get the fire going," he tells her gently. She arranges the things she's dropped and starts upstairs. Greg senses that there's something else. "What is it Lucille?" He asks.

"Oh, Honey, it's set now. We're going up to Lone Pine. We're going to start the show up there, and Marcus, that's the producer, has it set so that we're leaving Saturday."

"That's the day after tomorrow," he realizes.

"I know, Honey. It's all going so quickly. I told you it would be in about two weeks. I think we're in good shape. The cast won't arrive until Monday. Oh, Greg, it's going to be just freezing up there. Maybe that's why I've been so cold, just thinking about what it'll be like up in Lone Pine. You know, there's already snow on the mountains."

"Well, when I come to visit, maybe we'll go skiing," he laughs. "You'll be all right up there, but I'm going to miss you. Go change and tell me about it over dinner." She goes upstairs, and Greg starts for the fireplace, and then suddenly remembers what he was going to do. He goes to the desk where the albums lay as he had last left them. He's put bookmarks in the two places he found the clippings, and quickly finds them. Carefully, so as not to damage them, he retrieves them from behind the yellowed plastic covers, starting with the Betty Boudin article. He turns it over, and gasps. Written on the reverse side in French, are these words scrawled in pencil, now faded and barely legible:

Boudin was at least one of them; a vampire. I think Peter Weir is too. He killed Sally Smythe. . ...Ned Delacroix"

Quickly, he withdraws the other one. Again there is a note in the same script:

Jean Marc Descamps killed Jeff Smith. He was Peter Weir's little creation. He too disappeared. McCrae is right. April, 1955, Look to Zimmer. Vampires! All of them. . ..Ned

Greg stares at the two clippings in shock. Outside, he hears the wind rustling through the branches of the pepper tree. He too shivers. The wind envelopes him, making him feel very small and vulnerable in the clutches of the elements. He looks about. "Lucille!" he calls out for her, then remembers that she's gone upstairs. He rushes up the stairs. He needs to hold her, to know that she is all right.

He finds her standing in front of the dresser mirror. She is wearing a white terrycloth robe; open, so that her breasts and stomach are reflected in the glass. She stands there as if transfixed, with her right hand clutching the silver crucifix. Instead of turning on the lights, she has lighted scented candles, as she so often does before taking a bath. The effect is eerie. The window is open just a crack and Greg can feel the draught. It causes the candles to flicker, and all about the room, strange shadows dance a macabre dance. Hastily, he slams shut the window, then goes to her and wraps his arms inside the warm robe, holding her soft body with all his heart.

"Are you all right, Darling?" he asks in a hushed voice. She arches back into his embrace.

"Oh, yes, Honey. I was going to take a bath, and warm up. I was just thinking how much I'm going to miss you. You will come and see me, won't you? Won't you?"

"I'm going to miss you too, Baby. Of course I'll come up. And I want you to call me every day, just to let me know that you're OK. You hear?" He smiles at her pale face in the mirror.

"I will Greg. I promise." She turns to hug him. She kisses his cheek. "Of course I will. Every day!" They both smile. The shadows seem to have stopped their madness, now the room is bathed in a tender, yellow, light.

"Take your bath, Lucille. I'll set the fire and fix us a little something to eat. Take your time and relax. Everything is going to be just fine," he tells her, at the same time realizing that he is also reassuring himself

Greg throws together a quick dinner of linguini with a pesto sauce that he had picked up at the Theodor Carlo, the Italian deli, over on Magnolia. They eat it with a light salad, French style, with only lettuce and a French sauce of Dijon mustard, olive oil, vinegar, salt and pepper. They drink ginseng ice tea.

The fire burns in the fireplace, and the chill seems to have gone, along with the wind. She tells him her plans. They're to leave Saturday. The cast and crew have been booked into a ranch on Whitney Portal Road. It's a sizable place, often used by film crews, as it is so close to all the locations. The shooting schedule calls for a three-week stay up there.

"Dan asked me to drive my van up there, even though most of the crew is being bussed up by the company vans," she tells Greg. "He thinks that will be more practical, even though the Teamsters are supposed to do the driving. Sometimes, you need something right then. Emergencies are an everyday thing in the film business. Besides," she adds, smiling across the table, "when you come up there, if you fly, we'll have a vehicle to ourselves."

"You let me know when I should come. I'll work it out with Captain Magness and Eddy Cove. We're sitting pretty, right now. After that B. Of A. Business. I'm due for some time off.

During the meal, she relates little anecdotes about the film and the people she is working with. He knows just how pleased she is and is happy for her, but his concentration wanders. He keeps going back to the words his Uncle Ned left behind, scrawled on the back of the clippings. His mind wanders off to his meeting with old Jack McCrae, "Why they kill their victims and suck the body dry...dry as old dust!" He remembers Niki Starling telling him about waking, to find Zimmer's driver at her neck, and how his uncle and Pudge walked off the set, on some movie. In his mind's eye, he sees the sneer of the stranger in the taxi, the only stranger to show at McCrae's funeral. He thinks about Dorian Gray, about creatures that do not age, that live forever, and he ponders over the little green book, written at the turn of the century, by one, Dragan Radelescu.

Long after they have made love, and Lucille has fallen fast asleep, his thoughts drift. His detective's mind clutches at all the clues, the messages, and sometime during the night, perhaps after he has finally been drawn into sleep, his mind accepts the evidence, and his psyche finally embraces the reality, that they are out there. They are among us, and they kill, and in his acceptance, he makes a resolution that he will find out who they are, and some way, somehow, he will stop them, forever!

For Greg and Lucille, the next day, those few remaining hours they have together, fly by quickly, as quickly as bats in the night. They make the most of their remaining time, and when, on Saturday morning, the time has come, after Greg has helped Lucille pack all her things into the Volkswagen van, and the morning is still young, he leans into the driver's side of the car, and kisses her lips.

"I'll miss you, Darling. You work hard and enjoy it all, and you call me, and if ever there is anything that you need, anything, you call me right away, and I'll be there, just as quickly as I can be."

"Oh, Greg, I'll call every day. That's a promise. I already miss you, and, you know, I truly love you."

At the end of the block, just before turning the corner, she lightly taps the horn, and waves out the window, and then, she's gone.

He looks about the empty street. It's only six-thirty on a brisk Saturday morning. As he turns to go back inside, the gash from the broken branch catches his eye. He bought the sealer for the tree weeks ago but still hasn't found the time to paint it over the scar. "I'll take care of that this afternoon," he promises himself. Something about it offends him. He's not quite sure why, but his mind flashes back to the stranger in the back of the taxi. He goes inside, and returns to bed. This time his sleep is deep and long.

CHAPTER 12

George Zimmer, Ned and Pudge, And Paris

Both Lenny and Marcus, at that time, Theodore Schreppel, and John Joachims, were present, waiting patiently beside the silver finished coffin, when George Zimmer rose, literally, from the dead. After opening his eyes, they dressed him, again, like themselves, entirely in black. When it was completed, he climbed stiffly to his feet. Lenny rushed to his side to give him assistance, holding out his arm for Dragan to lean on. As he steadied himself on his feet, he looked into Lenny's loving visage, and with a smile on his finely honed face, greeted his servant.

"Hello, Old Hoss," he hissed, then threw back his dark head and laughed a laugh, so malevolent, that chilled the other two, to their very cores.

"You must be starved, Master," Marcus asked. "Shall we eat?"

"I'm famished," the new and still unknown, George Zimmer answered. "John, have you prepared us something to eat?"

"I, I thought that perhaps you would prefer to dine as in the old days, Master," Lenny stammered, "but I can quickly fix something to suit whatever taste you might have."

"No," Dragan stopped him with a wave of his hand, and a glance out the window at the crescent moon. "The moon is perfect for some liquid nourishment. Let us be off. Besides," he added, "you can show me Zimmer's new residence."

The following morning, three drunks, transients all, came into the Hollywood Squad room with a strange story. They had been sitting and sipping around a little campfire, up in Griffith Park, and had reached the point of mellow recollection, when they had been approached by three, strange, dark shapes, carrying gifts in the form of liquid spirits. They remembered accepting the gifts, but little more than that. All three complained of feeling weak, drained, and all three had some version of a story that involved getting bitten in the neck by these shapes. None of them could recall just what sort of creature had done the deed.

The officer at the desk, substituting for the sick desk sergeant, was the same officer who had driven Jack McCrae to the funeral. He knew that wild dogs roamed the park, and that fires were illegal, and he'd been on duty long enough to have heard all sorts of tales from drunks and dope addicts, so he dismissed the story along with the three men, giving them a warning about fires in the park, and firewater in general. Apparently, he thought the story amusing enough to share with his fellow officers, and in the telling, suggested that maybe the drunks had encountered McCrae's vampires. Jack McCrae happened to enter the room during the telling of the story. The young officer realized this, only at the end, when no one beside himself seemed to find it amusing, and was instead, focused on something behind him. When he turned to see what that distraction could be, he was met by McCrae, in full Irish. McCrae leveled him in front of the other men, asked him the whereabouts of the men he had released, and never again said another word to the officer, who asked for a transfer, and was gone, within the month.

For the next two weeks, Jack McCrae spent his free time searching Griffith Park, interviewing transients, in an attempt to find these three. Although he never did find them, he heard all sorts of stories, several of which were very similar to this one.

He did however; draw several conclusions from these interviews. He spoke of them to Ned and Pudge one morning over breakfast at Schwab's Pharmacy, on the corner of Crescent Heights and Sunset.

The three of them were sitting at the counter eating the breakfast special and consuming large quantities of coffee. As usual, the place was bustling with activity, full of young men and women, most Hollywood hopefuls, many, students from Hollywood High, and the remainder, the regulars, the locals, who lived in the neighborhood. The diner area was separate from the pharmacy itself, and both Pudge and Ned had long been regulars.

"Well, Lads, this proves a few things to me. Assuming that Descamps was one of them, and he's gone, then he's probably still around as something or someone else. They're still out there fellows. I figure they have to change identities. I'd say we had also better be careful. Old Descamps was on to me, and his friend, Peter Weir knew you were on to him Ned. The question is, who are they now?"

"Well, I'll tell you one thing, the studio shelved that film Descamps was going to direct, and that's a damn shame," Pudge grumbled. During the past eighteen years Pudge hadn't grown an inch, but he was as bald as an egg, and had taken to wearing a hairpiece. Each time he got agitated, he seemed to find something wrong with its fit. Ned, who still had a full head of hair, winked at Jack, as Pudge adjusted his hair and glared at his steaming cup of coffee. Jack smiled.

"And here's another thing, Lads, I figure that they can suck blood without killing the victim." He reached into his pocket and pulled out the little green book he'd acquired a month ago. He'd been hesitant about sharing it with his two friends. He didn't want to risk ridicule. He'd had plenty of that during the past eighteen years.

"What's that Jack?" Ned asked, while rolling a smoke.

"Well this here, is my little research book. I've read it through and through. It's kind of a manual on vampires, written by one, in fact. What's that?" he snapped, when Ned choked on the smoke he'd just inhaled.

"Nothing Jack, nothing. Still haven't got used to rolling, I guess."

"Now this book has all the information on these creatures, but it doesn't say anything about them changing identities, and it doesn't have any tips on how they suck blood without killing the victim." He opened the book to an ear marked page. This is all it says in that respect:

"Only occasionally do we need human blood to survive. We have adapted well to your ways. In fact we enjoy good food and fine wine. You humans have created so much confusion with your silly myths on a subject of which you have such little knowledge. This book is offered as a kind of reference on what we really are. I have chosen to give you some clues and to save others that I do not wish to share."

"So that was written by a vampire Jack?" Ned asked, with a straight face.

"That was written by a certain, Dragan Radelescu, who was born in Transylvania, my friend," Jack answered, with a look that almost convinced the two others. "It says that they moved to San Francisco, course that was some time ago." Jack paused and poked at his egg, sunny side up, with his fork, watching the thick yolk burst slowly and spread over the greasy white, until it settled up against the home fries. "I believe laddies, that this Dragan Radelescu is here, right now, and I think he's responsible for the murders of Jeff Smith and the two transients. And furthermore," he looked across the table at his two friends, "I believe that he could have been Miss. Betty Boudin, and either Jean Marc Descamps, or that little creep, Peter Weir."

During the weeks following their night sortie, the evening that the drunks in Griffith Park encountered the three dark shapes, Dragan, Marcus and Lenny, were busy setting up the next stage of their lives. Dragan had not yet moved into the house on Craig Drive, preferring instead, to keep a low profile by remaining at the manor off Sunset. The house on Craig Drive was in fact, not far from Griffith Park. It was on The Valley side of The Hollywood Hills. Were one to cut up the hill that now runs parallel to The Hollywood Freeway, up past Lake Sherwood, on the far side, the Hollywood side, one would practically stumble into the park. The three of them knew the park well. For years, they had used it as a location to hunt for their victims, when they needed only to taste the blood and not destroy the donor.

The first night that Dragan was to spend in the new house, Lenny prepared an Italian meal for the three of them. He grumbled about the insufficient kitchen accommodations, but nevertheless, adroitly managed to come up with an appetizing dinner, starting with an antipasto of melanzane al formaggio di capra, baked Japanese eggplant, goat cheese and toasted walnuts, followed by a linguine puttanesca, capers, black olives, garlic, and basil. This was accompanied with slightly chilled and quite excellent Chianti. Over the main plate of vitella pliccata, sautéed veal with capers and lemon in a white sauce, Dragan told the two of his plans.

"I have been thinking, my friends, that perhaps we should not yet surface as a trio in this new Hollywood. It's too hot. I can smell the smoke, and the smoke is Jack McCrae and those two cowboys, as well as the fresh string of murders. I know that he is looking for us, and it is the three of us that he searches. This veal is simply divine John," he complemented the chef, who smiled gratefully.

"Thank you Master. You have always been most fond of that dish. Ever since our days in Roma." Dragan smiled, as if at some long ago memory.

"It is fitting that we partake of Italian delicacies this evening, because it is of Europe that I am thinking, although my heart is set on France."

"I, I apologize, Master, I could have prepared a French plate," Lenny stammered.

"No, no my child, it is fine. It is the country to which I refer. I have decided that you and I shall go abroad for several years. We shall keep this house here. Theodore can do with it as he sees fit. It would make a nice rental property if he so wishes, or he can use it as an additional residence, or even as a sanctuary, should someone stumble upon the Sunset chateau." He lifted his wine glass, and regarded the fine color against the flames in the fireplace. The three sat in the dining room that shared a fireplace, on the other side of the wall, with the living room.

"It shall be as you wish and command, Master," Marcus answered dutifully.

"You've wanted to try your hand at the agent game, Theodore," Dragan chuckled. "This will give you the ideal opportunity. When we return, we shall continue as before, in the picture business. By then you should have all the connections necessary."

Dragan, as usual, was on the right track. He knew that McCrae was getting close. He had followed McCrae on his forays into the park, for information, and as Dragan had authored the little green book that McCrae possessed, he was well aware of just how much information on their kind, the detective had acquired. He was equally aware of Marcus' interest in delving into another aspect of the film industry. Agents had always been an important part of the movies, and prior to the movies, they were a necessity in the live entertainment field. The Broadway stage, vaudeville, and national tours, had traditionally been handled by agents, who represented the talent. The talent was not limited only to the actors. In Hollywood, agents represented producers, directors, directors of photography, and others as well. By the time the three had moved into The Valley, towards the end of the 'Forties, large agencies like The William Morris Agency and others, were putting together package deals that included as many of their people as possible on any one project. Any given film might include the leading actors, a producer and a director, all of whom were represented by one agency or a single agent. This allowed the agent to wield considerable power over the project. This practice has developed and refined itself to this day, where single agents and agencies have tremendous control, and are often viewed as bloodsuckers of a different breed than Dragan and his kind.

"It is settled then." Dragan said, sometime during the dessert course of profiteroles al cloccolata, (they all three, had a sweet tooth.) "We shall leave within the next few weeks. I have called a real estate agent in Paris, who as we speak is looking for an apartment for John and me. I've asked him to look in the eighteenth arrondisement, the area of Montmartre. It has always been my favorite part of that city. It is so, so old."

While Dragan and Lenny waited for news from Paris, and prepared for a lengthy sojourn in the city they had once called their own, Marcus set up shop in Beverly Hills. He called his business, "Agency Artists."

"It's got a catchy ring to it, wouldn't you agree?" he asked Dragan, one evening at Craig Drive. The three of them were sitting in the patio area off the living room, sipping a fine vintage, Cossart Gordon, Madeira and enjoying the pale light of a full moon. The crickets were chirping and an occasional cloud would break across the face of the moon.

"Very catchy," Dragan agreed. "Of course you are aware of the double A's and the other agency that employs that logo?"

"Yes, Master, I am quite aware of it," Marcus flashed his very white teeth, "I'm assuming that the connection will be subliminal, but will draw a substantial clientele."

By the time Dragan and Lenny left for New York City by train, from Union Station, on January 5th, 1947, Marcus's agency was established and already making deals for his first clients. Dragan's itinerary was to take an ocean liner to Cannes, in the South of France and leisurely travel North to Paris by train, with stops along the way for sight seeing and relaxation. He was in no hurry. Time, for his kind, was a commodity that need never be rushed. He had time eternal to fill. He would keep in touch with Marcus, who would let him know when the right time had come to return to Hollywood. As it turned out, Dragan did not return to America until the spring of 1953, seven years later, to direct *"Over The Edge."* The producer for that picture was one, Theodore Schreppel. Two years later, Dragan directed the cult classic, *"Biker Hell."*

Among Marcus' first clients, were two veteran cowboy stuntmen who had made the transition from doing their own gags, to directing others in the skills. Both Ned and Pudge had for some time, been directing second unit, on action pictures. Ned was at that time forty-six or seven years of age, and Pudge, just a few years younger.

"You know, Partner," Pudge said to his friend one morning over breakfast at Schwab's, "it's one thing to wait on these directors we know to give us work. You know John Ford always hires us when he can, but it sure would be nice to line up something with someone else, for those times in between."

"Hell, if Ford ever found out we got another job through an agent, he'd never hire us again," Ned laughed.

"No, seriously, we should find ourselves an agent. Old Knute Hopkins just signed with this Artists Agency, fellow name of Theodore Schreppel. Course, old Knute's been a bone fide actor for at least ten years now, but he says this guy is looking for producers and directors, even second unit ones like us."

So it happened. They set up appointments with Marcus, who, of course, knew who they were before they even came by, but for some perverse kind of amusement, decided, even before the interviews, that he would sign them on. Theodore Schreppel bore only the faintest resemblance to the vanished Peter Weir. Nevertheless, after signing with the new agent, while sipping a celebration drink at The Formosa, Ned brought up that very thing.

"Maybe it's the glasses he wears," Pudge suggested. "Certainly doesn't sound like him, or really look like him."

"Yeah, I guess you're right, Partner," Ned conceded, "Still, McCrae is convinced that they take on new identities. It's just possible.…No, the whole thing is too crazy" He faded off with his own thoughts.

Jack McCrae did not forget "his vampires"; he simply made the choice at some stage, not to share his theories with just anyone. He did share them with his nephew, Patrick who reminded Jack of himself. Patrick was the son that Jack never had, and a willing disciple. He never for a moment doubted his uncle's theory on vampires living and killing in Hollywood, and he was equally intrigued with Uncle Jack's tales of "The Little People" back in Ireland.

For the next few years, although Hollywood and Los Angeles suffered the usual amount of crimes, some being cold-blooded killings, McCrae did not encounter any suspicious deaths that involved tooth marks and bloodless corpses. And there were no more drunken tales of strange shapes in the night. Before his departure, Dragan had suggested to Marcus, that when the need arouse for him to taste human blood, that he should travel outside the city to find his prey. Had Jack McCrae wandered north to the high desert, the Palmdale, Lancaster area in The Mojave, he might have heard similar tales from the itinerant travelers and homeless drunks and others. Marcus grew fond of the desert. He felt at home with the scorpions and rattlers, and vowed to one day make another film, on its high, wind blown plains.

Ned and Pudge got plenty of work during those times, thanks in part to their agent, Theodore Schreppel. They still had their other contacts, directors with whom they had worked, who would directly hire them. In 1948, Ned worked with Yakima Canutt on *"Red Stallion of the Rockies"*, and both men were hired on by their old benefactor, John Ford, in 1949 to do the now classic Western with John Wayne and Victor McAllen, *"She Wore a Yellow Ribbon."* Most of their contact with Marcus was via telephone. He took his ten percent from their checks, which he rewrote, sending them the new ones, and keeping them informed on job bookings. His agency expanded to the point where he had three other agents working for him, along with a number of sub-agents, or apprentice agents who had not yet been franchised through Screen Actor's Guild.

There were many moments, during the course of building his agency that Marcus longed for the company of the forever young and lovely, Dorothy Doty. How he missed her. If only she had chosen to go along, to live forever, to be his bride for all eternity.

The Guild had come a long way since its early days. Ronald Reagan was its president, and it had become a powerful entity. And television had come to Hollywood. It would forever change the news, as with its advent, news events could be broadcast live. In 1947, KTLA became the first Los Angeles based commercial television station.

Dragan watched these events unfold from his spacious apartment on the fourth floor of an old apartment building at 18 Rue Gabrielle, above the many steps, on the hill at Montmartre. He understood that the world was shrinking, that it would become more and more difficult for the three of them to remain anonymous. His apartment, which was the whole of the fourth floor, gave view to the square on the hill where the Sacre Coeur is located. It was the closest he had ever lived to a house of God, and although Monsieur Zimmer was often seen at La Place de Tertre looking over various artists' shoulders as they sketched the tourists who constantly frequented the square and the church, he avoided The Basilica as one would The Plague. He was equally known by the merchants at the outdoor market on La Rue Le Pic, and in the many restaurants and cafes of Montmartre. He was often seen in the company of "the other one", the man known only as, "Jean", who everyone figured was his lover, (the French were far more sophisticated in these affairs than were the Americans, at the time), at Le St Jean. Le St Jean was a popular cafe on La Rue Des Abesses, and the locals would nod to Zimmer and Jean as they sipped a late afternoon beer, at one of the tables along the sidewalk. The locals also found it interesting that both men always wore dark glasses, even on cloudy, blowy, Paris evenings.

Dragan had delved into the art business. Paris was, after all, a city known for its famous art, and Dragan set himself up as a buyer and seller of celebrated masterpieces. As much of the artwork had been looted by the Nazis during the Second World War, and was just beginning to find its way back to its pre-war home, collectors and museums quickly become aware of the presence of this sophisticated dealer who spoke so many languages fluently, and seemed to have almost uncanny connections. As was usually the case, Dragan, in the brief span of time that he was there, amassed a considerable fortune, while at the same time, managed to keep his reputation, hazy and mysterious.

Between 1947 and 1953, Jack McCrae would have been interested to learn that in Paris, La Police were getting occasional reports of bizarre encounters between the "clodos", the town's many homeless drunks, and what they reported to be "strange shapes that offered liquid refreshments before biting gently into their necks." Perhaps it was because of these encounters, that Dragan's appreciation for truly fine wines, heightened, so that upon his return he drank only the best. He'd sampled enough of the cheap stuff intravenously.

One day around Christmas, during a particularly cold winter, just after completing a simple dinner, prepared by the ever diligent Lenny, a dinner of a roti de poulet with a light endive salad, Dragan received the phone call from Marcus.

"Master, I've done as you ordered. I have sold the business. It's just as well. It has recently bored me. I miss the real business of making moving pictures."

"That is good. I too have tired of my life here. Paris can be a very cold city you know. You might find this amusing," Dragan looked out the window at the large flakes of snow falling on La Place de Tertre, "but I long for the sunshine, and the palm trees, and I miss our home off Sunset. Each time I pass Notre Dame, and stare at the lovely gargoyles, my heart is drawn back to the castle of ours."

"Then the time has come Master. I have a wonderful script here. It is called *"Over the Edge,"* and I have put together a final package using almost exclusively my own artists. It would please me greatly were you to direct it. I, of course, would love to produce. I do miss the excitement."

"Then it shall be so," Dragan said. "John and I will return. We shall be there sometime toward the end of February. First, we shall take a little tour of our Europe. I should like to see the old country. Who knows when we shall be back?"

So it was arranged. As surreptitiously as he had arrived on the art scene, Dragan departed. His strange disappearance only added to his celebrity and mysteriousness. Of course art collectors and museum curators were distraught. They no longer had access to his sources, and the booming art market in Paris, for some years after his disappearance, suffered a horrible relapse. The next time Paris heard of George Zimmer, wasn't until 1955, when his film, *"Biker Hell"* broke all sorts of box office records in Europe and he and Theodore Schreppel were the star attractions at the '56 Cannes Film Festival.

Using the same real estate agent, whose discretion had first attracted Dragan, he quietly sold his apartment on Gabrielle. He would miss it, with the hand made wall paper that employed real leaves woven into its fabric, and the wonderful hand painted, tiled bathroom with the nudes carrying water and bathing in cool springs. And he knew that he would miss the heartbeat that is the life of Paris.

In Paris too, an era had come to an end and a new one, a post war era was just beginning. The Beats were just arriving in America; Jack Kerouac, Corso, Bourroughs and company, although their real influence wouldn't be felt until the mid 'fifties, but already, their message had crossed the Ocean and made its presence felt in Europe. American Jazz was played nightly in the underground clubs and caves of Paris and Frankfurt and Berlin, and American writers and musicians were again taking refuge in foreign capitols, where their artistic impulses could be played out.

Dragan, who knew so much, was keenly aware of the ever-changing world. Just before leaving "The City of Lights", during those last days and nights, there were many bitter winter nights, that he spent staring out at the Paris moon, reflecting on all his past lives, and wondering what this new future would bring.

When Lenny and Marcus did leave, they again left by train. This time they traveled East and North, through the old countries, Serbia, Croatia, and Hungary, all the way to Transylvania and the castle that had once been his. It was nothing more than a mound of ruble, high on a mountain trail that often slipped into the clouds, where the constant blowing wind was the only sound, that and the occasional wailing of a wolf pack. Dragan and Lenny spent two nights alone, sleeping out in the wind and clouds on the remnants of what Dragan had once called "home." If they felt the cold, or knew hunger or thirst, it did not show, so deeply were they lost in the old dreams, the dreams of the past, of the days when they ran with the wolves and flew with the mountain eagles.

Finally, when the dreams vanished with the morning mist, they came down off the mountain, and slowly, not before traveling through many lands, they returned to California, to their newest home, to Hollywood, and the movies.

"Over The Edge" was a success. It launched the career of the unknown George Zimmer. It was a psychological thriller, shot entirely around the Hollywood area, and it employed many of Theodore Schreppel's clients, although neither Ned nor Pudge worked on that one, both having found prior employment elsewhere.

Following that film, the team of Zimmer & Schreppel, did another film, titled, *"The Synergy."* It was a science fiction piece, and gained something of a following amongst the science fiction crowd. Zimmer moved into, and worked out of the house on Craig Drive, all the while maintaining the castle off Sunset.

Jack McCrae started hearing the same old stories from the occasional drunk who was hauled into the Hollywood Station. It had become company policy to interview the drunks when they had sobered up, before releasing them. Anyone with a strange tale was directed to McCrae. Although it was the policy, no one really took it seriously, it was just that Jack had acquired some tenure and rank and it was done on his orders, the orders of Lieutenant, Jack McCrae. The incidents were not lost on the wily detective. He started looking over his shoulder again, knowing that if they had gone for a while, now, they were back.

In early January, 1955, pre production was just getting started for a new film written by Theodore Schreppel. It was to be called, *"Biker Hell."* Biker movies were the rage. Marlon Brando had starred in *"The Wild One,"* and the studios quickly realized that teenagers, who were a large part of the paying audience, identified with the rebel image. Marcus, at Dragan's urging, knocked out a script in three days, and the two went about getting it ready for production. Among the people they hired for the project, was a young red headed ingénue, who went by the name, Niki Starling. They also took on two old faces; those belonged to Ned Delacroix, and Pudge McCoy.

"The rest," as they say, "is history."

CHAPTER 13

"Biker Hell"

It was a surprisingly warm day on February 27, 1953, when Dragan and Lenny arrived at Union Station; sometime around five in the afternoon, on the West bound train from Chicago. The weather in Chicago had not been friendly, and Marcus, who was dressed in a light summer suit, smiled when he spotted the two of them descending from the first class coach car, dressed for the cold. He was really very happy to see them. Even for an immortal, eight years can be a long absence from close friends.

After collecting the bags they had brought with them, (they had shipped most of their luggage) he took them to dinner at Charlie Morison's, Mocambo at 8588 Sunset Boulevard. As usual, the place was packed with celebrities, among them, James Cagney, and sitting in a corner, Jean Marc recognized the French singing sensation, Edith Piaf.

Later, the three of them sat outside on the patio of the house on Craig Drive, drinking expresso coffees and sipping a fine twenty year old Calvados that Dragan had brought back with the two of them. It was a lovely California evening. Dragan breathed deeply, inhaling the subtle smell of the magnolias, and the sweet orange blossoms, from the trees that surrounded his new estate.

"It's wonderful to be back, Theodore. We've missed Hollywood." Marcus just nodded. Now that they had returned, he was anxious to get back to the business he truly loved, the making of the movies.

"You know my friends; the movie business is rapidly changing here. Television is coming in, and the old studio system just doesn't work the way it used to," Marcus explained. "Many of the stars are no longer under contract to a studio, and to save costs, all the studios have cut back on personnel."

"That shouldn't affect this project," Dragan interrupted. "We've never really worked through the large studios."

"No, Marcus agreed, "but I want international distribution on this one, and the best way to produce, and then distribute it, would be through an in house deal. I've set that up with Jack Warner. We'll work through Fidelity Pictures. That's an in house production company set up at Warners, for Hitchcock. They'll do the distribution as well."

"The movies are your business, my friend," Dragan smiled across the darkened patio. "It's in your hands; I hope my directorial skills have not abandoned me."

"Why, Master," Lenny volunteered, "it's, as they say, just like riding a bicycle. It'll all come back just as soon as we get started."

Later, when the other two had left, Dragan sat long into the morning, sipping the Calvados, and listening to the night sounds, and before retiring to his room on the second floor, he prowled the premises, through the orange and lemon grove, to the edge of the hill. There, through the trees, he gazed down on The Valley which lay sleeping.

So through Fidelity, the team of Zimmer & Schreppel, made and marketed the two films, *"Over The Edge,"* and *"The Synergy."* Both did quite well at the box office.

Marcus had been for some time, even before the two returned, working on a new script, a motorcycle movie, and quietly setting up the production deal, both through Warner's and with his own connections. Part of the deal he made with The William Morris Agency, who bought Artists Agency, and with it, their entire roster of talent, was that he would have access to any and all of them for future projects, thereby making it a package deal. Marcus didn't really care about the money. Money had always been a commodity that required very little effort for the three of them to acquire. But as a business man, he understood the concepts involved in making a deal, so that when he signed the papers, William Morris was to get five percent of the gross on all the talent, while he retained the other five. As franchised agents, they were only allowed ten percent of the gross salary of any performer.

When the first day of filming *"Biker Hell,"* started on Saint Patrick's Day, March 17th, 1955, besides Ned and Pudge, and the comely ingénue, Niki Starling, The director of photography, production manager, first assistant director, leading man, (one Brick Lacey), as well as a number of the other members of the cast, who had all been represented by Theodore, now worked for him in his producer capacity.

The story that Marcus had developed was one of two rival motorcycle gangs whose territory was the San Fernando Valley. After months of tension between the two, they finally clash one weekend in the area of Van Nuys Boulevard and Victory. There was a love interest between a girl from one of the gangs, and a boy from the other, (Niki and Brick). When the cops finally come in to break the thing up, the two gangs join forces, and end up fighting their way out of the Valley. The idea behind the story was that, the then, two displaced gangs, are still out there, riding the highways like a band of nomads. Of course they are not really the bad guys, just a bunch of misunderstood youth.

It was the rebel thing that has always, and still does, pull in the younger generation of filmgoers.

Marcus had picked The Valley as the location for a few reasons. It was firstly, accessible as a location, being close to the rental houses and film and sound labs that alone, cut costs enormously. The Valley was also, at the time gaining some national recognition. It was an area with a young population. Cruising, as it was called, down Van Nuys Boulevard, reached its height during the, Sixties and 'Seventies. The police finally put an end to it sometime during the 'Eighties.

Ned Delacroix was hired on as the second unit director, whose job was to direct all the action sequences. Marcus got great pleasure from the fact that he had not only represented Ned as an agent, but was once again working with him in Theodore's role as producer. Ned had aged some since that first film up in Lone Pine. At the time they started *"Biker Hell"*, he was fifty-five or six. He had aged well. The hair had remained full, but was now white, and although the man who had seen Peter Weir running from the rocks after killing Sally Smythe, was almost thirty years older, he didn't really show his age. Of course Marcus, in his new incarnation as Theodore Schreppel, did not look much like the being he had once been. Still, for some reason that he couldn't quite place, Ned was once again reminded of Peter Weir when Marcus greeted him, the first day on the set.

"Well my friend, this should be different, I mean working with you as the producer and not the agent," Marcus greeted him at six-thirty in the morning, as they drank their morning coffees, and grabbed a quick breakfast from the roach coach.

"I suppose so," Ned agreed slowly. "I guess work is just work, Theodore, and I've got mine cut out for me on this film. I like the script. Nice job. You wrote some good action scenes in there too." Marcus beamed at the complement.

"Well, writing has always been a hobby of mine," he said modestly, while tugging at his left ear lobe. Ned looked closely at the little man with the dark glasses. During the time that Theodore had been his agent; the two of them had rarely met in person. Perhaps it was the early morning light, perhaps the fact that Ned hadn't gotten much sleep the night before, but something, some memory or vision, flashed across his mind's eye, and for the briefest instant, he remembered seeing the fleeing figure of Peter Weir, as he dashed out of sight behind the rocks, leaving the broken body of Sally Smythe behind. Ned shivered in the early morning chill.

Not far away, he spotted Pudge with a group of young stuntmen and women. Pudge had been hired on as the stunt coordinator, so the two of them were essentially working together. He noticed that his friend was wearing a cowboy hat that almost dwarfed him. Pudge had taken to alternating between wearing hair, or a hat. The first time he had tried wearing them both together during a shoot on an earlier picture, after a shot that he'd coordinated, one that went particularly well, when it was over, and he stood with the rest of the crew, whooping and applauding its success, in his exuberance, he'd lifted the hat from his head, and somehow, in the gesture, managed to remove his hair in the same motion. It took him a minute or two to realize that he was waving his hat, with his hairpiece attached. Worse than that, he overheard someone describe it as, "looking like a dead squirrel." For the next three or four days, he skulked around the set, wearing a new hat, one that was at least two sizes larger than the old one. Upon close inspection, Ned noted that there appeared to be no hair, real or false, under its wide brim.

"Hello, Partner," he said to his old friend, as Ned approached the group.

"Howdy Pudge, Fellows, Gals," Ned greeted the group. He knew most of them, this new breed of stuntmen. Many of the younger people in the business were the sons and daughters of the old timers, the cowboys he had known from his days at Gower Gulch, at what had once been called, "Poverty Row", that area on Sunset where the wranglers would assemble in the hopes of landing a job. There wouldn't be any horses in this picture, just motorcycles, fights, car wrecks, and a few falls. Each of these people had his or her specialty, although most of them were trained to do a bit of everything, including riding and falling from horseback.

Ned had already been introduced to George Zimmer. He'd never heard of this director who was introduced to him by Theodore Schreppel, one morning several weeks earlier. But Ned had been in the business long enough not to ask too many questions. If the guy was any good, he'd know right away. It's like that in the movie business. Anyone who's been around, had some experience, can spot an amateur immediately, and if the beginner is the director, the word spreads like wildfire through the crew. The two talked for a few minutes.

"I'm just going to introduce myself to the cast and crew, and then you can take your people and get started," Zimmer told him.

"Right," Ned said. "It's pretty straight forward stuff this morning. Shots from the picture car of the gangs riding, with a few little gags thrown in. I'll need Niki and Brick after lunch."

By the time Zimmer made his little speech of introduction, the sun had climbed up from behind the trees. The crew genuinely appreciated his talk with them. It was rare that a director started a picture like that. Time was money. "So let's do it people," he concluded, "you'll all miss the St. Patrick's Day parade this year, but hopefully you'll have a fine film to look back on."

Ned and Pudge took their people to the location they were going to use, which was close to the first unit crew. The teamsters had acquired the necessary motorcycles, and the extras that had been hired, all arrived with their own. Ned and Pudge, the camera operator and soundman, rode in the back of a pick up truck, in which the grips had mounted the camera, and they set up shots, following the gang down the road. It was all pretty basic stuff, but time consuming. At one o'clock, they broke for lunch, which was set up not far away, between the two film groups.

While Ned and Pudge were eating, Niki Starling sat with them and introduced herself. She was a cute gal, not more than nineteen, petite in build, with a very pretty smile and a head of gorgeous red hair.

"It's a pleasure meeting you," she said politely to the two men. "This is really my first leading role. I've only done a few films. Theodore said I should get to know you, that you'd been in the business for years and that if I had any questions, I should take them to you." Ned glanced at Pudge, who positively beamed, so taken was he with this girl.

"Why, you just do that Niki. Any time. We'd be more than happy to help you out. Right, Partner?" He turned to Ned.

"You bet, Niki," Ned agreed.

"Well," Niki flashed a sly smile towards the two of them. "I do have a question for you fellows." She waited just a brief second, then asked, "Just what do they call that dish there?" She pointed to Pudge's plate. Pudge, who had a big mouthful of it, just about choked. When he recovered, he lifted his plate up for closer inspection.

"Why, Miss. Niki, I do believe it's some kind of bird, could be chicken. Now a days, that's all they serve you on these shoots. Why in the old days, we had all kinds of good grub, when there was fellers like Cookie, making chilies and collards and great big old steaks."

So that was the introduction that broke the ice between Niki Starling and the two old cowboys. From that first day on, whenever they were working in the same location, Niki would spend as much time as she could with the two men. Pudge developed a real working crush on her, and Ned noticed that, once again, he started wearing his hair, and it wasn't the same old piece. Within days of that first meeting Pudge arrived on the location with a brand new, carefully groomed one. From that day on, whenever they could, they had lunch together. Pudge, with his boots on, stood no taller than Niki. In the old days, in the past, when they were still doing stunts, Pudge often put on a wig and doubled one of the actresses, when a gag was called for. He also had doubled for a number of children over the years. During the course of the filming, on *"Biker Hell"*, Niki asked all sorts of questions about the old days, and the two cowboys were only too pleased to fill her head with all kinds of stories. Among the stories they told, was the one about Sally Smythe, and the bizarre accident that befell her.

There were a few other introductions, that first day of shooting. Niki, although she was never formally introduced, did notice, for the first time, the strange driver that Mr. Zimmer had retained. For some reason, Dragan had decided that Lenny would drive him to the location each day. As Jean Marc Descamps, he had never employed Lenny in that service, but as Zimmer he did. Even Marcus found it a little odd at first, but figured that it was probably because the two of them had spent those years together in Paris, and Dragan had grown accustomed to Lenny's presence. Niki noticed him standing by the director's car, a 1955, blue Cadillac, and she didn't like his looks. She asked Ned and Pudge about him the next day over lunch.

"He's creepy looking," she whispered confidentially to the two men, over a meal of fried chicken and mashed potatoes. "Look at him," she said, jabbing a fork full of potatoes in the direction of Marcus who was seated next to Dragan at another table. Both men looked and Lenny stared back with a strange expression on his dull face.

""Don't pay him no attention, Niki," Pudge reassured her. "He's probably harmless. Besides, we'll keep an eye on him, won't we, Partner?"

"Why sure we will, Niki." Ned agreed. "I do like that car he drives though."

The other introduction of note that first day, was with the leading man, Brick Lacy. Brick was a tall, well built, and quite handsome fellow, standing about six foot, two, maybe a half an inch shorter than Ned. Ned had planned on doubling for Brick in one scene, a fight scene, where the actor was supposed to dive through a plate glass window. Brick, whose real name was Millard Michner, was a New York transplant, and was actually a fairly decent actor, despite the pretty face. He was just getting some recognition, having done some light comedy pictures, with a blond singer, dancer, named, Betty Shay, and both he, and his agent, Theodore Schreppel, had been looking for a more serious, manly role for his public persona. *"Biker Hell"* was the perfect format. Brick went on to have a very successful film career, as well as doing a famous television series. He was, for years, a favorite among the women fans, as well as the male leather crowd.

Ned got to meet and work with Brick the afternoon of the first day. The actor was walking with Pudge when he came over to Ned. "Hi Ned, nice to meet you," he extended his hand to Ned, and shook the stuntman's hand with a strong grip. "I guess we all have Theodore here in common. He told me that he represented you and Pudge as well." Ned was setting up for a traveling shot from the camera car, where he would follow Brick on his Harley. Brick was, of course, the leader of one of the gangs.

"Well Howdy, Brick, I guess we do have that in common. Now you say you've driven one of these before?" he asked.

"Yes, Sir, I've done some riding in the past," the actor responded.

"Can you drive it with Niki on the back?"

"Yes, Sir, I believe I can." He looked over the bike, admiringly. "This is a KR I believe. They use these on the flat track." Ned who was watching a grip secure the camera podium to the bed of the truck, looked up.

"That's right, son. This one here is bored out to nine hundred. Packs a kick. Why don't you give it a try." Without a moment's hesitation, Brick was on the bike and then took off. He did a couple of neat turns, dropping it low on each one, then turned back toward Ned and the rest of the scooters. Just before reaching them, he pulled the front forks off the ground and executed a short but perfect wheelie. Ned stood there for a second with his mouth open, before hearing Pudge and the rest of the crew laugh.

"Close your jaw, Frenchie," Pudge said to him. "Hell, I put him up to that. Knew he could ride. He used to race the dang things."

So that was how Ned met Brick. He liked the man, and during the course of the shoot, they got along well. When it came time for the plunge through the window, Brick insisted on doing it, as well as all his motorcycle gags, himself. One of the reasons that Brick later became such a box office draw, was the fact that the public knew that he did most of his own stunts. He was, during the 'Fifties and 'Sixties, one of the best known leading men.

George Zimmer ran a tight ship. For a director who had been a complete unknown to everyone, save maybe Jack Warner and Theodore Schreppel, he didn't lack for experience and know how, when it came to shooting action, in black and white. And Theodore Schreppel, whose previous credentials had only included, agent, seemed to be well versed in the production end of the business, as well as having written an excellent script. Neither Ned nor Pudge were ones to complain, especially when things went smoothly, but despite himself, something lingered malignantly on the past horizon of Ned's mind.

One day, about half way through the thirty-two day shooting schedule, again, over some version of a chicken lunch, he mentioned it to Pudge. It was a beautiful early April day, with a soft breeze blowing in from the ocean. By then, not only the two cowboys, but the entire crew, had grown so tired of chicken, that they had all signed a petition, requesting that the caterer either change the ingredients, or the production company change the caterer. There had been a footnote written on the petition, that "perhaps a certain black cook, known as Cookie, could be contacted."

"You know, Partner," Ned said to his friend, "remember when we first signed with Schreppel, back in 'forty- seven, remember that afternoon when we were having drinks at The Formosa, and I said something about him reminding me of that Peter Weir?"

"Yup, I remember," Pudge said, jabbing his fork into the crusty thigh on his plate. "Damn, this stuff is inedible. I told you it was probably the glasses."

"Yeah, that you did. But there's something else. I can't put my finger on it, but there's something about this Schreppel, maybe something he does, or says, that reminds me of Weir."

"I wish old Cookie was here. Besides the fact that he was a hell of a good cook, he never did like that Weir fellow. Maybe he could tell you what it is."

"Well, if you're so darned convinced that Schreppel is Weir, then maybe we ought to talk to old Jack McCrae, get him to come down. And if what Jack says is true and they do change forms, then maybe this Zimmer, this guy no one's ever heard of is that Jean Marc Descamps."

"I don't know, Ned, the whole thing's so dang crazy." Pudge laughed. "Hell, maybe we should have old Hoagie come down and kiss these fellers, and tell us which one is Betty Boudin!"

So that conversation ended, and Ned still didn't know what it was about Theodore Schreppel that set him off, but he decided to call McCrae and tell him his thoughts.

That weekend Ned called Jack McCrae. Lieutenant McCrae, like Ned and Pudge, hadn't gone for early retirement. That didn't come until three years later, the year Greg Delacroix was born, 1958. Although the cowboys hadn't seen Jack on a regular basis, they had remained in touch. There had been evenings, over the past years, when the boys would meet for a beer at The Formosa, or Musso's, both of which weren't far from the precinct, and Jack would join them after work. There had even been the odd time when Hoagie Coates, who had been retired for years, would venture off his Santa Monica ranch to meet up with his old friends, and the three of them would stay up until the wee hours of the morning, swapping tales of the old days. And even though a period of time had passed, when the strange blood sucking of transients in the park seemed to have ceased, and no bizarre, bloodless bodies had surfaced on the streets of Hollywood, or been found in prominent movie star's homes, Jack McCrae had never closed his file, and never stopped believing that a horror was alive, and living nearby. He had read and re-read the little green book, which, oddly enough he kept next to his bible, on the nightstand by his bed. By the time Ned Delacroix called him, that lovely Saturday afternoon, on April seventh, 1955, Jack McCrae could quote from his little green book, by chapter and verse, far more proficiently than he had ever been able to quote from The King James Version, of the good book. In fact, Jack really had no further need of the little green book, and had decided that the time was at hand to pass it on to the only person who was entirely convinced of Jack's own sanity, his nephew, Patrick.

"McCrae here," he answered the call, as was his fashion. He was sitting in the back patio of the house on Wilton, sipping iced tea, the house he shared with his nephew, Patrick.

"Jack, it's Ned, Ned Delacroix."

"Why Ned, how've you been, Laddie? It's been a darn long while." Jack took a pull on the straw, and leaned back on the bentwood rocker to better observe a pack of wild parrots in the tree, in the neighbor's back yard.

"What's that Jack? Can't hear you!" Ned hollered into the phone. "Sounds like you got a women's bridge party going over there!"

"No, no Ned, just a pack of wild parrots, makin a hell of a racket. Beastly birds."

"Uh huh," Ned answered, not quite sure of what he'd heard.

"How's Pudge?" Jack asked. "What are you two boys up to?"

"Well, we're working on a picture, out there in The Valley, Jack. Mater of fact, that's kind of why I'm calling. Got a favor to ask of you."

"Be glad to do whatever I can, Lad." At that moment, a car backfired on the street, sending the birds scattering off, in a confusion of squawking feathers.

"Well, that's better," Ned breathed, once the racket had ceased. "Couldn't barely hear you before. Look, Jack, remember that little creep, Peter Weir?"

"Why sure I do, Ned. He was one of them, them vampires, you know. Him and Descamps."

"Well, I guess you're right about that Jack. You know, after all these years, it's gotten a whole lot easier to see it your way."

"Well, thank you, Ned. You boys were the ones who saw the murder, up there in Lone Pine, when he killed that actress," he reminded Ned.

"Well I know that Jack, and that's just it. Now you said that these vampires change identities, that they kill someone and disappear and then come back as someone else. Ain't that so?"

"That's the way I got it figured, Ned. Nothing else makes any sense. Haven't seen hide nor hair of them in some time now, but I'm sure they're still out there, somewhere."

"Well," Ned said slowly, looking for the right words, and once again letting the doubts creep back in, "well, I'd like you to come out here to the set and take a look at something." Jack sucked up the last of the iced tea, then jabbed the straw at the ice on the bottom of the glass.

"Well, Jack, it's really someone I'd like you to take a look at. See we've got this here director, nice enough fellow, fellow by the name of George Zimmer. Anyway, he's not bad. Seems to know what he's doing, which is more than I can say for some of these youngsters that are coming into the business these days."

"Well, Ned. What's the problem with that?" Jack wanted to know.

"Well, it's not so much Zimmer, it's the producer, this Theodore Schreppel. Now I've known him for years. He was my agent. Didn't see much of him during that time, but there was always something that bothered me about him." Again Jack jabbed at the ice, this time a little more viciously.

"Now what could that be?" Jack asked slowly.

"That's just it. I can't put my finger on it. He doesn't really look like that Weir fellow, although he wore glasses too. It's something else. And another thing. Come to think of it, he showed up with a theatrical agency, just about the same time that Descamps and Weir disappeared. You see where I'm going?"

For just a second, Jack's heart maybe skipped a beat, as he felt a rush of adrenaline, and the old venom building up in his veins. It had been years since Descamps vanished, and during that time he'd had neither sight nor sound of the vampires re-emerging in any other form. They had vanished, but his detective's sixth sense had known that they weren't really gone. Now, his old friend, Ned, the same man who had been witness to the strange death of Sally Smythe, one of the few men with whom he had shared his theory, was telling him that perhaps, just perhaps, he had once again stumbled on to the creatures. It made sense too; Ned was talking about the producer and director of a feature film. Hadn't the vampires always been in the film milieu? Hadn't they always operated as director-producer, the two of them? And now Ned was telling him that this Schreppel, although he didn't look like Weir, reminded Ned of the little creep.

Jack grabbed the glass, and tossed what was left of the ice cubes, towards the tree where the parrots had roosted. "Yes, Lad, I see where you're going all right. When would you like me to pay a little visit to the set?"

"Can you come out Monday. We're shooting in Van Nuys. Make it about lunchtime. I'll call the station in the morning and give you the time and place. How's that?"

"Oh, that's just fine, Laddie. I'll be there, wearin' green."

"Thanks Jack. Have a lovely weekend." Ned laughed and was just about to hang up, when Jack cut in.

"Oh, by the way Ned, why don't you pick up a couple of crucifixes over the weekend, for yourself and Pudge, and you might want to get a few for some of your friends on the film, if you've got any," he added. According to this Dragan Radelescu, the author, vampires don't much like crucifixes, or anything else that reminds them of the church. And they don't take much to silver either. Apparently, it takes silver to actually kill them. I'll see you Monday!

So that weekend, Ned did just that. He bought two silver crucifixes for himself and Pudge, and just before he was going to leave the store, he got another one for Niki.

He gave them to his friends, the following morning, while the various crews were grabbing a quick breakfast, in between getting their first jobs of the morning in gear. On any film crew, there are individual crews, each performing its own function. The camera crew takes care of the film and anything to do with the camera. The grips, do the rigging, camera mounts, and operate the dollies and cranes, while the electrical crew handles all the cable, lights and such. There are property men and women, who gather and manage any thing that an actor uses, anything from weapons to watches, and there are art department people who collect the furniture and put together the decor. All these functions by the various crews, have been finely tuned over the years, and there is some crossing over. For example, the grip crew might hang a backdrop that the electricians will light, and sometimes the two will work together. Similarly, the set dressers might work with the property person. There are sound people, wardrobe, makeup, as well as the assistant director and the second assistant, and there are the actors, the stunt people, and extras. There are in fact, often, even more people than this, with more specific skills. For example, if animals are used, there are animal trainers. Often, there are dialogue coaches when a dialect is called for, or military, weapons specialists if needed. Each department has a first and second. The head electrician is called "the gaffer", and his second is called the best boy, (an old circus connotation.) With the exception of the director, these are the "below the line people." The above the line people, include, the director, the production manager, the various producers, the production designer and construction coordinator. There are also postproduction people like the editors, the music composer, and the musicians who actually play. There are publicists, and so on. Finally there are the distributors who distribute the finished product. The whole process of making a movie is like a ballet or a fine work of art, where every position has its function, and together, the end result brings about the completed movie.

Ned first got together with Pudge, who was holding court with some of his stunt people, reminiscing about the guts and glory days.

"Could I talk with you for a moment?" he asked his friend, drawing him from the crowd.

"Sure, Partner, what's up?" Pudge walked over with a cup of coffee.

"I talked with Jack McCrae over the weekend. He's going to come down and take a look at Theodore. Maybe he can tell us something." He hesitated. "Look, Jack told me to get a couple of these things." He pulled a crucifix from the light windbreaker he had on. "Told me that vampires couldn't stand them and don't much like silver either. Now you're Catholic, ain't you Pudge?"

"Well, heck yes. I ain't no Protestant!"

"Well then, why don't you just hang this around your neck. Just for the heck of it."

"Suppose I could do that," Pudge said, taking the crucifix from Ned and glancing around to see if anyone was watching the transaction.

"Good. Now I'm going to give this here other one to Niki, first chance I get."

Ned didn't get a chance to do that until lunch, over a plate of chicken and dumplings. He was sitting with McCrae, who had quietly appeared, and caught Ned's attention, after waiting in line with the rest of the crew, for the usual chicken lunch. Zimmer and Theodore, who were watching the dailies, (the footage they had just shot) had not yet appeared for the meal. "This here is an old friend, Niki, Detective Jack McCrae," Ned introduced the two. Jack stood not much taller than Niki. By that time, he too was as bald as Pudge, but he sported the natural look. He was wearing an emerald green windbreaker, as the day held a little breeze, and not much direct sunlight.

"Pleasure meeting you, Detective." Niki extended her tiny hand, which he pumped furiously.

"Oh, you just call me, Jack, like the boys here do," he said with a wide grin. Jack attacked his meal, while Niki and Ned picked at theirs, and the three talked about the movie and other things for a while before Ned produced the crucifix, and passed it to Niki.

"Jack here thinks it would be a good idea to wear one of these, just for good luck," Ned explained awkwardly. "You know that story we were telling you about that old nag, Sally Smythe, the one who got herself killed up there in Lone Pine? Well her death was a little strange." Jack cut in.

"Now, look here Niki." He looked around before leaning in to her and speaking earnestly, but in a whisper. "What old Ned is trying to say but can't quite find the words, is that we fellows know that there happen to be vampires around. And I happen to know that they're not to keen on crucifixes, especially these silver ones. We'd like you to wear this. For good luck!" he added, hastily. Niki giggled.

"Vampires? Oh come on, Jack. This is 1955!"

"Well, I know that Niki. And that's just the point. They've been here in Hollywood since the 'Twenties. They're all producers and directors, and Ned here thinks that this Theodore, might be one of em." Niki liked the detective and she was very fond of Ned and Pudge. Strange as she thought the request was, she didn't want to offend either man.

"Well, thank you, Ned. I'll wear that. Anyway, I'm a Catholic as well. Probably should have worn a crucifix a long time ago. Thank you." She smiled at the two men, and Jack McCrae grinned a wide grin in her direction, He too, liked this girl. It was just then that Theodore and Zimmer appeared for lunch. Like the rest of the crew, they stood in line. On a film crew, the working crew eats first, and being the director doesn't give one the right to walk to the front of the line. Zimmer knew this, even though he was a beginner.

"That's him Jack," Ned nodded in their direction. Dragan, maybe because he too, had a sixth sense, turned from the line and looked directly at McCrae at the instant that Jack had turned to observe Marcus and him. Marcus had not yet noticed McCrae, and was busy heaping a salad on his plate, but Zimmer did, and when he turned, he smiled. He had of course, immediately recognized the wily detective, but not wishing to play his hand, casually turned back to the job at hand, that being getting his meal. He did not indicate to Marcus that he had spotted McCrae, and neither Ned nor Jack, was really sure if the smile had been aimed at them. It had seemed natural enough. Jack was looking at Marcus, and took less note of the contact with Zimmer, than did Ned.

"I don't know, Ned," he said slowly. "He doesn't really look much like Weir, except for the glasses. I'd say he's taller too. You know I never really figured out what age that Weir was, but I'd guess this fellow to be maybe forty or so."

"You don't see anything there?" Ned asked again.

"It could be him," Jack answered. "Now you've got to understand that according to the book and my theory, these vampires, completely change when they take over a new person." He pulled the book from his jacket pocket and quoted:

"There are certain physical, as well as mental elements that are retained in the new incarnation. It is not an accurate science, and we have no way of knowing before The Change, just how the new identity will appear in its physical form."

"So you see, Ned, it could be him. Maybe it's something he does or says that reminds you of Weir."

"I don't know, Jack. It's just something."

"Well, there's one way of finding out," Ned, Jack told him, with a mouthful of dumplings. "You wave that there crucifix at him and see if he breaks out in a sweat." All this had happened as Niki sat there with the two men. She listened to this bizarre conversation with a blank look on her face, having absolutely no idea to what they were referring.

"Who are you two looking at?" She asked. Ned looked at Jack, not sure what to say. He didn't want to alarm Niki if he was wrong, but wanted to protect her, if perhaps, he was right. Jack took care of his dilemma by interrupting.

"Why we were talking about Zimmer and that Theodore fellow there, Niki," he explained, as if they were talking about the most ordinary thing in the world. "Ned and I figure they might be vampires."

"And I think that Zimmer recognized you Jack, when he smiled," Ned added. This was too much for the nineteen-year-old girl, who burst out laughing.

"Listen to the two of you! Vampires! Really. And Mr. Zimmer was smiling at me, like he always does. He's never even met you before, has he, Jack?" It was Jack and Ned's turn to feel foolish. What Niki had said, made complete sense, and Jack had never laid eyes on either one of them before.

Zimmer, on the other hand, knew immediately what was going on. He quickly realized that Ned had brought Jack out to the set, for just that purpose; that he had harbored suspicions about the two of them, and he had turned to Jack for some form of confirmation. After lunch, when they had a moment alone, Zimmer mentioned it to Marcus, who had not been aware that McCrae had resurfaced.

"We shall have to be very careful," he told him. "We don't want those two spinning any tales to Niki, or the rest of the crew. I want you to make sure that she spends as little time as possible with those two cowboys from now on."

After saying good by to Niki, Jack spoke with Ned. "Look here, Ned. I'd be very careful if I was you. If those two are who we think they might be, then they're already on to you. You keep thinking about what it was that reminded you of Weir. It's bound to turn up."

"It's right there, Jack. I just can't put my finger on it," Ned said. "Well, thanks for coming. I'm back to work. I'll be in touch."

"Right," Jack waved and started toward his car, which wasn't far away. Then, he stopped. "And Ned," he said, with a hard look in his eyes, "if ever, you get the chance to wave that crucifix at him, without getting fired or convicted to an asylum, you do that. I got a feeling it'll make him dance all right! And be careful!" he called out, just before getting into the car.

There were no further incidents for almost a week. The film was almost wrapped. There remained only four more days of scheduled shooting, and Ned had completed the most complicated and demanding of the stunts that had been called for. He was beginning to relax, knowing that the job had gone very well, and feeling proud of his part in it. He'd even begun to think that perhaps his suspicions regarding Theodore Schreppel were poorly founded; that perhaps he'd let his imagination run a little wild. The fellow seemed decent enough, and he was good at his job, and although there had been something about him, something he did or said that reminded Ned of Peter Weir, Ned still hadn't been able to place it.

Then, one morning, when he arrived on the set he heard a strange story. It was Niki who, upon spotting him, rushed over and in a breathless voice, told him of a frightening encounter. It was a gray morning with a light drizzle, not typical of an April day, and the forecast had been for rain. If it did rain, the plan was to move to a sound stage in The Valley, where a set of a small restaurant had been built, but the crew was on hold to see if they could go ahead with the regular shooting schedule, which was all exteriors. For that reason everyone was lingering around the trucks, or taking shelter under a plastic tarp that the grips had rigged. Ned and Pudge were sitting in Pudge's new red, '55 Ford pickup, sipping a couple of coffees, when Niki appeared at the window on the passenger side. Ned opened the door, moved over and let her in. He perceived immediately that something had happened. She was extremely upset, and he knew that she'd been crying.

"Niki, are you all right?" he asked. "What happened?" She sobbed, then put her head against Ned's big shoulder, and in a breathless voice, told him.

"That creepy driver that Mr. Zimmer employs, I was in my trailer last night. You boys had already left. Most of the crew had. I guess I wasn't feeling to well, I don't know, maybe just tired. You know I'm not used to this whole thing. Anyway, I must have fallen asleep on the cot in there, but something horrible woke me." Again she took a deep breath and kind of sobbed. Ned put his arm around her.

"What happened Niki?" He asked, now seriously concerned, and feeling the anger mounting like bile.

"That Joachims was on me. He had his hands on my head, holding it, and I felt his teeth on my neck. It was horrible!" Ned clenched his jaw. Somehow he had known that the story she was about to tell, would go something like this. All his suspicions came to light. He still couldn't place what it was about Theodore that reminded him of Peter Weir, but in that instant, he realized that his instincts had been on target. Zimmer, Schreppel, and Joachims, were what they had all suspected them of being.

"Did he bite you?" Pudge asked.

"No, he was about to when I awoke. I screamed, and he left. He ran out of the trailer, and I ran after him, and I practically ran over Mr. Zimmer. I told him what had happened. Joachims was just standing there, next to us, with his head down, and Mr. Zimmer grabbed him by the neck. He practically lifted him off the ground. I thought he was going to kill him."

Ned Looked over Niki's head at Pudge, whose hands gripped the leather cover on the steering wheel, while his eyes stared straight ahead, through the drizzle and mist to the tarp, where Marcus stood next to Dragan. When Ned followed the direction of Pudge's steely gaze, he saw the two of them huddled together, sheltered from the rain, and he could plainly see that both men were staring back at the three of them in the pickup truck. "Then what happened Niki?" Ned asked her, his eyes never leaving the two monsters under the tarp. "What happened to Joachims?"

"He didn't say anything. He just let Mr. Zimmer shake him. He couldn't look either of us in the eyes. Then Mr. Zimmer sent him home. He told him that he was banned from the set and that he would deal with him later."

"So he left?" Pudge asked.

"Yes, Pudge. He did. It's crazy, but even after what he did to me, I almost felt sorry for him. I've never seen anyone as angry as Mr. Zimmer. I don't know what he did to him later, or what he's going to do."

Then Pudge started the engine. Without saying a word, he swung the truck around, leaving a skid mark where it had stood, and just as quickly he sped off, taking a right on Van Nuys Boulevard, and headed South.

After maybe five or six minutes, he pulled over to the side of the road, in front of a little coffee shop. The rain still drizzled under gray skies. Neither Niki or Ned had said a word. When he had stopped and cut the engine, he looked at Ned. The two old timers, the two cowboys, who had spent so much time together over the years, these men who had known the hard life, and understood the necessity of making quick decisions when the time came, or when danger lurked, both knew what had to be done.

"We're quittin', Niki. We're packin our gear and taking our team with us." Ned told her. "Now we ain't telling you what to do. This movie is just about in the can. It's your first big part and you've done a swell job. There's only a few days left, and it means a whole lot more to you than it does to us, if we finish this gig. We ain't planning on ever working again for Zimmer or Schreppel." Pudge continued, picking up the thought where Ned had left off.

"We don't think you'll be in any more danger. Zimmer ain't going to let anything happen to you. He's got too much at stake. You can quit too, if you want to, but we're not recommending that you do." Again, Ned picked it up.

"No, Niki, we're just warning you. These men, if you can call them that are very dangerous. We never told you the whole story about that Sally Smythe, but we've got reason to believe, that the same thing that killed her, is the producer of this picture. We're not alone either. That's why Jack McCrae came down here. He's been following them for years."

"Yeah," Pudge said, "and it took us a heck of a long time to believe old Jack wasn't plum crazy, what with his theories and his little green book, but you, yourself heard what he called them the other day....."

"Vampires," she mouthed the word, almost inaudibly. But the two men heard, and they both believed, and they just glanced at one another, then looked at the pretty, terrified nineteen-year-old girl, and they nodded, yes.

"Whatever you decide to do, Niki," Ned said to her, "I'm sure it will be the right thing. The Lord looks over beautiful girls like you." Something in the way the cowboy said it to her, made all her fears wash away with the rain. She decided that she would stay on, and she knew, that she would wear the crucifix, just in case...

Both men hugged the little actress. "We'll miss you Niki. You take good care of yourself." Pudge said, starting up the motor.

"If I was thirty years younger, or you thirty years older, "Ned smiled, "why I'd sweep you right up off your feet and we'd ride off together into the sunset."

Pudge drove the truck slowly back to the location. By the time they got there, the rain seemed to have given up the effort, and allowed the sun to begin to break through the clouds. When he had parked, the two men got out and called their crew together. They explained that they were walking off the job. They didn't make any explanations as to why, they simply stated that it was a question of life and death and that one day it would all make sense and be explained. They thanked their people for the fine work they had done, and promised that they would keep calling them, that there would be other jobs in the future. It is an unwritten code or understanding in the film business, that if the department head gets fired, or walks off a job, that the rest of his crew goes with him. In any case, when he gets replaced, the new department head usually brings in his own people. This was a professional crew and they knew and lived by the rules. No one asked why, no one grumbled, or balked at leaving. They simply stopped working, and went about the business of packing up their gear.

The other crews were starting to set up. When Pudge's truck pulled back up to the location, Marcus spotted it. He stood there with Dragan, and watched the men call their crew together. Both Marcus and Dragan knew full well what had just transpired. They didn't know what the outcome would be. They didn't know if they would have to kill the two cowboys, and then go after McCrae. For that matter, they weren't sure what the two had said to Niki, and what she would do. Perhaps they would have to kill her too. Perhaps that morning, because of Lenny's stupidity, the film was finished, and they with it. Perhaps they would have to flee, and kill again to go through The Change. They stood there, waiting, waiting to make whatever decisions had to be made.

When they saw the stunt people packing up, and when Niki returned and reported to the assistant director, being the film makers that they were, they immediately understood pretty much of what had transpired, and both breathed a sigh of relief. The film would wrap. The stunt team would be replaced, the day was probably shot, but the project still lived, and with it, the three of them. What Jack McCrae would do, when he got the news, was still a question, but for the moment they had lost the day, but not the battle.

Ned and Pudge, when they had done, turned toward the two, still standing there, watching. They walked to them, the tall cowboy and his partner. Perhaps, they thought, these two creatures, if that was what they were, were the same two with whom they had worked, all those years ago, up in Lone Pine. Whatever the two cowboys were thinking, neither Dragan nor Marcus, had any way of knowing.

"We quit." Ned stated with a steady voice. "We're done with you, and our crews are done with you, and neither we or them, will ever work with you again." Dragan stared back at the tall cowboy and the short one, and both could see just how black were his eyes. But Marcus fidgeted, and at that moment, if Ned had harbored any doubts, as to whom these two might be, in an instant, no doubts remained. Marcus reached to his left ear and tugged at it nervously, and in so doing, thirty years flashed back in Ned's mind, and he saw again, Peter Weir, in the car, returning to the scene of the accident, where Sally Smythe's body lay bleeding and broken; Peter Weir staring at the man who had seen him fleeing the scene, Peter Weir, the same man as this one, tugging at his left ear as he stared into Ned's astonished face.

Ned and Pudge walked off the set. They never again worked for Marcus or Zimmer, nor did they see Niki again, at least not in person. Jack McCrae did, he interviewed her several days later, after he had met with Ned and Pudge.

CHAPTER 14

Post Biker Hell

Dragan's punishment of Lenny, was indeed as cruel as befitted one such as he. For the next year, he did not speak to, address or respond directly to his dark servant. For weeks after the incident, although they finished the movie and went about their daily business, they waited to see, what if any would be the repercussions, for his stupidity. Lenny continued with all his domestic duties. He received his orders from Marcus. Whatever remained of the hump he had once endured, seemed to have returned, so stooped with humiliation was he. Dragan would tell Lenny, in front of Marcus, what he wanted to convey to his menial.

The day after quitting the set, both cowboys got together with Jack McCrae. They met him at their usual watering hole, The Formosa Cafe, after his shift, around seven in the evening. The place was packed with its regular clientele, many of whom were employed at Paramount Studios, and Columbia. Pudge and Ned arrived within minutes of each other, and managed to get a booth when a grip crew with whom they had worked, got up and left it for them. The place was dark and intimate. All around the walls of the main room, hung pictures, eight by ten shots of movie and television actors, all signed. Some were of the famous, and some, of the then unknown. The Formosa, as the name implies, served a variation on Chinese food, although unlike other old Hollywood eateries, it was never known for its fine cuisine, but rather for its sympathetic owner, and personnel, as well as its reputation for honest drinks, and mellow atmosphere. It had been in the Jung family since the "Twenties. Many an actor ate for free, or ran a line of credit at The Formosa, until the time came when he could pay his debt. The boys had been going there for years. They still ran into some of the old timers, those of their generation in the film business, but that evening in April, 1955, there were many new, and younger faces.

Both men ordered beers with shots of Jamison's. Irish whisky had become de rigueur whenever they met up with McCrae, and both had need of something hard that evening. McCrae arrived around seven-fifteen, flushed, and somewhat out of breath. Ned hadn't told him much over the phone, just that they had walked off the set, and that they had something very important to talk with him about. When he saw McCrae come through the door, Lindy, the bartender, poured another shot and popped the cap off a bottle of beer, and placed them on the bar. Jack picked them up on his way to the booth.

"Evening, Lindy," rotten weather tonight, he said, knocking the rain off his windbreaker.

"Oh, you've got that right, Jack," Lindy smiled at him, but it hasn't slowed down business any." Pudge slid over in the booth, making a place for the detective.

"Hello, Lads, rotten weather out there," then noticing that neither of them was wet, asked. "You boys been here long?"

"'Bout fifteen, twenty minutes Jack," Pudge told him. "If it's raining now, must have just started."

"Well here's to better weather and brighter days," McCrae lifted the shot glass to his lips and downed it in one gulp. "What have you Lads got for me?"

"Well Jack," Ned began. "You know we walked off, took the entire crew."

"So you told me," McCrae nodded, catching Lindy's eye for another round.

"Well, something happened to Niki. That driver, Joachims, attacked her in her trailer. She woke up to find his teeth on her neck." McCrae whistled.

"Yeah, Jack, just like a real vampire," Pudge cut in.

"Did he bite her?" The detective asked.

"No, she woke up just in time. Ran him out. Apparently Zimmer almost killed him. Anyway he threw him off the set for good." Ned explained.

"Well, when she told us that, we figured you was right, Jack," Pudge told him. "They have to be what you called 'em."

"Yeah, but that ain't all." Ned, slammed down the shot that Lindy had delivered and took a long pull off his hand rolled cigarette. "You remember me telling you there was something about that Schreppel, something I couldn't rightly place, that reminded me of that creepy Weir?"

"'Course I do Ned. That's why I came to the set. But you couldn't place it."

"Well, I placed it now. Didn't have it figured until we were saying our good- byes. Then it hit me square in the jaw, like a mule's kick."

"Go on," Jack said.

"It was that ear tugging thing that Weir did when he got fidgety." Jack just stared blankly at his friend. "Weir used to tug on his left ear. He did that in the car, when he returned seconds after killing that Sally Smythe, when he saw me looking at him. He did it a few times, nervous habit, I guess, but Schreppel did the same thing. Did it just like that Weir used to. I know they're the same." All three of them finished their drinks, letting that set in. Then Jack spoke.

"Well, there you have it. Just what I figured. He produced the little green book from a pocket inside his raincoat, and laid it on the table in front of himself. He then placed his hand on the cover, as one places his hand on the Holy Bible in court, before swearing the solemn oath to tell the truth. "It's all in here, Lads. This Dragan Radelescu, who wrote this here book, was one smug son of a bitch. He swears he's one of them, and he must be, cause no mortal man could possibly have known all these little details; and everything he says seems to have happened."

"You think, he's one of them, this Zimmer, or Schreppel?" Pudge asked. He was wearing his hair that day, and he kind of arranged it as he asked the question.

"Yes Lad, he's got to be one of them too. I'm thinking that one of them, maybe it's Zimmer, is this Dragan. I think that Radelescu is here now, in Hollywood and has been, since leaving San Francisco."

Lindy brought over another round, and for a while they just drank. No one wanted to say anything, but all three had the same question in mind. Finally, Jack broke the silence. "Listen, Lads. I'm going to talk to Miss. Niki. See if she can add anything to this story about the driver. Now, these creatures know that we are on to them. They might come after us. You boys wear those crucifixes, and keep your windows shut at night too. If anything happens; if you even get suspicious, a hunch, or anything at all, you let me know. I'm going to watch this Zimmer. I'm also going to run a little background check on him."

"All right, Jack, we'll do that," Ned said, glancing at Pudge, who had a scary look in his eyes. Ned recognized the look. It was the same one he'd seen in his friend, every time someone had pushed him a little too far. It was, what Ned called, "his fightin' look."

"Now we've got to look out for each other," the detective said to his two friends, in the little space that was the entrance to the restaurant. "And don't get too wet on the way home," he called after them as they dodged the rain on the way to the street and their cars.

Jack did get a hold of Niki, but it wasn't until the movie had been wrapped. She had just found a little apartment on Cochran Avenue, and had paid for it with some of the money she had made from the movie. She really didn't have much to add to the story that Ned and Pudge had relayed to him. Only that she had always had a creepy feeling about the driver, and that her instincts had proved right. She served Jack a tall glass of mint iced tea, on the balcony that overlooked the street.

"I thank you, Niki," Jack said, shaking her tiny hand, as he was on his way out. "If you don't mind me making a suggestion, I'd keep that crucifix on your person or in your house. You never know when it will come in handy. I picked one up for myself too," he put his hand to his neck, where she could see it under his shirt.

"I'll keep that in mind," she smiled at him. She still wasn't entirely convinced of the story, and with time, the memory of Lenny's aggressive act seemed to have faded. Besides, Mr. Zimmer had treated her with the utmost courtesy. "You know he invited me to go with him to the opening," she said at the door. "You're invited as well, Jack. It will be June 15th at Grauman's Chinese."

"I'll make it a point to be there," Jack assured her. He had every intention of making that party, and was pleased with the invitation. "You be careful, Missy," he called up to her from the street below.

McCrae knew that he was due for retirement in just a few years. He knew that he was not crazy, despite his maligned reputation. He understood that the creatures that, for several years, seemed to have disappeared, were now back. With the help of the little green book, which he was about to present to his nephew, and some hard facts, he rationalized that George Zimmer was probably one of these most recent incarnations. He suspected that the blood letting in the park would probably recommence, and he was aware that, if they had panicked, Zimmer and company might disappear, as they had in the past. He also reasoned out, that they had too much at stake to do so. The word was already on the street that *"Biker Hell"*, was going to be something special, and that its two leads, Niki Starling, and Brick Lacey, were about to take off as pop stars for the younger generation. "As big as Elvis," was one of the phrases going about the gossip mill. Louella Parsons had already interviewed both actors, and although the film had not yet been released, it was already booked into the '56 Cannes Film Festival. Jack knew that the last thing Zimmer and Schreppel wanted to do, was to vanish and have to start all over again. Knowing that, made his own position even more precarious. He hadn't exaggerated the warning to the two old cowboys. They were all at risk.

In between his regular police work, he ran a background check on the three men. He found out that Zimmer and Joachims had spent a number of years abroad while Schreppel ran the agency. They had social security numbers. (These later, proved to be false), and he found bank accounts and license numbers. What he didn't find was any kind of a past, and only a very superficial present. There were no records of doctors or dentists, no credit reports, no pending or past lawsuits, or legal papers filed, and no real family history. It was like they had been invented as characters in a movie. So if any of this information was proof, perhaps the proof was in the general lack of information.

He mentioned that to Ned, several weeks after their Formosa meeting, through a phone call.

"You boys be specially careful, Ned. These vampires are an invention. Just as I suspected. Problem is, they're legal, and they haven't committed any crimes. Not even a parking ticket from that driver."

"So what does that mean, Jack?"

"What that means, Lad, is that they are clean. And until they do something otherwise, I got nothing on them."

"I'll explain that to Pudge," Ned told him. "He's been in a vicious state of mind for a while now."

"Well, keep in touch, Lad," Jack told him, before hanging up the phone.

Dragan, had he known of McCrae's summation to the two cowboys, would have agreed. The three of them did have a lot at stake, and murder was not an imminent option. He didn't have any idea what kind of information McCrae had spread around, nor to whom. For the first time since writing it, Dragan regretted the impulse, the vanity, or had it been boredom, that had led him to write the little green book. In all their years together, nothing like this had ever happened. During the time together in Paris, Dragan had grown fond of Lenny, and his servant's impulsive stupidity hurt even more because of that attachment.

"We shall continue as before," he told Marcus one evening, while sipping a Pastis, on the patio. "I believe we have covered ourselves. As long as we don't make any more mistakes, McCrae can't do a thing."

"Perhaps, Master, we should continue to go north when the urge comes to taste human blood. It's beautiful desert country up there near Palmdale, and the pickings were very good during your absence." Lenny stood by the door, head bowed, waiting to refill the glasses, when called for. His shame and humiliation were complete, and so distraught was he, that despite preparing all the meals, he hadn't eaten in days.

"Yes, we shall venture outside of Los Angeles. You can inform John of that, should he ever recover his appetite," Dragan said, knowing full well that Lenny heard every word. "Meanwhile, we must complete the post production on the film so it will open as scheduled."

"You know, Master, those two cowboys are on to me. Perhaps, we should arrange a little accident?" Marcus suggested, but Dragan cut him short.

"We will do nothing for the time being. When the time is right, if such a time comes, then, and only then, will we take care of that!"

The film did open. On June 15th, there was a huge gala opening at Grauman's, on Hollywood Boulevard, complete with spotlights, celebrities, motorcycles, and leather gear. The trade papers unanimously gave it rave reviews, and within days, it opened across America, to full houses. Shows were sold out in advance. Harley Davidson sales soared, and, across the country, from the cities to the small towns, young people sported, black leather jackets and caps. There was even a migration of young folks from all over, who came to Van Nuys, as they would come ten years later to San Francisco, to the Haight Ashburry area. Both Niki and Brick gained heroic stature among the younger generation that lasted for years and for a while perhaps, they were "bigger than Elvis."

Jack McCrae, who by then, knew the contents of *"The Real Vampires"* as well as a Boy Scout knows the oath, handed over the little green book to his nephew, one sunny July day in 1955. They were sitting on the patio at the house on Wilton, drinking mint iced tea. Jack had taken to drinking mint iced tea since his meeting with Niki. He, like the two cowboys, had taken a liking to the girl. She was a sweetheart, and had even greeted him personally at the opening. Both Brick, and Zimmer had accompanied her to the event, (for a while there were rumors that Brick and she were an item. This was, of course, not true), and when she spotted Jack, she had stopped and called his name.

"Mr. McCrae. Detective," she called. They were ambling down the red carpet, like royalty, just about to enter the theater. When McCrae walked over to her, amidst the flashing bulbs, and general commotion, she introduced him to Brick and Zimmer.

"I believe we know one another," Jack said, shaking Zimmer's cold hand, and staring hard into his black eyes."

"That's impossible, Detective," Zimmer laughed, "We've seen each other, only once, and were never introduced."

"Not in this life," Jack muttered.

"What's that Jack?" Niki asked, not having made out what he had said.

"It's nice to see you Niki," McCrae answered. "Good luck with the film. I'm looking forward to seeing it."

His words were not lost on Dragan, nor was Dragan's sneer lost on Jack. That had been it. Later, Jack had reported the encounter to both the cowboys.

Patrick received the heirloom with all due reverence. For years, he had seen his uncle produce it as a reference guide, and Patrick was almost as familiar with its contents as the man who had failed to return it to the public library. But Patrick was a true believer, and accepted the little green book, as one.

"Now it's important that others learn of these creatures," Jack said, over a cool sip. "Problem is, most people think you're crazy if you mention them. Now I don't know for how long The

Good Lord's planned for me to hang around, but you keep this, and memorize it, and when you meet someone who you trust, who doesn't take you for a dang fool, why you pass it on."

"You bet I will, Uncle Jack," Patrick eagerly took the book. "And I'll make sure, when the time comes, to hand it over to the right person."

That time didn't come until 1995, when Patrick turned it over to a psychic he had been seeing; a middle aged lady, with beautiful, long grey streaked hair, named Andrea Poe, who had a little shop of the occult, over on Melrose.

Ned and Pudge didn't have to wait long to pick up another job. The mid 1950's was the era of the television Western. There were many of them filming, among them, *"Wagon Train," " Gunsmoke," "Wells Fargo," Rawhide,"* (staring a young Clint Eastwood,) and a series starring Richard Boon, called, *"Have Gun Will Travel."* The principal director on that show, was a fellow named, Andrew V. McLaglen. He was the son of Victor McLaglen, who was part of John Ford's stock company, and another Irishman. Pudge and Ned, of course, knew all these people, and when the call came from Andy McLaglen, to work on the series, the two of them jumped at the chance. The studios used to send their cars, the stretch-out limos, out to the corner of Sepulveda, and Ventura Boulevards, to pick up the actors and stunt people and drive them to the various locations. So every morning, by six-thirty, a crowd of players would gather at the corner, to pick up a ride, much as they had gathered years earlier, at Gower Gulch. As the limos would pull up, each would have a placard with the name of the show, in the window. Most of the locations weren't far from The Valley, but a lot of *"Have Gun Will Travel"* was shot up in Lone Pine. Ned and Pudge had, over the years, returned to Lone Pine, but when they signed on to *"Have Gun,"* they spent a lot of time up there. They used to stay at the Dow Hotel. Both men liked the star, Richard Boone. He was a talented actor, good director, and he knew how to have a good time too. The two saloons in Lone Pine were familiar with all three men as well as most of the cast and crew. McLaglen also directed a great many episodes of *"Gunsmoke,"* and the two old timers, had plenty of work cut out for them all through the 'Fifties.

In May, 1956, Dragan and Marcus went to The Cannes Film Festival. Lenny was not included. Although, he was allowed to address Dragan personally, he had not been entirely brought back into the fold. That was to be a long process, over a number of years. Both Brick and Niki, accompanied the director and producer to Cannes. *"Biker Hell"* opened the festival at Le Palais. All four of them stayed at L'Hotel Carlton, where they were treated like royalty, constantly besieged by the media, and by mobs of young fans. The film had been a huge hit in Europe, and caused the same kind of cultural stir over there, that it had wrecked on America. Brick and Niki were astonished, that both, Mr. Zimmer and Theodore, spoke so many languages fluently. They conducted their interview with the foreign press, in German, Italian, Spanish, Portuguese, and French. That skill alone gave them greater coverage, and helped elevate the already, well received film. The fact that this Zimmer spoke fluent French, as well as all the other languages, and the pictures of him that ran in the papers, made their way back to Paris. His name, once again started popping up in the art world. When a very well known dealer arrived in Cannes, sometime toward the end of the festival, and encountered Dragan on the terrace of the Carlton, Dragan decided that it was time for them to return to America. They had accomplished all they could over there.

Upon their return, both Niki's and Brick's careers took off, even more so than they had prior to the event in Cannes. Both went on to have successful careers, Brick's lasted longer than Niki's, but she outlived him. He passed away during the early 'Eighties. Niki continued working through the 'Sixties and 'Seventies. She became well known in Europe, after marrying Daniel Prest, a wonderful French director, and part of "La Nouvelle Vague" of young, creative artists. She worked a great deal in France and Italy, returning to The States, in 1974, when her husband was killed in a plane crash. She never did have children, or re-marry, and did a little work in television, before retiring to her apartment on Cochran, to paint.

Jack McCrae retired in 1958, the same year that Greg Delacroix was born. McCrae had started as a cop in 1923, at the age of twenty-two, and made his detective grade late in 'twenty six. At his retirement party, at the Roosevelt Hotel, when the time came for Jack to make his speech and receive the plaque, he'd downed more than a few shots of Jameson's, some of his fellow cops got up with him, and after receiving the plaque, they handed him a box. When Jack gratefully opened the box, a live bat shot out and took desperate flight about the room. Jack then, let loose with an arsenal of Irish vulgarities, and chased the officers out of the hotel, and on to Hollywood Boulevard, thereby causing several, near collisions. The next day, the word had traveled from the Hollywood division, all the way down to the Rampart one, about the incident.

"Can you believe it, Patrick?" Jack asked his nephew, the following morning, while nursing a ferocious hangover with a green, ice bag. "Those sons of bitches still don't get it. A bat, for the love of Mary!"

"Just keep that on your head, Uncle Jack, and don't get yourself too worked up," Patrick advised him.

"And that Zimmer and Schreppel, are still out there too. I bet they've already heard about that little prank, and are having one hell of a good laugh, thanking their lucky stars that no one believes that they could possibly exist."

"Well, I believe you, Uncle Jack, and I'll keep my eyes open." Patrick promised.

For the next thirty-five years, Jack lived with Patrick in the house on Wilton. His retirement package hadn't been enormous, but between it, and Patrick's salary from Guinness, as a beer distributor, the two managed to live quite comfortably. McCrae never did give up on Zimmer. There had been evenings when the two of them would get in Patrick's car, and cruise over the hill, past the house on Craig Drive. Jack never again saw Zimmer in person. From time to time he'd read about him in the trades, but even Zimmer seemed to have grown away from the Hollywood spotlight.

One day in July, the fifth, 1984, Jack went back to the old precinct to say hello to the few officers who he still knew, and to leave a message. The message was in the form of three spiral notebooks that he'd kept over the years. They were his notes on the Roland Jordan, and Jeff Smith murders. He had put the notebooks in a manila envelope, but before so doing, had added a message on the last page of one of the three. His plan was to put the envelope in with the old files on the murders, the files they still kept in the Records Department. His hope, was that someday, someone who had made the connection between these murders, and whatever the next one that involved the vampires, was to be, would find the notebooks, and finally solve the mystery. He put the manila envelope in the inside pocket of his jacket, borrowed Patrick's car, and drove the short distance to the station. It was a lovely summer's day, and with this as his mission, Jack felt some of the old excitement.

He was surprised at the changes at the station. "Nothing like it used to be here," he told the captain, a fellow named, Mike Keenan, who he'd known as a very young officer. Kerry Magness had not yet been transferred to the Hollywood Division. "Whole town ain't what it used to be. Used to have some glamour. Look at Hollywood Boulevard now. Full of runaways and drug addicts."

"You've got that right, Jack," the man agreed. "Just dopers and scumbags."

"Why I remember when folks would get dressed up and walk the boulevard. I used to see old John Carradine, in tails, up there at Hollywood Billiards. Now the whole place is a dump."

"Well, times change Jack, times change," Keenan mumbled. He really didn't have time for the ex-cop. Somehow, Jack had managed to corner him in his office, just as he was about to leave for lunch. Keenan kept glancing at his watch.

"You fellows ever hear any strange stories from the drunks in Griffith Park?" he asked. "I mean crazier than the usual. Stories about creatures biting them and such."

Eddy Keenan darted a look at Jack. He suddenly remembered Jack's penchant for vampires. "Just an occasional dog, Jack. Nothing strange that I can think of. Course half them drunks have brain damage. Look, Jack," he said, getting to his feet, "I really have to get going."

"Well," Jack said, "if ever you do hear anything, anything about creatures like vampires," he handed the man a card, "you call me OK Mike."

Keenan took the card and shook his head. "My God, Jack, you're not still chasing those vampires, are you?" McCrae glared back at him.

"What I'm chasing, ain't any of your damn business, Laddie. What I'm asking, is that you'll let me know if your boys report any strange stories about dark shapes offering liquid refreshments of the alcoholic variety. That's how they used to do it, and I know they're still out there." With that, Jack walked out of the captain's office.

But before leaving, he managed to charm one of the female clerks into the room next to Evidence, where they kept the old files, the old records. It took him little time to find the files from the Jordan and Smith murders. No moment of nostalgia, inspired him to re-read anything that he had written so many years back. He knew it all by heart. He'd gone over and over it, time and again. He only hoped, that when the next murders happened, when Zimmer decided it was time for the three of them to move on, that someone, would draw the connection, and go through the files, thus finding his notebooks, as well as the warning he had written in the one.

That day finally came in October, 1998, fourteen years later. Mike Keenan had retired, and been replaced by Captain Kerry Magness, and Greg Delacroix, the great nephew of his old friend Ned, a man who had not yet been born when Zimmer first came to life, was the first one to make the connection and contact Jack.

Jack had been living in the retirement home on Melrose since '95, when he had fallen in the patio of the house on Wilton. He'd slipped on some ice cubes that still remained on the stone pavement, after tossing what was left of a tall, mint ice tea, at the old flock of wild parrots. The parrots made an annual migration to the tree, and over the years, their incessant squawking, had come to drive old Jack half crazy. Perhaps their racket had come to represent his failure at destroying the other flying creatures that had mocked and tormented him all those years. In any case, when he did fall, Jack broke his pelvis and both hips. The doctors told him that he was too old to get a hip replacement, and the hips never did mend. He had great difficulty getting around, and was eventually confined to a wheel chair. It was Jack's idea that he move down to the retirement house in West Hollywood.

"Why, I'll be just fine down there," he argued over Pat's protestations. "It's a lively little neighborhood and you can visit when you want. Besides, I've never seen any damn parrots on Melrose, just a lot of pretty girls."

So it was settled. Patrick moved his uncle in and visited him regularly. Before Pat discovered "Gino's," he liked to wheel his uncle over to "Johnny Rocket's" for burgers, fries, and shakes.

In 1965, seven years after Greg was born, Ned sold his house on Los Feliz to his nephew, Henri, and his wife, Greg's mother, Beatrice, and Ned moved to a small place he bought off Gower and Santa Monica, right near the police precinct. By then, both he and Pudge had pretty much retired. The movies had been good to them, and when television had come along, all the Western series that were shot during the 'Fifties and early Sixties, kept them busy enough. When the Western series started to go the way of all things, by the mid 'Sixties, both of them figured that the time had come to throw in their hats. Pudge found a place right around the corner from Greg.

Warm sunny weekends would often find the two of them fishing off the Santa Monica pier with a third man, one Hoagie Coates. They spent some time up at his ranch, as well, riding the trails, and musing over the good old days. And they did not abandon their cherished haunts. They still breakfasted occasionally at Schwab's, ate at Musso & Franks, and drank at the Formosa Cafe, where they were often joined by Jack McCrae, and still served by Lindy, the bartender.

Greg didn't see much of his uncle, Ned, while growing up, and he was really too young to have seen all the changes that came to Hollywood during the 'Sixties. Hollywood, in the 'Sixties, saw the completion of many new high rise office buildings, which brought a new influx of businesses to the town, and with that, an increase in population, crime, and deterioration. The porno industry, thanks to the changing laws, boomed, and with it, drugs and prostitution. Old houses were torn down and replaced with apartment facilities, doubling the housing population from what it had been in 1944. Television had to some extent replaced much of the film business, which moved to locations outside of town, and the music business was born. The Capitol Records building on Yucca and Vine, was a monument to the thriving industry, and clubs along Sunset Strip, clubs like, The Whisky-A-Go-Go, The Trip, The Daisy, and Gazzari's, featured local musicians and bands. Groups, such as, The Byrds, The Mamas and the Papas, and singers, like Johnny Rivers, Frank Zappa, and Tim Hardin, who became nationally known, only accelerated this music phenomenon.

The whole of the country was going through a major metamorphosis, with the youth movement, and Hollywood, perhaps more than other places, epitomized it. There were "Sit Ins" and "Love Ins" at Griffith Park, Hippies and runaways, dealers, and pimps, on Hollywood Boulevard, confrontations with the police, as well as demonstrations against the war in Vietnam. It was a time of great change, and with it came all the negative a well as positive accouterments.

Greg grew up in the house on Los Feliz, and when the time came, attended Hollywood High, from which he graduated, with good grades, in June, 1976. From there, he went on to UCLA as did so many of his contemporaries, where he majored in liberal arts, graduating in 1980. After college, he joined the Marines, putting in three years, including a stint in the Falklands, during the war there. In 1983, he returned to Los Angeles, and tested for the police department, graduating from The Police Academy, in '84. By 1990, he had made his detective grade.

If one had asked him, "why the police department?" Greg would have been hard pressed for an answer. His great uncle, Ned, could probably have answered that question. Maybe it was due to the same spirit of adventure, adventure with risk that had brought his ancestors, from the beaver streams, and mountains of Canada, through the old West, to Hollywood, and the world of the movies. Maybe it was just because he was really, a son of Hollywood, and as such wanted to contribute something to the town in which he had grown. He certainly could have chosen another profession, and one that paid better. The Los Angeles Police Department was under the leadership of Chief Darrel Gates, at the time, and had not yet suffered the criticism that almost brought it to its knees, following the Rodney King incident. When Greg joined, the police still exercised some authority, and although not with all the population, some respect.

Greg liked fast cars, as Ned had loved fast horses, and he was an adventurer. He'd seen action in the Falklands, played football at UCLA, and enjoyed rock climbing, to which he had introduced Lucille, early on in their relationship. They often traveled to, and camped out, in Joshua Tree, out in the desert.

He did well as a patrolman, showing initiative, and imagination, and had done equally well as a detective. He was well liked and respected by his fellow officers, and Captain Kerry Magness did not ignore his abilities. Greg was a practical man, and not prone to exaggeration. The Marines had instilled discipline and practicality, as had, athletics. Although he rarely saw his uncle while he was growing up, and never knew Pudge or McCrae, he'd never heard Ned mention anything about vampires. The idea that vampires were roaming the streets of his city, would have struck Greg as some absurd fantasy, some Hollywood movie, and hardly the cause for strange murders and disappearances. Years later, when the Zimmer disappearance was dropped on his desk, and he had discovered the articles in the family albums, with the notes written by his uncle on the reverse sides, he wished that his uncle had said something, and at the same time, Greg wondered why he never had. But by that time it was too late. Ned had passed on.

Hoagie Coates was the first of the three to go. Hoagie came down with flu, while riding his horse down Hollywood Boulevard, during the Bi Centennial Parade. It had just been bad luck that it happened to be a miserable, misty day, that day. Ned and Pudge were also in the parade on horseback, but neither one came down with so much as a sniffle. Of course they were both more than ten years younger than Hoagie, who, in 1976, was in his late eighties. His two old friends took him back to his ranch, tucked him under a pile of blankets, and gave him a good dose of hot rum toddy.

"Hoagie," Ned told him. "We really should call a doctor, and have him take a look at you." He was sitting on the edge of Hoagies bunk bed.

"That's right, Partner," Pudge agreed. "You don't look so good. Why you're sweatin like a horse in labor, and you ain't got no color in your cheeks."

"No boys, don't need one," Hoagie kind of choked out the words, as he came down with a coughing fit. "I feel just about as miserable as I can ever remember. I got a strong feeling that this here, is how this old cowboy's going to see his last sunset. I don't want no doctor to make my life miserable. It's been a damn fine ride, and if this is the end of the trail, so be it." Both Ned and

Pudge looked grimly at one another. They too had pretty much come to the same conclusion.

"Well, is there anything we can do for you, Partner?" Pudge asked.

"Why, yes, old friend. Just set me in my rockin chair out there on the porch, so's I can watch that old sun set."

So the two men, who were themselves, both in their seventies, carried Hoagie out to his rocker, fetched the bottle of rum, and made sure he was wrapped up tightly, and warm enough. Sure enough, by then, the rain had stopped, the clouds cleared, and one of God's most perfect sunsets fell over the hills, and down into the great Pacific, and the three of them watched it go down all the way. They put Hoagie to bed, but when Ned went to check on him in the morning, the old cowboy was quite dead.

"Hoagie would have liked a party," Pudge told Ned, "a real rip roarer."

So for his funeral, the boys threw him the biggest party the ranch had ever seen, and all his old friends, the living ones, as well as hundreds of people he never knew, showed up for the event.

Three days later, when the last of the guests had finally left, Ned turned to his pal. They were on the porch, watching another beautiful sunset. "You know, Pudge, I sure will miss that old timer. Too bad he wasn't here to enjoy it. Hoagie would have loved the hell out of his send off."

Pudge was the next one. It happened the following year, on a beautiful spring day, while riding a horse on a washed out trail up in Griffith Park. Something spooked his horse, and Pudge who had ridden all his life, and piloted trails much more hazardous than that one, was thrown, as the horse bolted. Just before flying over the horse's head, he grabbed for his crucifix, and suddenly realized that he had forgotten to wear it that morning, and in the same instant, Pudge got a glimpse of what had caused his horse to spook like he had. As he sailed over, he spotted a horrible, dark shape, perched on a low hanging branch of the California Oak tree. He came so close to the thing, that in that brief instant, he smelled its horrible breath, and under the frigid, black eyes, he saw the great-yellowed fangs, and felt the beast's cold breath.

Ned who knew his friend, probably better than any living man, and understood that when it came to riding, Ned was no slouch, had a terrible time believing that he had simply fallen. After the funeral, which was a very private affair at a little funeral home on Bronson, Ned mentioned it to their old friend, Jack McCrae.

"Doesn't make much sense. Old Pudge knew that horse and he knew every trail in the park. Didn't matter what kind of weather, the man could sit on a horse, without getting throwed. Something must have spooked the two of them."

"Those vampires might be back. They always loved the park for their pickings. Wouldn't surprise me one bit if Zimmer and company had something to do with it," McCrae said, thoughtfully. "I've got some checking to do. I'll let you know."

The two of them had Pudge cremated, as he had wished, and took the urn of ashes out to Hoagie's ranch. There, they scattered his remains around another California Oak, not far from the gravesite where Hoagie lay buried.

A week later, Ned got a call from Jack. "Look here, Lad, I checked with the Hollywood Precinct. Just checked to see if any of the officers had heard any strange stories from the drunks and transients that they sometimes pick up in the park."

"Yeah," Ned said, softly.

"They're back, Ned. The bastards have to be back. There were three separate incidents told by three drunks. It was the same old scenario; the black shapes in the night, with the liquid refreshments. I think they got Pudge," then McCrae lowered his voice to almost a whisper, "and I think they might be after us too. You watch your back, Laddie."

Three weeks later, they got to Ned. He hadn't been doing very well since his old friend had passed on, and he'd even taken to drinking more than he could handle. It was almost like a relapse to the time when he had lost his Suzanne Farley. Maybe, because of that, he too, hadn't worn the crucifix the night it happened. That night, after a long afternoon and evening at Musso & Franks Grill, while walking home, somewhere on Yucca, at a location where the already dark street was even darker, because of a few blown out street lamps, Ned saw a dark form approach him. He had trouble making his eyes focus on it, partially because of the light, but also, due to the quantity of Jameson's that he had consumed. As he stumbled on toward it, it suddenly stopped in front of him. For a moment he too saw the ghastly fangs, and smelled the foul breath. Then the thing reached up, and tugged at his left ear, as if mocking Ned, before letting loose a piercing cackle, and reaching for Ned's throat.

"Weir!" Ned screamed, grasping for the missing crucifix. "You son of a bitch. It was always you!"

Only Greg's father attended the funeral, which was held at the same place on Bronson, as was Pudge's. Greg was no longer living at home. He'd rented an apartment in Westwood, with some other guys from UCLA. His father told him about his great uncle's passing, by phone. Greg couldn't make it because he had just started a summer job for Mayflower, the trucking company.

Afterwards, Jack and Patrick, who had introduced themselves to Henri, took him out to Hoagie's place, and did for Ned what they had done for Pudge, spreading the ashes around a tree, not far from either site. Jack said a few words.

"This was a fine man. He was a good man, and a straight shooter. To watch him ride a horse, it was a thing of beauty. I'll miss them both now, as well as old Hoagie." Then he took a long look at Henri, Ned's nephew, and added, "They don't make them like that anymore."

Privately, he spoke with Patrick later at the house on Wilton. "Pat, these vampires are surely back. They've gotten my two best friends, killed them dead, and I fear I'll be the next one to go."

"Well, we won't let them get either of us, Uncle Jack! No sir," Patrick vigorously shook his head." McCrae wasn't too sure of anything at that point, and didn't want to alarm his nephew, but at the same time, felt he should make some plans.

"Listen here, Pat," he went over to the old metal file cabinet, in the corner of the den, and sifting through it, returned with three, spiral notebooks. "If anything should happen Laddie, I want you to take these down to the Hollywood Division. Somehow, you've got to slip them in the Records room files, in with the Roland Jordan murder. You understand?"

"You bet I will Uncle," he again nodded his head.

For the next several months, Jack kept an eye peeled, and didn't venture much from their house. Unlike Ned, he made sure to always wear his crucifix. Like Ned, he kept company with the Jameson's bottle, but when nothing happened, he settled down some, and returned to drinking mint iced teas.

Dragan, as Zimmer, had gone for a lower profile. Following the success of *"Biker Hell,"* all sorts of offers to direct, came his way, but he chose not to follow up on any of them. Money had never been a problem for the three of them, and they didn't have to work, had they not wanted to. Lenny's stupidity had brought McCrae out of the woodwork, and he knew that the two cowboys, and perhaps Niki, had their suspicions.

As Theodore had suggested, when the times came, and the old craving for human blood had to be satiated, the three of them headed north, and out to the desert. No longer was Griffith Park, the hunting grounds. Dragan spent much of his time wandering through the various museums and libraries. He loved fine art, and had been fortunate enough to see many of the world's great masterpieces at the time they had been created, and had even known some of the famous artists of the past. His wanderings through the museum halls, gave flight to his memories, and seemed to relax him. From time to time, he attended various Hollywood functions, but chose to keep his name and face out of the headlines, as much as was possible. Marcus took to driving, and took long sight seeing trips. Besides the desert, he especially liked the drive up Route One, The Coast Highway. He spent a lot of time up in Big Sur, and Monterey Bay. Lenny, stayed more or less house bound, administering his domestic duties.

In 1977, Dragan gave Marcus the permission he had asked for all those years earlier. It was Marcus, who spooked Pudge's horse, and taunted Ned Delacroix, before breaking the old cowboy's neck.

On October, 10, 1998, bored after years of near anonymity, and longing to return to the business he loved, with his old adversary, Jack McCrae confined to a wheelchair, Dragan made his move. For the first time since arriving in Hollywood, Dragan did not purchase another residence in which to establish his new identity, which he had chosen to be, a Richard Stewart. He had decided to simply abandon the house on Craig Drive, furniture and all, and return to the place off Sunset. He figured that George Zimmer had been around far too long, and a complete disappearance was in order. Oh, there would be a body left behind, there had to be, but there was no one that he could think of that could place him, Dragan Radelescu, at the house with the towers and the turrets. They had successfully kept that place, their little secret.

Both Theodore Schreppel, and John Joachims, had just gone through The Change, and were established in their new identities as Marcus Banning, and Lenny Fields. Marcus had opened a production office at Raleigh Studios, and had already started pre-production on a movie called, *"Life-Blood, The Last Vampires of Hollywood."* Richard Stewart would direct it, a vampire thriller, and he would do so in one of his old and favorite locations, Lone Pine, California. With this movie, he hoped to destroy some of the myths that humans had manufactured about his kind. As with the little green book, Dragan felt a need to explain.

"Marcus," Dragan called his servant out to the patio, where he was sitting, staring up into the night's bright stars. An owl, a very rare bird to be seen, sat perched on the pepper tree that gave shade to the patio. Its eyes too, sparkled, as it scanned the hillside for rodents, and other vermin.

"Yes, Master." Marcus appeared in the doorway.

"It shall be tonight. I shall find an unknown, perhaps a homosexual, one of the prostitutes on Santa Monica Boulevard. He must be healthy, of course, and strong. Lenny will drive me, as he always does."

"What do you wish me to do Master?" Marcus asked.

"You will arrange the coffin in the great room at the chateau. Tonight we leave this place, as is, for good."

"It shall be as you order." Marcus answered, simply.

And so it was. At about ten, as Marcus left in the silver

Mercedes convertible for the place off Sunset, Lenny opened the door of the black one for his master, Dragan Radelescu. It was a pleasant autumn evening, a good night for a drive. They drove to Santa Monica Boulevard, where young men sold their bodies for a few dollars, or a place to eat and spend the night. It didn't take Dragan long to spot the one he wanted. He was older than the others, perhaps in his late twenties or early thirties. Dragan knew that most of them didn't survive that long, and that the men who paid them, were generally interested in the younger ones. This one, was well built, with dark shoulder length hair.

He quickly did the transaction, not wanting to loiter long enough to get pulled over by the police, who regularly patrolled the street. He simply told the man that he wanted him to spend the night; that he would feed him, and pay him very well, and that if the man pleased him, it might be possible for the relationship, and its financial rewards, to continue indefinitely. It was an offer that the man immediately seized, as Dragan knew he would.

Lenny drove the two back to the house on Craig Drive. There, he prepared a meal for Dragan and his prey, served it, and retired to one of the guest rooms. During dinner Dragan interviewed the man thoroughly. When the meal was done, and the second bottle of wine consumed, and Dragan was quite satisfied that this one was the one, he suggested that they retire to his room. There was no need for a seduction. The man followed Dragan to the bedroom, where Dragan indicated that he should enter. As he did so, with an incredible quickness, like a jaguar, another creature that hunts at night, Dragan was on the man, and before he could even open his mouth to gasp, Dragan had sunk his teeth deep into the flesh.

Lenny came to the doorway and waited, wondering if perhaps this time, the Master would take on another form, but again, he didn't. He simply walked outside, leaving the lights on and the door open, and waited by the car until Lenny opened the door for him.

Lenny drove him to the castle, where Marcus had prepared the casket with the satin lining. Together they helped their master into its confines, where he reclined.

Exactly six days, one hundred and twenty four hours from the moment that George Zimmer had sucked dry the corpse of the transient that he had housed and so carefully prepared for this moment, at twelve, midnight, on the morning of Friday, the sixteenth of October, Richard Stewart blinked once, then slowly opened his dark eyes.

CHAPTER 15

Lone Pine, 1998

It's a beautiful morning for a drive, with high cirrus clouds and a cool breeze. It takes Lucille little time to climb out of Los Angeles, on her way north. The traffic is light, and she makes good time. Somewhere up by Four Corners, up there in the high desert, a silver Mercedes rushes past her, almost forcing her off the two way strip of road. She has enough time to straighten out the Volkswagen, and still notice the driver of the other vehicle. She recognizes Marcus. She sees him hunched behind the wheel, alone in the car, clutching the steering wheel with both hands, both hands wearing black leather driving gloves. She shivers, slightly unnerved by the near accident, and the shock of having recognized the driver, the producer of the film she is about to start.

By noon, she reaches the Inyo Mountains, and pulls into the little town of Lone Pine. Looming high above, and reaching into the clouds, she sees Lone Pine Peak. At its sight, she is reminded of the wonderful history of film making that has taken place in this remote spot, at the same time realizing that she is about to become a part of that history. On the way into town she notices the tiny airport, and thinks of Greg. It will be their first time away from one another since living together. She has a map that the production office supplied with directions, on her lap. At the stoplight, she turns left, on to Whitney Portal Road, and toward the mountains.

The company is booked to stay at Esmerelda's Dude Ranch, just up Portal Road, before Movie Road. She has no trouble finding the sprawling ranch with the individual cabins. As she drives through the wooden gate, she sees that other company members have already arrived. She immediately spots Marcus' Mercedes, and sees Dan out in the yard, in front of the office and main house. He's speaking with part of his crew, Barb, Beth, and Jake.

"Lucille!" He comes over to her car as she parks it and gets out. "No trouble getting up here?"

"No," she tells him, throwing a glance towards, Marcus' car. "No trouble at all. Boy, it's kind of nippy up here. Lot's of wind too."

"You'll get used to it. There's already snow right down to the base of the mountains. Perfect for what we're shooting. Listen," he adds, "I got you a small cabin to yourself. It's the smallest one here, but most everyone else is pairing up. The two girls are down there, and Jake is bunking with the assistant prop man."

"Thanks, Dan," she says appreciatively, "I know that wasn't easy." He laughs, pleased by her gratitude.

"Well, Marcus seems to like you, and I know just how busy we shall be. Listen, we're going to eat in the main house here. They've set up tables for everyone and most of the meals will be here. The location isn't far away, just off Movie road," he says, pointing toward the mountains. "A place called Lone Ranger Canyon."

"Have you been there yet?" she asks.

"Just got back," Dan tells her. " Went up there with Marcus and the Production Manager. The set's all built and they've got wardrobe and makeup trailers all set up."

For a moment Lucille is tempted to tell Dan about the incident with Marcus, when he almost ran her off the road, but she decides against it. He must have sped all the way up here. Perhaps he was simply late, she decides. "Well, it should be exciting," she says. "Guess I'll unpack."

"You do that Lucille." He rubs his bald head reflectively, then remembers. "Here's the call sheet for tomorrow. Six AM for us. Seven for the main crew. Tonight we eat at six."

"OK, Dan, she says. "Now, I guess I'll unpack."

"Cabin, number eleven." He points her in the direction. "See you at dinner, and Lucille. Try to get a good night's sleep."

At dinner in the main house, Lucille's reminded of the first day of a summer camp she attended as a teen. The dinning room is large and rough in a western way, with dark stained pine walls and furniture, long wood tables and benches, and mounted on the walls, riding gear, reins and saddles. An ox yoke hangs over the wide fireplace, which burns, warming the room, and scenting it with a rich outdoors smell. The meal is good, with plenty of dishes from which to choose, and the ambiance over the first dinner is as warm as the fire. The feeling seems good. Old friends greet one another, while others get acquainted. It's a young crew mostly, with mainly relatively unknown actors. She spots Marcus and Richard sitting at a nearby table with the male and female leads of the show. Marcus sees her look, smiles, and waves to her. She decides to tell Dan about the little encounter.

"Well," Dan explains to her. "Probably, he was running a little late and not paying attention. I wouldn't worry about it. You made it OK," he laughs it off.

"You're right Dan. It's strange though. I remember seeing these gloves he was wearing, and his hands were so tight on the steering wheel. It was creepy, and scary."

"Lucille," Dan gets up from the meal. "I'm going to bed. I suggest you go soon. It's going to be a long hard schedule, and we've got to stay healthy. Goodnight."

"Wait," she says suddenly, "I'll go with you."

Outside, they both feel the night's cold wind sweeping down off the mountains. The western sky is alive with thousands of twinkling stars. She slips her hands into the pockets of the blue ski parka she's brought, and shivers.

"It's truly beautiful, isn't it? Isn't it, Dan?"

"That it surely is. Sleep well, Lucille."

In her tiny cabin, Lucille lights one of the candles she has brought with her, and prepares for bed. She thinks of Greg, and decides that she will call him tomorrow. Already, she misses him. The bed is a single wood framed one, set against the wall. There is one window with blue denim curtains, a chair and a small chest of drawers. There is also, a simple bathroom, with a sink and shower. The accommodations are to say the least, rustic. Before pulling the red Starling's Bay wool blankets up, she opens the curtains to get a clear view of the starry sky. In bed, she blows out the candle, and just before falling off to sleep, reaches for the crucifix that she wears around her neck. As she does so, she suddenly realizes that she forgot to bring some for Dan and the rest of the costume crew. For a moment, she feels just awful that she had let it slip. It would have been so easy, but then, she rationalizes, that there had been so many other things to think about, things pertaining to the movie, she's sure that if Dan remembers to ask her about the crucifixes, that he won't make anything of the fact that she forgot, just as long as she does her job well here, here in Lone Pine.

Lucille is wide-awake with the first ringing of the alarm at five-forty five. She showers, relishing its warmth, dresses quickly, and goes to the main house for breakfast, which is already laid out, buffet style. Again there's plenty of food, coffee and tea, but only a few crewmembers in the room, as her call for work is earlier than for the others. As she carries her plate down the serving line, filling it mostly with fruit and a croissant, she recoils, as someone touches her sleeve. She turns. Marcus stands inches from her, holding his own plate, smiling.

"Oh, Mr. Banning, you frightened me," she smiles back. "I didn't hear you. And there's practically no one else here yet."

"Lucille. I certainly didn't mean to," he tells her. "And please, call me Marcus. I like these early mornings, before the sun has come up. I'm really a night person, you know, even though movies are a day job."

"Well, I had no trouble getting up this morning," she says. "I guess we'll all get used to the hours, won't we, Marcus." He laughs.

"Of course we will. It's always that way when we start a new project." He pours her a cup of coffee. "Shall we sit together?" He indicates the nearest table. It is empty. She looks toward the door, hoping that Dan will show up. She feels strange, being alone with the producer, in this large, almost empty place. Despite that, she sits where he has indicated.

Lucille wants to talk about the movie, but Marcus steers her away, preferring to ask her questions about herself; where she is from, her schooling, her ambitions. As she talks, she seems to relax somewhat. Before she realizes it, she's told him a great deal about herself. "I've worked on a lot of commercials, but not too many features. This is a wonderful opportunity, and it's a period piece. I especially like that. It's so much more creative." She laughs. "I had to explain to my boyfriend that a period piece, is a film that's set in a different time." Marcus smiles, knowingly.

"And what does he do? What are his interests?" he asks. Suddenly Lucille once again, feels uncomfortable. Perhaps she has talked too much already.

"Oh, she mumbles. "He's a police detective, homicide mostly."

"Really?" Marcus responds. "How fascinating. He must have some interesting stories. What's his name?"

"Greg," she says, softly. "Greg Delacroix." Marcus' initial reaction to that information, does not in any way surprise the girl. Had Ned Delacroix been witness to it though, he most certainly would have grabbed Lucille and taken her as far from Marcus Banning and Lone Pine, as quickly as was possible.

"That's a most interesting name," he says, instinctually reaching for and then tugging on his left ear. "That's French, I believe. Same name as the famous artist, isn't it?"

"Why yes, I believe so," she says, at the same time noticing that Dan is about to join them at the table. She's relieved to see her boss. Marcus too, sees Dan, and has by then finished his plate, as it has been Lucille who has done most of the talking. The coincidence has not been lost on him, and he wants to relate it to Dragan.

"Hello Dan," he says, standing. "Lucille, it's been a real pleasure getting to know you. We shall spend more time together. Bye. See you both on the set."

"I see you're getting acquainted with Marcus," Dan says. "He's very talented you know."

"Yes, perhaps," she says quietly, returning to what is left of breakfast. Something about Marcus disturbs her. She's not sure what it is, but she knows that she feels vulnerable, and open in his presence, and there is something in that, that frightens her.

Lucille and Dan drive to the set in one of the company vans, with the other members of their team. Lone Ranger Canyon is not far from the ranch. Over the years, many films and

TV shows have been shot at this location, including "Hop A Long Cassidy," and "The Lone Ranger." The set has been constructed in an area known as, Yellow Sky Arrista.

"Wow," Lucille utters, as she gets out of the van, "look at that! Isn't that something!"

"And the wardrobe trailers are right here," Dan points at three trailers set among other ones, right where they've pulled up. Unlike his assistant, he's already seen the set.

The set is of a complete western mining town, complete with a saloon, general store, horse livery, mining office, sheriff's office and jail. "The mine is located at what they call, "Hoppy Rocks," Dan explains. "They're over there," he points across an outcropping of rocks. The film calls for lots of special effects. On the nearby mountains, Lucille sees that the snow line has dropped to only several yards above the town's elevation. Since the story involves horrible weather, with tempests, snow and floods, all the equipment necessary to create these effects will be brought in, and any long shots that include the mountains, will show the natural snow. The disaster scenes have to be shot at the end of the shooting schedule, so as to not, destroy the town. Everything else will be shot first, before the effects team wrecks havoc on the construction.

Dan shows his crew the trailers and helps them set up. He's not going to spend much time in either the trailers or on the set, as he'll be doing all the ordering and organizing, leaving those duties to the others.

"I want you to keep checking, going on the set, whenever you can," he instructs Lucille, just before leaving. "I'm leaving Barb and Jake as the on set dressers, and Beth will work with you in the trailer. But you should be available to Richard and Marcus, as much as possible. Besides, Marcus seems to have taken a special interest in you, and that should keep everything running smoothly."

"I'll do that Dan," the young woman answers, at the same time, feeling unease come over her.

The morning goes smoothly. Beth and she seem to work well together. Beth is younger than Lucille, only twenty-two. She's slightly overweight, but very pretty, with bright cheeks, blue eyes, and rich, dark hair. She's a Hollywood girl, whose dream is to design costumes for big budget features. Although she hasn't had much experience, Lucille recognizes her talent, and her willingness to work and learn. She is not at all competitive with her older boss, and the two share a similar sense of humor and outlook on life. Beth too, has a boyfriend who is a rookie cop, and works down in Central Division, which is a mixed bag of crime, well blended in poverty.

Lucille makes several trips down to the set, where they are shooting exteriors. It's a fine, late autumn day. The night's cold has given way to a pleasant breeze, and the sun shines. Jake and Barb have things under control. She's been around long enough to know that one of the principal understandings, while shooting anything, is that the director should not have to wait unduly, on any of his crews. Jake and Barb, have the actors dressed, in the proper wardrobe, and set ready, before they are called for, and therefore, are adhering to that principal. Marcus is also pleased with not only the wardrobe department, but with the entire crew, which despite its youth, work with a veteran professionalism. Just before they break for lunch, while they are waiting for the electrical department to finish a lighting setup, he calls Lucille over.

"Lucille, your people are doing just fine, and the wardrobe is terrific, now that I see the actors wearing what you've done, I appreciate what you've done, all the more." Lucille is a bit surprised by his somewhat patronizing comment. The film is just starting and compliments are usually saved until the end, if mistakes and disasters have been circumnavigated.

"Thank you, Marcus. We've got a good crew. We hope to keep everything running smoothly. If you need me, I've got a walkie-talkie in the trailer, and I'll be right down."

"I'll do that if I have to," Marcus tells her, as she turns to go, then stops her. "Lucille, why don't you join me at lunch." He catches her indecision, then adds, "It would be my pleasure."

"Thank you. I guess I can, if Dan doesn't need to discuss things with me."

"Oh," Marcus answers quickly, "Dan, won't be here for lunch. He had to run down to Lone Pine for something. He asked me to let you know."

"Oh, Well OK," she says, surprised that Dan didn't tell her himself. "Is everything OK?" she asks. He smiles, reassuringly.

"Everything's fine, nothing to do with the show. Just a personal matter." That makes her feel better about his not telling her.

"Sure," she says again, "I'd be happy to."

The crew stays on the set for lunch. A catering company has set up tables and brought in a catering truck. The meal centers around chicken. Lucille arrives after most of the crew is seated, and after getting her plate, spots Marcus sitting at a table with Richard Stewart, the production manager, and several actors who she's already met.

Marcus, immediately after breakfast, found Dragan and filled him in on the conversation.

"I think this boyfriend might be related to that old cowboy," he tells Dragan.

"If he's the same cop, I saw at McCrae's funeral, I'll know it if I see him. The problem is that he'll recognize me as well," Dragan says slowly.

"Why don't I get her to sit with us at lunch," Marcus suggests. "That way we can pump her for more information."

"Yes," Dragan agrees. "You do that."

So the entire morning, during the filming, Dragan reflects on this new information. He's too adept as a director to let it interfere with his work, but despite his extreme self-confidence, made more so by the fact that he has managed to live as long as he has, he is troubled.

As Lucille walks towards the table, Marcus smiles at her and indicates a spot next to the two of them. She sits. Richard Stewart makes the obligatory introductions around the table. "Wardrobe's fine," he tells her simply, when the introductions are over.

"Thank you, Mr. Stewart," is her response.

For a while they all eat. As the conversation at the end of the table gets animated, and seeing that the others are not paying attention to Dragan's end of the table, he starts working on Lucille. "Marcus tells me that you're from the East Coast," he starts.

"Yes, sir. Boston, in fact," she says, picking at the chicken in front of her, wondering why she was getting this special attention, usually reserved for the actors, at least on the first week of a shoot.

"Please, Lucille, call me Richard," Dragan says charmingly. "I know Boston. In fact I used to live there, some time back." Marcus darts a look at his master. Some years back, was more like two hundred years ago, when they had first arrived on these shores of America.

"Really, she says, "what part of town?"

"I used to live down by the port, the Haymarket area. Of course, I understand that it's completely renovated now. Nothing like it was when I was there." Marcus smiles. He understands Dragan's ironic sense of humor. He's come to, after the hundreds of years they have spent together.

Dragan continues to converse with Lucille, who doesn't have much of an appetite. She wishes that Dan were here, or that there had been two places at the table, and that Beth was sitting next to her. Eventually, Dragan leads the conversation back to Greg. "I understand that your boyfriend is a cop, a detective?"

"Yes," she smiles, "I hope he'll get a chance to come up here. He's supposed to have a few days off."

"That would be nice, Lucille. Of course, we shall be extremely busy until the end of the shoot," Marcus interrupts.

"What kind of cases does he work on? Dragan presses.

"Oh," she says innocently, "whatever they put him on, mostly murders, he's homicide." She laughs, "It's funny, you know, he was working on this Zimmer disappearance. Maybe you knew him? George Zimmer, the director of "Biker Hell? He thinks there might be vampires involved!" Again she laughs. For a moment she wants to mention the crucifix, then thinks better of it. It seems so silly in front of these two men. Neither Marcus or Dragan look at one another, but it is Dragan who fields the question.

"I know who George Zimmer is. I heard he'd vanished. Hard to believe, isn't it? I doubt that he's really gone. Either he's dead, or he'll show up somewhere. Don't you agree Lucille?"

"Well, I suppose so," she says, looking at her half eaten plate of chicken, and the salad she barely touched.

"The police don't really believe that there are vampires out there, do they?" Dragan continues. "I mean, other than these silly kids with their vampire clubs and makeup, so they can go on shows like, "Jerrry Springer."

"Vampires are pure show business," Marcus chuckles. "That's why we're doing this film. People love the fantasy. We just want to make this one, one that they'll remember. This is just fun and fantasy, and hopefully big box office." They all laugh at that.

The second assistant director announces that the time allocated for lunch, is over and everyone finishes up, and goes about getting back to work. Now Lucille is glad that she never brought up the crucifix. As Richard and Marcus explain it, the idea is really rather silly. She'll call Greg tonight.

"Lucille, it's been nice getting to know you," Dragan says, as she gets up. "We'll have a good time on this one, I'm sure."

"Well, thanks, I guess I'll get back up to wardrobe. I'm on the walkie-talkie, if anyone needs to get a hold of me."

Both Marcus and Dragan watch her leave. "I don't want that boyfriend coming here for a visit, Dragan hisses. "This is so, so.... inconvenient. He watches the crew assembling around the camera, which is all ready for the next setup. Already, they are waiting on the director. The assistant director starts to walk toward the two of them. "Perhaps it would be best to just fire her, find some reason to get rid of her now."

"Perhaps not, Master," Marcus intercedes, cutting short, the idea. There is something about this girl that has awakened and stirred an old emotion, an emotion that he has known on only several occasions over the many years that the three of them have roamed the earth. The last time he felt this stirring, was for his beloved Dorothy Doty. He had given her almost everything, humanly possible; riches, renown, as well as a form of love. To give to her, his full and total love, required her to make a choice, that being immortality. To achieve that, he needed to make love to her in a way no human ever could. She also needed to accept that proposal, and to invite him to love her then, and thus forever. When he made the proposition to her, her reaction was not at all what he had longed for, or expected. Instead of embracing the opportunity, and the monster that could deliver it to her, repugnantly, and with absolute horror, she rejected both. If Marcus had still had a heart, Dorothy destroyed it. He had no choice, but to kill her.

Prior to Dorothy Doty, the only other woman Marcus had fallen for, since coming to America, was a girl in Salem, Massachusetts, a girl by the name of Pamela Smith. Unfortunately, this was during the time of the witch-hunts. Marcus, Lenny, and Dragan, barely managed to escape the throng that arrived at the gates of their house, the throng, armed with silver stakes and carrying burning torches. The girl was less lucky. They found her first, and by the time the three ancient ones fled on horseback, Pamela Smith, the only daughter of the Reverend Cotton Smith, was burning at a stake in the village square. Unlike Dorothy, Pamela thought that the reality of eternal life on earth, as opposed to that, in an unknown heaven, was one that she could live with.

There is something about Lucille that has brought out that old emotion, and the last thing Marcus wants, is for Dragan to get rid of her. Of course, he knows better than to let The Master become aware of this feeling. He knows the rules. He remembers Lenny's almost fatal mistake, when he attacked Niki Starling. He is acutely aware of the fact that Dragan, had he chosen to do so, could have easily killed Lenny in the briefest of seconds. He is not sure as to what it is about this young woman that so attracts him, but he is determined to find an alternate solution to her simply being fired from the movie.

"There has to be a better way," he calmly reassures Dragan. "We have no grounds to fire her, and doing so at this stage, would only create tension with the entire crew."

"Perhaps," Dragan says, "but I don't want this other Delacroix in my sight!"

"Let me work on it," Marcus coaxes. "I'll take her under my wing. She is most impressionable. I'm sure that within a few days, she will listen to any and all advice I give."

"Very well then," Dragan gives Marcus an odd look. " I shall give you a few days, but at the first sign that this cop is on his way here, she's history!"

The rest of the day's shooting goes very smoothly. Although no one on the crew has ever worked with this, Richard Stewart, or for that matter, Marcus Banning, most of the crew find the two of them to be not only skilled and efficient at what they do, but also, rather fun to work with. Richard Stewart's sense of humor, keeps his camera, grip, and electrical department amused right through the last shot, the "martini shot," after which, the assistant director calls, "That's a wrap folks. Pick up your call sheets, and we'll see you tomorrow."

In the evening, before and after dinner, some of the cast and crew wander into the town of Lone Pine for a little recreation and exploration. A number of them end up at DBL Cocktails, others at Bo Bo's Bonanza. Some just wander about town. Lucille chooses to stay at the ranch. Dan was back for dinner. He mentioned nothing about the personal matter, and she didn't ask, not wishing to intrude. Later, she calls Greg from one of the pay phones in the main yard.

"Hi, Honey."

"Lucille, it's so good to hear your voice," he smiles.

"I miss you already, Honey."

"How are you? How's it gone so far?" He asks.

"Oh, Greg, it's so beautiful here! I'm standing outside, looking at about a million stars shining over the mountains. It's really magnificent. You've got to see it!"

"Are you doing OK?" He wants to know.

"Everything's fine. It's cold up here. You know, there's snow on the mountains. You've got to come and see it."

"I'll get up there soon enough," he says. "How's the job going?

"Oh, Greg, everything's going almost too well. Of course, it's only the first day, but so far it's just fine. We've got a good crew, and everyone seems to get along. I had lunch with the director and producer. They seem to like me, and are happy with our work. "Did you hear that?" she asks excitedly. Listen!" Lucille holds the phone out in the courtyard. From the hills, come the yipping and long howls of the coyotes.

"Sounds like you've got company," Greg laughs.

Lucille goes on to fill Greg in on everything that has happened since arriving. She describes her little cabin, where they eat, the rest of her crew, and just how the first day's shoot went.

"Marcus, that's the producer, he almost ran me off the road on the way up," she tells him. It scared me. I guess it was nothing. He was just in a hurry. Dan said that he was almost late or something. Anyway. Everything's fine. He seems to like me. I'm sure I'll be all right, but I miss you, Darling."

"Well, I miss you too. I 'm due for some days, and I'll come up. Look, if you need me for anything, and you can't reach me here, you've got the cell phone number, and if you have to, call the station and ask for Jim Diehm."

"Oh, Honey, I will, but everything's fine. I'm going to bed now. We've got early calls every morning. I love you."

Later, Lucille blows out the candle, and pulls the warm blankets up. Through the window, she sees the night's stars, twinkling like a million dreams, and just before drifting off to sleep, once more, she hears the lonely wail of the coyote pack in the foothills. They seem to be so close.

The day after talking with Lucille, within minutes of his arriving at the station, a call comes in. It's a homicide, an apparent murder in the Hollywood Hills, off Barham Boulevard, on a street that winds up the hill from Craig Drive. Both he and

Cove are sent to the house where the crime was discovered by the Spanish maid, who had arrived that morning to find the door open, and the elderly gentleman for whom she cleaned, dead, on the living room floor.

By the time the two detectives get there, the uniformed cops who had first arrived on the scene, have cordoned off the drive and are trying to move the curious neighbors, away from the house. "In here, Detectives," a young patrol officer directs the men.

"Jesus," Eddy mutters, will you look at that!"

"Nasty business, Detective," the officer agrees.

The victim is a man, probably in his sixties, dressed in a bathrobe and pajamas. His body lies crumpled on the floor, just in front of the door, which is the main entrance. His throat has been slashed so deeply, that the mortal wound has almost left him decapitated. As the detectives look about the room, it's obvious to them, that in addition to the murder, some sort of robbery was also committed. "Looks like he answered the door for the murderer," Eddy says.

"Forensics team is on the way," Greg tells the uniformed cop. "Just keep everyone out for now, and make sure that no one tramples around outside, as well. We'll take a look around."

Greg and Eddy spend the morning, along with the other teams, investigating the crime scene. Upstairs, they find the place in turmoil. It's obvious that the place was robbed after the owner was killed, but it looks to the detectives, as if the perpetrator was also looking for something specific. This is just their initial take on the situation. The two men discuss it over lunch at Gino's.

"You know, Eddy, I was scheduled to get some days off," Greg tells his partner over a lunch of spinach pasta, and a salad. The day is warm for this time of the year, and they take advantage of the weather by sitting outside on the terrace.

"Good luck with that now, Partner," Eddy tells him. "You were planning on going up to see Lucille, weren't you? Where is she again?"

"Place called Lone Pine, up north in the mountains. She says there's snow on them. Hard to believe," he says, looking around. "It's beautiful here."

"You think there's any connection to this thing and that Zimmer case?" Eddy asks. He's ordered a steak. Unlike Pat McCrae, Eddy likes his meat cooked. "I mean, it's practically next door."

"Too early to tell," Greg answers. "Zimmer's place was just abandoned. Nobody took anything, not even Zimmer. Does seem a little strange though. Could be. Damn, I really wanted that time."

"How's she doing up there?" Eddy asks him.

"Everything sounds like it's going OK. Still, I worry about her some. This is the first time she's ever had to go out of town for one of these things."

"I'm sure she'll be OK," his partner reassures him, "and maybe we'll get lucky and break this thing in a couple of days."

"Yeah, maybe," Greg mumbles, unconvinced himself, as Gino comes out to greet the two men.

"Greg, Eddy," he shakes their hands. "How's life treating you?" Greg tells him that Lucille is out of town working on a movie, and that they just got hit with a homicide, just when he'd planned on taking some time off and going to visit his girlfriend.

"Bad luck, Greg. You know, I haven't had a day off since, geez, I can't even remember."

"Gino," Greg asks the owner, "I hear you've got a new customer now, Pat McCrae?" Gino wipes his big hands on his apron, and laughs.

"Oh yeah, he's quite the character. Comes by every now and then, ever since you bought him that steak. Calls me, Dino." Gino points to the sign over the front door, that clearly reads, "Gino's"."

"Yeah, he's a character all right. So was the uncle."

"He brought him in a few times. Said he'd passed on. A retired cop, right?"

"Yeah. He was ninety seven years old," Greg says, thinking of old Jack.

"This Pat," Gino goes on, "he has this theory that vampires are running the movie business." He laughs, "Of course I've served a few of them here before, but they don't look much like bloodsuckers, although some of them have nasty, spoiled little attitudes."

"Yeah, you know Gino," Greg glances at Eddy, "there is something strange going on around this town, and it's been going on for a long time."

"What do you mean by that?" Gino asks.

"I don't know, maybe this Pat McCrae is not as crazy as he sounds," Greg says slowly. Gino laughs, and heads back inside.

"Well, if you catch one of them, bring him by for lunch. I'll fix him up some blood sausage linguini."

The first week on the film continues as smoothly as did the first day. Gradually the various crews get familiar with one another. Some of this takes place on the set, and some when they are not working. So far, all the shooting is taking place at the one main location, that being the western mining town. The actual mine is at the Hoppy Rocks, not far away, and there are other rocky locations planned for other sequences. The snow line is right at the base of the mountains, and Richard Stewart shoots as much footage of the mountains as he can get, as the weather is cooperating with the script. For the crew, the mornings are chilly, and as the sun begins to drop in the evening, the cold creeps back in. There have been a few very windy days, but despite having to suffer the wind, Marcus and Dragan, make the most of it, by not having to use wind machines. Once the sun drops below the mountains, the show is wrapped for the day, although the electrical truck has lights available, big HMI, twelve K lights, should Stewart choose to use them.

When Lucille called Greg, the second day of shooting, she was disappointed to learn that he had been put on another case.

"Do you still think you'll be able to get away?" she had asked him.

"I don't know, Darling. This is our case now, and we're not about to turn it over to anyone else. Besides," he added, "Magness thinks that there might be something tying this one in with the Zimmer one. I'm not so sure of it."

"Well, if you could maybe even drive up for the weekend," she suggested. "You know we get Sundays off." Greg thought about that for a second.

"Maybe, I can make it next weekend, after your second week. I know it's a long time, but I'm jammed with other things here too."

"Well, Honey, we're only going to be here for three weeks, so if you can't make it this weekend, it will have to be the second weekend."

Since that call, she had been in touch with him every night. Friday night he asked her if she was still wearing the crucifix every day.

"Of course I am. I promised you I would." Dan had forgotten all about them, and she was just as happy that he had.

"You know Lucille," he says to her, "I went back to that shop on Melrose, the place I picked them up, and talked to the lady, Andrea Poe. Pat McCrae seems to think that she's some kind of psychic. I don't know maybe she is, if you believe in that sort of thing."

"Oh, I believe that there are some people who have some psychic abilities," Lucille cuts in. "What does she say?"

"Well she knows Pat McCrae. He's the one who gave her the little green book I have, and she is convinced that there are vampires out there. It's a long story, but that's not what I wanted to say.

"What do you want to say, Honey?" she giggles.

"Well," Greg starts slowly. "She described you to me. I hadn't even mentioned you, and she described you pretty accurately."

"Wow," she exclaims, "that's amazing!

"Yeah, it kind of was, but there was something else. She told me that she could see you in some place with snow, someplace where there are wild beasts. And she said you could be in danger." Lucille shivers at the pay phone. Every night she has heard the coyotes. The evening before she went to the window during the night, when something woke her, and she saw three of them loping past the cabin, running toward the main house. And even on the location, she had spotted them not far from the trailers. But she had figured they were just after food, now that all these people were here. Besides, coyotes wouldn't attack human beings!

"Well," she says, pulling the parka tighter about her, "it's probably the coyotes that she sees, but coyotes won't go after humans, will they Greg? Will they?"

"Of course not," he reassures her, "They're probably after food, scraps, you know."

"That's what I thought too. Don't worry about me, Honey," she tells him, feeling better herself now.

"Well," he says with some urgency, "you just take good care of yourself. I promise I'll be there next weekend. Meantime, if anything happens, anything at all, you call me right away. I can and will get away if I have to."

That night Lucille sleeps restlessly. She keeps thinking of the little lady in the shop, the lady she's never met, but who seems to know her, and when she does finally fall asleep, she has a horrible nightmare. In it she once again sees Marcus speeding past her in the silver Mercedes, hands gripping the wheel like a vice, but this time, he is not alone. Sitting in the car with him, are two coyotes, shaggy, yellow beasts, with sharp fangs, dripping foul saliva, with eyes, blacker and colder than night. And in the dream, something else happens. As the car shoots past her own, the driver and the coyotes, turn and glare malevolently at her, and as she starts to scream, her van is suddenly caught and pulled in behind the Mercedes, where the two creatures glower at her through the back window, as her Volkswagen, with Lucille trapped in it, gets sucked closer, and closer to certain death.

CHAPTER 16

Radelescu

That first weekend, Lucille spends mostly at the ranch. She and Beth take a hike Sunday afternoon, up into what is called, "The Alabama Hills, the hills named after a civil war battleship, by Southern sympathizers, during the same war. They are the group of hills located on the other side of Portal Road. It's a fine day, and the two young women take a picnic with them, which they share in the area known as, "Khyber Pass." It's one of the locations used during the shooting of, "**Gunga Din**." She wishes Greg could have made it up there. Her dreams still frighten her. She's been hearing the howling of the coyotes more often, and now, their wild sounds are unnerving. The two girls don't wait for the sun to set before heading back to the warm security of the ranch.

Monday morning work continues. The first part of the week calls for a new location. The Teamsters, over the weekend, have relocated all the trailers to the Hoppy Rocks area, where the mine is supposed to be. It's a little further away from the ranch, a little less convenient. Dan, feeling confident with Lucille's ability to handle the wardrobe from the set and trailers, has spent less and less time at the shoot. He usually stops by around lunch, just to check with his crew, and join the others. On Monday, the catering truck is set up at the Hoppy Rocks location, when lunch is called. Dan joins Lucille, Beth, Barb and Jake at a table.

"I'm getting tired of this chicken," Jake comments, while picking at a lump of it on his plate. "I think they've served it just about every way humanly possible."

"It's Richard and Marcus," Dan tells them. "They both have a thing for chicken, although I hear that tomorrow, we're going to have a barbecue, with steak and Maine lobster that Marcus is having flown in."

"That'll be a nice change," Lucille agrees. "I'm kind of tired of chicken myself." Just as she says that, Marcus approaches the table, with a plate of his own.

"How's that chicken?" he inquires of the group.

"I was just telling them that you've got some lobster and steaks coming in tomorrow," Dan says, covering for the less than enthusiastic response to the question.

"You bet," Marcus smiles, and sits next to Lucille. "You like lobster, Lucille?" he asks her.

"Why, yes, I love lobster," she says, surprised that he addressed the question to her. Ever since that first nightmare, the week before, she's tried to avoid Marcus, who seems intent on cornering her, every time he sees her. He's even made trips to the wardrobe trailers, ostensibly, work related, but Lucille feels that there are other motives. She's not sure if it's a sexual attraction on his part, that is drawing him to her, or if it's some other thing. On several occasions, he's gone on about this Dorothy Doty, who was some kind of portage. He's compared Lucille to this Dorothy. Perhaps, Lucille thinks, he's got some sort of mentor-student obsession with her. Whatever it is, it has been making her extremely uncomfortable. He's the producer of the movie, and she's simply one of the staff, not even a department head. And the dreams don't seem to stop. Each night since the first one, she's trembled through some variation of the same one. Each time, she sees his Mercedes and the two coyotes, and now, when the real ones howl, nearby, their cries send shivers down her spine, and Marcus' face flashes charmingly before her. She's been tempted to mention Marcus' behavior to Greg, but hasn't, not wanting to worry him, not quite sure that she hasn't imagined all this.

"The wardrobe looks great," Marcus tells the crew, as he gets up after the meal. "You're all doing a great job." This he says, looking directly at Lucille. Again something makes her blood run a little cold. Dan notices her reaction.

"Is everything all right, Lucille?" he asks her when the others have left.

"I guess so, Dan. It's just that Marcus seems to pay me a lot of attention, and I guess it makes me kind of nervous." He nods

"I've seen it, Lucille. I wouldn't worry about it if I were you. You are doing a good job. This film, so far, is running smoother than others I've worked on. Hopefully it will continue" He sees Lucille glance toward the icy, mountains, now partially hidden by dark cumulous clouds. "And hopefully, this weather won't turn south on us. It sure does look stormy up there doesn't it?"

"Yeah," she answers softly, "and the coyotes keep coming closer. They frighten me, Dan."

"You just button up, and keep warm." He pats the shoulder of her heavy parka. "Everything will be just fine."

Later, those words of his, come back to haunt her. She would remember the dark clouds over the mountain, and Dan's hand on her shoulder, because by Wednesday, the storm came, and when it did, all Hell broke loose.

The storm that Lucille saw building its wrath over the mountains, was an angry southern one that had started somewhere over the Pacific, swept in over the Baja Peninsula, growing in fury, and would reach Los Angeles, by Tuesday night. El Nino had played havoc on the California coast, throughout the winter of '98, and was due for one final assault. Perhaps what they said was true; that like the desert winds, the Santana's, El Nino, besides destroying homes and lives, also made men mad. Whatever the case, or the cause, Tuesday night, after years of abstinence, years of sublimating his urgings, following the debacle he had caused on the set of "Biker Hell," Lenny, once again took to the streets.

He took the black Mercedes. The rain had not yet started when he pulled slowly down the drive of the house with the turrets and towers, and weaved his way down the hill, down to Sunset. For maybe an hour, he cruised the boulevard, searching for someone, a woman, with whom to spend a moment of passion, before tasting her blood. He was looking for a runaway, or a party girl, preferably someone who had had enough to drink, or ingested a sufficient amount of a controlled substance, that when morning came, she would have little, or no recollection of what had transpired the night before.

Around ten, just as the first drops started to fall, and the hills rumbled with distant thunder, he found one that seemed to fit the bill. She was staggering slightly, on the curb, in front of Carlos & Charley's, but she was alone, and although a few cars had slowed down for closer inspection, no one had yet stopped, when Lenny pulled easily to the curb and offered her a ride. She looked at the slightly hunched man behind the wheel, before getting in.

"Are you looking for a date?" she asked.

"Perhaps for the entire night," he suggested. "I'll pay you well." She was high, but not too much so to let this opportunity pass, not with the night ahead, and the foul weather rapidly approaching.

"It'll cost you five hundred for the night," she told him, figuring that he could meet the price.

"That will be fine," he said, as she had expected he would.

He took her back up the hill, to the only sanctuary that the three of them had known, since first coming to this town, to the place that they had so successfully managed to keep secret, during all those many years. As he pulled up the drive, all those thoughts played madly in his head. He knew that he was about to break the cardinal rule, and perhaps destroy everything Dragan had created and maintained throughout the centuries, in countless lands. Perhaps El Nino had rendered him impotent to do anything but this, perhaps all the years of loneliness, no longer seemed worth the price of immortality. Whatever the reason, even as he rushed her out of the pounding rain and into the warmth of the great house, even as she undressed and lay beside him, he knew that his commitment was complete, the die had been cast, and there would be no turning back.

He made love to her over, and over again. He tasted and touched every part of this woman, and he did so with a passion and a need, that was born in years of desperate deprivation, and terrible longing. And to her surprise, despite her familiarity with the act, she responded to this strange little man, with the unbridled emotion, and she found herself swept away by it and him.

Later, sometime in the early morning hours, after he had satiated his need, and she had fallen asleep, completely exhausted, she awoke in horror. At first, she thought it was the rain that had wakened her, she could hear it beating unmercifully down on the hard tiled roof, but when she opened her eyes, she saw this thing hunched over her partially clothed body, and she felt the first pressure of its fangs as it started to pierce the soft flesh of her neck. She screamed, in shear terror, knowing that she was all alone with a monster, knowing that the wind and rain would never allow the scream to be heard by any mortal being, and knowing that if she did not flee, that death was imminent.

As she screamed, she clawed at the face over her head, and for a moment it moved away. In that moment, she rose from the bed, and fled from the room, down the stairs, and through the long halls, to the front door, then out, into the night!

For some reason, that he would never know, when she screamed, Lenny recoiled, and as she rose, he did nothing. He could have killed her in a breath, an instant, but he didn't. Maybe it was because he no longer cared, he knew that it had all come to an end. As he watched her flee from the room, he knew then, that he would have to tell Dragan. He was sure that Dragan, in his supreme fury, would probably kill him. At the window of his room, even as he watched the half naked woman running down the drive, he knew that had he had the desire, he could have leapt from the window, and killed her. But he couldn't. It was too late. It was all, too late.

All night, as the storm raged outside, Lenny stood by his window. All his lives, his histories, flashed across the windows of his memory, and with the vast melancholy he felt, came a sense of relief in understanding, that he would soon be, at peace.

Sometime in the morning, as the storm raced north, Lenny descended the stairs, for what he was sure would be the last time, and in total dejection, and quite soaking wet, he started the engine of the black car, and headed north, to Dragan and final redemption, or death.

Greg arrives at the Hollywood station Wednesday morning, early and dripping wet. As soon as he comes through the door, Jim stops him.

"They've got a woman in there," he indicates the back, and the interrogation rooms, "who's got some strange story. You might be interested."

"The Baxter murder?" Greg asks, referring to the elderly man whose throat was slashed.

"No," Jim answers, and his tone, for once is not derogatory. "It's along your vampire line. Someone bit her."

Greg heads immediately toward the back of the station, brushing water from his jacket. "In there," someone points. He opens the door. Cove is standing with his back to the window. Rain beats steadily on the glass. Sitting at the table, in the center of the room, Greg sees a youngish, blond woman. She's wearing a dark colored raincoat, wrapped tightly around her thin figure. Her entire look is disheveled, with wet and unruly hair, and makeup that has smudged and run. She turns and looks at the detective as he closes the door behind him. In her eyes, he sees something akin to the fear he saw in the eyes of some of the men with whom he fought, while in the Falklands.

"This is Meredith McBride," Eddy introduces them. "Detective Logan. Why don't you tell him the story you told me." The woman takes a deep breath, and turning away from Greg, stares out the window at the pounding rain. Then she talks.

She tells how she got a ride from a guy. She was standing in front of Carlos & Charley's waiting for a bus, just as the rain started, and some guy came by and asked her if she needed a lift. They ended up back at his house, a mansion off Sunset, with towers and gargoyles. They made love, for hours, before she fell asleep. Sometime during the night something unsettled her. She awoke to find this guy on top of her, but this time he was more like some creature, than the guy with whom she had made passionate love. His breath was foul, his face had changed, and his teeth, well they weren't really teeth, they were fangs, and they were on her neck. She screamed and pushed him away, then ran. She hasn't slept, and came here, first thing in the morning.

Greg stands there, in shock, listening to the onslaught of foul weather outside.

"Look!" she says, unbuttoning the raincoat, then tearing a gauze bandage from her neck. Both men move at the same time. Her neck is slashed slightly, where the blood has dried, but clearly, Greg and Eddy see the impression left by two large teeth.

"Are you all right?" Greg puts his arm on the woman's wet sleeve.

"I, I guess so," she stammers. "I've never been so scared. I was sure that I was dead." It's a simple statement, an acknowledgment of what is obviously, the truth.

"Do you remember the house?" Greg asks, desperately. "Can you take us to it?"

"Yes, yes I can. I'll never forget it," she says, absolutely terrified.

"Let's go then," Greg says, slipping on the soaking jacket. "Take us there, now!"

They take the Mustang. The girl sits up front, with Eddy squeezed in the back. It feels to Eddy that they race to the place. All the way down Sunset, Greg ducks in and out of the traffic, which is just holding its own in the torrent of endless rain. Near the 9000 building, off Sunset Plaza, she directs Greg up the hill, then right, up the drive. As soon as he reads the address, painted on the curb, he calls the station on the cell phone.

"Call in a search warrant," he tells Jim, and gives him the address, "and tell Captain Magness that we're on to them, to the vampires!"

The drive is empty, and the place looks deserted, and when Greg stares up, it seems to be guarded only by the fierce gargoyles, perched high on the tiled rooftop. He pounds on the door, and to his surprise, it swings open by itself. As they enter by the great living room, they see the remnants of a fire in the fireplace, casting shadows on the heavy curtains. Quickly, but cautiously they make their way through the castle. She shows them the room upstairs, the dark room in oak, with the frilly white curtains on the soiled bed. She sobs, and leans against Greg, who hurries her from the place.

"Do you want to wait in the car?" he asks her at the foot of the stairs.

"No," she says. "Don't leave me alone. I'll stay with the two of you."

Together, they inspect the entire place. When they come out of the kitchen, Eddy spots a door. It looks like it might lead to the cellar, but is closed with a small padlock.

"Get something from the kitchen," Greg tells his partner. "We'll break this thing."

Eddy returns with a metal mallet. They slam it against the lock, finally tearing it loose from the hinge, then push the door open. Greg fumbles for the light switch, finds it and flicks it on. They stand there, all three of them, in shocked silence.

The room is like a museum. There are all sorts of items, antique clothing and paintings, coats of arms, and ancient weapons, all arranged and carefully displayed. The shelves hold souvenirs of all kinds, letters and photos, many yellow with age, some almost in ruin. Among the photos is one in which he recognizes two people. It is a picture of George Zimmer and a young Niki Starling, and they are standing outside the Chinese Theater, in front of the marquee, which reads, "Biker Hell." As he stares at the picture, he feels something in his soul, gasp, then grow numb. He looks beyond. At the far end of the room, overlooking all of it, is a family crest, very old, and very ornately wrought in iron, and etched into its mass, is the name, "Radelescu."

"My God," Greg mutters, as his incredulous eyes take it all in. "They're here!"

There is some furniture. It is simple and modern in design, just a coffee table and two stuffed armchairs, both deep red in color. On the coffee table are several papers and magazines, left as if someone had looked through them, and just discarded them afterward. Greg picks up a copy of The Hollywood Reporter. It's dated from a month earlier, and it's open to a page containing several photographs. There is a short article. He sees immediately that it's about the movie, "Lifeblood, The Last Vampires of Hollywood." He pulls it closer to better see the photo.

"My God!" he screams. "Eddy!" Desperately, he thrusts the magazine at his partner. The caption underneath the photo says, "Richard Stewart, director," and even before he has read it, as if he had always known, he recognizes the face, as belonging to the same man who taunted him from the back of the taxi. Faintness grabs him by the chest, and he clutches for the back of the armchair. "Lucille," he barely manages to breathe.

Dragan rises early, Wednesday morning. The clock in his room reads: 4:40. He's unsure whether it is the rain and wind beating on the cabin, or the dreams that he has had that has roused him. The wind and rain are but the elements, wild and unpredictable , like him. He has loped through fields of rain, and flown across wet skies, but the dreams he's been having are unsettling. He has been dreaming of eternal fire, and horrible, excruciating pain, and worse than that, in his dreams, he is always alone in his suffering. The business about the wardrobe girl disturbs him too. He should have found some excuse to have her fired, and never agreed to Marcus' plan. He can't allow the boyfriend, the cop to come to Lone Pine. And he has been watching Marcus. Dragan too, sees something of Dorothy Doty in the girl, but then, unlike Marcus, he had no attraction to that girl, Dorothy. He had learned years ago, that avoiding physical attraction, was but one of the prices one must pay for eternal life. But Marcus' fascination with this Lucille, is obvious. He has talked with him about it, but each time Marcus rationalizes that the attention he pays her, is strictly professional, and only for the good of the show.

The picture is going well. He remembers coming to Lone Pine as the actress, Betty Boudin. The place hasn't changed much. The rocks are the same, and the coyote packs still roam the rough terrain, but the times have changed, and in the air, he feels a terrible transition coming. He stands by the window until dawn breaks, watching the lightening play havoc over the snowy mountain.

Dragan decides that they're going to go ahead with the filming this day. The weather that El Nino has unleashed on Lone Pine, is far more realistic than anything the special effects team could come up with, and there will be no waste of time setting up the shots for each effect. They'll simply move the camera to fit their needs.

Over breakfast with the production manager, and the first assistant director, he plans the day's filming, jumping off from the prearranged shooting schedule. They will use the real weather to portray the fictional storm's first assault on the little mining town called, "Hollywood." The various crews, who had been on a weather standby from the night before, gather in the main dining room, and are handed the revised call sheet. They've all come to Lone Pine prepared for any kind of weather, and are bundled up in warm, wet weather gear, as the Teamsters drive the vans out to the location. The weather rages. Over the mountain, Lone Pine Peak, lightening dances, cutting through the dark, overcast sky.

"Wow, it's just wild, isn't it?" Beth says to Dan, Lucille, and the others, as their van slips and slides over the deep ruts of Movie Road.

"It's beautiful," Dan answers, "but we're going to have a lot of work to do with the wardrobe tonight. Everything's going to be soaked and muddy." Lucille stares out the window. She doesn't like the weather at all. She thinks of the pepper tree back home, and how it brushed menacingly against the window, and how warm the fire was, when they burned that horrible branch.

"I hate this weather," she tells the others. "It scares the hell out of me. Especially the lightening."

"You'll be fine," Dan reassures her. "You and I will work in the trailers. Beth, I want you on the set with Jake and Barb today." Somehow, that makes Lucille feel better. She'll be all right with Dan, but she can't help but think of Greg. She wishes that she was in his arms, far away from Lone Pine, with its coyotes and rain.

Bud, the driver, drops Dan and Lucille off at the wardrobe trailer. "Don't catch cold!" he hollers to them, as they dash for warmth and cover. It's about a five minute walk from the trailer to the set, and the walkie-talkies are the only connection between the two, those and personal visits. After settling in, maybe an hour later, Lucille checks the walkie-talkie, since she hasn't yet heard from the others.

"You guys OK down there?" she asks Jake.

"Christ, it's wet," he curses. "Lucille, the whole of Main Street is turning into a river. It's unbelievable. Richard's all over the place. He's shooting as fast as he can. Looks like a mad man. He's really in his element. We're just trying to keep up. It's insane. Can't wait for lunch. How you doing?"

"I guess we're the lucky ones. We're high and dry up here. Where's lunch going to be?"

"Oh," Jake says, "the driver's are going to take us back to the main house at 'one. Hey, gottah go!"

"Jake," she stops him before he can sign off, "Dan just told me to tell you that he'll be down there in ten minutes, he knows you guys are jammed, and he'll fill in."

"Great," Jake says, and clicks off.

Dan bundles into his rain khaki rain gear and boots. "We'll swing by and pick you up for lunch," he tells her, at the door. "I like the weather. Reminds me of back home in Seattle. Call, if you need anything. Bye Lucille." With that, he slams the door shut against the wind, which seems to be getting worse. Lucille makes sure that the door is tightly shut, and pauses at its window, gazing out over the hills, toward the nearby mountain. The clouds swirl, and beat violently across the peak, and lightening flashes in the darkish sky.

Marcus, who's been on the set all morning, sees Dan walking down the trail towards them. He looks at his watch. It's eleven: thirty. He knows that the entire wardrobe crew, except Lucille, is now accounted for, on the set. Dragan is so completely involved with the weather and the set ups, that he won't even notice Marcus' absence. Marcus is by now, well aware of Dragan's disapproval of his relationship with the pretty wardrobe assistant, who reminds him so longingly, of his beloved Dorothy. Perhaps, he reasons, she will be more receptive to his advances and ultimate offer, than was Dorothy. For the last three days, he hasn't been able to think of anything, but this girl. He feels emptiness in his heart that only she can fill. He can wait no longer. The time is right, and it's now. He decides to pay her a visit. As he starts his way up the muddy trail to the trailers, what he doesn't know, is that Dragan, who's just finished a shot, and has a moments break, while the crews set up for the next one, sees Marcus leave. Dragan knows where his associate is headed, and is not pleased. He decides to go ahead with the shot and then have a little chat with Marcus, before they break for lunch.

As Marcus is slowly negotiating his way up the slippery trail towards the wardrobe trailers, Lenny is behind the wheel of the black Mercedes, focusing through the blur of the wipers' blades, as they shear the rain from the window. He drives solely on instinct. He does not hear the roar of the thunder, and is oblivious to the torrential rain. Driving is what he has always done. In the old days, he drove teams of horses or oxen, but since the arrival of the automobile, he has driven almost every make and every model, ever manufactured. Driving, is second nature to Lenny. Lenny's mind is neither on the driving, nor on the weather.

As he speeds through the green light at Four Corners, his mind is on only one thing. There is but one face that he sees in his mind's eye, and that face belongs to his master, Dragan Radelescu, The Eternal One. From the moment the girl fled down the drive, Lenny has seen only Dragan's image embossed in his head. He had nowhere to go, but to his master. There is no place on earth where he could hide. He had destroyed that most sacred of traditions. He had revealed their secrets. He knew that the police would come. He was terribly aware that they would eventually stumble on the little room next to the kitchen. He knew that if Dragan spared him, if they managed to escape, and flee to another land, that his retribution would take years. However, he doubted that Dragan would give him another chance. He was fairly certain that the Master would kill him, and strangely enough, Lenny felt that perhaps the time had come. He was not afraid. In fact, with this certainty, if anything, he felt a certain absolute peace.

Greg too, was on the road. From the house off Sunset, they'd dropped Meredith off at her apartment, then returned to the station. Magness had the search warrant and was waiting for the report.

"They never made an "X Files," like this one, Captain," Greg told him, breathlessly. "Old Jack McCrae wasn't seeing any leprechauns. They're here all right, and they've been here for a long time, and my girlfriend's, right this minute, up in a little town called, Lone Pine, and the director of the picture she's on, is one of them."

Kerry Magness might have enjoyed the fantasy offered up by a TV show like "The X Files," but he had, for some time, suspected that McCrae might have been on to something. When he saw the two faces before him, and heard the story, any doubts he might have still harbored, vanished. "I'll contact Lone Pine," he said. "Who's the director?"

"Zimmer," Greg spit the name from his lips, "but not really, anymore. He's made The Change. Now he calls himself, Richard Stewart. He's got a new face, and a different physique, but he's still the same bastard that Eddy and I saw at McCrae's burial."

"Jesus, Lord," was all that Magness could utter.

"Look, Captain, I've got to go up there." He pulled the little green book from a pocket inside his dripping jacket. "It's all here. This Radelescu, who wrote this book, well we found his family crest at the castle. He's Zimmer and all the other ones before. They never left, just kept killing to get new identities. I know what to do, how to destroy them. Captain, I've got to go, to do it. If you call the locals, they'll botch it, and the bastards will be gone, and Lucille is there. They've got her!"

Magness pauses. "All right then, but I'm sending Eddy with you."

"Sorry, Captain, but I'll need him here, and I've got to do it myself. Besides, he's the only other one besides the nephew, who knows anything about these monsters. I've got to go myself, and you've got to give me some time, before you contact Lone Pine. I've got my cell phone. I'll be in touch. Please, Captain!" It was a plea, so desperate, that the captain agreed. He'd call Lone Pine anyway, but he would wait to hear from Greg.

"Well, OK. I guess if they've been here all this time, a couple of hours won't make much difference. But you better keep close touch. How far is it up there, anyway?"

"It's about a hundred and fifty miles, Cap. With this rotten weather, I'll need a couple of hours just to get there. I'll call when I hit town." Magness looked at his watch.

"OK, he said, "it's a go. Is there anything else you need?"

"Yeah, Greg told him, "I need to find out if there's some gun shop, or place that supplies ammo to the local cops."

"What for? You arm yourself before you hit the road." Magness said. Greg shook his head, and even managed to smile, almost bashfully.

"Lone Pine used to be a silver mining town. There's still silver up there, and I need a gunsmith who can cast me some forty five caliber bullets, in silver, like immediately!"

"You're kidding?" Magness chuckled. "You mean like, in Dracula?"

"No, I'm serious, Captain, like in "The X Files," Greg said, then turned to his partner. "When I call in, give me a name and a place, Eddy, where I can pick them up on my way to the movie location." That time, no one laughed. The captain, and Greg's partner, just nodded. It was settled. The vampires were real, and they were operating out of Lone Pine.

The first thing Greg does, is to stop at his house. There, he picks up some rain and warm weather gear, climbing ropes and boots, and the Springfield Armory, 1911 model, forty-five automatic that he owns, the one with the silver grips that he bought down in Mexico. The rain is relentless. As he scurries for his car, he touches the silver crucifix that he still wears around his neck, and says a silent prayer that Lucille is wearing hers.

Greg works his way out of town. The traffic is a mess with the lousy weather. Maybe, he thinks, it will work to his advantage. He's read the little green book from cover to cover, and although it's on the seat next to him, he no longer needs it for reference. What he needs, is an edge, and surprise has always been a good one, in any dangerous situation. He gets on Interstate 5, and climbs rapidly out of town, flying with all haste up to the desert, and Highway 14, past towns like Palmdale, and Lancaster, then on to Mojave and Red Rock Canyon, another location where Westerns were shot. All the while, El Nino, beats down, like a wrathful god. At Homestead, he turns the Mustang off the 14, and on to the 395, for the final leg to Lone Pine, and Lucille.

Lucille has her back to the door when she hears the knock, followed by a gust of wind. She turns, startled, to see Marcus standing inside the trailer, smiling benignly. His dark raincoat drips puddles onto the carpeted floor.

"You frightened me," she tells him bluntly. "What's wrong? Why are you here?" He takes off the wet apparel, and drapes it over a folding chair.

"I'm sorry, Lucille, there's nothing to be afraid of, and everything's all right." He chuckles, "Just bad weather, that's all."

"Do you want some coffee?" She goes to the table and a Mr. Coffee machine, and pours a cup.

"No, thank you," he says, still smiling strangely. "I simply wanted to see you again Dorothy." Lucille shudders, and almost spills the coffee.

"What?" she asks, astounded. "What did you say?"

"We don't need any coffee, Dorothy. I just had to see you again. It's been so long, so long." He tugs on his left ear, watching her, bleakly.

"Mr. Banning," she starts, and retreats a step or two, "It's…" But he cuts her short.

"I'm so sorry. So sorry. How will you ever forgive me Dorothy?" Lucille backs against the table and the coffee machine, still holding the steaming cup in her hand.

"Who are you?" She demands. "I'm not this Dorothy. I'm Lucille!" she screams, but Marcus no longer hears her, or even sees her. He sees only his cherished Dorothy, and feels a horrible loss and sense of guilt for his part in her demise.

"Oh, Dorothy," he sighs, then slumps into the folding chair. Lucille stares at him, at the same time, both terrified and bewildered. The water from his coat, slowly soaks into the black turtleneck sweater he wears. He covers his face with both hands. "Dorothy, I didn't want to kill you. I loved you, my Darling. I've always loved you. We could have had anything, the two of us. The world was ours, forever, for all eternity.

"My God," Lucille mutters. Marcus looks up at her, as if just now noticing her. But again, it is not Lucille that he sees.

"Do you know what it is like to live forever? Can you imagine the wonders that one sees, the places one goes? I would have given you all that, Dorothy," he sobs. "I still can!" Now he looks directly into her eyes, and what she sees, absolutely terrifies her. His eyes are black and so, so deep. They are the cold eyes of an ageless demon. In the instant that she sees into him, everything falls horrifically into place. This isn't a man at all. It's the thing that Greg feared, the beast for which he is searching, and the beast is here, in the trailer, far away from the man she loves and on whom she counts, here in a blinding torrent of lightening and rain, high up, in the loneliest spot on God's earth.

"Love me, my Darling," he says, staggering slowly to his feet. "Love me, Dorothy," he moves toward her, and as he does, the eyes darken, as the face changes. It no longer bears any semblance to the human form that it once was. The nose lengthens, and hair sprouts on its forehead, and the teeth are not teeth. They jut viciously from the muzzle of the beast, like fangs, like the fangs of a wolf, or a coyote. In complete terror, Lucille screams, and throws the steaming coffee at the muzzle. Instinctively, she grabs for the crucifix, hanging from her neck. She rips it off, tearing it loose from the chain, and thrusts it toward the creature, as she rushes past the thing, to the door. She feels its cold, fetid breath on her neck. As she flings it open, she screams again, but the scream is lost in a clap of thunder, and a torrent of blinding rain.

At the same time that Lucille throws open the door, Lenny turns off Portal Road and on to Movie Road. When he reached Lone Pine, he stopped at a store called, "Lloyd's Boots and Shoes," and asked for directions to where the movie was being shot. Of course, everyone in town knew about the movie. Many of them had already appeared as extras, and it was the only film shooting, at the time.

"Why, of course, the cashier answered amicably. The vampire flick." Lenny winced at that. "Why you just go to the light there," he indicated, "turn up Portal Road, 'til you see Movie Road, take a right, and park at the area where they got the trailers. Can't go any further anyway. You got to walk down to the set. It's about a five minute walk." He looked the stranger up and down, and seeing that Lenny wasn't really attired for the weather, added, "If you need some wet weather gear, a raincoat, or a poncho, I got 'em stocked here," he offered, walking back towards the racks.

"No," Lenny said almost sadly, "I don't need anything now. Just have to go. Got to see the director." He started to leave, when the cashier called after him.

"Hey, Buddy, you got a part in the flick?" At the door, Lenny just turned.

"Huh?" was all he mumbled.

The cashier, a young guy, just out of high school, looked at the diminutive, slightly hunched man, who was about to walk outside into a raging storm, dressed in only a dark leather vest.

"Nothing, Buddy, just take a right at the light."

Just past Four Corners, Greg had called Cove, back at the station, on his cell phone. "What have you got for me, Partner?" he asked. "You find me someone?"

"Yeah," Eddy said. "I found you someone. I just hope you know what you're doing. A couple of silver bullets doesn't sound like much firepower to me."

"Believe me," Greg said. "One of them will do, if I get the chance and the shot. Where is it?"

"Little place on the left, when you first get into town, place called, "Lee's Frontier." They supply ammo to the local cops, and deal in some antique guns. Ask for Peter Grau, German guy. He's got two clips worth for you. He knows you're a cop, and asked me if you were the Lone Ranger, and what the hell you wanted with silver bullets. I told him that it was for a forensic study, and that we were in a rush. They're ready."

"Thanks, Partner, Greg said. "Magness hasn't called in the local law, has he?"

"No, he's going to wait for you to let him know when."

"Good, I don't want to spook the bastard," Greg had signed off.

At Lee's, he'd introduced himself to Peter Grau, and fielded the questions he had already figured were coming, as to what kind of forensic tests they were conducting with silver bullets, why they didn't have them cast back in Los Angeles, was it a homicide, why he needed to know how to get to the movie location, the weather, etc. Etc. Peter seemed like a descent enough fellow, but he was of a curious nature, and Greg neither had the time, nor the inclination to hang around and swap detective stories with the man. "Thanks, Peter, I appreciate your getting this done as quickly as you did. I'll let you know how the tests turn out," was what he said, on his way out.

"Let me know, Greg. Next time you swing by I'll show you some real beautiful antique guns," Peter called to him.

"I'll do that," Greg conceded. He was enough of a cop to know that Peter hadn't really bought into the story, and figured that within minutes, he'd be on the phone to a friend, maybe a cop, relating how some Los Angeles detective was up in Lone Pine, picking up silver bullets. They used to shoot the "Lone Ranger" series up here. Greg guessed that by the next morning, there would be a whole new set of Lone Ranger jokes running around town. He just hoped that by that time, he'd have Lucille with him, safe and unharmed, and that the monster, Radelescu, would be, forever dead!

Back in his car, he called Cove. "Thanks, Partner. I got the ammo. I'm on my way to the location. I'm taking my cell phone. I'll let you know if , and when I need backup. The rain's just pouring down here," he told Eddy, staring up at the looming height of Lone Pine Peak.

As Greg turns up Portal Road, just ahead of him, the black Mercedes makes the turn onto Movie Road, and there, by the wardrobe trailers, Lucille rushes into the downpour, and headlong, into the arms of Dragan Radelescu!

When Marcus made his way up the trail towards the trailers, and Dragan was waiting for the next setup, the assistant director approached him. "Richard, this is going to take a while," Doug said. "We've got the camera truck stuck in the mud. Maybe we should leave this shot and do it latter, you know, pick up something else?" It was a question, that on any other occasion, the director would have agreed to. Time, is always money on a movie set. But this time, Dragan made a quick decision.

"Thanks, Doug, but I'll wait for you to get the truck out, and go as planned. Listen, I'm going to the wardrobe trailer. I should be back in fifteen minutes. That should give everyone enough time."

Dragan had decided to clip in the bud, the growing obsession that he had been observing in Marcus. Marcus' behavior had puzzled and disturbed Dragan. It wasn't simply this strange obsession with the wardrobe assistant that bothered Dragan. Marcus, who had always, in each reincarnation, been sharp and concentrated, now seemed scattered, and strangely distant. It was more than disturbing. His distraction could prove dangerous, and this Lucille was the catalyst.

"Thanks Doug," Dragan says, adjusting the brim of the Stetson he's wearing, "I'll be up there if you need me. He nods towards the trailers, and bows his head into the wind. Marcus has by now, passed out of sight.

As Dragan arrives within several yards of the trailer, through the sound of the howling wind, he hears Lucille scream, and with the scream, Dragan sees his world start crashing down around him. Seconds later, the door flies open, and she rushes out into the rain. In her hand is a silver crucifix, and on her face is a look of absolute terror. And right behind her, is Marcus. But Marcus Banning no longer resembles the man who goes by that name. His passion has brought about the physical transformation that Dragan Radelescu described in the little green book.

"When we drink the blood of humans, our bodies take on the form of the beast. The jaw protrudes, and large canines jut forth. Hair grows on our faces, and our look is more animal than human. It is for this reason that when we do feed, we find drunks, and such like, as in the morning, when they awake, they will be unclear as to exactly what transpired. In the rare case when we initiate a mortal to the joys of everlasting life, then too, we take on this form. The act is both beautiful and repugnant for the recipient, and he, or she must be a willing participant."

It was written, and Greg had read it, as had both Patrick and Jack McCrae, and as Lucille rushes headlong toward him, among the things that flash through Dragan's head, is a terrible regret for the moment of vanity that had led him to write the book, thereby, revealing the secrets.

He grabs her free arm, the one not holding the crucifix. Even then, the pain he feels radiating from the thing is so intense that he has to concentrate, just to maintain his grip. With his other arm, he clutches Marcus by the neck. There is an instant when the two creatures regard one another. In that look, countless lives flash before them. They have been companions for centuries, and lived lives that no mortal man could imagine. But they both know , that now, those times have ended, probably for both, but most certainly for Marcus, whose neck Dragan now snaps, as a child would snap a nasty twig. As Marcus Banning falls to the ground, Lucille witnesses something that very few humans have ever lived long enough to see. The body, even as it falls, seems to shrivel and turn to ash, or dust, so even as it lands on the wet ground, what is left of it, washes away, and disappears in the rain

"Farewell, my brother," he mumbles. Then turning to Lucille, he violently slaps the arm that holds the crucifix. "Now for you!" he hisses, as the crucifix flies from her hand, landing on the other side of the road, in a muddy puddle. As it does, the black Mercedes slides to a stop just in front of them. Dragan has no idea why Lenny is here, nor does he have any time to consider. He has to dispose of the girl. Somehow, he'll figure out a way to cover her disappearance, at least until he can come up with another plan. He knows that the game is up, and that at the very least, if he and Lenny are lucky enough, they might just be able to flee the country. It takes six days to go through The Change. It will be impossible. Time is not on their side, and any fortune has vanished in an instant.

"Get in!" he commands her, at the same time opening the front door, and pushing Lucille through. He slips in next to her, knocking the Stetson from his head. "Turn around, and drive!" He snaps the order at Lenny, who has barely come to a stop, and instantly turns the car toward Portal Road and the mountain. The rain is incessant, and the road slippery and gutted. Lenny deftly maneuvers the car through the mud. Halfway to Portal Road, Greg's Mustang flies past them. Dragan turns and looks out the back window, seeing the red brake lights flash on the Mustang. "Faster!" he screams at Lenny.

The moment that Greg passes the Mercedes, he sees everything. The monster, Radelescu is in the passenger seat, glaring at the intruder, another man, at the wheel, and squeezed in between the two of them, wearing a look of utter dread, the girl he loves, Lucille. Even as he passes them, Greg hits the brakes and starts the turn. By the time his car is faced around, the Mercedes is several hundred yards further on, and making the turn on to Portal Road. He floors it, throwing mud and water in his wake, then he too, turns right on Portal, and sails after the speeding Mercedes, up the road, toward Lone Pine Peak, and the blinding snow.

The two cars race uphill toward the snow line. It's no more than several hundred yards beyond now. Greg wonders what kind of tires the Mercedes is using, knowing that his own will never negotiate through the sleek snow. It's going to be a foot race. He speed dials the station.

"Captain Magness!" he hollers, "Quick." Magness gets on the phone. "Captain, call them in. We're on Portal Road, but we'll be on foot in a minute. At the snow line. Got to go!"

He's wearing his hiking boots. The clip containing six silver bullets, is already loaded in the gun, with one in the chamber, and the other clip is tucked away in his jacket pocket, but easy to reach. The Mercedes plows into the snow that descends from the mountain, whose peak, is hidden in the swirling clouds. Within seconds, it skids off the road and wedges itself in a rut. Lenny squeals the tires to no avail. Both doors open, as Greg pulls to a stop, and as Lenny gets out from the driver's side, Dragan hauls Lucille out the other door. He throws but a glance in Greg's direction, yells at Lenny, Get him!" then heads for the rocks.

If Lenny were to have one defining moment in his many lives, he knows that it is now. His disgrace has been complete, and if there is to be any redemption, it will come only if he can save his master. As he turns to face the detective, he knows that he is not afraid of the alternative. In one leap, he cuts in half, the fifty-yard distance between Dragan and Lucille, and Greg. It takes Greg entirely by surprise. He's never seen anything like this, and knows that a vault like that, is not humanly possible. The driver of the Mercedes is no hostage. He is one of them! It takes Greg only that instant to recover and draw his gun. The second leap will bring the creature on top of him. With a dead calmness that comes only in times of great crises, Greg cocks, and raises the gun with both hands, then gently pulls the trigger, with the tip of his index finger. The deathly roar of agony that comes from Lenny, drowns out the explosion of the gunpowder. The shot is straight to the heart. Behind the driver, Greg sees Dragan turn, and just before Lenny falls to the ground, Greg swears that he sees a smile, almost a look of gratitude, pass across the lips of the thing he just killed. As Lenny falls, the body disintegrates, crumbling before Greg's eyes, to dust, but Greg doesn't wait to see it. He is already moving forward quickly, his boots, sure in the slippery snow.

Dragan is having more trouble. Lucille is not making it easy for him to advance, and the ferocious wind carries with it, a deluge of snow and sleet, and there are flashes of lightening on the mountain. When Lenny fell, Dragan knew that the man in pursuit, had armed himself with silver, and that Lenny's fate could befall him as well. His only protection is the girl, that and the cover of the nearby rock outcroppings. And Dragan is no stranger to these rocks. He filmed here once. Well, at that time, he wasn't the director, but the star of the picture, the female lead, Miss. Betty Boudin. What Dragan does not know, but what would have appeared ironic, to say the least, to Greg's great uncle, Ned, is that the rocks to which he was moving, were the same ones that Marcus used to kill Sally Smythe, the rocks known as, Three Passes. And the rock which he is now frantically climbing, is the one from which the gin soaked actress fell to her death.

Greg follows, scrambling up the rocks, the forty-five in his right hand, using the left, to pull himself upwards. He wants to shoot the creature, but can't risk injuring Lucille. Dragan, with Lucille, disappears behind a boulder. The sleet is dangerous, and blinding. He pauses, to catch his breath, and hears nothing but the roar of the wind. He stops, waiting for Dragan to make the next move. He knows that they are both probably only yards away. Greg wonders when the backup will arrive, and when they do, if that will make things worse. At the moment, it's a standoff.

Dragan has also stopped. He stands on the icy ledge, one hand over Lucille's mouth, in a grip that not only prevents her from screaming, but also, it is a hold, so powerful, that she has no way of moving. The minutes pass, with neither of them moving, each waiting for his opportunity. Finally, Dragan breaks the silence.

"I know you, Delacroix, and I knew your uncle as well. We killed him and his little friend Pudge, and I can kill you too!"

"No one else is going to die here," Greg lies, "not if you let Lucille go!" Dragan laughs, and the harsh cackle cuts through the wind and the weather, like a butcher's knife.

"I've got your woman. I could break her in two with my little finger. Do you know that?"

"Then, you will die, you bastard!" Greg screamed, over the wind.

"You can't kill me, Greg. Didn't you know it? I will live forever."

"If you don't release her now, you're dead. I read your little book, you sick son of a bitch. I know you as well as old Jack McCrae did, and I can kill you." Dragan, for maybe the first time since becoming what he was, feels fear. He knows that Greg could kill him, and he understands that the cop has no intention of letting him get away. His only hope is to negotiate an escape, using Lucille as the hostage.

"You still there, Radelescu?" Greg shouts. "Or do you prefer that I call you George Zimmer?"

"I'm here Delacroix, and so is your sweet little girl." Greg says nothing, waiting, letting the monster play his hand. Dragan continues. "You let me walk away. I'll take your car. I'll drop your playmate off at the stop light in town. You should get there in an hour or so. Why don't you pick her up at Bo Bo's Bonanza." Again he laughs. "I'll buy her a coffee, on my way out of town." Dragan's laugh is hollow. He has already heard the sound. His hearing is far keener than is Greg's or Lucille's, and he knows that the game is about to shift in Greg's favor.

"She'll walk away now, Zimmer, or should I call you, Jean Marc?" Greg calls, and as he does, he too hears the unmistakable sound of chopper blades on a turbo prop helicopter. The sound rumbles and lumbers through the wind. He also knows that they would have trouble spotting the people on the ground.

Dragan knows that the time has come. He's trapped behind the rock, with Greg holding the ground to the only way out. Suddenly, he appears, at the side of the boulder, on the narrow ledge that separates them from the ground below, the same rocky ground that proved fatal for Sally Smythe.

"There you are," Greg says, gun drawn, and seeing his enemy for only the second time. He bares little resemblance to the neatly dressed, well kempt man Greg first saw at the funeral. This, Richard Stewart, is soaking wet from head to toe. His hair is a snake pit of unruliness, and his face no longer speaks the cockiness, that Greg remembers. He can see the contempt in Dragan's demeanor, but mixed in with it, Greg sees the fear, and he has seen the face of fear before. He holds Lucille in front of his body, like a shield. Overhead, the sound of the choppers is carried closer by the wind.

Greg whips the crucifix from his neck and thrusts it at the beast. Dragan flinches.

"Let us pass," he snarls. "Let us pass, or I shall jump. I can survive the jump, but she won't."

"Let her go, Radelescu," Greg orders him. "Let her go, then you jump." Dragan looks to the sky. Spotlights play across the rocks, searching for them. He moves to the very edge of the ledge.

"I'll jump," the monster says. "Maybe you'll get me, but I doubt it. In any case, she dies!" As he speaks, Greg sees his legs tense, coil up for the spring off the boulder. Greg knows now that Dragan will jump, that he's about to. As Dragan starts to adjust his grip on the terrified girl, as he looks to the ground below, Greg runs out of time. He fires the gun, aiming for the shoulder, knowing that he can't kill the thing with Lucille in its arms, but hoping to wound him enough for him to loosen his grip. The bullet strikes Radelescu's shoulder. He screams in agony, and at the same time lets go of Lucille, who rushes into Greg's arms. With Dragan still screaming, Greg aims for the heart, but as his finger starts to squeeze the trigger, with a horrible scream, Dragan leaps, and as he leaps, the thing that he's waited, and prayed for to happen, does. They are not feet, which leave the rocky heights, but claws. And the shoulder that Greg clipped with the shot, suddenly, is no longer a shoulder, but a bleeding and injured wing, and the creature attached to it is some loathsome form of a bat. With a taunting screech, it takes to the air, and just as quickly, vanishes in the sleet and snow.

Greg stands there with Lucille clinging to him, her head buried on his chest, sobbing uncontrollably. A beam of light stabs down, encircling the two of them. "Are you two all right?" is amplified from a speaker in the helicopter. Greg waves to them. "Where are they?" they ask. Greg shakes his head and waves the chopper away.

"It's gone," he says softly to the woman he loves. We're going to be all right." He kisses her. "Can you make it down with some help?" he asks.

"I'm OK, yeah, Honey. I can make it. Oh, it was so, so horrible." They start to make their way down the slippery face. She hangs on to his hand and squeezes it. "Is he really gone, Greg?" she wants so desperately to know.

"Yes," he says simply, but knowing better. "Yes, he's really gone, Darling. Come on now, they're waiting for us."

Down on the lower ground, the helicopter has landed. The two men who were in it, are standing outside on the snowy ground. Down Portal Road, Greg can see other people approaching. "It's some of the crew," Lucille tells him, and moves behind him.. The pilot shakes Greg's hand. "You all right, Buddy?" he asks curiously.

"Yeah," Greg assures them, "we're just fine."

"What was all that about?" the other cop asks. "Where's the perp? We heard some wacked story about a vampire, and silver bullets." He laughs. Greg looks at Lucille, then smiles too.

"They're shooting a vampire movie here," he explains. "My girlfriend, Lucille, she's working on it. That's all."

"Well where did the guy go?" the pilot persisted. "Why did you cut us loose. Is he dead? We didn't see a body." Greg looks the man steadily in the eye.

"You won't see a body. And no, he's not here." Greg takes Lucille's hand, and starts walking to where his car is parked. "Thanks, if I forgot to tell you. You guys got here just in time, and don't worry, I'll do the paperwork. Come on, Honey, we're getting out of here!" He nods at the quickly approaching group. "These guys are missing a director, and there's going to be too much explaining to do." He opens the door for her, and quickly gets in himself, then starts the engine. It sounds rich, and smooth. He smiles. They pass the approaching crowd. Lucille ducks down, so as not to be spotted.

"Come on, Baby, we're going for a long drive."

Down the road, before they reach the stoplight, he turns. "Did I ever tell you how much I love you, Lucille?" he grins, and she reaches for his hand.

"Just about every day, Honey. Yeah, just about every day."

END OF BOOK TWO

EPILOGUE

They found Richard Stewart's Stetson several days later, when the Teamsters started hauling the trailers back to Hollywood. There wasn't much left to it. The weather had taken its toll, as it, and the events had, on the entire crew. Later that evening, Lucille returned to the ranch. The afternoon's incidents, at least what the crew knew of them, had left everyone and everything in a state of shock and amazement. Lucille and Greg had decided that the best approach, was to say nothing, and let the mysterious disappearance work its way through the usual gossip channels. Without Marcus, who had been the driving force behind the picture, the movie was never completed, but the rumor mill spinned, as Greg had foreseen. Through Peter Grau, and the local cops, word soon spread of vampires, and silver bullets, and the fact that the movie that was shooting in Lone Pine, was a vampire movie, only lent credence to the myth. Someone got a hold of the film footage already shot, spliced it together into a documentary form, and released it to the general public. It created quite a stir. Marcus would have been proud to know that all the trade papers gave it favorable mention, and that like, *"Biker Hell,"* it too, acquired a cult following among the vampire crowd.

Greg did give a full accounting of the encounter to both Eddy, and Captain Magness. He did so the following morning. El Nino had run its foul course, and the sun, once again shined in Hollywood. Magness had shut his office door so that no one could pick up the smallest inkling of their conversation.

"Jesus," he muttered, when Greg described the final transformation, as Radelescu leaped into the air, "and poor old Jack McCrae got a bat for his retirement, for all his years of chasing the bastards."

"What are we going to do, Captain?" Greg asked. It was the obvious question.

"Well, boys, I'm coming up for retirement myself, and I'll be damned if they hand me a live bat, and a legacy like the one they gave to old Jack. I think the best thing to do is to bury this, and say as little as possible, when asked. What do you think?" He looked hard at the only other two men who knew the terrible truth. They both nodded agreement.

"What about the house off Sunset, the castle with the gargoyles?" Greg interjected. "There's a fortune in there. There's even a letter from Marie Antoinette of France. Can you imagine, Captain?" Magness looked out the window. A bluebird stood teetering on a branch of the Magnolia tree.

"Yeah, Greg, I can imagine all right, and that's the problem. Like I said, I want to leave a descent legacy when I'm gone, and you boys, why you're both good, honest cops, aren't you?" They all smiled. The door to the office, was indeed closed.

"Ain't life something?" Greg laughed.

"Guess, it'll just have to become the property of the State of California? Right, fellows?" the captain smiled kindly at Eddy and Greg.

So, that business was cleared up. Not much of an investigation was launched by the authorities in Lone Pine either, and more than a few of the local population figured that perhaps vampires weren't that much of a stretch of the imagination. After all, things had happened up there before. Strange things always happened, where movies were involved, and legends and myths were a kind of lifeblood for the mind.

One day, several weeks later, Greg drove the two of them over to the little shop on Melrose. In his pocket he had the little green book, and in his heart, a few words of gratitude for the shopkeeper with the long, darkly streaked hair, Andrea Poe.

"This is Lucille, the girl you saw in your vision," he introduced the two.

"Yes," Andrea said brightly, "it is you, and the pleasure is mine. I see it all worked out."

"Yes, so far," Greg told her. She nodded. "Thank you for everything. Maybe you don't know it, but in a way you were a huge help to me." Lucille looked about the shop, full of its sights and smells.

"Please, Lucille," Andrea said, "have a look around." As Lucille wondered about the shop, Andrea looked carefully at Greg. "He's still out there, isn't he?" she said. It was really not a question. Greg nodded, and told her how it went in the end.

"Here," he concluded. "Here is the little green book. I won't be needing it again. I know it by heart, and in my soul too. Perhaps someone else will be able to use it. I hope not, but you never know, as long as he lives."

"Come by again," Andrea said, walking them to the door, and the afternoon sunlight. "You'll both be fine. I can see it!"

Dragan Radelescu sat at his favorite cafe in his new neighborhood in Paris, the sixth arrondisement, at Montparnasse. It both amused and irritated him that the name of this favorite of cafes, was Le Cafe D'Argent, which in French, means, money, or more specifically, silver. His arm was healing, slowly. He had spent many sleepless nights, since fleeing America, enduring the searing pain in his shoulder, but it was healing, as he knew it would. There were other things of which he was less than sure. He liked the cafe for its ambiance, but also because when there wasn't a soccer game playing on the TV, over the bar, the owner, a Monsieur Jean Luc Chenebenoit, let CNN run its news. Dragan was an avid follower of the news. He sat at his spot in the corner, away from the door, and savored a heaping plate of Spanish mussels and fries, accompanied by a 1996 Jean-Claude Chatelain, Pouilly-Fume Pilou.

He had just managed to get out of the country. He had been pleasantly surprised to learn that Interpol had not been contacted by Delacroix & Company. He didn't know that Magness had decided to bury the thing. Perhaps, one day, he would have to return to America and take care of Greg Delacroix. They should have gotten rid of the uncle, and that McCrae as well.

After arriving safely in France, Dragan had promised himself that in the future, he would not let vanity in any form, play into his actions; it had already caused permanent loss, and great sorrow. He had lost his two companions. For centuries, they had wandered, through countless lands, and many lives, and now, they were gone, forever!

Dragan Radelescu took a thoughtful sip of the wine. He would have to find a new project. The movies had been fun, but were now just another part of the past. He had dipped his hand in the art business, the last time he had been in Paris. Perhaps he would try that again, perhaps, something different. He needed a diversion, but before anything, he needed an associate, a companion. The Change could not be accomplished without assistance. He could only remain in his present shape for a number of years. Even then, he wasn't sure. Perhaps they were looking for him. They had the face of Richard Stewart. No, he needed to find someone right away. He needed to go through the process, and abandon this form. Besides, he was so, so lonely.

He looked about the cafe. In the far corner, sitting alone, was a young woman. She had long, dark hair, and her face was pale, and distant. Dragan liked pale faces. She turned, sensing that he was there, and their eyes met. Dragan nodded, and she smiled back. Dragan looked deeply into her raven black eyes.

THE END

Dragan Radelescu & The Vampires of Paris
The sequel Also on Amazon

Made in the USA